Chapter One

The last time Fancy Holleday robbed a train, she did it in her bloomers.

On that singular occasion, she'd had only one hired gun to distract from his duties. Tonight, the train carried a railroad detective *and* a deputy U.S. marshal. As skilled as she was at disposing of lawmen, even she had to admit she had limitations.

Fancy scowled, careful to hide her tapping boot beneath her skirts. She'd made the unfortunate decision to concentrate her charm on the marshal, since she reasoned that a federal tin-star could do her mission more damage than the detective. Cord Rawlins, however, had barely glanced her way. Now her time was running out.

Perhaps the Texican had grown too fond of his horse, she thought uncharitably. How else might she explain his indifference? Other men positively drooled over her lavender eyes and bulging bustline; Marshal Rawlins acted as if beautiful women were as common as fleas on dogs. She had half a mind to plop down on his lap to see for herself if he were bull or steer.

She smirked at the thought—until she heard the clock

chime the quarter hour. Her heart lurched. Only fifteen minutes remained before the other outlaws boarded. Only fifteen minutes were left to prove to her Spanish lover that she was still valuable to him, in spite of her twenty-five years.

Damn that Marshal Rawlins. Did she have to look like a beefsteak to interest the man?

Gazing past the scurrying waiters with their trays of crystal and gleaming silver, she glared once more at her mark. He had made a face at the menu's exotic selection of blue-winged teal and had specially ordered beef. His suffering waiter had been sent back twice with orders to "burn" the steak. Now Rawlins was shoveling beans down his gullet with a slab of cornbread.

Fancy sniffed. As far as she could see, Rawlins's badge was the only thing that distinguished him from a cowpoke. She supposed she had expected more from a federal tin-star. Foolish of her, really. She had yet to meet a lawman whom she could respect. The ones in San Francisco all seemed to be more crooked than she was. That was why she never had qualms about drugging them when they interfered with her lover's casino business. The way she saw it, laudanum was a far kinder fate than anything Diego might have planned.

But Rawlins, of course, was oblivious to the favor she'd tried to do him. He had refused to sneak off with her to the sleeping car, and he had declined her invitation to dine. Now, short of cracking open his skull in full view of a dozen witnesses, she didn't see how she could possibly render him unconscious before Diego's thugs derailed the train.

Diego Santana, so help me God, this is the last time I will ever participate in one of your heists.

She winced inwardly as she remembered their last job, when she'd had to strip to her underclothes before the laudanum finally took effect on the railroad detective. Her gun hand quaking as much from cold as from guilt, she had herded the pajama-clad passengers from the sleeping car to the snow, where Diego had looted and ridiculed them.

She had hoped then, as she did now, that Diego would come to appreciate her loyalty and that, finally, he would ask her to marry him. Although she and Diego had had their differences of late, tonight he was counting on her to crack the safe in the express car. He had given her another chance, thank God, even though he'd been furious with her for begging him to forget his dreams of a counterfeiting empire. Arguing with him had proven useless, so she had finally swallowed her misgivings and agreed to help him accumulate the kind of wealth he would need to control the Barbary Coast. Although she didn't share his new fondness for armed robbery, she loved him. That would have to see her through this ordeal.

Uh-oh. Fancy's heart tripped. Marshal Rawlins was on his feet. He was heading for the door! If she bungled this job, Diego might send her back to the whorehouse! She would never see an altar, then. There was only one thing left to do. Make a scene. Hadn't Diego always said that scene-making was her second-greatest talent?

With theatrics worthy of the great Laura Keene, Fancy bounded to her feet, swept the china from her table, and loosed an ear-splitting shriek.

"You cad!" she exclaimed, looming over the innocuous-looking gentleman who sat behind her.

Until that moment, her neighbor had been staring dreamily out the window at the starlight and pines rushing by. Now he turned, blinking owllike at her through thick, round glasses. Only then did Fancy notice his black frock coat and starched white linen collar. She nearly groaned aloud. Her mark was a *preacher!* Why in God's name had she let herself be seated next to a preacher? Convincing Rawlins that this worm of a creature had tried to fondle her would demand the performance of her lifetime.

She let her forefinger shake as she leveled it at the cleric. "Loathsome man. Never in my life have I been so . . . so *vilified!* And you, a pillar of the church. Have you no conscience? No shame?"

The parson had yet to recover his wits, and Fancy glanced hopefully at Rawlins. The marshal looked like he was about to yawn—or worse, to continue on his way. She battled a wave of panic.

"How *dare* you hide your depraved, disgusting behavior behind the trappings of your office!" She flared her nostrils at the man.

"My dear young woman, I think you must have mistaken—"

"Charlatan!" She filled her lungs until her breasts nearly spilled from her artfully rigged corset. "You lie! You would have these good people questioning my integrity. Marshal!" Her bellow rattled the windows and caused at least one passenger to douse his lap with turtle soup. "Arrest this man!"

Rawlins folded his arms across his chest. Straddling the threshold, with the gaslight slanting across his shoulder, he looked like one of the gunslingers that always seemed to adorn the covers of penny dreadfuls.

"You want the preacher cuffed, eh?"

"Yes, sir, I most certainly do!"

"What in blazes for?"

Fancy hiked her chin. Obviously, Mama Rawlins had neglected to teach her son the finer points of etiquette.

"Because that—that *beast* of a man dared to—" she paused dramatically, "to grope me!"

Rawlins chuckled, a rich, warm sound in the breathless silence of the car. "Whoa, darlin'. No one was over there groping anything that you didn't give away a good long time ago."

She bristled. Rawlins's drawl was so pronounced that words like "whoa" and "thing" dragged on for nearly three syllables. But that wasn't the worst part. The worst part was he had seen through her ruse. Despite her stylish emerald traveling suit and the demure black ringlets that framed her face, Cord Rawlins had pegged her for a trollop. She wasn't sure she could ever forgive him for that.

"If you're not man enough to defend my honor," she said coolly, "then I shall be happy to speak to the railroad detective whom I saw dining here earlier."

Every eye in the car shifted eagerly back to Rawlins. He

appeared undaunted. Hooking his thumbs over his gunbelt, he strolled to her side. She was surprised when she realized he was only about three inches taller than she. Standing in the doorway, he had appeared much larger. Nevertheless, the lawman exuded an aura of command. He reminded her of the wild mustang stallion that Diego had corralled last spring.

"Well, Preacher?" Rawlins tipped his Stetson back with a forefinger. A curl so dark brown that it verged on black tumbled across the untanned peak of his forehead. "Speak your piece."

The cleric continued to gape. "Well, I, um . . ."

"Spit it out, man. Did you or did you not grope this . . ." Rawlins paused, arching an eyebrow at the straining buttons of Fancy's bodice. "This, er, lady."

She glared narrowly into his dancing eyes. They brought to mind the jade dragon Diego had won for her—then gambled away. The hurtful memory only made her twice as determined to dislike Rawlins. Fortunately, the man had dimples. Bottomless dimples. They looked like two sickle moons attached to the dazzling white of his grin. She thought there should be a law against virile Texicans with heart-stopping smiles. Cord Rawlins had probably left dozens of calf-eyed sweethearts sighing for him back home on the range.

"I'm sure there must be some reasonable explanation," the preacher babbled. His scarecrow's body trembled as he towered over Rawlins. "I'm sure the young lady just made a mistake—"

"The only mistake I made," Fancy interrupted tartly, "was thinking that this lawman might come to the defense of a lady. No doubt Marshal Rawlins finds such courtesies an imposition on his authority."

"Begging your pardon, ma'am." He indulged her this time with a roguish wink. "I thought you did a mighty fine job of defending yourself."

Oh, did you now? she thought, seething. *Then just wait till you get a load of my .32! If only that blessed moment would come. Where in hell was Diego?*

"Show's over, folks." Rawlins waved his audience back to their meals. "Your pigeons are getting cold."

"That's it?" Fancy gaped at him, forgetting to hide the embarrassing gap between her front teeth. "That's all you're going to do to help me?"

"'Fraid so, ma'am. You aren't any the worse for wear, as far as I can see. And I reckon Parson Brown isn't any worse off, either."

"Why, you—!" Fancy remembered belatedly that ladies didn't curse. "You can't just walk away," she insisted, grabbing Rawlins's sleeve and hoping he would mistake her panic for indignation.

"Says who?"

A nerve-rending screech pierced the expectant silence in the car. Fancy had a heartbeat to identify the braking of iron wheels. In the next instant, the floorboards heaved, throwing her against Rawlins's chest. Silver, crystal, and a diner's toupee flew. She cringed to hear the other passengers scream as she clung to Rawlins's neck. His curse ended in an "umph." Fancy was grateful he'd sacrificed his own spine rather than let hers smash against the carpet. For a moment, Rawlins's tobacco and leather aroma and wiry musculature imprinted themselves on her senses. Then her mind whirred back into action. She had to get his Colt.

Having made a career of outsmarting men, Fancy found it no great feat to shriek, thrash, and wail in a parody of feminine terror. She wriggled across Rawlins's hips and succeeded in hooking her heel behind his knee. She knew she could pin him for only a moment, but a moment was all she needed to slip her Smith & Wesson from her boot and jam its muzzle into his groin.

"Whoa, darling," she taunted above the distant sounds of gunfire.

His face turned scarlet, and she knew he had correctly assessed his situation. He couldn't reach his holster without first dumping her to the floor. And that would be risky, she gloated silently. Most risky indeed.

"Have you lost your goddamned mind?"

"My dear marshal, you really must learn to be more respectful of ladies," she retorted above the other passengers' groans. "Now real slowly, I want you to raise your hands and put them behind your head."

"The hell I will!"

She cocked her .32. "Then you'll have one helluva time explaining to Mrs. Rawlins why you can't father a little lawman of your own."

His eyes darkened to pine-needle green. Fancy felt herself grow uncomfortably warm beneath the challenge of his gaze.

"You're all spit and no claw, girl."

A sudden blast of winter air raced down Fancy's spine. She glanced up to see masked men swarming into the car.

"Perhaps, señor, you are right," said the lean, elegantly dressed man who stalked toward them. "My Fancy, she is just a woman after all. But I am fond of watching *federales* bleed. Too long have I been denied the pleasure."

She caught her breath, recognizing Diego's muffled Castilian accent and his immaculate black frock coat and shirt. Squinting against the wildly swinging gaslight, she saw four of his men race into the next car. Two others remained behind, waving revolvers at the diners. Gold, watches, and jewels plunked into grain sacks; a pile of holsters, guns, and knives accumulated at the center of the car. Diego stopped to stand beside that small arsenal. Above the silk neckerchief that covered two-thirds of his face, his coffee-colored eyes were bright with the thrill of his conquest. Fancy shivered a little. She couldn't help but notice the bullwhip on his hip.

"Now then, señor. I suggest you do as the señorita says, unless, of course"—Diego's revolver glinted like a black diamond in his fist—"you wish to piss lead for the rest of your life."

Rawlins wore a poker face. No one would have guessed that his heart hammered against her breast or that his thighs tensed beneath hers like straining ropes. He was a cool one, this Texican.

"I might have guessed that the dove was in cahoots with someone." Rawlins's lip curled, leaving no doubt in her mind that he considered her a very soiled dove indeed. "But you're wrong, dead wrong, mister, if you think you can get away with this."

"Big talk wastes time, little man. Raise your hands or lose your pecker."

Fancy's eyes locked with Rawlins's. The outrage that blazed there reminded her again of Diego's mustang, a spirited young stallion that he'd whipped to a bloody death. Would Rawlins actually sacrifice his manhood for a show of proud heroics? She found herself holding her breath, half-fascinated, half-frightened by the thought. Having lived the last seven years on the Barbary Coast, she was not accustomed to stubborn displays of grit. Most men met their deaths from behind in the alleys of San Francisco's tenderloin district.

Diego, please, she prayed silently, *you promised there would be no killing. No killing except in self-defense.*

An eternity passed. Finally, Rawlins ground his teeth and raised his hands. Fancy's breath raced from her lungs in a gust of relief.

"Bueno," Diego taunted. "The marshal's gunbelt, Fancy, *por favor."*

Her hand shaking, she groped blindly beneath her skirts. She found the lawman's buckle, but the brass was slippery and the belt leather stiff. She fumbled as she tugged. Diego cursed her slowness. With another barrage of Spanish, he shoved her backward. She cried out when her buttocks struck splintered crystal. He sneered, reaching for the buckle himself.

"On your feet," he snapped, slinging Rawlins's gunbelt over his shoulder.

Diego barked a second order in Spanish, and an unwashed wall of flesh stepped forward. Fancy's nose recognized Bart Wilkerson. The outlaw grabbed Parson Brown and shoved him toward the door. When the preacher resisted, his gangly legs tangled, and he sprawled across the threshold.

"Clod!" Wilkerson bellowed, kicking the parson in the

buttocks. "Get up. Get your scrawny ass up before I fill it with lead!"

The preacher squealed as Wilkerson booted him into the snow.

"Your turn, Marshal," Diego said.

Rawlins's eyes narrowed. His gaze flickered to his captured holster and the civilian weapons that lay beyond his reach. Then he glared at the gunmen who threatened the diners.

"What about the rest of them?" he demanded.

"That depends entirely on your cooperation, señor."

Fancy pictured the thin, cruel smile beneath Diego's mask. *"Andale!"*

Diego gestured with his .45. Rawlins's fingers whitened where he'd laced them behind his head, but he kept his peace as he stalked to the door. Diego turned and sauntered after him. Furtively rubbing her buttocks, Fancy clutched the lucky coin she wore around her neck and hurried after Diego.

Outside, a macabre hissing echoed in the valley. The locomotive had capsized, and the ruptured boiler spewed clouds of steam over the twisted spine of the train. Rawlins's jaw hardened as he gazed upon the scalded remains of what must have been the engineer; Fancy quickly averted her eyes.

Caring is weakness, and weakness is death.

Chanting the old adage over and over in her mind, she stripped off her skirt, revealing the trousers she had concealed underneath. Ribald hoots and cackles encouraged her from the trees, where a handful of outlaws covered the wreckage with their rifles. Strewn across the blood-stained snow, the dozen contorted bodies of soldiers and deputies attested to the gunfight that they'd lost shortly after derailment. She shuddered, trying to think of those men as faceless enemies, nothing more, as she tramped past them.

Diego forced Rawlins to crunch a trail through knee-high drifts. The express car lay behind the parlor and sleeping Pullmans, which the rest of Diego's gang were now looting. Fancy knew that most of the outlaws considered this robbery routine. Only she and Wilkerson knew of Diego's plot to steal U.S. minting plates.

In fact, she had been the one to discover the hidden papers ordering coinage operations to commence at Carson City's branch mint. According to the federal agent she had duped, the necessary machinery would be secretly shipped from the Treasury Department's San Francisco office. That was why the army and the U.S. marshal's office had teamed up to ride shotgun on this train.

"Now to business, Marshal," Diego said as Wilkerson shoved the hostages to their knees. "Call to your men. Tell them to open the door and throw out their weapons."

"And if they refuse?" Rawlins challenged.

In answer, Diego fired. Parson Brown yelped as the bullet clanged into the car's metal wall, just inches beyond his ear. Rawlins's jaw twitched. He tossed a calculating glance at Fancy's .32, which she aimed steadily despite her shivers. He probably thought she would be the easiest to overpower. He would not be the first man to make such an error.

"Hamilton! O'Reilly!" he finally called, his face ghostlike in the stars' frosty light. "It's Rawlins. Open up."

A faint scratching answered his bellow. When the door did not open, Diego arched a brow.

"Your men do not seem overly concerned for your welfare, Marshal. Remind them that we have a train full of passengers and enough bullets for each."

"Why don't you just blow the car to kingdom come?" Rawlins retorted. "Or did you idiots forget the dynamite?"

Diego stiffened. Rawlins had called the outlaw's bluff. Dynamite was out of the question, and Rawlins knew it, if the outlaws hoped to keep the plates intact.

"Call your men again." Diego ground out the words, his eyes glinting like twin stilettos, "Or the first bullet sends the preacher to his maker."

Brown's eyes brimmed with tears, and Rawlins clenched his teeth, forced to relent.

"All right, Hamilton. Enough. Open the goddamned door."

"Sorry, Marshal. I got my orders," came the muffled reply from inside the car.

"To hell with your orders, Captain. They're holding hostages out here!"

Diego, who had taught Fancy everything she knew about theatrics, gestured to her. She nodded in understanding.

"Please, Captain Hamilton," she begged, adopting her best scared-witless tone, "do as they say!"

"They got a woman out there?" called a second voice from inside the car.

Wilkerson jammed his revolver beneath Rawlins's chin before he could answer.

"Yes!" Fancy wailed. "Please, oh *please* open the door. They said they'd kill me! And Parson Brown too!"

"I don't want no preacher's death on my conscience, sir—"

"Shut your mouth, O'Reilly," Hamilton said with a growl.

Fancy could see that drastic actions were required. She gestured for Diego to play along. "Stop!" she sobbed. "You —you're hurting me!"

"I'm just getting started," he snarled on cue.

With extra flair, she tore the false sleeve of her gown from shoulder to cuff. It ripped loudly, and she screamed. The door clanged open.

"Take your filthy hands off her, you sons of—"

"Dammit, O'Reilly! Close that door—"

The soldiers' threats died simultaneously on their lips. Gaping, they blinked at the .32 in Fancy's unwavering fist. The captain's gaze flitted to the hostages. His grip tightened on his rifle.

"You probably think you can kill one of us," Diego said, his voice pleasant despite his sinister words. "You might be right, señors. But then you would die, and the preacher would die, and the fine young marshal here would join you all in hell. You see that stand of trees?" Diego waved toward the grove, no more than thirty paces away. "My men are covering you from there. So you see, you would be wise to throw down your weapons."

Captain Hamilton, a grizzled bear of a man, glared at Rawlins. "I'll have your hide for this, Texican," he said in unmistakably New England accents. He tossed his rifle so that it jutted from the snow crust; the Irishman did the same.

"Out of the car," Diego ordered, motioning the soldiers to their knees. When they were at last shivering beside Rawlins, Diego pulled two grain sacks from his frock coat and thrust them at Fancy. "Empty the safe."

Her heart quickened. Shoving her revolver into her waistband, she furtively crossed her fingers before hoisting herself into the car. She had to stumble over crates, bruising her shins and banging her knees until she finally found a lantern. She congratulated herself for having had the presence of mind to stash a flint inside her pocket. Living a life on the run, she had learned to survive by her wits.

The wick flared, and light bloomed inside the globe. She retreated hastily, unable to quell a sudden shiver. The outlaws always whispered that a fluttering lantern flame portended death. She glanced over her shoulder, and Rawlins's gaze snared hers. She felt as if he'd pinned her to the wall.

"Christ, what are you standing there for?" Wilkerson bellowed. "Get a move on! Crack the safe, bitch."

"If you'd keep your sewer mouth shut for a minute, maybe I could," she fired back. She trusted Wilkerson about as much as she trusted a rattlesnake. In camp the other night, he hadn't been pleased to learn she no longer sold her services. Fortunately Diego had been sober enough to protect her—and himself—from a bullet.

Shaking away those thoughts, she knelt and pressed her ear to the door of the safe. She turned the dial with painstaking slowness, her ears straining for the faint echoes that would betray the lock's combination. Once, twice, three times, she tried the handle and failed. It was nerve-racking work. She didn't realize that she'd worried her lip until she tasted blood.

"We're gonna freeze to death before that slut figures out

what she's doing," Wilkerson grumbled. "Let's blast the damned thing open and be done with it."

"You don't have the brain that God gave a cockroach," Diego retorted. "Shut up."

"Stinking greaser! I'll carve out your tongue and serve it for breakfast—"

The door swung open. Fancy caught her breath. Never before had she seen so much silver! For a moment, as the car walls reverberated with Wilkerson's tirade, greed whispered to her heart. Only Rawlins watched her now. She could feel his eyes stabbing through her, but he couldn't stop her. Not with Diego's gun trained on him. She could stash a few bars inside her pockets and no one would be the wiser. . . .

Visions of Diego's bullwhip quickly negated that idea. Shuddering, she reached for the nearest bar of ore.

The silver was heavy, and she wasted precious time lifting the bullion from the safe. As if that weren't bad enough, she quickly found that Diego's sacks were too small. No matter how she restacked and rearranged, she couldn't fit all the silver and the four minting plates inside. The canvas seams were in danger of splitting; she wasn't even certain she could hoist the sacks. She needed to find another way to carry the two remaining plates.

Biting her lip again, she gazed around her. Dangling from the corner of a nearby crate was a heavy woolen duster. Judging by its lingering odor of tobacco, Fancy decided the coat belonged to Rawlins. She couldn't help but smile to herself. How ironic that a marshal's coat would help her commit a federal crime!

Thrusting her arms through the long sleeves, she turned her back on her cohorts and stuffed two minting plates into her pants. She used her belt to strap them to her waist before she stashed her .32 in a pocket and buttoned the coat to her chin. The voluminous duster disguised the lumps against her stomach. Still, she felt clumsy and not at all certain she could ride a horse, despite the coat's accommodating rear slit. Whenever she bent forward, the leaden plates bludgeoned her ribs. She was beginning to think there must be a better solution when Wilkerson stuck his head into the car.

"What're you up to, slut? Whatcha got that coat on for?"

She blushed, and was glad the lantern threw her face into shadow. Diego's eyes had narrowed as he, too, noticed the duster. She stooped hastily, dragging the sacks forward.

"I'm cold. I ripped my sleeve, remember?" she said, trying not to imagine what Diego would do if he thought she had cheated him.

"Get down, *querida.*"

She swallowed. "But Diego, I couldn't carry all the—"

"Get down."

She thought better of defending herself. He wouldn't believe her, anyway.

As she eased to the ground, snow flurried, dusting her eyelashes. She blinked, squinting toward the outlaws who had mounted their horses and were waiting in a cluster near the tracks. At their forefront was Gonzalez. The heavy-set Mexican was recognizable by the double set of cartridge belts that he wore slung across his shoulders. He rode forward, leading Wilkerson's horse. Fancy's heart quickened as he approached the express car. Only one horse? What was the idiot thinking?

Uneasily, she drew her .32. Wilkerson grabbed the silver bags. Carrying them to his horse, he strapped them behind the saddle. Diego waved to Gonzalez.

"Our friend Wilkerson is finished now," he said.

"*Sí.*"

Fancy dashed a hand across her eyes. The snow was so deceptive. For a moment, she actually imagined that Gonzalez had turned his rifle on Wilkerson's back. Had Diego conspired with the Mexican to kill Wilkerson?

A shot rang out. Grunting, Gonzalez pitched forward. His horse reared, bolting, and his unfired Remington sank beside his lifeless body in the drifts.

"What the—?" Wilkerson grabbed a shotgun from his saddle. "Who the hell is shooting?" he shouted as gunfire spat again from the windows of the train. Near the grove, a mounted outlaw crashed to the snow. The bandits scattered, but three more fell before their horses reached the trees.

"My God, it must be the railroad detective," Fancy said, glancing nervously at Diego. "He must have stashed rifles on the train and passed them out to the passengers!"

Diego bit out an expletive as he rounded on her. She heard his gun chamber click, and for a split second, she thought he might actually shoot her. Then she spied a whir of movement.

"For God's sake, woman, run!" Rawlins shouted as he dived for an army rifle, snapped its breechblock, and fired. Never before had Fancy seen a man move so fast. Diego shrieked when the bullet ripped through his shoulder. Blood spurted, and his gun arm dangled. A second shot smashed through his leg. He crumpled to the snow, and Rawlins rolled beneath the train.

"Diego!" Her stomach crawling to her throat, Fancy ran toward him. She slid to a halt before the threat of O'Reilly's rifle.

"Drop the .32. Drop it!" the young corporal shouted, his voice high and wavering.

The gun slid from her shaking fingers.

"Diego?" she whispered again.

He didn't answer. He didn't move. His blood seeped into the snow in widening circles. This time when she blinked, she felt the hot sting of tears.

She turned to run. O'Reilly wouldn't shoot her, she reasoned wildly. Not a woman. Not in the back!

"Halt!"

Warning bullets burrowed in the snow around her boots. She stumbled, glancing fearfully over her shoulder. O'Reilly hesitated, and Wilkerson's buckshot drilled through him. She was nearly deafened by the second blast that tore Hamilton's chest in two.

Rawlins loosed a retaliatory volley, and Wilkerson screamed. His shotgun clattered across a patch of ice. Fancy almost retched to see the weapon's trail of blood. Gathering her wits, she raced for the horse Gonzalez had been leading.

"You ain't riding off without me, bitch!" Wilkerson cried as she wrestled with the frightened animal. She threw her boot into the stirrup, and Wilkerson drew his .45. Blood bubbled from his chest as he rose, firing at the entrenched lawman. Bullets pinged off the iron rails, and Rawlins yelped. His curses were vehement when Parson Brown appeared, dragging him back beneath the belly of the train.

"Wilkerson!" Fancy struggled to sit his skittering mare. "Mount up! Grab my hand!"

He grunted, nearly dragging her to the snow as he threw himself behind her. More bullets whined past her ears. The mare half reared as Wilkerson raked his spurs across her belly.

Minutes passed like hours. They galloped through the maze of trees, leaving the gunfire and shouting behind. The snow began to fall so fast that Fancy could see little beyond the horse's ears. She was grateful for the flakes on the one hand, for they would delay pursuit and cover their tracks. On the other, she feared she might freeze to death before they found decent shelter. The rifles had long since fallen silent. She couldn't tell where the rails were, much less the train and the surviving outlaws.

"Slow up." Wilkerson's voice was raspy. "Can't you see Bessie's laboring?"

He wrenched the reins from her hands, and the mare stumbled to a halt, her sides heaving.

"Get down," Wilkerson said.

"What?"

"Get down, you stupid whore!"

Fancy quailed when his gun hammer clicked in her ear. "All right! All right! Take it easy, Wilkerson."

Careful to keep the plates anchored to her waist, she jumped, landing knee-deep in a drift. "Where are we?"

"Hell, I don't know. A mile, maybe two, north of Carson." He doubled over, clutching his chest, then wrenched the horse's head around. She gaped.

"Wilkerson, wait! You can't just leave me here."

He laughed. The sound was cruel and pitiless before it wheezed into a cough. "You are stupid." His hand shook as he holstered the gun. "I got the plates and the silver. I don't need nothing else, 'specially no aging, smart-alecky whore."

"You need someone to bind that wound!" she said desperately. "You'll bleed to death before you reach Carson."

"This ain't nothing. The Yanks shot me up a sight worse at Chickamauga."

"But I'll freeze!"

"Then you best start walking, eh, long legs?" He cackled as he spurred the mare. "See ya in hell."

"Wilkerson!"

Her cry echoed off the valley walls. He never looked back as he cantered away.

She railed. She cursed God, Wilkerson, and the elements. She damned Diego for letting himself get killed. But most of all, she damned herself for surrendering her .32.

Her throat burned from yelling, but the rest of her felt cold. Thrusting her hands into Rawlins's pockets, she rummaged inside. Her fingers were stiff despite her kid gloves, and she had trouble pulling out the pockets' contents: tobacco, jerky, riding gauntlets, and a whittling knife. She felt a grudging gratitude for Rawlins's possessions until she remembered how he'd shot Diego.

And quite possibly saved her life.

She hurriedly dismissed such a notion. Diego had loved her; he would never have betrayed her as he'd tried to betray Wilkerson. She would make Cord Rawlins pay for killing Diego. But first, she would have to survive.

Her hands quaked as she tugged on the gauntlets. She reminded herself that she'd lived through tougher spots than this. She had her flint, and a knife. She could eat. All she had to do was keep moving. She knew that every lawman in Nevada would be looking for her and that they'd start in Carson City, but it couldn't be helped. It was either Carson or freeze.

A pearl-gray dimness heralded the rising moon. Clouds

dumped less snow now. Tucking her fists beneath her arms, she trudged south into the dwindling storm.

Lawmen were just men, she comforted herself grimly. And there wasn't a man alive she couldn't seduce, outsmart, or bribe.

Chapter Two

Cord Rawlins squinted at the crudely painted sign. It was supposed to proclaim the shack before him as the Diamondback Saloon. He wasn't much good at letters, but he recognized the snarling rattler with its exaggerated fangs. Little else distinguished this pinewood shanty from the dozen other saloons on Main Street. One-story beer joints with their false fronts and swinging doors were as common as dust in Hell's Half Acre.

Cord swung down from his saddle and tied Poco to the crowded hitching post. At high noon, the Diamondback was already rowdy. Piano music tinkled above the laughter and cursing that floated outside. A gunshot suddenly hushed the din, but the noise quickly roared back to normal. Cord smiled mirthlessly and unhooked his holster's trigger guard. Near the door, another sign demanded that all patrons check their weapons with the sheriff. The ordinance was largely ignored now, but five years earlier, Cord had strictly enforced it when he kept the peace here as a Texas Ranger.

"Think she's in there, Cord?"

Nodding, Cord donned his sternest expression for the

eager sixteen-year-old who had refused to stay out of trouble and on the range, where he belonged.

Undaunted, Wes Rawlins jumped down from his horse. His red-gold head rose four inches higher than his brother's.

"Hey Zack, get your nose outta that paper," Wes said, slapping a hand across his double-holstered rig. "We're gonna catch ourselves a real train robber!"

Zack's high, thoughtful brow furrowed as he studied Fancy Holleday's wanted poster. At seventeen, he had taken it upon himself to be a gentling influence on his two more willful brothers.

"Are you sure we're on the right trail, Cord?" Zack asked. "I mean, Miss Holleday looks too purdy to be an outlaw."

Wes snickered, elbowing Cord in the ribs. "Zack's in love with the bandit queen."

"I am not!"

"You are too."

Zack blushed to the roots of his chestnut hair, and Cord shook his head. He wondered for the hundredth time why he hadn't cuffed his brothers to the breakfast table—as he'd had half a mind to do—when he left Aunt Lally's ranch. For two days, Wes and Zack had dogged him north through desperado country. Fearing they might get their fool heads blown off, he had finally let them catch up.

"Quit your squawking," he told them. "I want the two of you to wait out here."

"Nothing doing, Cord."

"That's right," Zack chimed in. "We're going in with you. We promised Aunt Lally we'd bring you back safe in time for droving, and safe you're gonna be."

Cord sighed. He figured it was useless to remind his still-wet-behind-the-ears brothers that he'd survived the War Between the States, several Indian raids, and countless shootouts without their help. Arguing with them now would only waste time, and God knew, he had wasted enough of that by tracking Fancy Holleday.

Never mind that hundreds of ruthless men were preying on decent folks across the territories. He had been ordered to hunt down a gun-toting floozie. But that wasn't the worst part. The worst part was that Fancy's dining-car antics had been reported to the U.S. marshal's office by irate passengers, who had blamed Cord for the robbery's success. Never in Cord's thirty years had he felt like such a laughingstock. Even if he did manage to arrest the hoyden before she reached Mexico and tried to unload the minting plates there, he wasn't sure he could ever repair his reputation. He only hoped to God he could keep his humiliation from his brothers. He didn't think he could bear it if they learned what a jackass "purdy Miss Holleday" had made out of him.

His face heated at the thought.

"If you boys are so bent on being deputies, then you best start following orders. Think you can do that for once?"

They nodded, their stubbled faces bright with anticipation.

"Good. Then keep close."

He crossed the heat-warped porch and halted before the swinging doors. As eager as he was to teach Fancy Holleday a lesson, his first priority would have to be his brothers' safety.

Warily, he surveyed the room beyond. Cattle season was still a month away, so drovers were sparse among the buffalo hunters, desperadoes, and whores. Stale beer and tobacco juice had attracted a never-ending stream of flies that buzzed past the open shutters and lighted on the bar. Behind the pistol-packing barkeep, a cracked mirror had been white-washed with the words "Lunch, 25¢."

"Is that her, Cord?" Zack whispered, pointing at a flirtatious young woman who sat playing five-card stud at a center table.

Cord nodded. That was her, all right. He would have recognized that wicked little hellcat smile anywhere. It was the same smile she had worn when she cocked her pistol at his pecker. Just last night, he'd had another nightmare about that .32 and had sat bolt upright, sweating like a plow mule.

Nope, he wasn't likely to forget that gun. Or that grin. He figured the little minx must always smile like that when she was up to no good. Like cheating.

He was too far away, of course, to tell if she was really palming cards, but he wouldn't have put it past her. His only consolation came from watching the poker players, who were faring no better against her than he had. None of them seemed to realize they were being fleeced.

Of course, there was always the possibility that none of them *cared* they were being fleeced, Cord thought dryly. He might not have minded a fleecing so much, either, if Fancy Holleday sat an arm's length from him with her corset rigged like that. Plump and delicately powdered, her breasts rose and fell hypnotically in a bodice that threatened to spit out buttons.

He tore his gaze away. Only then did he notice Wes. The boy was grinning like a coyote in a henhouse.

"Hoo-dogie. That poster didn't say nothing 'bout teats the size of—"

"That's enough, boy."

Zack chuckled, and Cord glared at him in turn. He didn't need to be reminded that his would-be prisoner was a desirable woman—or that the brothers he'd been raising since childhood were turning into men.

"All right, listen up." He pulled them into a huddle beside the doors. "Here's the plan. Zack goes in first. Then you, Wes. You cross to different sides of the room. You stand with your backs to the wall. You don't talk to anybody; you don't look slantways at anybody. You keep yourselves out of trouble while I make the arrest. Got that?"

"Shoot," Wes grumbled. "That sounds about as exciting as shooing flies off the back porch."

"You want excitment? I'll tan your hide."

"Aunt Lally tried to wash his mouth out with soap once." Zack smirked, winking. "That was exciting."

"Tattletale!"

"Donkey brain."

Cord frowned. He was sorely tempted to lock them both in the local jail, but a three-nail hoosegow wouldn't keep two Rawlins brothers safe for long.

"You boys done cuss-fighting?" He shot them each a warning look.

They fell silent instantly, nodding as they reddened.

"Good. Then let's get started."

His hand on his holster, Cord watched as Zack pushed inside. The boy could usually be counted on to follow orders. Still, Cord found himself holding his breath until Zack skirted the billiard table and took a stance near the caged rattlesnake that gave the saloon its name.

Wes followed a few moments later. To Cord's consternation, the boy stopped to tip his hat to a flock of soiled doves. Cord thought he would have to go in and drag the rascal off by his ear, but Wes eventually remembered his mission. Amidst a great deal of cooing, he swaggered off and propped a shoulder against the saloon's half-hinged alley door.

Cord released a ragged breath. At last it was his turn.

Hooking his thumbs over his gun belt, he shouldered his way through the crowd. A drunkard lurched forward, waving a handful of markers in his face, but Cord shook his head and pressed on. Most of the wagers being made by the game's spectators favored Fancy. The gamblers were lauding her as the "Princess of Poker" and "Fortune's Fancy."

"Huckster Holleday," he thought grimly, was closer to the mark.

He halted behind his quarry. He'd arrived just in time to watch her shuffle. Flawlessly manicured, her fingers cut, riffled, and folded the deck like greased lightning. Cord found it impossible to follow every gesture. In his gut, though, he knew she was cheating. He also knew he would risk a shootout with her admirers if he interrupted her deal. In order to haul her off without protest, he would have to prove she wasn't playing square. He forced himself to bide his time, watching her silver ring flash as she doled out the first round of cards.

"Uh . . . I'll bet a dollar," said the charcoal-smeared giant sitting to her left.

"A whole dollar," she purred, her voice throbbing with false praise.

The giant blushed like a schoolboy, and Cord recognized Dolf Vandermeer, the town blacksmith. The other players, a grizzled drifter and a sun-blackened mule skinner named Turk, both raised Vandermeer's bet.

Fancy dealt again. Cord watched her narrowly through the next three rounds. He was careful to keep his shadow off her cards, a precaution born of habit rather than necessity. She was too busy flirting and carrying on to notice a lawman at her rear. The girl was in her glory, all right. Judging by his neighbors, there wasn't a man in the saloon who wasn't smitten. With her heart-shaped face and violet-blue eyes, she had every rowdy fantasizing about meeting her in a hayloft. If that tongue of hers hadn't come with the package, Cord might have hankered for a rendezvous too. He wondered if there was a man in the room who could straighten her out and settle her down.

"And the dealer takes a lady," she concluded, setting the rest of the deck on the table. "Possible three-of-a-kind."

It was the fifth and final round. Vandermeer had already folded. He looked glassy-eyed from staring down Fancy's cleavage. Turk was drooling like a coonhound. Only the drifter seemed unmoved by her charms. In fact, the man looked downright sinister as he watched her play, his hat slanting across his gunmetal-gray eyes. Cord racked his brain, trying to remember which wanted poster the man resembled most.

But if Fancy was unnerved by the drifter's stare, she didn't let on. She simply treated him to a loins-stirring smile.

"Your jacks bet again, Mr. Slade."

Slade's expression never wavered. He threw a double eagle onto the pile of gold pieces. Turk chewed his bottom lip. Shrugging, he finally called. Cord estimated that the kitty was well worth two hundred dollars when it came Fancy's turn to wager.

"You have quite a show of might there, Mr. Slade, with your three jacks and a king. I so adore a man of might," she crooned, lacing her fingers beneath her chin. "But luck is a lady, so they say. So I'll see your twenty dollars, sir, and raise you twenty."

Cord arched a brow. She'd made a helluva bet, considering she only had two queens showing against Slade's three jacks—and his possible full house. Did she have the third queen or was she bluffing? Cord wasn't sure, but he would have wagered a month's worth of pay that Fancy knew what card Slade was holding. The only question was, How?

Turk grimaced and folded. Slade fingered his coins. His eyes were so cold that Cord worried he might have a dead prisoner on his hands if he didn't end Fancy's cheating soon.

"All right, woman, I call," the drifter growled, tossing in his gold. "Whatcha got?"

With a deft flick of her wrist, Fancy turned over her hidden card. The queen of hearts fell into place by her sisters.

"My calling card," she said sweetly.

Slade's face darkened. She resumed her coquettish pose. The glint of her ring attracted Cord's eye once more, and he suddenly understood how she must have rigged the game.

"Hold on, Slade," he called. "Don't bother to show Miss Holleday your hand. She' knows you don't have that full house. Fact is"—with the speed of a gunfighter, he grabbed her wrist and turned the flat, polished surface of her ring to the lantern—"she used this little mirror here to see exactly what she did deal you."

A grumble of discontent circled the crowd. Slade hiked an eyebrow. But not until Vandermeer lurched to his feet did Cord realize the extent of Fancy's popularity in this woman-scarce cowtown.

"Listen here, lawman," the giant rumbled, "wearing a badge don't give you the right to call a lady a cheat."

"You misunderstood me, Dolf. I called Miss Holleday a cheat."

The goliath was unarmed, and Cord stared him down. Fancy looked a little shaken to see her champion sit. She was a brassy piece, though, and she didn't let her worry show for long. She twisted in her chair, and he almost admired the saucy way she raised her chin at him.

"Well, well, well."

Eyes as purple as a summer thundercloud raked him from hat to toe. "Marshal Rawlins, isn't it? Why yes, I do believe it is. I don't often forget a"—her dimples peeked—"pair of chaps."

Whoops of laughter erupted around him. Cord carved his lips into a tight smile. She was brassy, all right. Brassy and tarnished.

"The game's over, darlin'. Give the nice gentlemen back their money, and we'll be on our way."

"Just what did you have in mind, handsome?"

"A date with a Nevada judge."

"Do tell?" She lowered fluttering lashes over anxious eyes. "And would this be a marrying judge?"

More hurrahing from the crowd. She was playing to please her audience. No doubt she thought her supporters were her only hope. And she would have been right—if he'd been the kind who let roughnecks set his knees to knocking.

"Can't say that he is."

"Pity." She shrugged with catlike grace. "I guess you'll have to ride the lonely trail alone then, cowboy."

"I got a better idea. How 'bout I get my rope?"

The mockery froze on her face.

Slade struck a match. It hissed into life in the breathless silence.

"Is cheating a federal crime now, Rawlins?"

Cord glared at the drifter. In spite of the casual way Slade puffed his smoke, his demeanor was full of challenge.

"You know a lot about crime, mister?"

"Mebbe," Slade drawled, his lips twisting in a thin smile. Cord couldn't help but notice how the man's amusement never lit his eyes.

"Mr. Slade's a bounty hunter," Fancy said, her voice dripping honey for her newest champion. "Sheriff Applegate sends him out after cutthroats and road agents. Isn't that right, Wilton?"

Slade ignored her. Propping his heels up on the table, he leaned back in his chair. "Seems like a waste of time for a federal lawman to be chasing down a card sharp, don't it? 'Specially one wearing a skirt."

"I got my reasons," Cord said gruffly. He didn't much like bounty hunters. Most of them were no better than paid assassins. Some were so greedy that they killed at random, bringing in any corpse that might fit the description on a wanted poster.

He kept a wary eye on the manhunter as he turned back to Fancy. "Well? You coming peaceably? 'Cause it wouldn't grieve me any to have to hog-tie you."

"How manly of you." Her smile looked tense in her come-hither facade. "Tell me, Marshal. Do you tie up all your women? Or just the ones who get away?"

Someone snickered. Cord ignored the man. Instead, he took a deliberate step closer to Fancy, leaning down and placing his hands on each arm of her chair.

"You know something?" he said quietly. "I thought you were smart. I thought you could spot an ace in the hole."

"Meaning?"

"Meaning I just might be the only thing standing between you and a tomahawk on the trail."

"Now that sounds too good to be true."

He snorted. "Don't go celebrating just yet, darlin'. You aren't done wrangling with me." He yanked her chair around, and was rewarded to hear her sharp intake of breath. "On your feet. I won't be saying it again."

He thought she'd turned a full shade paler. He'd been waiting a long time for her comeuppance, and he planned to enjoy every moment of it. He watched her eyes flicker left and then right, as if she were seeking a savior—or gauging her chance of escape. The odds were against her this time.

He straightened, folding his arms across his chest, and smugly wondered what she would do. Would she get weepy and beg for his mercy? Would she turn to sugar and start to apologize?

He should have known better, of course. She gazed past him toward the swinging doors, and a sudden flood of relief washed the uneasiness from her face.

"Er . . . Marshal, you didn't happen to stop by Sheriff Applegate's office on your way to harass me, did you?"

He eyed her suspiciously. "I don't answer to Tarrant County."

"Then mebbe it's time you did, mister," boomed a canyon-deep voice from behind him.

"Who the—"

The sound of a priming rifle jarred Cord's spine. He froze in midturn.

"I'd just as soon shoot you as look at you, mister, so keep your hands high."

Fancy laughed, the sound warm and sweet with triumph. "Why, Sheriff Applegate. What took you so long?"

Cord ground his teeth. If she thought a swaggering, granddaddy of a sheriff was going to keep her out of a federal reformatory, she had another thing coming.

"Blast it, Applegate. It's Cord. Cord Rawlins. You going to let me turn around?"

"Cord?" The sheriff sounded skeptical. "I heard you were scalped by Comanches."

"Then you heard wrong."

"Hellfire." Amusement crept into Applegate's gruff voice. "I shoulda known you'd be too ornery to die. Turn around, son, and let me look at you."

Cord found himself grinning as he obeyed. Fourteen years ago, he'd hunted cattle rustlers alongside Clem Applegate. A prosperous rancher, the man had been a law unto himself in Tarrant County. Then the war had come, and with it confiscation—or Reconstruction, as the Yankees liked to call it. Clem had lost his livestock, his spread, and just about everything else, except for his belly.

Yep, Applegate was still as wide and red as a barn, with whiskers big enough to match. Of course, the sheriff's beard was a little grayer now, his brow more lined, but Cord felt certain that the sixty-year-old lawman could still shoot out the eye of a rattler at fifty paces.

"So they went and made a U.S. marshal out of you, eh?" Applegate said, studying the star on Cord's vest. "That explains the gunfighter my deputy saw going inside this saloon. 'Course, it don't explain what you're doing 'round these parts. Ain't seen hide nor hair of you for two years, Cord, not since that wife of yours passed on."

Cord stiffened, feeling Fancy's speculative gaze upon him. He wished Applegate had kept his mouth shut about Bethany.

"I'm here to make an arrest."

"An arrest, eh? Hot damn." Applegate stepped forward and menaced Turk. "What did the mule skinner do this time? Lynch a lawman? Drown a baby?"

"I didn't do nothing!" Turk wailed.

"Sure you did, you stinking heap of cow turd. I just didn't find out about it yet."

Cord shook his head. He was used to Applegate's style of peacekeeping. "Turk's all yours, Sheriff. I came for Miss Holleday."

"You came to arrest Fancy?" Applegate's brows rose, then he donned a lopsided grin. "Aw, what did she do, son? Steal your heart?"

The crowd behind Applegate dissolved into back-slapping and guffaws. Cord felt his ears burn, knowing his brothers were probably laughing with everyone else. He tugged a wanted poster from his pocket and thrust it at the sheriff.

"Train robbery, eh?" Applegate tossed the paper aside, and it fluttered to rest beneath Slade's chair. "Looks like you're roping the wrong steer. Or in this case, the wrong heifer. Miss Fancy don't look nothing like that wanted poster. She's purdier."

"Why, thank you, Sheriff."

"Sure 'nuff, sweet thing."

Cord swallowed his oath. He'd often wondered these last four months how Fancy had escaped two jail cells and a dozen posses before he could arrive in time to haul her back to Carson City. Lawmen all across the west had reported that they'd lost her—and they didn't quite know how. They didn't quite know how, his rear end! If just one of them had thought with his brain instead of his pecker, Cord could be hunting a murderer or counterfeiter worth hanging by now.

"Look, Applegate. I was there. I saw her crack open the safe on that express car."

"Well hell. Then how did she get away, son? Did she take your gun?"

He felt his face heat.

"Clem, really. You're embarrassing Marshal Rawlins," Fancy said in her syrupy alto. "Why don't you tell Sheriff Applegate what really happened, Cord? You can't let him go on thinking that I"—she smirked—"robbed you of your piece."

He wanted to wring her neck. No, better: he wanted to spank the living daylights out of her. His handprint on her behind ought to keep her biting her tongue when she was bouncing in a saddle back to Carson.

"The fact is, Sheriff, this woman robbed a train on the Central Pacific railroad."

"Well . . ." Applegate still didn't look convinced. "It serves them prairie diggers right. You know we ain't too partial to the railroad 'round here. Fort Worth's still waiting on its feeder line."

"It's not that simple, Clem. She stole valuable government property."

Applegate snorted, hiking his breeches. "Now you'd be talking about the United States government, wouldn't you, Cord? We ain't too partial to that 'round here, neither."

The crowd rumbled in approval. Twenty pairs of burning rebel eyes drilled into him. Cord's jaw twitched, and he glanced at Fancy. Smirking, she looped a curl around her finger like a hangman's noose.

"Look, Clem," somehow, he managed to keep the frustration from his voice, "I've got a job to do. I'm talking to you lawman to lawman. Texican to Texican. I've come for my prisoner, and I'm not leaving without her."

Applegate shifted uncomfortably, his gaze straying to Fancy. "Well, seeing as how you put it that way . . ."

She looked stricken, her eyes brimming, and Applegate's

resolve weakened visibly. Cord could practically map its retreat across the man's craggy features.

"I reckon you'll just have to tell that Yankee judge of yours to wait his turn," Applegate finished finally.

"His turn for what?"

"Well, you see, Cord, Miss Fancy's done rustled, thieved, and bamboozled half the cowpokes in Tarrant County. If she weren't so goldurned pretty, they'd have strung her up by now. Ain't that right, Slade?"

"Is a pig's butt pork?" the bounty hunter growled.

Applegate winked at Fancy. She flashed him the most delightfully wicked smile that any man could hope to withstand and still keep his pants on. Cord struggled with his patience.

"Reckon we'll be keeping the little darlin' safe till Judge Crowley rides back to town," Applegate continued. "There's a big hanging trial going on out Dallas-way. Crowley won't be back this side of the Trinity River for a month. Mebbe two."

"Two months!" Cord nearly choked on the string of curse words that he forced back down his throat. "You can't expect me to sit around here just whistling at the moon."

"Well, son," Applegate patted his Winchester, "I don't see how you got much choice."

An expectant hush settled over the room. Cord glanced at his brothers. They just might run half-cocked to his rescue and try to tangle with Sheriff Deadeye. He decided he'd better try to reason with the man.

"All right, Applegate. Supposing I let Tarrant County take first crack at her. Supposing I agree to wait out your trial. What makes you think Miss Holleday won't hightail it down to Mexico the first chance she gets?"

"I got the lady's word."

"Her *word?*" Cord's jaw dropped. "Dadblast it, Clem, her word's about as good as a tin quarter!"

Applegate frowned. "In case you're forgetting, Mister Yankee Marshal, around these parts, we don't talk about a lady like that. Now, you want to tell Miss Fancy you're sorry? Or you want to step outside?"

Cord ground his teeth. He should accept Applegate's invitation and lick some sense into the old skirt chaser. Problem was, he had a soft spot for the man. He didn't want to be the one to show Tarrant County what a fool Fancy Holleday was making of its sheriff. So once again, he'd have to bide his time—until night fell, anyway.

Leaning forward, Cord planted his hands on the table and lowered his face to hers.

"Reckon you're right pleased with yourself, eh?"

She tilted her chin, and he was struck again by her eyes, two shimmering violet oases.

"You're not much of a sport, are you, Marshal?"

"Cord?" Applegate shouted. "You apologizing over there?"

"Sure, Sheriff. I'm apologizing."

He watched the ripple of triumph in those bottomless eyes. "But don't deal me out just yet, sweetheart," he added, lowering his voice so only she could hear.

"Mmm."

Her moist cherry-red lips curved in such a tantalizing smile that his traitorous mouth actually watered.

"Then by all means, Marshal," she said softly, "welcome to my game."

Chapter Three

Later that evening, Fancy sat demurely on a jail cell bed. Sipping coffee as thick as a river bottom, she took great pains to look and act at ease. She winked and flirted, coaxing an occasional blush from the two lawmen who guarded her, but on the inside, her stomach was churning fast enough to make butter.

She kept telling herself that surrendering to the sheriff had been a smart idea. Thanks to Cord Rawlins and that damned wanted poster, jail was now the safest place in town. She'd felt doomed when she saw Slade reach beneath his chair and tuck her likeness into his pocket. A professional manhunter wouldn't have wasted his time tracking her across the country for the original $50 bounty. But the reward for her capture had climbed to $500. Now she worried every cold-blooded killer in Hell's Half Acre would be on her trail.

Fancy swallowed hard. She needed time, time to find the Wilkerson gang. Then she could make Cord Rawlins pay for killing Diego. She would tell the other outlaws that he had inflicted the wound that eventually caused Bart Wilkerson's death. Hearing that, Bart's cousin Ned should be pleased to get rid of Rawlins for her.

She smiled, relishing the thought.

Yes, she would have both of her revenges after all. She had vowed to make Bart rue the day he left her to freeze to death in Nevada. Tracking him south, she had figured he was heading for New Mexico and his estranged kinfolk, but his trail had ended in Hell's Half Acre. By the time she caught up with Bart, the snake had died of his gunshot wound.

Fancy had felt cheated of Bart's plates, the silver, and her vengeance until she stumbled across Bart's doctor in a saloon. The drunkard had bragged of meeting Bart's cousin, the notorious Ned Wilkerson, when the outlaw came to Bart's deathbed. Apparently Ned and his gang had been lured all the way from Lincoln County, New Mexico. The ailing Bart had promised to split his profits with his cousin and the other outlaws if they helped Bart get his minting plates to buyers in Mexico City.

"'Course, by the time Ned got there, ol' Bart was weak as a newborn," Doc Tate had slurred in his rummy voice, "so I told Bart to stay abed. I told him all his boozin' and whorin' was gonna do him in, and damn if he didn't prove me right. Not an hour later, he knocked hisself clean out. Dropped like a rock, he did, when he hit his head on the stone wall outside of Cattleman's Bank. Meanwhile, Sheriff Applegate got wind of Ned hidin' out in the Acre, and the next thing we knew, Ned was hightailin' it out of town like his britches was on fire."

Upon hearing this story, Fancy had concluded that Ned must have fled with Bart's plates. Planning her own safe passport out of Texas, she had promptly sent wires to Lincoln County in the hopes that one would reach Ned. She had offered to cut him in on the deal she would make with Mexican nationals for her own two minting plates if he returned and escorted her safely across the border.

Ned was due to ride back into Fort Worth that very night to discuss their partnership. Considering the stakes, Fancy was betting he wouldn't leave her in jail for long.

A deep rumble of laughter broke her reverie and brought her attention back to her pathetic excuse for a holding cell. She couldn't help but wonder if a strong wind had ever knocked the building down, especially when the roof creaked and groaned.

"Hey, Fancy's gone and made the news," Applegate said, shaking open an outdated copy of the Dallas *Herald*. Winking at her, he turned back to the town marshal, a surly, one-eyed war veteran named Brand.

"Listen here. Says Fort Worth imported itself a lady card-sharper 'cause none of the Tarrant County boys knows how to play a man's game of poker."

Brand snorted. "That's worse than the *Herald*'s last whopper 'bout a panther falling asleep on Main Street 'cause there weren't nothing better to do in Fort Worth. When are you taking a posse over to Dallas County to put a stop to them cock-and-bull stories?"

Applegate chuckled, gesturing toward the Fort Worth *Democrat* that lay on the table beside Brand's freshly cleaned Winchester.

"I reckon I'll do that after you put some pressure on your friends to quit spinning yarns about Dallas County."

Fancy only half listened. Her ears had pricked to another series of creaks and groans. This time, she could have sworn they were accompanied by the muffled jingle of spurs. Her heart quickened. Had Wilkerson's gang finally arrived?

She cast a nervous glance at the lawmen. She was beginning to wonder if she should somehow lure them into the next room, when a lanky youth burst through the door.

"Marshal Brand! Sheriff Applegate! You gotta come quick," the boy shouted. He slid to a sudden halt, as if arrested by the sight of her bodice.

"Yeah?" Brand growled. "What for?"

The boy seemed to collect himself. Clutching his chest, he made a great show of panting and stumbled to Brand's desk. "The Carson boys just rode into town. They say they're looking for Pete Hancock. They say they've come to even the score after ol' Pete pistol-whipped Jim-Bob Carson!"

"Tarnation," Brand grumbled. "Can't those boys cheat trouble for a spell? I just arrested the whole Carson clan last Saturday for shooting up the big coffeepot over Jim Bradner's tin store."

"That was five nights ago," Applegate said. "You know

better than to ask a self-respecting cowpoke to pass a whole week without mischief."

The messenger nodded, his Stetson plunking down over the bridge of his nose. He blushed as red as his hair. Hastily shoving the hat back, he hooked his thumbs over his double-holstered rig.

Fancy couldn't help but find the youth familiar, even though she had a keen memory for faces and she knew she'd never seen his before.

"Yeah?" Brand said to Applegate, rising and snatching up his rifle. "And just what are we gonna do with them rowdies once we round 'em up? We can't throw them in the hoose-gow with Fancy."

"Not we, son. *You,*" Applegate said, settling his girth back into his chair and spreading out his paper. "This here's Fort Worth business, not Tarrant County. 'Sides, I kept the peace today at the Diamondback, when you were losing your shirt at craps."

The young messenger's face fell. For a moment, he looked so crestfallen that Fancy was surprised—and more than a little suspicious—when a scheming look broke across his features. He was quick to hide it.

"There sure were a lot of them Carson boys, Sheriff," the youth said, sounding grave. "I reckon I could watch your prisoner a spell if Marshal Brand needed a neighborly hand from Tarrant County."

"Much obliged, son," Brand snapped back, throwing his rifle across his shoulder. "But they'll see snow in San Antone before Applegate squeezes his bulk outta that chair."

"Aw, you're just sore 'cause you're sweet on Fancy," the sheriff taunted as Brand stalked into the street. The door swung open after him.

Applegate chuckled. Fancy forced herself to join him, if only to ignore the lonely, wistful feeling that arose whenever she considered her odds for a proper courtship. For at least the hundredth time, she comforted herself with the thought that Diego would have wed her—eventually. Cord Rawlins had stolen her one and only chance for happiness, and she would never forgive him for that. Never.

The redhead was fidgeting. Suspicion pushed aside Fancy's grief. She wondered why he hadn't run after Brand to get a front-row view of the excitement. Frowning, she watched the boy. He was gesturing urgently, albeit furtively, and she realized he was communicating with a masked man who had appeared at the front window. The man shook his head as if in disgust. Fancy felt her heart leap.

So Ned Wilkerson *had* come to break her out of jail! He must have sent the boy to lure Brand and Applegate away from her cell.

"Something ailing you, boy?" the sheriff demanded, craning his neck over his shoulder. The masked man ducked hurriedly out of sight.

"Er . . . no, sir. What makes you think that?"

Applegate pursed his lips and glared at the youth. "'Cause you're jumpier than a long-tailed cat in a room full of rocking chairs."

"Well, I . . . just thought I heard something, is all."

"Heard something, eh?" Applegate's eyes narrowed as he studied the youth from head to toe. "I reckon you ain't from 'round these parts, son. 'Cause if you were, you'd know we don't cotton to firearms in Fort Worth." Applegate jabbed a finger toward the slingshot protruding from the youth's rear pocket. "We ain't especially fond of peashooters, either. So it's a darn good thing you've come here, to the marshal and me, to hand over your weapons."

The youth's chin jutted. He looked ready to square off for a fight.

"Heavens, Sheriff. A slingshot?" Fancy intervened quickly, fearing the youth's flare of temper might spoil her rescue. "You can't really believe this young man's a threat to law and order. Why, he ran all the way over here to warn you about the Carson boys."

"Now don't you be taking sides, Fancy," Applegate said. "I've seen more fools than I can count get their heads blown off 'cause they sport fancy shooting irons that they can't aim."

"Well, I can aim. And damned straight too," the boy said.

Fancy cringed at his outburst. *No, no, no!* she wanted to shout. *Stupid boy, you'll ruin everything!*

Suddenly a nerve-jarring whoop shook the walls of the jail. That Rebel yell echoed again and again, keening above the thunder of gunfire and the pounding of hooves.

"What the devil?" Applegate heaved himself to his feet as a frightened team of horses galloped down the road, hauling their careening wagon after them.

"I bet that's those Carson boys," Fancy said, praying that Applegate hadn't noticed, as she had, that the wagon carried no driver.

"Yep, that was them," the youth chimed in. "Looks like Marshal Brand's been out-coyoted."

"Confound it." The sheriff muttered a second, bawdier oath. "Send a boy to do a man's job . . ."

Applegate hiked his breeches over his belly, crammed his hat on his head, and stomped onto the porch. He'd no sooner stepped across the threshold than gun barrels appeared at either side of his head. He froze in midstride.

"We're not looking for trouble, Sheriff," a muffled voice warned. "We just want the girl."

Fancy nearly crowed with relief. "Wilkerson! Thank God. I knew you would come. I knew you wouldn't let me—"

"Shut up," that muffled voice snapped. Its owner gestured to another youthful accomplice. "Take the sheriff's Peace-maker."

"Now hold on a minute, mister. You're barking up the wrong tree if you think I'm gonna—"

A .45 jammed into Applegate's ruddy neck. The sheriff tensed, slowly raising his hands. His gun belt fell away.

"Good," came the distorted voice again. "Like I said, we don't want any trouble."

The masked man waved to the redhead. The boy grinned, snapping to attention.

"Get the horses."

A scowl replaced the boy's mirth. "Aw, why do I always have to—"

"Get the damned horses!"

Sulking, the redhead waited for his cronies to back Applegate into the room before he ran off on his errand.

Fancy clasped her hands, hard-pressed not to clap with glee. They were really doing it. They were breaking her out of jail!

"All right, son. Get the keys."

The younger-looking of the two masked men hurried past the window with the black SHERIFF'S OFFICE arcing across it, to Brand's battered three-legged desk. Rummaging through the drawers, the youth scattered dice, faro markers, and the calling cards of a dozen scantily dressed bawds. He'd turned as red as his neckerchief before he finally emerged with his prize.

He approached her sheepishly.

"I won't soon forget this, friend," she murmured, favoring him with her most stunning smile.

The boy's brown eyes widened, and she nearly laughed when the keys slid from his fingers to clang in a heap across his boots.

"Ignore her," his leader barked. "Brand could wake any minute from that knot on his head."

Fancy's humor ebbed. Savior or not, Wilkerson and his rudeness were beginning to wear on her patience! Rising on tiptoe, she peered over the younger man's shoulder as he opened the cell door. Suspicion needled her spine. The way Wilkerson held himself, the way he snapped orders and stumped around on those bowed legs of his, she couldn't help but think that he bore an uncanny resemblance to—

"Rawlins?" Applegate boomed. The sheriff squinted more closely into his captor's masked face. "Well, I'll be good and damned. It *is* you! Who went and put a cockleburr under your saddle, son?"

Rawlins had the decency to blush; Fancy cursed under her breath. Rawlins! Of all the rotten luck.

"This isn't a personal matter, Sheriff. Don't make it one."

Rawlins's pine-green gaze stabbed at his deputy. "Well, what are you waiting for? Drag her out of there."

Fancy hiked her chin. Her heart was pounding so hard, she could scarcely breathe. Still, she hadn't built her reputation as a high-class sharper by folding under pressure.

"Forgive my ignorance, Marshal." She managed to sound derisive. "I must be operating under the misconception that kidnapping is still a crime."

"You think I give a hoot about the rights of some lying, cheating thief?"

Applegate scowled, his raised hands twitching as if eager to get at Cord's gun. "There's still a law in this land, Rawlins. And U.S. marshal or not, you ain't above it."

"Don't start preaching to me, Applegate. After what I've seen around town today, I could have your badge. Brand's too."

"Yeah? Well, we could have your hide!"

"I reckon you boys'll have to wait in line, then. Now get inside that cell."

Applegate grudgingly obeyed. Rawlins's deputy extended a hand to Fancy.

"Come on out, ma'am," the youth said gently. "There's no use in arguing."

"Oh? And just what does Marshal Rawlins think he's going to do if I refuse? Kill me? Odds are he'll never find his precious minting plates then."

"I can think of a dozen ways to get my satisfaction," Rawlins said, "and killing you's the least of them. Now get your cheeky little tail out of there, or you'll be walking every blessed inch of the way back to Carson."

Fancy stiffened, her fingers curling clawlike. Applegate shook his head.

"Go on, girl. You best do as he says. Don't you worry none, though. Me and Brand ain't going to let this rest. There's nothing worse than a Texican who turns against his friends. And Rawlins has got a lot of countryside to travel before he makes the New Mexico border."

Fancy's eyes narrowed. She didn't take much comfort in

Applegate's promise. His vendetta was a personal one, and she knew her freedom mattered little to him. She would have to rely on herself.

Hiking her skirts, she knocked the deputy's hand aside and swept haughtily past him. When she tried to sail past Rawlins, though, he grabbed her arm.

"Not so fast, darlin'. I've got a present for you. A couple of silver bracelets."

He pulled her to his side. Outgunned and outnumbered, she knew better than to resist.

"Afraid I might get the jump on you again?" she taunted, taking advantage of their proximity to rub her hips against his.

"You think right highly of yourself for a girl who's been mounted more times than a cowpony," he retorted, snapping his cuffs around her wrists.

She flinched. His manacles didn't hurt nearly as much as his insult.

With his arm clamped around her waist and his revolver pressed against her ribs, Fancy stalked outside. She spied a pair of boots lying toes up in an alley, and she guessed that Brand had been dragged there, out of sight. She hoped he hadn't died in the meantime. To pass a dead man lying on the ground could only bring her more bad luck, and she desperately needed a change.

She considered her alternatives. Since Rawlins and his deputy were both wearing masks, someone might actually come to her aid if she screamed. Of course, she'd have to yell loudly to be heard over the whoops, bets, and curses that accompanied the cockfight raging a block or so away. She wondered next how she would explain her handcuffs to her eventual savior.

Suddenly she spied a man-shaped shadow flitting behind a chimney. She tried not to look too closely for fear of arousing Rawlins's suspicions, but her heart soared to think that she had been right. Someone was prowling the jail's rooftop!

Who else could that someone be but Ned Wilkerson, coming to rescue her?

Chapter Four

Cord tightened his grasp, driving Fancy before him over the rutted road. She had proven again and again that a gentle hand couldn't rein her in; still, it chapped Cord's hide to treat a woman harshly. He'd been raised better. So had his brothers. Why, already Zack was casting sheep's eyes at Fancy. Given half a week more, she would have Wes tripping over his tongue. The boys just didn't understand how dangerous she could be.

"Where do you reckon Wes went?" Zack murmured, glancing anxiously toward the cracked blue lantern that singled out the livery from the neighboring red-lighted cribs. "I don't see the horses anywhere. You don't suppose he ran off to scare up mischief, do you?"

Cord was wondering the same thing. In fact, he considered taking a switch to his youngest brother's behind. Then a thump and a muffled jingle pricked his ears. He tensed. When Fancy caught her breath, suspicion galloped down his spine. Cocking his .45, Cord started to turn, but a rifle lever snapped. He froze, instinctively tightening his arm around Fancy. They were fully exposed in the wash of the moon.

"Drop your guns," ordered a guttural voice from the shadows.

Cord remembered that voice. "Slade? Is that you?"

"Mebbe."

Cord squinted, trying to decipher features in the hulking, heavily shrouded frame. All he could see clearly was a pair of polished boots and the glint of moonbeams off a Henry repeater rifle. He thought he could strike that rifle—maybe even the chest of the man who wielded it—but he didn't dare risk a shootout. Not with Zack by his side.

"You boys deaf," Slade threatened, "or just plain stupid?"

Cord hardened his jaw and nodded for Zack to disarm.

"You been deputized, Slade? Or are you just fond of corset-busting cheats?"

Slade snorted. "I'm fond of five hundred dollars."

Cord understood now. It wasn't love of Fancy or loyalty for Applegate that motivated Slade. In fact, Slade probably would have gunned down the sheriff if Applegate had refused to surrender her. Fancy wouldn't have fared much better.

"Seems like my partner and me saved you a heap of trouble by breaking the girl out of jail." Cord counted on his mask to keep his identity hidden while he stalled and planned. "How about us making a three-way split?"

Fancy's breasts heaved above his arm. "You're not bargaining with that rabid, trigger-happy butcher, are you?" she whispered.

"Keep quiet," he whispered back. "And keep those manacles hidden in your skirts."

"No splits," came Slade's reply.

"Well, Slade, I reckon I'll just have to kill her then."

"Kill me?" she repeated, choking. "You wouldn't dare, you lying son of a—"

Cord's .45 ground into her ribs, and the rest of her oath wheezed into silence. He thanked God for that. She should be smart enough to realize he was trying to save her.

Then again, the only reason she was footloose was because every lawman she had met recently was as crooked as the devil's backbone. She probably thought he was too.

"I gotta agree with the whore," Slade jeered. "Dead, she ain't worth a plug nickel."

"Hell, I don't care about the money as much as I do my

satisfaction," Cord retorted. "She killed my brother. He was the engineer on that Central Pacific train."

Zack looked so stunned that Cord feared the boy might actually speak out against him. For once, he wished Zack was more fond of yarn spinning, like Wes.

"Yeah?" Slade's tone was sharp and angry, as if he half believed Cord's bluff. "Well, that don't mean nothing to me."

"It should, seeing as how my itchy finger could rob you of your bounty."

"You ain't going to rob me of nothing, mister," Slade said, training his rifle on Zack. "Now throw down your gun. I ain't gonna say it again. I'm just gonna put an extra pair of holes in your pardner's head."

Cord's gut knotted. Minting plates or no, he absolutely would not risk Zack. He muttered an oath and tossed aside his Colt. At least Wes wasn't at risk too. Unless that shadow creeping up behind Slade belonged to the youngest, hot-headed Rawlins.

Slade was gloating over Cord's disarmament. "Now send the woman here."

Fancy shrank against Cord's chest. He clasped her protectively. To send her into that alley would be lower than a snake's belly. And he'd rather be damned.

"You scared or something, Slade? You got the gun. Come on out here and get her yourself."

The manhunter's teeth showed in a snarl. "You don't listen so good, mister. I said, send that whore over here."

"Shoot, mister," came Wes's sudden, cheerful challenge from the alley. "Didn't your mama ever teach you any manners?"

Cord choked, spying the glint of a gun behind Slade. The bounty hunter whirled. For a heartbeat, Cord could see nothing in the web of moonlight and darkness. Then gunfire spat. The double report was deafening.

"Wes!" Zack dived for his .45, his cry ricocheting off the walls. Cord had to grab the boy's collar before he could charge headlong into the alley.

"Look after the girl," he snapped, thrusting Fancy into Zack's arms.

Grabbing his Peacemaker, Cord bolted for the jail's porch. His head pounded with the cadence of his pulse as he cocked the gun hammer. Willing himself to caution, he sidestepped with his back against the wall until he could peer around the building's edge.

"Wes! Can you hear me?"

"'Course I can hear you. You're shouting in my gol-durned ear."

Cord's heart nearly stalled. There, framed in the feeble light of the jail's back window, Wes stood with a smoking six-gun in his right hand and Slade's rifle in his left. The bounty hunter rocked back and forth on his knees, his teeth clenched and his face ashen as he clutched his bleeding elbow to his chest. Despite his agony, he wore a look of murderous vengeance.

"Were you hit, Wes?" Cord forced the words past the lump in his throat.

"Naw."

Cord didn't know whether to clasp Wes to his breast or to scold him as an uncurried young fool. He decided against making a scene.

"Where are the horses?"

"Behind the jail."

"Good. Ride to the livery. Tell the stableboy to fetch Doc Tate. We'll wait ten minutes. You know where."

Wes grinned, saluting with Slade's rifle. Cord took the prize away.

"Get a move on, boy."

"Aw, Cord . . ."

Slade roused himself from his pain.

"Cord? Cord Rawlins?" the bounty hunter croaked. His features screwed into a mask of fury. "I'll track you down, you bastard. There ain't a hill too high or a river too wide. I'll snuff you out like a candle in a whirlwind. You and your wise-cracking friend."

Cord had heard similar threats before. Last December,

Diego Santana had threatened to burn his ranch, rape his woman, and murder his children. Cord smiled grimly to himself. If Santana ever got out of state prison, he was going to be sadly disappointed to learn that his enemy had little more than a horse to wreak vengeance on.

"Much obliged for the warning, Slade. I'll be sure to keep a chamber loaded just for you."

By the time Wes caught up with his brothers and Fancy at the city limits sign, he was grinning.

"What are you so chock full of glee about?" Zack grumbled, shifting in his saddle to better glare at his brother. "Hell, you're late again."

Wes reined in, tossing Fancy a roguish wink. "Seems to me you could keep a civil tongue in your head, seeing as how there's a lady present and your skull's all in one piece, thanks to me."

Zack muttered an oath, betraying none of the misty-eyed relief he'd exhibited when Cord had told him Wes was unharmed.

"If you'd done what you were supposed to do when you were supposed to do it, then no one would have been shot up, and we'd be half way to Caddo Peak by now."

"Caddo Peak?" Wes's eyes grew star-bright and eager. "But that's south of here, ain't it, Cord?"

"Applegate expects us to head east toward Dallas, so I figured we'd ride south a ways, through the hills."

Wes was practically jumping up and down in his saddle. "Think we'll meet some Injuns?"

Fancy stiffened in Cord's arms, and he smiled wryly, kicking her skirts out of the way to spur Poco. The odds of running across Comanches weren't good in this part of the country; still, he couldn't resist the temptation to rib her a bit.

"Maybe," he said.

Delighted, Wes began whistling some ditty off-key. Zack, who could sing a ballad almost as well as he could rope a steer, threatened to tie his brother's tone-deaf ears in a knot.

Wes retorted that he would nail Zack's hide to an outhouse wall.

And so the bickering continued.

Cord didn't bother to shout at them for silence. He'd learned from experience that anything short of a gag would prove a waste of time.

Besides, he had plenty to think about. Every lawman in Texas would be gunning for him if Applegate really did spread the word. Wilton Slade would hound him until one of them woke up dead. And then there were Fancy's friends— his enemies. She'd been downright livid when she learned he wasn't one of the Wilkerson gang.

Cord could only guess at the plot she'd been hatching with New Mexico's notorious outlaw clan. If minting plates were involved, then Cord figured he and his brothers would be ambushed at least once before they reached a train depot. He decided he'd have to ditch Zack and Wes before he got them killed. Either that, or he'd have to turn Fancy over to the outlaws.

Cord's chin jutted at the thought.

In a pig's eye! No one got his prisoners except the judge.

He turned his attention back to his renegade. She was quiet now—like the eye of a hurricane. He wondered why she hadn't given away his identity. Maybe she figured he was an easier mark than Slade. Or maybe she was just plain scared of the manhunter. What had she called him? A rabid, trigger-happy butcher?

Cord remembered how Fancy's voice had quavered when she sassed him. He wouldn't have called her yellow, though, not by a long shot. The fact was, she'd impressed the devil out of him. He'd seen grown men wet their breeches when a gun was trained on them. Fancy had done little more than cringe.

He had often wondered what it would take to frighten Fancy Holleday. The law hadn't. Crossfire hadn't. Hell, he sure hadn't. She was quick tongued, and fast thinking, and too damned ornery for her own good. He couldn't remember meeting another woman like her.

Least of all, Beth.

Looking back on his marriage, Cord remembered his wife as being scared and crying most of the time. The disloyalty of his recollection made him wince inwardly. But then, memories of Beth never failed to make him writhe with guilt. He should have come home to her more. He should have tried to make her happier. The problem was, he'd been so damned unhappy himself about their life.

He gave himself a mental kick. Thinking like that was hardly fair to Beth. She'd tried, in her own way, to be a good wife. Looking back, and knowing what he knew now, he couldn't say she'd asked for much. Not really. But the thing that she kept demanding, the thing that she had asked for most of all, was the one thing he should never have given her.

That was why he kept her picture in his breast pocket. When he got too randy, it reminded him what a bastard he had been. Aunt Lally had tried to comfort him, saying he hadn't been wrong to want his wife. He disagreed. He had known the consequences. Beth would be alive right now if it hadn't been for him.

"It sure is quiet over there. What do you suppose those two are up to?"

Wes's exaggerated whisper tugged Cord from his thoughts.

"Nothing," Zack shot back. "Mind your own beeswax."

"Aw, you're just sore 'cause I'm a hero."

"Hey, Cord," Wes said gaily, "you aren't nodding off or anything, are you?"

Cord tossed his kid brother a quelling glare.

"If you want to, we can stop for a spell," Zack said more discreetly.

"Or Miss Fancy can ride with me," Wes quipped. "It's a far piece to Caddo Peak, and we wouldn't want Poco to get himself all lathered."

Fancy smiled at the boy, and Wes's grin grew wider. Cord bit his tongue on an oath. If Fancy sat in the boy's lap, the only one who would get all lathered would be Wes.

"Much obliged, boys, but I was thinking we'd ride on a

ways. Put in three, maybe four hours. Bed down again about dawn. You game?"

"Sure, Cord," they said in unison.

Fancy shot him a glare. Turning back to the road, she gingerly shifted her buttocks. He couldn't help but smile then. It looked as if she'd be saddle sore by sunrise. And a heap less trouble too.

He knew his amusement was less than gentlemanly. After all the trouble she'd put him through, though, he figured she deserved a sore rump at least. Why, even now his body was responding to her in ways that it knew full well it shouldn't. Her cascade of blue-black curls had risen on the breeze and were tickling his nose. He supposed he could put an end to that temptation if he found her a hat.

But there was also the matter of her breasts. They nudged his forearm with each step of his horse. Her buttocks, God help him, were cuddled against his thighs. Even a saint would have trouble minding his hands. He worried that Beth's picture might not be enough to keep his mind off such a lapful.

Damn. It looked as if he would have to waste time finding a nag to put under the girl.

Either that, or lose his honor on this trail ride.

As morning filtered through the clouds, Zack circled back from his scouting mission to report he'd found a stream, a cave, and a good lookout post on the cliff face above.

The current was fast and shallow, perfect for watering horses but a little too cold for bathing. The boys dismounted, stretching belly-down on the bank and dunking their heads into the water. Cord waited his turn, using his hat to dust his chaps.

"Marshal?"

He pressed his lips together. Even if circumstances permitted, it would have been mighty hard to ignore Fancy. She sat astride Poco with her skirts hiked up to her knees and the ruffles of her drawers staring him square in the eye.

"What?"

"Would it be within my legal rights to take a walk?"

His eyes narrowed at her silky tone. Despite their long ride, she still managed to look appealing with her hair in windswept disarray and her cheeks as bright as apples. He didn't think she needed the exercise.

Drawing his tobacco from his pocket, he began to roll a cigarette. His motions were casual and deliberate as he licked the paper, tamped the end, and lit a match. He watched her from the corner of his eye. He thought he saw her frown through the curling tendrils of smoke.

"Well?" she asked.

"Well what?"

She looked down her long nose at him. "You haven't answered my question."

"Seems to me I did."

He was rewarded to see her chin rise. She looked like a queen sitting up there on her high horse.

"I see," she said. "And I suppose it would also be out of the question to get down off your paint?"

"Now that all depends."

"On what?"

He folded his arms across his chest and blew out a long trail of smoke. "On how well you cooperate, *querida.*"

She stiffened as he mimicked Diego Santana. The idea surprised him at first. He'd spent more hours than he cared to remember hauling Santana's scrawny rear to Carson City and a doctor. The outlaw had been about as companionable as a rattler, and Cord just couldn't see why a woman would get riled up for him.

Then again, after being the butt of so many of Fancy's jokes, he wasn't at all opposed to seeing her spit and claw and lose control for once. He waited expectantly for her outburst.

He was disappointed.

"Really, Marshal," she rallied with a disdainful smile. "I've tried to be delicate about this, but I can see I'll have to put it another way. Might I have a moment of privacy to, er, visit the bushes?"

He felt his face heat. He'd been so bent on bringing her in, he hadn't given much thought to the complications involved. Now he wondered how he was supposed to keep an eye on the woman when she was off taking a . . . Well, when she was off doing *that*. And with Zack and Wes dogging his heels, he had to worry about them getting an eyeful too.

"You mean you want to go now?"

"Why, yes. Now would be a rather good time."

He muttered an oath. She was wearing that wicked smirk again, so odds were, she was up to no good. Still, he didn't see how he could refuse her request without sounding like a cad.

"All right. Get down."

"Perhaps you'd care to lend a hand, Marshal." She raised her wrists, and sunbeams glinted off her cuffs like silver rowels. "I fear I'd be rather clumsy in your bracelets."

He jammed his hat back on his head. Tossing aside his smoke, he reached up and locked an arm around her waist. He didn't waste time on ceremony; he just dragged her from the saddle. The air whooshed from her lungs, and she flailed for a moment until she could loop her arms around his neck. Then she hugged him closer. Hooding her eyes, she parted her lips and let her lush curves slide down every inch of his length. He felt his pecker stir. The girl wasn't as helpless as she liked to pretend, he thought darkly.

"Let's get something straight," he growled, wresting himself free. "I'm not interested in what you're giving away. You're wasting your time playing coy with me."

"Have I been coy?" She feigned distress. "Oh, dear. And here I thought I'd been rather direct."

He bit his tongue. She'd been direct, all right. His loins still throbbed where she'd rubbed her hips against them. But that was what she wanted, right? To start him thinking with his poke?

It occurred to him then he'd be in for one hot and sticky ride if he didn't rein himself in. He needed to do something —anything—to keep his concentration. Making her look less like a female might help. He could rest a whole lot easier if her bawdy charms weren't luring bounty hunters and woman-starved renegades.

Or his brothers.

He grimaced at the thought.

Besides, he'd started to wonder what those bawdy charms were hiding from him. He suspected that more was concealed beneath Fancy's skirts than long legs and firm buttocks.

The sound of a snapping twig jerked him from his musings.

"Something wrong, Cord?" Zack asked, halting beside him.

"Yeah. You look ready to burn some gunpowder," Wes said, his speculative gaze traveling from Cord's squared jaw to Fancy's fluttering lashes.

"Nothing's wrong, boys." He managed to keep his voice even. "Did you bring any spare duds, Zack?"

"Yeah. I got an extra shirt and some jeans in my saddle-bag."

"Good. Mind if Miss Holleday borrows them? I reckon she'll be more comfortable—and a sight less troublesome—when she sheds those frills."

"You gonna let Miss Fancy wear *Zack's* clothes?" Wes pouted. "Shoot. He's too long and gangly for his rigging to fit her."

Cord didn't bother to remind Wes of his own height, which was well over six feet and made him a danger to low-flying birds.

"Zack's duds will have to do. In the meantime, you can lead the horses up the hill. Miss Holleday will want her privacy."

Cord could almost hear the "Aw, Cord" of Wes's thoughts.

"Maybe I should stay and keep a watch with you—on account of Injuns, pumas, and such," Wes said gravely.

"That would certainly ease my mind," Fancy drawled.

She shared a look with the boy that made Cord fear for his brother's innocence—if, in fact, innocent was a term that could ever be applied to Wes.

Fortunately, Zack stepped between them to push a checkered shirt and some faded blue jeans into Cord's hands.

"C'mon, churn head." Zack grabbed Wes's arm. "You aren't wanted here. Three's a crowd."

Cord felt his neck heat. He wasn't sure why, but his brothers seemed to have concluded that he was desperate for a woman. Desperate enough to lose his head—and his job— over one buxom, violet-eyed outlaw. He would have to set them straight about that later.

As Zack dragged Wes around a rocky outcropping, Fancy eyed Cord's saddlebag speculatively.

"I don't suppose you carry any . . ."

"Leaves?" he finished dryly. "Sure. We got plenty of leaves."

She made a face. "Never mind, Marshal. I'll manage." She held out her wrists. "Now if you'd be so kind . . . ?"

He hiked a brow. "Well now, removing cuffs is a privilege. If you want privileges, you're going to have to earn them."

The ghost of suspicion haunted her face. "Earn them? Just what did you have in mind . . . Cord?"

The way she purred his Christian name wasn't lost on him. No doubt she'd had similar conversations before with lawmen—all of which she'd finished on her back. The thought annoyed him somehow. He sure as hell wouldn't do her that way.

"Tell you what," he said, tossing Zack's clothes over his shoulder and fishing in his pocket for the key. "We'll make a deal. You hand over your weapons, and I'll keep the cuffs off."

He unsnapped the manacles, and their eyes locked. Hers turned smoky blue with triumph.

"My weapons?" she repeated archly. Raising her hands to the sun, she made a great pretense of studying her fingernails. "Well, I suppose I could break them off for you, if you insist."

That girl. She had more nerve than a toothache. He knew she was armed. The only reason he hadn't frisked her so far was because he felt uncomfortable about such a search in front of his brothers. They were gone now, though, and her cuffs were off. And so too were his kid gloves.

He reached for his Colt. His draw was so fast that her blood was still draining from her face when he finished.

"Yep," he said. "I insist. Next you can hand over that .32 you carry in your boot and the knife you've stashed in your collar. Oh, and don't forget the pins in your hair. I reckon they could stab a man's eye out in half a second or less."

Fancy felt her heart crawl slowly north from her toes. How the devil could Rawlins draw so fast? And how did he know about the stiletto? Only iron self-discipline kept her from groping behind her neck to see if the sheath had jarred loose during their ride. She suspected there was little she could do except kiss the knife good-bye, but she really hated giving up without a fight.

"I'd like to help you, Marshal, really I would," she said in her sweetest, beast-soothing voice. "But Sheriff Applegate already confiscated my knife and my .32. He said I might hurt myself."

Rawlins snorted. "I think you've got your facts all tangled. Now, we can stand here trading whoppers till sundown, but I'm hungry. My patience wears mighty thin when my belly feels hollow. Nevada may want you alive, but they didn't say anything about teaching you some respect for the law. So what's it going to be?"

Fancy's eyes narrowed. She suspected that Rawlins didn't make idle threats. Perhaps she should count herself lucky. After all, he hadn't ripped off her clothes to search her yet.

Even so, there was a part of her—a lonely, hurting part— that wondered why Rawlins wasn't eager to grope beneath her gown. Whether farmer or banker, railroadman or sailor, men gawked at her breasts and leered at her buttocks. Every man, without exception, tried to put his hands on her.

So why didn't Cord Rawlins?

She remembered the train and how he'd ignored her best efforts to entice him. In the jail, he'd looked more irritated than interested when she rubbed her hips against his. What was wrong with her that he found her so unappealing?

On second thought, what was wrong with him?

Deciding to find out, she donned her best disarming smile.

"All right, Cord. You win," she lied. "But you can hardly blame a girl for trying."

She bent at the waist and extended her right leg. Pointing her toes, she raised her skirts, taking extra care to expose the creamy flesh below her drawers. She ran a suggestive hand down her calf before drawing the Smith & Wesson from the holster inside her boot.

"Toss it aside."

She obeyed, continuing to smile.

Straightening leisurely, she smoothed stray curls from her neck and reached for her collar. His suspicious gaze followed every movement of her hand as she withdrew the stiletto, dangled it suggestively before her rocking hips, then let it plunge into the earth near her gun.

She thought his breaths had quickened, but it was hard to gauge the rise and fall of his chest beneath his linen duster.

Sliding her fingers through her hair, she plucked the four-inch pins from the mass one by one. The tendrils delighted in their freedom, bouncing and slithering over her shoulders to sway against her breasts. She shook her head, and the remaining strands cascaded down her back. She let the pins trickle through her fingers.

"Shall I continue?" she purred.

He eyed her the way he might have eyed a loaded pistol. "Continue what?"

"Well, I'm assuming you want all my weapons," she replied in velvet tones. "And some of them are . . . well, not as close to the surface as the others."

"Get on with it, then."

Fancy hid her disappointment. She had hoped the thought of her nakedness would make him sweat. Or make his pants bulge. The very least it should have done was make his gun-hand quake! Instead, he looked as steadfast as an oak. A traitorous side of her admired his restraint, but the rest of her was miffed. Could she have underestimated the love that Cord Rawlins still felt for his wife?

The idea unaccountably troubled her, so she pushed it aside. There wasn't a man alive who could resist a willing woman. She simply had to work harder on Rawlins.

Brushing aside her hair, she made a great show of unfastening her bodice and tossing aside the hollow buttons one by one. A pity she had to lose them; they had served her well in the past, hiding small stolen jewels.

Next she raised her shoulders, executing her most provocative shrug. Her silk poplin bodice fluttered to her waist. The alabaster tops of her breasts were revealed, and she waited expectantly for his reaction.

He never batted an eye.

She did, in disbelief.

Freshening her smile with the tip of her tongue, she reached for the hooks of her skirt. A sultry, well-rehearsed wiggle shed the gown, and it rustled into a magenta puddle at her feet. She swayed her hips to shake out the pleated flounces and lace-edged train of her jaconet petticoat.

Again, no visible response from Rawlins.

She considered walking over and slapping him a time or two, but that would have been akin to admitting defeat.

Hiking her buttocks, she bent at the waist. Her bosoms all but spilled from her stays as she reached into her petticoat's hidden pockets. A pouch of sewing needles, a knuckle duster, a pair of files, and a straight razor soon joined her growing arsenal. She even tossed in her ring shiner and the widdy she used to jimmy locks on hotel doors and traveling trunks.

Rawlins looked vaguely amused.

Fancy barely mastered her scowl.

Slipping the silken ties at her waist, she stepped from her petticoat. All that remained were her corset, chemise, and drawers. The latter hid the tops of her stockings, which camouflaged her derringer and a small bottle of laudanum. She kept the sleeping draught as a precaution against aggressive admirers. Seven years ago, when Diego rescued her from the whorehouse, she had vowed never to return to her mother's way of life. The laudanum—and the derringer—had allowed her to keep that vow. She had shared no man's bed other than Diego's in all that time.

She cast a sidelong glance at Rawlins. To keep her weapons secret, she had to keep her drawers on. They didn't appear in immediate danger, however, judging by the lack of interest on his face. She vowed to scratch his eyes out if he yawned.

"Satisfied?" She barely kept the caustic edge from her voice.

His stare drilled into her bodice. "What's that strung around your neck?"

"You mean this?" She touched her silver chain with a sheepish kind of reverence. Diego had never had much patience for her superstitions, and she suspected that no-nonsense Rawlins would feel the same.

"It's nothing. Just a necklace."

"I can see that. What's hanging from the end?"

She blushed. The last thing she wanted was to give Rawlins the same ammunition that Diego had used to wound her. Breathing deeply, she swelled her breasts to their best advantage, and the chain slithered into her décolletage.

"It's nothing, Marshal. Nothing of value. But you're welcome to come see for yourself."

He frowned and stalked closer. She caught her breath. She hadn't dreamed he would take her up on the invitation!

His hand plunged into her corset, and she had to bite back a squeal, willing herself not to retreat when his yank retrieved the chain. The attached medallion flashed like a beacon in the sun's white-gold rays.

His dimples began to show.

"Two bits?" His infuriating shamrock eyes danced a jig. "You punched a hole in a two-bit piece?"

She felt her face flame. If his Peacemaker wasn't pointed at her ribs, she might have told him to board the next train to Hades.

"I told you it was nothing of value," she retorted with as much disdain as she could muster.

"That you did, darlin'." He chuckled, letting the coin flop back against her breasts. "Imagine me not taking you at your word."

She really wanted to punch his lights out then.

"Got anything else hidden in there?"

She sniffed. "Why bother to ask? You clearly won't believe me. Why not just rip off my underclothes and see for yourself?"

"I reckon you'd like that."

"I most certainly would not!"

"No?" The amusement faded from his eyes. Shaking his head, he holstered his Colt. "You're a fine piece of work, Fancy Holleday."

He retreated to a safer distance, but his hand hovered ever-ready near his gun. "Go on. Do your business." He tossed her Zack's clothes. They nearly hit her in the face.

"And be quick about it," he called as she stomped off toward a tree. "I'm not going to have you parading around naked in front of my boys."

The contempt in his voice made her wince. She quickly squared her shoulders.

Why should she care what some Texas chawbacon thought about her? Cord Rawlins wouldn't have known a desirable woman from a wooden Indian. She should have realized she was wasting her time on a man who'd spent more hours in a saddle than a bed. Besides . . .

She sulked, hardly conscious of her pout.

. . . the man had dimples.

Chapter Five

As Fancy waved her nose in the air and stalked toward the tree, Cord discreetly adjusted his chaps. His pecker throbbed so hard, he feared his fly would burst. He'd started sweating too. He'd heated up hotter than a fox in a forest fire, but he didn't dare shrug off his duster. He'd be damned if he'd let her see how she'd gotten to him again.

Chafing inside and out, he grimaced. Half of him wanted to take a switch to her behind; the other half wanted to follow her into the bushes and find out if she were really worth the tumble. How in tarnation had he let some snippy little tease fire up his blood? It wasn't as if he'd never seen a half-bared breast before.

Many burlesque shows played the cattle trails between Fort Worth and Abilene, Kansas. In the last two years Uncle Seth's drovers had dragged Cord to them all, but their good intentions had been for naught. He hadn't been able to free himself from the specter of Bethany. Once in a while, when he got drunk enough to see double, he could bring himself to crawl into a woman's bed. Using a faceless body had never set well with him, so he would quickly slink out again, hating himself ten times worse when the act was over. God knew, he didn't want to go on feeling ashamed of a need that was so natural, but he didn't know how to forgive himself. And he didn't know how to let Beth go.

His throat tightening, he let his eyes stray once more to Fancy. She was a woman. What would she think if she knew his seed was poison? Chances were, she'd run screaming through the bushes. Hell, she'd avoid him like a pestilence, then. If he went and told her that he'd killed his wife, he could curb her wanton ways and get himself some peace.

The problem was, peace was the last thing he wanted.

He smiled grimly at himself, at the weakness that had brought him so much grief. Fancy Holleday was a long-legged, sable-haired hellion who filed her nails on a whet-stone and clawed a man's heart for fun. Every now and then, he had to tell himself that. Reminding his pecker that she was his prisoner and that he just couldn't have her didn't seem to be cooling him off. He still burned with longing when he thought of those rounded buttocks. The memory of her lilac scent, so sweet and alluring on the wind, was enough to make him groan.

In desperation, he conjured an image of Beth's cool and placid smile. For the first time in months, it brought him no relief. He wasn't sure anything could. Fancy was standing just a stone's throw away, jumping and wriggling, wrestling Zack's jeans up over her rump. Cord blushed to think how he must look to her in turn, stamping and pawing like a stud pony that had been fenced away from his mare. If the girl wasn't so underhanded, he would have done the courteous thing and turned away.

At least, he liked to tell himself that.

He liked to tell himself, too, that the only reason he'd looked at her drawers was out of self-defense. God knew, she was probably hiding a torpedo in there. Nothing would sur-prise him now.

He stifled another groan. She was strutting back toward him. Seeing how Zack's shirt fit her, he tried to console himself that he'd been right to make her shed her frills. Weapons weren't likely to go undetected beneath that shirt. Aside from the sleeves, which hung at least six inches too long, the flannel fit her snugly. Too snugly, he confirmed with a second uncomfortable glance. Only Fancy Holleday could don a red flannel work shirt and make it look indecent.

"Fasten the rest of your damned buttons," he said, managing somehow to drag his gaze away from her plunging neckline.

She had the audacity to smile. He really hated it when she smiled like that. It made him remember he'd gone four months without a woman.

"I'm afraid buttoning the shirt would be quite impossible," she said. "You see, your brother's chest is a good deal smaller than mine."

"I can see clear down to your navel!"

"Well then . . . *Cord.*" His name rolled off her lips with some wicked, hidden meaning. "I suggest you stop looking."

He ground his teeth. "Here." Tugging off his neckerchief, he thrust it into her hands. "Cover yourself."

"Why, thank you, sir. How kind you are to worry about me exposing my tender parts to . . . er, the sun."

When he scowled, Fancy's pride ached a little less. Finally she had managed to do *something* to irk him. She was beginning to think she'd lost her touch. To feel that way rattled her nerve far more than she cared to admit.

The smell of mesquite-cooked frijoles wafted down from the cave. Fancy wrinkled her nose at the woodsy odor, and her belly rumbled. Ordinarily, she wouldn't have been eager to eat beans, but Applegate's biscuits had tasted like boot leather. She couldn't afford to be choosy; she was starving.

Still, she couldn't help but worry when she remembered Rawlins's taunt about earning her privileges. If relieving one of her most basic human needs was a privilege, might he not consider food one too?

She cast him a sidelong glance as he dumped her weapons in the stream. With his jaw set like that, he didn't seem predisposed to acts of kindness. Perhaps it was time to befriend his young deputies.

Gathering her petticoats, Fancy wrapped them carefully inside her gown. The ensemble had cost her one rustled horse. Normally her winnings would have paid for two such outfits and all the frills—a hat, a parasol, ammunition—but pickings had been slim in Fort Worth. Until she found a high-stakes poker game, or better yet, a casino that hired faro dealers at $100 per week, she had to take extra care not to damage her gown. She'd have trouble earning her living in the coming months without it.

"Give me that," Rawlins said, snatching the bundle from her arms. "The trail's too rugged. You'll need both your hands."

She glanced toward the steep, boulder-strewn path. It looked as narrow as a hair ribbon. Rawlins might be right. She indulged in a grudging moment of gratitude that her enemy would carry her clothes for her.

A heartbeat later, he had tossed her gown into the stream. She choked back an oath as she watched it bob and unfurl, strewing her underclothes among the rapids before sinking in a purple froth of dye. Rawlins grunted his approval.

She vowed to move her derringer to a handier location the second the louse took his eyes off her.

A pot of coffee was simmering beside the boys' kettle of beans when Fancy at last hauled herself over the lip of the cave. She was panting, thirsty, and tired, but she did her damnedest not to show Rawlins as he scrambled up behind her.

She shouldn't have worried. He was apparently so intent on filling his belly, he hardly glanced her way as he took her arm and escorted her to the circle of firelight. Only when she wrenched herself free did she earn his attention. His eyes drilled into her with their no-nonsense glare.

"Sit down."

She pursed her lips and knelt beside Zack. He offered her a tin plate heaped with beans.

"You sure do look purdy in red, ma'am," the youth said shyly.

"Shoot. Miss Fancy could turn heads in a gunnysack," Wes said, snatching the coffeepot out of Cord's hands.

Cord cursed, but Wes ignored the oath. He scrambled to

Fancy's side and wedged himself between her knee and Zack's.

"Hey!"

Wes ignored Zack too.

"Bet you're thirsty, ma'am." He grinned at her in unabashed admiration. "Want some belly wash? I made it myself."

She smiled back. "Why, thank you, Wes." This was going to be easy. Much easier than she'd thought. "That's awfully kind of you."

Zack looked ready to wring Wes's neck. Cord looked ready to help.

"Which one of you boys is taking the first watch?" Cord asked.

"Zack is."

"I am not!"

"Sissy."

"That'll be enough."

Cord glared at Fancy as if she were somehow to blame. She smirked. How in the world did a deputy U.S. marshal bring fugitives to justice with these two puppies tagging along?

Zack looked to his oldest brother for support. Cord sighed.

"Seeing as how you boys can't decide for yourselves . . . Wes flapped his jaw, so he volunteered."

The boy's face fell.

"And while you're at it," Cord added, "you can fetch my bedroll."

"Aw, Cord."

Zack nodded smugly. "Mine too."

Wes sniffed and turned his shoulder on Zack. "What about Miss Fancy?"

"What about her?" Cord mumbled through a mouthful of beans.

"Is she gonna sleep with you?"

Cord choked, turning scarlet. Zack had to reach over and

slap his brother's back before Cord could manage a swallow. He coughed, wiping his mouth with his sleeve.

"No, she's not sleeping with me!"

"But we only brought three bedrolls," Wes persisted, braving Cord's malevolent glare. "Where's she gonna sleep?"

"She can sleep in mine," Zack offered gallantly.

Cord scowled. "Forget it."

"Geez, Cord. You can't let Miss Fancy sleep on the rocks."

"I am quite aware of that, Zack, thank you. Miss Holleday will sleep in mine."

"Alone?" Wes asked suspiciously.

"Yes, alone!" Cord's jaw began to twitch. "I'll sleep in your bedroll, and you can sleep in Zack's after he goes on watch."

"When will that be?"

Fancy suspected Wes was in serious danger of getting his ears boxed.

"Next Christmas, if you don't get your mulish hide up on that hill."

Zack snickered, and Wes sulked, slinging a Winchester over his shoulder. Spinning toward the trail, he jammed on his hat, then hesitated, turning back and tipping the brim at Fancy. It hung at a jaunty angle, and his grin crept back across his face.

"See ya later, ma'am."

" 'Bye, Wes." She grinned back, wondering where the boy had learned his good manners.

Then she felt the warning stab of Cord's glare.

Obviously not from his brother.

After their hurried meal and four restless hours of sleep, Cord roused them all to "hit the trail" again.

The trail wasn't all that Fancy wanted to hit.

Every bone in her body ached, every muscle groaned in protest. She didn't know which was more difficult to bear: the rocks, or Cord's saddle. Even if she could have dozed, she wouldn't have dared—not with his thighs squeezing her hips like sunbaked rawhide. His arms were wrapped around her, too, holding and confining her like a corral.

A much too intimate corral.

She tried to straighten her spine, to separate their torsos, but the fraction of space she earned brought her little relief. His maleness was pervasive, a primal heat that invaded every pore. His scent, a heady blend of leather, musk, and tobacco, was more aphrodisiac than opiate to her senses.

She didn't think the ride would ever end.

Fortunately, the horses grew tired, and the sun eventually set. Cord Rawlins might have needed less sleep than a night owl, but his deputies were nodding off in their saddles. Neither of the boys complained, of course, but Cord conceded that the time had come to make camp.

Fancy wanted to kiss Zack and Wes both.

If Marshal Charming hoped to keep her too tired and sore for escape, his plot was working. She didn't bother to protest when Zack cooked beans again and shoved a plateful into her hand. Then she collapsed on Cord's bedroll. She figured she had six hours to sleep.

Or rather, six hours to sneak her derringer to a more accessible location.

Cord took the first watch. Knowing he was out in the bushes somewhere, watching every movement, every shadow, was nerve-racking. Fancy didn't dare go through the gyrations necessary to retrieve her pistol and its holster from the hem she had rolled inside her boot. The fact that Cord hadn't suspected the gun was the first stroke of luck she'd had since meeting him. She didn't plan on tempting fate.

Resigned to waiting, Fancy dozed. She tuned her ears for the scrabble of Cord's boots on the rocks or the murmur of his voice as he woke one of the boys. Instead, it was the howl of a coyote that jerked her from sleep. Her heart raced. Turning her head stealthily, she searched for signs of Cord. She found him sitting about five feet away, on a log by the fire. If he had heard the cry of the scavenger, he didn't seem alarmed. Nor did Zack, who had apparently taken the second watch, because his bedroll was empty.

Fancy released a slow and lengthy breath. Cord hadn't realized she was awake—yet. He was too engrossed in the daguerreotype in his hand. As much as she wanted to crunch down beneath her blanket, unhook her holster, and sneak it to her wrist, she willed herself to resist. Since she was lying so close to his knee, the odds of his noticing her were still too great. Damn the man. Did he never rest?

She reined in her frustration. Forcing herself to lie motionless and to even out her breaths, she watched him through half-closed eyes. In the ruddy emberglow, his profile looked carved from bronze. A cigarette burned forgotten in his left hand; a cup of coffee steamed in the ashes near his boots.

She wondered what was so moving about that dog-eared picture card, for it had transformed Rawlins. The steely U.S. marshal who had gunned down Diego was not sitting on that log. Instead, she saw a haunted man. The angles of his face were stark and naked with emotion; his shoulders were bowed, as if burdened by guilt. Her heart reluctantly went out to him. What memory tormented him so?

She had to find out. Rising cautiously on one elbow, she kept the rising moon behind her as she strained to see past his fist. She forced herself to ignore any lingering traces of compassion. After all, Cord Rawlins was her enemy. She needed to learn his weakness.

Fancy felt no triumph, though, when she glimpsed the prim young woman staring back from the card. Fair-haired and slender, with delicate eyebrows and intelligent eyes, the woman projected an air of breeding that suggested old wealth. She looked to be everything Fancy was not—and everything Fancy could never hope to be. A pang of jealousy stabbed through her.

Clearly this was the woman Cord had taken as wife.

He turned his head then. Some instinct must have alerted him to her observation. Their eyes locked, and his stare bored into her. She couldn't help but flinch. She had expected to feel superior, smug. She had expected to discover some new secret weapon. Instead, she had learned why Cord Rawlins found her unappealing. And the reason made her feel flawed.

She raised her chin to show him—to show herself—that she didn't care. Not one whit.

He said nothing.

Slipping the daguerreotype inside his breast pocket, he raised his cigarette to his lips. The tip brightened, glowing scarlet, before he exhaled. Tendrils of smoke wrapped around his neck, hugging him like a lover. She wondered what he was thinking. Was he comparing her to his wife? The idea was somehow wounding. What had been so special about that prim and proper slip of a girl? What had she done to get Cord Rawlins to pledge his love to her for the rest of his life?

Diego had never pledged himself that way.

A lump formed in Fancy's throat. The bitterness was hard to swallow. She had always had more than her share of admirers. Oglers, really. But when it had come to courtship and sharing vows, those admirers had always tucked their tails and run. Diego had seemed to be her best bet for a normal life—normal, that was, for the preferred paramour of a Barbary Coast kingpin.

She wondered what life with a lawman would be like.

Cord's gaze had not yet broken from hers. The intensity of his stare was unnerving. Her pulse began to flutter so shamefully, she felt she had to say something to prove her mettle.

"What's wrong?" she taunted softly. "Can't fall asleep?"

"Don't need much."

"No?" She managed a provocative smile. "I thought maybe your dreams had gone . . . bad."

"Don't dream much, either."

She was disappointed when he didn't rise to her bait. Perhaps he truly wasn't like the other men she had known. Perhaps the only corsets and garters he enjoyed viewing were his wife's. She felt a growing resentment. Just what did a widower like Cord Rawlins *do* until he re-married?

"I guess a man who doesn't—" she paused suggestively, *"dream* much doesn't get tired like other men."

"Could be."

His lips curved, and she felt her insides heat. She recognized that look. It was the look of a man who could take what he wanted. A man restrained by his integrity, nothing more. It unnerved her more than she cared to admit.

She tried again. "It's a pity, Cord, you being dreamless. Every night, all night long."

Those penetrating eyes continued to hold her. Even if she wanted to, she couldn't have looked away. She sensed a wanting deep inside him, a gnawing hunger he chose to ignore. If he should ever yield to that need, she knew she'd be overcome, the way a brass rod must bend to steel.

Her stomach quivered at the thought.

Still, some perverse side of her kept pushing, kept needing to feel his edge.

"The night's a whole different world," she whispered. "A world of fantasy. A flight of fancy."

The breathless quality of her voice surprised her. She'd meant to sound husky, alluring. Not eager.

"The night's the best time for a man's dreams to come true," she added.

Something flickered in his eyes, something turbulent and hard to fathom. Then his lids drooped and his guard came up. He took another draw on his cigarette.

"Reckon you dream a lot, eh, Fancy?"

She felt her face burn. *Oh, brava, Fancy girl.* First she'd set herself up, then she'd let his barb sting. She didn't know which was worse. Either way, she felt like a prime candidate for a fleecing.

"It takes practice to do it right," she rallied lamely.

He chuckled. The sound reverberated through her, warm and rich with genuine mirth.

"You best get to it then. The night's nearly over."

Her breath caught when he rubbed out his cigarette. Her heart leaped when he dumped his coffee and rose.

But if some tiny part of her had hoped that Cord Rawlins would fling his honor to the wind, that he'd crawl inside her bedroll and love away the emptiness eating at her soul, that part of her was disappointed. He crossed to Zack's bedroll, stretched out on his back, and propped his hat across his face. After a few minutes, his breathing grew deep and regular. She noted in growing annoyance that his hand hovered near his six-gun, even in his sleep.

The son of a . . .

She bit her tongue. It was insulting that she had such a negligible effect on the man. And it was aggravating that he was not the kind of whorehound she could despise.

Feeling cheated somehow, she resigned herself to her original plan and stealthily strapped her derringer beneath the rolled cuff of her sleeve. Not that she would ever *need* the pistol, she thought acidly. Never in a million years was she likely to be defending her virtue against Cord Rawlins!

Her chin jutted, and she glared up at the stars. She comforted herself that there were still Indians. And outlaws.

And Slade.

Chapter Six

The next two days dragged by. Bitter cold followed a moist heat, and then came the rain. Zack found another cave. The roof leaked, the walls stank, and bats squealed overhead. Fancy huddled under Wes's slicker. She sat as close to the daylight and as far from the sheeting water as possible. Not even Cord had been able to start a fire.

She would have liked to say that she was glad for the downpour. It spared her hours of humiliation, bouncing between Cord's knees, squirming in his arms, inhaling his tobacco-and-musk scent.

His manly odor titillated her from his bedroll too. It wafted through her dreams and often stole away her sleep. She would lie there, staring at the heavens, and feel herself ache. Really ache.

Sometimes she found herself watching him. Sometimes she caught him watching her. He would lie so still that she could hear his breathing. She would gaze into his firelit eyes, eyes as green and deep as the sea, and she would think about reaching out to him. Touching him. The notion would tempt her, but he would always look away. He would always reject her.

She'd remind herself then that she hated him. She would hammer the words again and again into her brain: *I hate him. He killed Diego.*

Because of Cord Rawlins, she was loveless and miserable.

Because of Cord, too, she was forced to sit through a bone-chilling downpour. She feared the rain would wash away her trail and keep Wilkerson from finding her. What was worse—far worse—was being trapped with bats and a man she loathed.

On the morning of the third day, the rain tapered to a mist. Cord, who'd been pacing through the night like a caged mountain lion, announced that he would take Poco and scout ahead.

"Need a pardner, Cord?" Zack asked.

"Yeah, you'll need four eyes to see in this fog," Wes added hopefully.

Cord looked her way, and the corners of his mouth began to twitch. She suspected his amusement had something to do with her, and she fumed, adding another insult to the list of offenses she was building against him.

"You boys aren't bored with deputy work already, are you?"

"'Course not!" they chimed in unison.

Cord hiked a brow. "But you'd leave Miss Holleday alone with these bats?"

Zack and Wes blushed, both glancing at her. Next they peered at the ceiling. Wes fidgeted.

"Aw, Cord. Them bats aren't gonna carry Miss Fancy off or anything."

Cord folded his arms across his chest. He looked the picture of parental authority. "I reckon they won't have to, son. Not if you let your prisoner walk out of here on her own. Are you forgetting the first duty of a deputy?"

Wes dug his toe into a crevice. "Never take your eyes off the prisoner."

"That's right. See that you don't." He squeezed the boy's shoulder. "I'm counting on you, Wes. Zack too."

Hoisting his saddle, Cord shot Fancy a don't-even-think-about-leaving glare before he dissolved into the mist. Zack began to chuckle.

"And you want to round up outlaws like Cord?" he said to Wes. "A fine lawman you turned out to be."

"Shut up, Zack."

The morning heated up. The sun dissolved the mist, and the cave's yellow-gold walls began to gleam. Fancy shed Wes's slicker and stretched her cramped limbs. She might have tried to escape if she weren't so sore, not that she would have gotten far. Cord had camped them miles from the nearest town. As for food, a one-shot derringer was little good for hunting. She would have had to trick the boys, steal their guns, round up their horses, and disappear without a trace.

She was good, she thought dryly, but not that good.

Wes crept closer and sat down beside her. His expression was a tad sheepish, and she suspected he was feeling guilty for his earlier outburst about the bats.

She smiled. To her surprise, it was genuine. She'd tried her damnedest not to like Cord's deputies. Wes had insisted she wear his slicker, though, and Zack had given up his only blanket, and the two of them had vied incessantly over fetching her water, spreading her bedroll, and cooking her meals. In truth, Cord's brothers had made her feel more valued than she had ever felt in her life. She still struggled to harden herself against them, but some treacherous part of her preferred to feel the warmth, not the hate.

"I reckon we'll be riding soon," Wes said.

"I reckon you're right," she teased gently.

His freckles crowded closer as he grinned. He glanced toward Zack, who had leaned his shoulders against the wall. In the sunlight, Zack's chestnut curls most closely resembled Wes's hair, but Zack's chiseled jaw and full, firm lips showed his blood ties to Cord. When he raised his harmonica to his mouth, Fancy spied the Rawlins-family dimples.

"Hope you're not mad, ma'am," Wes said as Zack began to play. "About the bats, I mean."

"Nope. Not one bit."

Relief flooded his face. She couldn't help but notice how it made his shamrock-colored eyes shine—like Cord's.

"Well, bats are really good luck, you know," he confided.

"I once heard of a poker player who tied a bat's heart to his arm with red thread. He said he got the best cards that way."

Zack's music wheezed to a halt. He shook his head, but Wes ignored the warning and gave Fancy a conspiratorial wink. She found herself remembering just how intrigued Wes had been when she placed her boot toes outward near the foot of her bedroll. She'd explained rather abashedly that she was protecting herself against nightmares. Wes hadn't batted an eye.

Zack began to play again. Fancy recognized his spritely version of "You Never Miss Your Sainted Mother Till She's Dead and Gone to Heaven."

"I've been meaning to ask you, ma'am . . ."

Wes tossed his brother another furtive glance and sidled closer to Fancy.

"Yes?"

"Well, um . . . it's just that I was wondering why you went and robbed that train."

The harmonica made another wheezing sound. "Geez, Wes!"

"Well, shoot. It ain't every day you get to meet a lady train robber. 'Sides. You want to know just as much as I do, so don't you go acting like you don't."

Fancy knew she had blushed. She just didn't know what she should say. Looking from one pair of inquisitive eyes to the other, she saw no reason to lie. Why had she robbed that train? As she took a moment to recall that night—the fear, the violence, the bloodshed—it didn't seem worth all the pain it had caused. Diego was dead, and she was alone. And all because of greed.

"Well . . ." Folding her hands, she sighed, staring at the red and purple wildflowers on the sunny ledge below. "I suppose I did it for Diego."

"Diego?" Zack hurried forward to sit at her other side. "Who's Diego? Your husband?"

"No."

"Your brother?"

She almost smiled at Zack's innocence. "No, my lover."

"Oh." He reddened.

Wes frowned. "Well, if he loves you, why did he go and make you rob a train? That doesn't seem right."

Fancy winced. She'd heard a truism in that question that she didn't wish to hear.

"Tell me, Wes. Have you ever been in love?"

"Well . . . no."

"Then how would you know what it's like?"

He hiked his chin. "'Cause I watched Cord. He treated Beth real fine. He didn't ever make her do things she didn't want to do."

"Geez."

"Geez yourself, Zack. Don't you think Miss Fancy deserves someone treating her fine, like Cord?"

Zack had turned brighter than Wes's freckles. "Sure I do. But it ain't right, you asking her questions like that."

"Shoot, she ain't mad." Wes cast her a worried, sidelong glance. "You ain't mad, are you, ma'am?"

"No."

She smiled in spite of herself. The boy obviously idolized Cord. Personally, she couldn't fathom how anyone could adore the man, but since Zack also worshiped his older brother, Fancy reasoned that kinship must be to blame. As for herself, she had grown up in an upscale whorehouse, a mistake on her mother's part. She had never known a brother or sister. She had never known much in the way of maternal love, either, so it was hard for her to understand just how binding a blood tie could be.

"You needn't worry about me, Wes," she said.

"Someone's got to. This Diego feller ain't around, and Cord's still got his head all muddled over Beth."

"Wes!" Zack looked as if he might shove his harmonica in his brother's mouth.

"Well, he does, doesn't he?" Wes said. "Even Aunt Lally says she ain't ever seen a man get so torn up over a woman's death. For almost two years now he's been mooning around, thinking he killed her."

"Did he?" Fancy prompted, half-hoping to hear the

worst. It was high time she dispelled her silly notion that Cord Rawlins had made a good husband.

"'Course not."

"You have to understand, ma'am," Zack interjected quickly, tossing his brother a quelling glare. "Beth was kind of frail—"

"Yeah," Wes said. "You couldn't look sideways at her without her getting sick."

"And she just wasn't suited for fighting coughs and fevers and such."

"Or birthing babies."

Zack drew a sharp breath and punched his brother's arm.

"Ow! What'd you go and do that for?"

"'Cause you're talking like a biscuit head."

Fancy wasn't sure she was following this conversation. "So you mean to say that Beth . . . er, had trouble conceiving a child?"

Wes set his chin and rubbed his bruise; Zack avoided her eyes as he pushed stones over the hill. The silence lengthened. Fancy could hardly stand it.

"What happened?" she asked softly.

Wes shrugged.

Zack cleared his throat. "Well, um, you see, Beth was reared out Galveston way," he began reluctantly, "and she was kind of genteel. She didn't take a shining to the ranch. The rattlers, coyotes, and scorpions all scared her. She didn't leave the house much in the heat, and I reckon it got lonesome for her sitting around, waiting for Cord to ride home. She used to spend her time worrying about him getting gunned down somewheres, and she started thinking that a baby would keep her busy. She started wanting that baby real bad."

Wes nodded gravely.

"Now, Beth wasn't ever what you'd call hardy," Zack continued. "The doctor told her no babies, 'cause he said birthing might . . . er, snuff out her candle. Cord told her no babies, too, 'cause he couldn't bear it if she died. But Beth could be real stubborn once she got her dander up. She pleaded, and she begged, and when she saw her tears weren't working, she threatened to pull up stakes and find herself a new husband.

"'Course, Cord couldn't let her do that," Zack said. "So he finally let her have her way. About six or seven months later, the baby came. The boy was stillborn, and . . . well . . ." He dropped his eyes. "Beth never left the birthing bed."

"It wasn't Cord's fault," Wes said in a low, fierce voice.

"'Course it wasn't," Zack said.

Fancy was silent. She wasn't sure what she had expected to feel, but sympathy for Cord Rawlins had never been a consideration. It stunned her when it wrapped around her heart. For a moment, she wondered why she grieved for him. After all, he wasn't the only one who'd lost a loved one. Hadn't she lost Diego? And hadn't Cord been to blame?

Still, to lose a son. . . . And to know that son—his seed —had been the death of his beloved wife.

Fancy repressed a shudder.

Why had Beth done it? Why had she insisted on conceiving a child when she knew the baby would be a death sentence?

Fancy asked herself those questions again and again, but the conclusion always proved the same: Beth must have loved the devil out of Cord. Fancy didn't know if she could be as selfless. She didn't know if she could sacrifice everything for love.

The scrabbling of rocks roused her from her brooding. From somewhere below, she heard a masculine oath. The sound of labored breathing quickly followed, and the boys jumped up, their fingers flexing over their holsters. Cord's head bobbed into view.

"I told you boys to watch her!"

Zack and Wes exchanged dumbfounded looks.

"But Cord, we *were* watching—"

"The hell you were."

Cord hauled himself into the cave, and Fancy quailed. He loomed over her. His face was florid, and his hands were fisted so tightly, his knuckles were white. For the first time since she'd met him, she knew genuine fear. She scrambled to her feet.

"What is it? What's happened?" she asked.

His eyes glittered like emerald shards. "Don't play games with me, woman. What did you do with the horses?"

Chapter Seven

Cord watched Fancy blanch. If he hadn't known her better, he might have believed he'd really scared her this time. He might have felt guilty for it, too, except that he'd seen for himself the slender, female-sized footprints where the boys' horses had grazed.

At first, he hadn't thought it likely that someone as sharp as Fancy would run off her only means of escape. Then he reminded himself how sneaky she could be. He hadn't bothered looking for more proof after that.

"Sorry to disappoint you, Marshal," she answered with an asperity that returned the color to her cheeks. "As delightful as your company has been, I wouldn't have idled my morning away here if I'd had access to a horse."

"She didn't go anywhere, Cord. Honest," Wes said, standing staunchly by her side.

Zack nodded and frowned. "Still, it's not like Shawnee and Trail Boss to wander away. Do you reckon the thunder spooked them?"

Before Cord could answer, a piercing neigh shook the walls of the cave.

Zack caught his breath. "Isn't that Poco?"

Thrashing and snorting accompanied the horse's cries. Wes peered over the lip of the cave.

"Uh-oh. We got company."

Cord's heart leaped. He, too, had spied the slender, breechclouted youth wrestling with the paint. The Indian looked a year or two younger than Wes.

"Hey!" Wes shouted, bristling for a fight. "Take your thieving hands off our horse!"

Cord choked back an oath. He grabbed for Wes's collar, but the boy ducked and charged down the hill. A heartbeat later, Zack had snatched up two rifles and was racing after his brother.

"Zack! Wes! Jesus." Cord drew his Peacemaker. "Stay here out of sight," he snapped at Fancy.

"But there's only one Indian. Surely Zack and Wes can—"

"Comanches don't travel alone. Ever."

He leaped to the ledge below and scrambled around a boulder. To his consternation, Fancy jumped down after him. Her jaw was set, despite the grayish tinge that mottled her cheeks.

"Confound it, woman, I told you to stay put!"

"I'm not staying here alone—especially without a gun."

Cord cursed. She had a point, and he didn't have time to argue. "All right, give me your hand."

She obeyed for once. Her fingers felt like ice, but they didn't quiver as they wrapped around his own. She swung down beside him, and their eyes met. Determination overshadowed the fear in hers.

"Brave girl," he said, nodding. "Stay close, now."

She surprised him when she kept pace, leaping from rock to rock with the grace of an antelope. He'd feared he would have to throw her over his shoulder to make better time, but when he reached the wooded plateau, she was only three steps behind him.

As they ran into the clearing, Poco was bucking harder than a mustang. Shrilling his outrage, the gelding jumped in punishing circles beneath the lowest boughs of a cedar. Cord had taken special pains to train Poco so that rustlers and fugitives couldn't get the drop on him and ride off on his horse. Under different circumstances, he might have allowed himself the satisfaction of watching Poco make short work of his thief.

When the Indian hit the dirt with a thud and an "umpf," though, Cord knew there would be hell to pay.

Wes and Zack stood laughing over the youth.

"Reckon that ol' paint was more than you bargained for, son," Zack said.

"Yeah. I don't guess you've got much future as a horse thief." Wes grinned, sticking out a hand to help the boy up.

The Indian colored a full shade darker. Slapping Wes's hand aside, he bounded to his feet and loosed a barrage of virulent Comanche. Wes tipped back his hat and scratched his head.

"Shoot. I can't make heads or tails of what he's saying."

The Indian shouted again, stomping his feet. Cord feared that the young warrior sought retribution. Although Comanches accorded high honors to braves who stole horses from enemy camps, they accorded even higher honors to warriors who killed enemies in hand-to-hand combat.

"Back off, Wes," Cord warned.

Shadowy riders began to materialize along the tree line as the young Indian swooped for his ankle sheath. A bonehandled hunting knife appeared in his hand.

"Look out!" Zack raised his gun. "He's got a pig sticker!"

Cord knocked down Zack's rifle. "Dammit, Wes, I said back off!"

"Aw, Cord. I can take him."

"I know, son." Cord struggled to keep his voice even. "But he's not likely to quit while his brothers are watching. You'll have to kill him, and then the whole tribe will be after our blood."

Wes glanced uneasily toward the half-dozen braves and their outmoded Enfield rifles, then his gaze shifted to Fancy. She stood pale and rigid, her hair floating around her shoulders like a storm cloud, her eyes flashing like blue lightning. She stood defiant in the face of the Comanche threat, and for a heartbeat, Cord couldn't remember ever seeing anything so beautiful.

"For Miss Fancy's sake, I'll keep the peace," Wes said at last, retreating two steps.

This show of timidity only enraged the Indian. He began to shout, slicing and jabbing the air. When this challenge also failed, he screwed up his face and spat on Wes's boots. Cord watched his brother's face turn red.

"Ignore him, Wes," Fancy said quietly, moving close behind him. "He's a spoiled, undisciplined child trying desperately to prove he's a man."

The Indian snorted. Pointing at Wes's hair, he called to his comrades in contemptuous tones. They started to laugh. Before Cord could guess the boy's intentions, the Indian shoved Wes out of the way and grabbed Fancy's arm.

Cord's heart nearly stalled. All manner of horrors raced through his mind. He rushed to save her from rape, mutilation, or worse, but in the three seconds that he took to race to her side, she'd spun, blocked the boy's knife, and rammed her knee into his loins. The Indian howled, doubling over.

Rumbles of displeasure replaced the horsemen's mirth. Zack tossed Wes a rifle. Cord hastily pulled Fancy behind him. He could feel the pulse hammering in her wrist.

"Hellfire, girl," he whispered. "Who taught you how to fight like that?"

She drew a shaky breath. "My mother."

After a moment of silence one of the Indians rode forward. He was large and powerfully built despite his wrinkled skin and the silver hairs that twined through his fur-wrapped braids. From the top of his head fell a scalp lock, which he'd adorned with a yellow feather, and he had painted the center part of his hair red, like the tattoos on his face and chest. No brows or lashes framed the keen black eyes that gazed into Cord's, for the Indian had plucked his body hairless, as was the Comanche custom. Still, the white man's influence was evident in this warrior's choice of weapons—a double-action Remington revolver—and in the oversized dice that dangled from his belt.

The warrior's shadow fell across the youth. It acted like a

tonic on the boy. Rousing himself, he reached for his knife, but Cord stepped on the handle.

The boy's eyes grew murderous, but the warrior berated him in cool, crisp tones. The youth staggered to his feet. Muttering what must have been oaths, he limped to his horse.

"The boy has brought great honor to himself and to your people," Cord said in Spanish, hoping the warrior would understand the dialect of Aunt Lally's vaqueros. He knew that Comanches often traded their rustled horses and cattle for guns with Spanish-speaking New Mexicans. "He has stolen two ponies from our camp. Now we want them back."

Again those keen black eyes locked with Cord's. He thought the Indian must have understood him, for the warrior's gaze shifted to Zack and Wes. Their repeating Winchesters could easily have gunned down the entire Comanche hunting party—assuming, of course, Cord thought grimly, that the Indians missed with their one-shot Enfields.

"I am Standing Bear," the warrior said at last in stilted Spanish. "Blood Wolf is my son. That which he took from you is now his. Be grateful that he left your scalp."

Standing Bear turned his horse's head around. Cord caught the reins.

"The great Standing Bear would not return to his people with only two ponies when he could have had three. He would lose face."

The warrior looked down his long, flat nose at Cord. "There is no shame in two ponies."

"No shame to Blood Wolf, who caught the ponies. But Standing Bear has nothing of his own to show his people. The tribe will whisper. They will say he is old. Unfit to raid."

The Indian stiffened, and Cord knew he'd figured right. Standing Bear must have had trouble persuading the tribe's more venerable warriors to join him. He was aging. He was losing respect as a hunter. That was why four of his six braves looked no older than Zack.

"We will trade," Standing Bear said abruptly. "I will take your rifles and your squaw. You may take one pony."

"One pony?" Fancy exclaimed. "I'm worth only one lousy pony?"

Cord hid his smile. Apparently Fancy understood Spanish too.

"Actually," he said to her, "Standing Bear figures you're worth something closer to a quarter of a pony."

She turned crimson. "Well, you just tell Standing Bear he can go to hell!"

"I'm not sure Standing Bear would understand, considering how the Injuns don't have fire-and-brimstone preachers. You have any other ideas?"

She glared at him. "As a matter of fact, I do. You need to play Standing Bear for the horses. He's wearing dice, so he must be a gambler."

Cord had been thinking the same thing. In fact, his initial challenge had been headed that way. There was just one little problem.

"I'm not good at dice."

"I am."

"That's only because you cheat."

She dug her fists into her hips. "Look here, Rawlins. Do you want those horses or not?"

"I want them all right." His humor ebbed. "But not your way. I don't cheat. Never have. And I'm not going to start now."

"Oh. And I suppose you think Mr. Standing Bear is going to roll a square game?"

"It doesn't matter. A man's got his honor."

"Honor?" She tossed her head. "Well, I've seen more honorable men than I can count wind up dead. You know what your problem is, Rawlins? You've been a lawman for too long."

Before Cord could stop her, she marched straight up to Standing Bear and tapped a forefinger on his buffalo leggings.

"Excuse me, sir," she crooned in lilting Spanish. Her smile was sweeter than a honeycomb. "My husband and I were just talking. We figured that because of the baby and all"—she laid a loving hand on her belly—"you'd consider a different trade. You see, I won't be much use to you for . . . oh, another six or seven months."

Cord's face flamed. One of his brothers snickered. He shot them each a withering look, but he couldn't tell which one was guilty. They both wore poker faces.

Standing Bear frowned at Fancy's bulgeless womb. "Consider?" he said. "Very well. I will take instead the pistol in your husband's belt."

Cord's patience completely unraveled. "Look here, Standing Bear. I'm not parting with that pistol. Or the woman, either."

"No pistol? No deal."

Fancy laughed in musical tones. "Darling," she said lightly, her eyes piercing through him like flint, "don't be such a ninny. I think Standing Bear's offer is more than fair. Only . . ." She fluttered her lashes. "I was wondering, Mr. Standing Bear. Is your six-shooter just for show? Because my husband's a fair shot with his. He can knock out the eye of a squirrel at sixty paces. Can't you, darling?"

Cord understood now where Fancy's guile was leading. The girl was smart, all right. Smarter than a tree full of owls. "Sure I can . . . sweetheart."

She rewarded him with a heart-tripping smile. "Can you shoot like that, Mr. Standing Bear?"

"Your squaw talks too much, white man."

"Maybe." Cord hooked his thumbs over his holster. "Or maybe Standing Bear can't hit the side of a barn."

The jibe worked. The Indian set his jaw and dismounted. "Name your target."

"First, the terms. Six shots at sixty paces. Best dead-eye wins. If it's you, you get the horses and rifles. If it's me . . . well, I just want the horses."

"Agreed."

"It's a trick, Father. A white-man's trick!" Blood Wolf cried. Apparently recovered, he cantered forward, waving his

Enfield. "I say we kill them now. Take the guns, the horse, and the woman!"

Standing Bear raised a hand. "No. I have agreed."

"But the horses are mine!"

"Do you wish to compete for them?"

Blood Wolf hesitated, but only long enough to leer at Fancy. "I will whip this paleface dog and teach his woman what it means to know pain."

Fancy stiffened. On impulse, Cord dropped an arm around her shoulders.

"Listen here, Standing Bear. I don't give a damn which of you I shoot against. I'll take you both on, if you want. But the woman's not part of the deal. You got that?"

Standing Bear nodded. Blood Wolf sneered. Jumping to the ground, he traded guns with his father.

"Cord, what if it *is* a trick?" Fancy whispered in English. "What if Blood Wolf tries to shoot you?"

Cord gave her a light squeeze before he set her free. "Don't you fret. Zack and Wes will cover me."

"But you've promised Standing Bear the rifles and the horses."

"That's because I don't plan to lose."

Her gaze was so troubled, he almost believed she was concerned about him.

"Here now," he said gruffly, discomfited by the feelings of warmth that her worry roused in him. "Don't you think I can hit a knothole at sixty paces?"

"Of course you can. It's just that . . . Well . . ." She frowned. "You're too honest, Rawlins."

"You make it sound like a hanging offense."

She reddened. "Well, where I come from, honesty's a weakness."

Turning on her heel, she marched off to join Zack and Wes. Cord shook his head. Now she was acting more like the Fancy Holleday he knew. He probably shouldn't care, but . . . Why did she always believe the worst of his good intentions?

Standing Bear led his son's horse away, and the other

Comanches entered the clearing. Fancy willed herself to stand firm, meeting their eyes with defiance. Some of them gestured obscenely at her despite Zack, who stepped forward to shield her, and Wes, who snapped his rifle lever in warning. She tried to tell herself that no matter what happened, Indians were just men. She could handle them.

Still, stories of Comanche brutality crowded her mind. The prospect of captivity left her cold. The most frightening part of all, though, was that she was actually beginning to fear for Cord and the boys. Her enemies.

Caring was weakness. And weakness was death. Diego had taught her that lesson well.

She tried to discount her feelings. She told herself that worrying about the Rawlins brothers was only natural, since they were protecting her from Blood Wolf and his kind. Her derringer would be useless under these conditions. And she had no way of surviving out here, alone, against Indians who intended rape, or worse.

She swallowed hard.

While his braves gathered behind the firing line, Standing Bear paced off fifty yards and plunged his knife into an oak. A breath of wind riffled the leaves, and Fancy could vaguely discern a knothole in the dappled play of light and shadow.

Blood Wolf shoved past Cord. With a show of arrogance, the youth indicated that he would fire first. Cord shrugged.

Wes snorted. "Shoot. Knotholes are nothing. If the Injun can't hit a sitting target, he doesn't deserve his gun."

The Indians grew breathlessly quiet. Blood Wolf raised the Remington. Firing in rapid succession, he split the knife handle, shattered the blade, and carved the knothole from the tree. He accomplished all this with five bullets. The Indians whooped.

"Not bad for a windbelly," Zack murmured. "Reckon he can aim at that."

Standing Bear searched for another target. Claiming the knotholes were all unsuitable, he hung his dice from a low-hanging cottonwood bough. Each die was crudely carved

from bone and measured about half the circumference of
Blood Wolf's target.

The wind shifted, and the cubes began to twist and sway.

Fancy's heart quickened. "Blood Wolf's mark wasn't
nearly as difficult!"

Zack smiled grimly. "Don't you worry, ma'am."

"Yeah, Cord'll get our horses back," Wes said. "Plenty
pronto too."

Cord stepped to the line. The Comanches all shouted and
jeered. He ignored them. Turning his shoulder, he raised his
Peacemaker and fired so quickly that the three reports
sounded like one. His first bullet pierced the right die's center.

His second punched out the left's snake eye.

The third shot sawed the rawhide cord in two.

Spinning his .45, he shoved it back into its holster before
the dice could rattle to the earth.

The braves sobered, falling silent.

"Looks like I get the ponies," Cord said dryly.

Blood Wolf turned a shade of plum. "No! The horses are
mine."

"The agreement will be honored," Standing Bear said,
nodding at Cord. "I gave my word."

"Your word is not mine!"

Blood Wolf raised his gun. Fancy cried out a warning
along with Zack and Wes.

Cord turned, reaching, but it was too late. The Indian's
gun blazed. The charge was deafening as the revolver
backfired, exploding in the young Comanche's hand. His
high-pitched screams froze Fancy's pulse. Stunned, she could
only stand in horror, watching the spray of blood from the
grotesque remains of severed fingers.

Cord was the first to reach Blood Wolf. Ripping off his
shirt, he pinned the writhing youth and wrapped his gushing
wounds. Standing Bear fell to his knees at his son's side. The
old warrior's face looked pale despite his unyielding features.

"He needs a doctor. A medicine man," Cord said
brusquely, binding Blood Wolf's arm to his chest.

The boy began to shake and chatter. He curled into a ball. "Is your camp nearby?"

Standing Bear nodded stiffly, then called to his braves. Two scrambled forward and carried their comrade to a horse.

Cord rose. Standing Bear joined him. Only then did Fancy realize she'd twisted the chain of her lucky coin so tightly, her fingers had chafed near to bleeding.

"My son would have killed you." Standing Bear's voice was hoarse with restrained emotion. "Why did you help him?"

Fancy wondered the same thing. If Diego had been in Cord's shoes, he would have gunned the boy down—after prolonging his agony, of course. She waited shakily for Cord's answer.

He fidgeted, seeming uncomfortable with Standing Bear's question. Many seconds passed before he finally met the old warrior's eyes.

"Because it was the right thing to do."

Fancy couldn't stop thinking about Cord's answer. She thought about it that afternoon as he helped escort Blood Wolf to the Indian camp. She remembered it again when Cord returned, sporting a deerskin shirt, hunting knives for the boys, and a strawberry pony for her. Later, she thought about it on the trail, when his brothers began teasing him, and his rough, embarrassed voice silenced their yarns about Cord, the death-defying Ranger.

Fancy thought a lot that day. She reflected on honor and compassion, hatred and vengeance. She remembered how she had vowed to punish the lawman who had killed Diego. She knew her lover's soul could never rest until the deed was done, and yet, a part of her yearned to be excused from the treacherous task she'd set for herself. Maybe, just maybe, a man like Cord Rawlins deserved to keep living.

Never had she expected to think of a federal marshal as anything other than a mark. Cord wasn't just her enemy, though. He was a widower grieving for his wife and son. And he wasn't just her captor, he was a brother, dedicated to protecting two young hotheads. She tried doggedly to harden herself against him, to strip him of every attribute except his badge, but the more successful she became, the more alone she felt.

When the sun began to sink, Cord ordered the boys to make camp. Wes hunted rabbits for dinner, and Zack warmed the inevitable beans. Fancy sat idle.

If she'd still been dealing faro, twilight would have signaled the start of her busiest time of day. She tried to reflect fondly on those nights of humbugs and shams at the Golden Garter. Instead, she kept recalling the endless waiting for Diego, his cursory lovemaking, his drunken rages, and his flagrant affairs. Sometimes it was hard to remember the silver-tongued caballero who had been so enamored of her, a girl of eighteen, that he'd staked his beloved casino to win her from the whorehouse.

Of course, Fancy knew now that Diego's sacrifice hadn't been as great as it seemed then: He'd cheated. As he always had.

Her gaze strayed to Cord. Bare-chested and dripping, he was returning from the nearby stream. She watched his approach furtively, telling herself she must study his habits. How else could she apprise Ned Wilkerson of them?

He stopped by the fire and used the rag that once had been his shirt to dry himself. The fine coat of sorrel hair blanketing his chest formed ringlets as water dribbled over his ribs. Rolling past the hardened planes of his stomach, the droplets trickled into the dark recesses of his breeches. She grew warm, despite her stubborn efforts not to imagine where those droplets had come to rest.

Next, he shook his head. Water sprayed, leaving his mane unruly and spiked until his sun-bronzed fingers curried the mess. She couldn't help but admire how his hair glinted like copper fire against the red-gold horizon. He appeared oblivious to her regard, though. In fact, the entire time that he rubbed and stretched, working his naked muscles before her, he seemed to concentrate on Zack.

"We'll be heading east a ways now," he said. "I reckon

we'll come to Fort Graham in a day, less than two. It's high time I sent you boys home to Aunt Lally."

Zack's brow furrowed, and Cord steeled himself for an argument. Now that the boys were enamored of Fancy, it would be even harder to send them back to the ranch. Even so, he couldn't let them anywhere near Carson City's courthouse. They would insist on attending Fancy's trial, and when she was sentenced, all hell would break loose. He had nightmares about Zack and Wes breaking her out of jail, using the ruse that he, God forgive him, had taught them. They'd either get caught, or shot, or live like wanted men, hiding out in the hills with Fancy.

Cord wasn't sure which was worse.

One thing was certain, though. The girl had an appetite. If she ever feasted her eyes on Zack or Wes, those same, hungry eyes that were devouring his naked flesh and heating up his insides, then the boys he knew would be lost to him forever.

"You're worried about those Comanches, aren't you, Cord?" Zack asked.

Cord fidgeted. He supposed he was, but it was hard to concentrate on Indians when a woman was staring his pants clean off him. In a way, her wanting him was flattering. Most women didn't let on that way. Beth sure never had. Just knowing Fancy sat nearby, ripe and ready and certain to please, jangled his nerves. He felt as he had at sixteen, when he was falling head over heels for Lila Mae Clegg. Restless and hot-blooded at the age of nineteen, she had lured him to her daddy's hayloft one night to teach him everything she knew about loving.

And Lila Mae had known plenty, he thought with a lop-sided grin.

"Cord?"

He started, his face flaming. Zack was eyeing him as if he'd gone deaf. Or daft. He figured daft was closer to the truth. How the devil had he let himself get so randy?

"Er . . . Comanches. Yeah."

He glanced furtively at his fly. It didn't look as strained as it felt—yet. If his pants got any tighter, he would have to take another dip. Either that, or carry Fancy off into the bushes. The idea made his pulse pound, and he nearly groaned aloud.

Confound it, he was playing right into her hands. Horny with his pants down was exactly how she wanted him. He had to get ahold of himself. He had to think of Beth, instead of wondering if one tumble with Fancy was worth a whole night with Lila Mae.

Zack cleared his throat. "The way I figure it," he said, his eyes shifting curiously to Fancy, "Standing Bear's braves are just strays. The Quahadi and Peneteka bands aren't likely to leave their hunting grounds and come this far east."

Cord smiled ruefully. So Zack could sense the sparking going on. Bless the boy's discretion. Wes would have made at least a dozen wisecracks by now.

"Maybe. Or maybe we were just lucky." Cord drew a ragged breath and forced his brain back to Indians. "Whatever the case, I'm not taking any chances. We'll be safer heading east. And you boys'll be safer at home."

"Well . . . that's fine by me, Cord. Ever since Uncle Seth died so sudden last winter, Aunt Lally's been relying on me to get the beeves ready for Abilene. But Wes—" Zack shrugged, his smile bordering on apologetic, "he isn't gonna like it, you sending him back to the range."

"Then we'll just have to rope him to a fence post, won't we?"

Zack laughed. Cord did, too. He worried that he'd have to carry out the same threat on himself if he wanted to keep his hands off Fancy Holleday. Somehow she'd gotten under his skin that day, and she'd done it with a good deal less than her usual effort.

That was the unsettling part.

He'd worked all afternoon to forget how she'd impressed him by single-handedly defeating Blood Wolf. He'd worked even harder to forget how gut-deep scared he'd been when he realized she was in danger. Perhaps it was understandable to worry about a prisoner who was his sole hope of recovering vital U.S. minting plates. It was not understandable, however, to miss the nudge of her buttocks against his inner thigh. Or the flutter of her heart against his forearm. His saddle felt empty without her.

And that was the dangerous part.

Hardening himself against his baser instincts, he turned suddenly, thinking to grab his deerskin and cover himself. His eyes met Fancy's. She blushed and glanced away. If he hadn't known her better, he might have thought he'd actually flustered her. Now that would be a switch, wouldn't it?

A slow grin stole across his face.

"You best quit your staring, girl, or your eyes are going to bug out."

Her color deepened, and he smirked. Well, well, well, he thought. Madam Hellcat did have the jitters!

"I . . . don't know what you mean."

He folded his arms across his chest. She trained her gaze behind him. Or above him. Anywhere but *on* him. The devil sneaked inside him, then. Maybe it was time for a little harmless retribution.

"A smart lady like you? I think you do know."

Fancy hiked her chin. She could feel her face flaming, and the knowledge rankled. For some unfathomable reason, she was having a hard time recovering her composure. It wasn't as if she'd never seen a naked man before. In fact, she'd seen so many more than her share that she thought she'd lost the ability to appreciate one. Yet here she sat, going weak on the inside just watching Cord put his trail-hardened muscles on display.

"I'm not the only one who thinks 'right highly' of myself, it would seem," she said tartly. "It just so happens I was watching the sunset."

"The sunset, eh?" He tossed a "sure you were" grin at Zack, and the boy chuckled. "Now don't you go getting any ideas about mischief making after dark. You wouldn't last an hour on the run in this country. Not with those Injuns prowling around."

She wished she could slap that smirk right off his face. "I suppose that's your way of trying to frighten me."

"I've seen desperate people do desperate things."

"Your concern is truly touching, Marshal. But like you said, I'm smart. And those 'Injuns' are nothing more than men to me."

"You've got us menfolk all figured out, eh?"

"What's to figure?" she said haughtily. "You're all pitifully simple. You get hungry. You get amorous. And you butt heads to determine king of the herd."

He looked amused. "Sounds like a mighty limited view, if you ask me."

"Oh, so you're miraculously different?"

"Well . . ." His eyes twinkled. "I reckon I can't answer that, on account I couldn't be a fair judge."

She pressed her lips together. She didn't know what was worse, his teasing banter or the butterflies it had launched in her belly. It scared her to death to think she might actually have come to like this man. First, she'd doubted her right to hand him over to Ned Wilkerson. Next, she'd started mooning over his flexing muscles!

Something was wrong, terribly wrong, if Cord Rawlins could make her blush. She decided she'd better start an argument before she did something really foolish, like lose her heart to him.

"The fact is, you couldn't possibly be objective," she goaded. "Why, you've got two brothers who worship the ground you walk on. And your wife was probably even more starry eyed."

The humor drained from his face. "You don't know a damned thing about my wife."

"I know her type. A virgin till her wedding day. Sheltered, helpless, and pure. At least, that's what she had everyone thinking. She had you eating out of the palm of her hand, didn't she, Cord?"

"That's enough."

"Enough of what? The truth? But surely that couldn't be. An honorable man like you would respect the truth."

"You wouldn't know the truth if it were a snake that crawled up and bit you."

"Maybe." Her lips carved out a mocking smile. "Or maybe you're not a fair judge of that, either."

His face darkened. Her heart hammered, but she steeled herself for the worst. She expected an explosion, a slap, perhaps even a good, hard shake. Instead, he reached for his shirt and yanked the deerskin over his head. He grabbed his Winchester next.

"It's almost dark," he said gruffly. "I'm going to see what's keeping Wes and those rabbits."

Zack shot Fancy an accusatory glare. She did her best to ignore him. This was her moment of triumph, and she wanted to taste the sweetness.

As she watched Cord stalk away, though, she tasted nothing but ashes.

Chapter Eight

That night, Fancy dreamed about the whorehouse. She saw herself as she'd been at the age of eighteen, trapped in a life she abhorred.

Then, from out of the mists of Portsmouth Square, a man entered the chandeliered foyer. He was not overly tall, but he appeared broad shouldered and narrow waisted beneath his long, flowing overcoat. He surrendered his gloves to the porter, but not his hat, and try as Fancy might, she could not see his face as he wandered through the plush velvets and rich woods of the parlor.

The madam rustled forward, intercepting the gentleman with two glasses of champagne. He graciously declined her most coveted of invitations. This night, he had come for a virgin, he said, and he inquired after Fancy. The madam smiled and nodded. She accepted his purse, and Fancy knew a moment of panic. Surely the madam would not pass her off as a virgin!

The gentleman approached her, and her heart plummeted. She thought to protest when he took her hand, but his white teeth flashed in a disarming smile. For a moment, she was too dazzled to speak.

The next thing Fancy knew, she lay naked before him. The bed was like an island in a sea of candleglow. He came to her, and the gauzy bed hangings swirled behind him, distorting and muting the light. She tried to see his face once more, but the shadows favored him so, that her eyes grew weary and soon fluttered closed.

She retreated to the furthest corner of her mind then, a place where she need not think or feel. She surrendered her body dutifully to his pleasure, not her own. Never her own.

Her lover would not let her escape him so easily, though. His hands were callused and gentle as they roamed over her, chasing tingles across her skin, coaxing tremors from her limbs. She was amazed and not just a little frightened when she responded to him in ways she had never intended. She thought she should tell him of the madam's hoax, but when she tried to warn him, when she tried to push him away, his arms folded her to his heart, and his lips wooed hers with tender kisses.

He whispered Spanish love words, words she had despaired of ever hearing. She listened in growing wonder. Perhaps it was not so wrong to let him love her, she mused hopefully. Perhaps he wouldn't care that she was unvirtuous and impure if she could only find the way to please him.

She wove her hands through his hair—thick, rich waves of darkest brown. He murmured encouragements. His fingers delved lower, stroking her thighs. She thought she must go mad for the sweet, unfulfilled promise of his passion. She started to moan. He clasped her closer, and her nipples buried in the soft sorrel down of his chest. His kisses grew hungrier, deeper. She gasped, her eyes flying wide. Finally she could see his tanned face. She tore her mouth free to cry out his name.

"Cord!"

No. It couldn't be.

Her heart racing, she replayed the scene. She tried to re-create that precious moment of discovery, when she at long last gazed into Diego's dark eyes.

But the gaze that returned her own was forest green with wanting.

"No! Not Cord . . ."

Her cry was desperate this time. She panted. Dear God,

how could this be? How could she have surrendered her dreams, the only refuge she had left in this world, to Cord Rawlins?

"Fancy."

His voice filled her head, and she thrashed harder, succumbing to an uncontrollable fear.

"Leave me be!"

A weight pressed down on her shoulder. "Fancy. Wake up. Wake up, darlin'."

She gasped and blinked. The stars spun into watery focus. Next came Cord, silhouetted against the dying campfire. His hand squeezed her shoulder.

"There. That's better."

Her pulse thundered in her ears; her breaths rasped.

"You're safe now," he said.

But she wasn't safe.

She sat hastily, retreating from his touch. For a moment, all she could do was crouch there, gulping down air, feeling like a first-class fool.

"You were dreaming," he said softly.

"It was a nightmare!"

He nodded. She could see his eyes now that her own had adjusted to the firelight. They fairly glowed, but with concern or amusement? She couldn't say.

Oh God, did he know? Did he hear her cry out his name?

"Were you dreaming about Blood Wolf?"

Visions of the Indian's twitching stump of a hand stole into her mind. She shuddered. Even that ghastly image would have been better—far better, she told herself weakly—than visions of making love to Cord Rawlins.

"No. Of course not. Indians don't scare me. I told you that."

"So you did."

He was close, so close. The bedroll was like an island in a sea of emberglow.

Nonsense, she thought. She wasn't dreaming now.

Still, it was hard to forget. And it was hard not to wonder.

Would his touch move her as it had in her dream? Would he promise her love? Would she let herself believe?

His warmth lapped gently over her. She could hear the lulling rhythm of his breaths. Her senses expanded, drinking in each nuance of man—the sheen of his hair, the scent of his skin, the intoxicating light in his eyes. She could have drowned and refused to revive. She could have reached out and . . .

"I dreamed about prison," she said hastily. She had to break the spell. Lying didn't feel good; it just felt familiar.

"Prison, eh?"

She hiked her chin and nodded. He sat back on his heels.

"I reckon prison can be a scary place."

She said nothing. Her mind flashed back to a time long ago, a memory she thought she had buried. Her mother, unable to cope with her fading beauty, had thrown herself from a third-story window. Fancy had been thirteen. Packing her meager belongings, she had run away, but the madam's thugs had hunted her down. The first time they dragged her back, she had merely been beaten. The second time, she had been locked in the cellar. For three endless days, she'd huddled without food, warmth, or light. She hadn't dared to run away again.

"You know, Fancy, you could keep away those nightmares," Cord said quietly. "You could make your life a whole lot easier, if you'd just tell me where those plates are."

Idiot. She cursed herself. Why had she confided her fears about prison? He was her enemy. Had she thought he would sympathize?

"Why should I tell you anything?" she asked hoarsely, forcing the lump from her throat.

"Because I could tell the governor how you cooperated. Get him to shorten that prison sentence you're bound to get."

She gave a short, hollow laugh. "You'd do that for me?"

"Yes."

She was afraid to believe the sincerity in his tone. "Why? Don't tell me it's the right thing to do."

"It is the right thing to do," he insisted, his eyes captivating hers. "That and . . . Well, hell. A girl should settle down. Find herself a man. You don't need to be running from town to town, cheating and stealing to get by. That's no kind of life. You can do better, Fancy."

She wanted to believe him. God, how she wanted to believe. But she knew better. She was a realist. No man, no good and honest man, would want her. She was on her own unless she found another Diego. Until she did, she'd spend her days cheating and stealing. She had to. She would never, ever, go back to whoring.

She looked away from him. "I like my life just fine, Rawlins. I don't need some tin-star crusader preaching salvation at me."

"My offer still stands."

Damn him, why was he doing this? Why was he making it so hard to hate him?

"Forget it," she said. "I'll take my chances in court. Providing I get there, of course."

He shifted closer. His heat had so charged the inches between them, she felt rather than saw his ripple of movement.

"And why wouldn't you get there?" he murmured. "Is Santana's cavalry on its way?"

She cursed herself a second time. Why didn't she just blurt out that she and Ned Wilkerson were going to sell their plates to Mexican nationals?

"I just figured that between the bats, pumas, and Comanches, I was going to end up buried in this godforsaken wilderness you Texicans call home."

He didn't look convinced. He smoothed back her hair, catching a lingering tear on his thumb. She felt her heart leap.

"Is there something you're needing to tell me?" he asked gently, his palm coming to rest along the traitorous pulse in her throat. "Something about your friends?"

"I don't know what you mean."

"I think you do." The sea-green depths of his eyes threatened to drown her. "Santana's men are coming for you, aren't they?"

She swallowed.

"Fancy?"

She felt herself sinking. She tried to twist away, but his hand was her anchor. It was all she could do to stay afloat, to remind herself who he was and what he'd done to Diego. She couldn't let Cord Rawlins tempt her when she had failed so miserably to tempt him.

And yet, as he leaned closer, she felt reality slipping away. The tip of his nose nearly brushed hers. If she tilted her head, if she parted her lips, she could kiss him. She could run her tongue along that mobile mouth and sip the tangy-sweet flavor of man. Already his tobacco and leather scent had drawn her taste juices. She could nibble and lick; she could savor that secret, indelible seasoning that was unique to Cord Rawlins. And what was worse, she wanted to.

"It's not like you to hold your tongue, darlin'."

Her palms moistened at the husky timbre of his tone. "Let me go."

"Let you go?" He smiled. "That's all? No lies? No insults?"

"Let me go, damn you!"

His mesmerizing gaze lowered until it was fastened on her mouth. For a moment—one breathless, stunning moment— she hoped he would kiss her. His lips had already parted; moist and soft, they invited her own. If she hadn't known him better, if he hadn't proven time and again that he found her so unappealing, she might have believed he was tempted too. His breathing had quickened. She heard the cadence of his heart—or was it hers?—echoing all around them.

Her belly heated. Some primal, unthinking part of her took control. She swayed nearer. Her lashes fluttered, and she sought the lips she couldn't bear to admit she wanted.

"Let you go?" he whispered as her mouth hovered a fraction from his own. His thumb brushed her cheek. "No one's holding you back this time, darlin'."

She blinked, then stiffened. Humiliation seared through

her like a freshly forged blade. She recoiled, hating him for the truth of his words, hating herself for her weakness.

"Are you quite finished harassing me, Marshal?" *God, Fancy, how could you have fallen for your own scam?* "I'd like to go to sleep now."

His brows arched over those gemstone eyes.

"I reckon so. You've told me everything I wanted to know. Except of course"—his dimples peeked in a wistful kind of smile—"why you called out my name in your sleep."

Fancy nearly died. She wished she had. Her face flamed hotter than a Chinese firecracker. "That's preposterous."

"Don't remember, eh?"

"No, I do not!"

He chuckled warmly. "Now there's that lie I was waiting for. And here I thought I'd go disappointed."

"You can go to hell!"

She flopped down, tugging the blanket to her chin. When she rolled over in a huff, he laughed again.

"Pleasant dreams to you, too, darlin'."

He moved away. She watched his shadow as it played over the ground, slipping past the saddles and Wes's bedroll. Only then did she realize the boy was awake. He'd been lying there, watching them, listening to every blessed word they'd said! He grinned when she noticed him, and she thought about crawling under a rock.

Squeezing her eyes closed, she prayed fervently that Ned Wilkerson would hurry up and find her and put an end to her misery.

"Wake up. Breakfast is waiting."

Cord started, eyeing Zack curiously as the boy snapped at Fancy. It wasn't like him to be so brusque. Nor was it like him to stomp off to the fire without so much as a "Good morning, ma'am."

What was eating the boy?

"Looks like someone got up on the wrong side of the bedroll," Wes quipped, withholding the coffeepot from Zack's outstretched hand.

"Give me that, peabrain."

"Uh, uh, uh. Ladies first."

Cord's gaze shifted to Fancy. She looked a little disconcerted as she blinked after Zack, but he attributed her confusion to being jolted from sleep, not to the boy's behavior. She wasn't likely to care whether Zack was upset. In truth, if she cared anything at all about Zack or Wes, she would have confessed to the things she knew about Santana's men.

Damn her, anyway.

Cord sipped his coffee. He'd spent a restless, guilt-ridden night, but lying awake until dawn had given him plenty of time to set himself straight. At first, he'd been moved when he heard her cry out. The tremor in her voice, the misty violet of her eyes, had led him to believe that prison truly frightened her. He had never jailed a woman before, and he had worried that the courageous, quick-witted girl he'd so admired the day before would be broken by the reformatory. So, like a fool, he had softened, offering to plea-bargain for her.

She had refused to come clean, though. She had refused to discuss the plates or the outlaws. He figured she was hoping he would be ambushed and herself rescued. The more likely outcome, of course, was that she would be murdered—along with Zack and Wes. Couldn't she see that he and the boys were the only ones keeping her off of boot hill? Couldn't she have been honest, just this once, and admitted their danger?

His jaw hardened as he fortified himself with the dispassion required by his badge.

Fancy Holleday had broken the law. No one had put a gun to her head and forced her to rob that train. That being the case, it was his job to bring her to justice. She could lie and cry and lure him to sin as much as she wanted. None of it would keep him from handing her over to the courts.

But if anything happened to his boys, anything at all, she'd have hell to pay.

"Morning, ma'am," Wes greeted her as she dragged her feet toward the campfire. He favored her with a dimpled grin as he patted the log beside him. "Ready for some flapjacks? I saved you the unburnt ones. I reckoned you'd be hungry after all those nightmares."

Fancy felt her face heat. Remembering her dream naturally brought to mind how she had tried to enact it, right there, by the campfire, with Cord Rawlins. God, she felt like such a cat's paw! She didn't know which was worse: facing him then or facing him now.

"Thank you, Wes," she murmured, taking the plate he offered.

She sat between the boys—and as far from *him* as she could possibly get. She needn't have worried, though. Cord Rawlins was too decent, too *honorable* a man to mention how he'd answered her cries, how he'd brushed away her tears— or how he'd resisted the temptation to bed her when she had been weak and willing.

God, how she hated him.

She frowned down at her breakfast. She was too tired to be hungry. She hadn't slept much, thanks to her encounter with Cord. And Zack had ended her doze rather abruptly when he barked at her to wake.

She glanced at the boy. It wasn't like Zack to be so surly. Most of the time, he was shyly attentive. This morning, though, he seemed so distant. He hadn't spread his coat to keep the dew off her britches; he hadn't offered to roll her bedding; he hadn't even vied with Wes to serve her flapjacks. A twinge of concern stirred an uncharacteristically maternal emotion in her. Was something ailing the boy?

"How are you feeling this morning, Zack?"

"Just dandy," he growled.

He sat grim and rigid, refusing to look her way. She was amazed that his snub should hurt her. She glanced at Cord for some clue to the boy's behavior, but he said nothing. He simply smoked his cigarette and watched her, his eyes narrowed in speculation.

"Don't pay Zack any mind, ma'am," Wes said, sidling closer with the coffeepot. "He went and lost his harmonica last night. 'Course, I say good riddance to the darn thing, but Zack stayed up till dawn, bawling like a lost dogie."

.Zack said nothing in his defense. Fancy felt herself empathizing. On impulse, she touched his sleeve.

"I'm sorry about your harmonica, Zack."

He recoiled as if he'd been burned. "No, you aren't! Don't go pretending. You aren't our friend. You never were. The sooner Cord's done turning you in, the better!"

She caught her breath. So did Wes. His face darkening, he reached over and punched Zack in the shoulder.

"Take that back, you weasel mouth! I won't have you talking bad about Miss Fancy."

"Wes."

Cord's quiet voice averted what looked like a sure-bet brawl. Zack's fist relaxed. Wiping his hand across the back of his mouth, he fished his toppled plate from the ashes.

"Seems to me you've got some bedding to roll, Wes. Saddle up while Zack eats."

Something in Cord's manner must have made Wes think twice about arguing. He mumbled an apology, touched Fancy's shoulder, and ambled away.

Silence settled over the campfire. Fancy was amazed to feel how fast her pulse was pounding. Zack's harsh rebuke shouldn't have troubled her in the least, yet here she sat, hurting. Worse still, she was hoping that Cord would insist Zack was wrong, especially about turning her in.

Cord said nothing, though. His eyes were cool. The tender caring that she'd spied the night before was thoroughly extinguished. How could she have been so naive? She had almost believed the man when he offered to speak to the governor!

The morning clouds burned off. The day grew warmer, but Zack's demeanor didn't. By late afternoon, Fancy was convinced that she, not the missing harmonica, was responsible for the boy's mood.

Wes rode like a champion by her side, quick to deflect Zack's dour looks and sharp comments. For the most part, though, Zack ignored her. She wasn't exactly sure why his behavior toward her had changed, although she thought her ridicule of Beth might have offended him. Or perhaps he was angry because she had used Beth and the things Zack had said about her to hurt Cord.

How amusing.

At least, that's what Fancy kept telling herself. She told herself, too, that she should use Zack's disapproval to her advantage, but her heart just wasn't in the game. It wouldn't take much skill for a sharper like her to play the boys against each other, now that Wes was taking her side and Zack was taking Cord's. Besides, Wes wasn't in possession of all the facts. He still blamed Zack's hostility on that "consarned harmonica."

Cord seemed to understand Zack better. When the boys struck a truce long enough to water the horses, Cord pulled her aside, folded his arms across his chest, and fixed her with what she'd secretly come to think of as his gunfighter's showdown glare.

"All right, girl. Out with it. What did you do to Zack?"

Fancy hiked her chin. She was in no mood for his accusations. Dusty, tired, and saddlesore, she wanted nothing more than a private moment to bathe herself. Instead, she was being harangued by a man clearly impervious to trail hardships.

She swore that Cord grew more handsome the harder the sun beat down on him. She couldn't remember ever seeing teeth so dazzling or eyes so verdant. His six-day growth of beard made him look more ruggedly virile, not grizzled and crusty the way most men would look. The man was simply gorgeous. And that meant war.

"What did I do to Zack?" She donned her best smug smile, the one that always seemed to rub him raw. "Why don't you ask him yourself?"

"Because I'm asking you."

"Really, Marshal. I'm surprised at you. You can't hope to get a straight answer from me. I'm a lying, cheating thief, remember?"

His jaw hardened. She was amazed to see the proof of her score. Something must really be eating at him for her to have taken the advantage so easily.

"You tried crawling into Zack's bedroll, didn't you?"

She started. She hadn't expected this line of questioning, and it stung far more than she cared to admit.

"Why, I do believe you're jealous, Cord."

"Just answer the goddamned question."

"What lady could refuse such a charming request? And yet if I tell you no, you'll think I'm lying. And if I tell you yes, well . . . you'll wish that I was."

His eyes slitted. Stalking forward, he reminded her of a puma, all muscle and menace.

"Now you listen to me, girl." He pushed his face down into hers. "You keep your claws out of my boys. Got that?"

Fancy steeled herself against her rising indignation. As if she would lay a hand on either one of his precious brothers! She liked to think she had a few redeeming qualities, and refusing to seduce innocents was one of them. Her own innocence had been forcibly taken at the age of twelve, and she'd always made it a point to turn blushing youths away.

But she wouldn't let Cord Rawlins know that. Let the Texas chawbacon go right on thinking the worst of her.

"Come now, Cord. Where's your sense of humor? A girl like me isn't accustomed to"—she leaned closer, walking her fingers up his chest—"all these lonely nights."

He pinned her hand. She felt his heart hammering beneath her palm. For a moment, as his eyes locked with hers, she knew a bittersweet triumph. She'd piqued him. That was all she'd really wanted. Now he would recall his proper little wife, turn a bright shade of red, and save himself from sinning —as he always did—just in the nick of time.

A heartbeat passed. Then another. His heat rolled over her, and she felt herself flush. What was he waiting for? Didn't he know his part of the game? He was supposed to free her now. She considered jerking loose, then quickly rejected the idea. Retreat was for the fainthearted.

"It's your turn, Marshal. Unless, of course, you plan on giving me the last word."

"Think you've won, do you?"

"Don't I always?"

Suddenly his arm dropped to her waist. She gasped, too

surprised to protest when he pulled her length against his. Wiry musculature folded around her, molding her softness to his ruggedness. It was unsettling to admit how good all that potent masculinity felt. Rallying her wits, she grabbed for his Colt, but he caught her hand with the speed of a gunfighter. She scowled. He chuckled.

"Yep," he said. "Just as I figured. Call your bluff, and you get all skittish."

"Skittish?"

"Sure. What would you call it?"

"One breath shy of suffocation. Whoever taught you how to kiss anyway? Babe the Blue Ox?"

He arched a mocking brow. "Don't tell me I've bruised your delicate sensibilities."

"Crushed them would be more accurate."

"Well now." His lips twitched, betraying his dimples. "I surely do apologize, ma'am. Reckon I might have been a bit careless at that, you being so fragile and all."

He leaned forward, his eyes aglow with mischief. "Seems like the least I can do is try to patch things up. You just tell me where it hurts," he whispered, pressing his lips to her temple. "Here?"

She tensed in reflex.

"Or here?" he murmured, his lips touching hers.

It was the barest caress, but she felt her pulse leap. For a moment, she couldn't decide whether to protest or yield, but he had already shifted, nuzzling the corner of her mouth. Her lips turned traitor. When they parted, she felt him smile, victorious. Still, he ignored her invitation. Teasing with featherlight persistence, he trailed kisses along her jawline, down to her pulse, up to her ear. He nibbled leisurely on the lobe, making her belly flip. But when his tongue flicked inside, shooting sparks to the base of her spine, she couldn't bear his assault any longer. She hiked her shoulder to nudge him away.

"You're just one hot little tease, aren't you, Fancy?" he whispered, his mouth hovering a bare inch above her own.

She drew a ragged breath. "Amateur."

"Oh, I reckon I am—next to you. Think you've got something to teach me?"

She felt her heart trip. He wasn't serious, was he?

"You've piqued my curiosity, Marshal. What kind of student would you be?"

"There's only one way to find out."

She fanned her lashes downward to hide her uneasiness. What had happened to the grieving husband? To Marshal Do-Right, ad nauseam? This wasn't the Cord Rawlins she knew. This was a wild card.

Still, she was the mistress of gaming, was she not? She could match any ace he had hidden, and then some. She'd make this one showdown Cord Rawlins would never forget.

Rising on tiptoe, she touched her lips to his. She expected him to stiffen; instead, his mouth slanted, demanding more of her kiss. She obliged. Gripping her buttocks, he ground his hips into hers, and she gasped, feeling his manhood strain hot and hard against her thigh. His heat was electric, shooting up her spine, charging every nerve.

She told herself she had no business liking the way her flesh tingled, or the way her nipples grew taut in response, but desire was like a firecracker bursting in her brain. Her limbs trembled, and her breaths rasped. The thunder of her pulse drowned out the last cries of her reason. Arching up, she pulled him closer, eager to feel her breasts flatten against his chest, eager to mold her every quivering curve to his sinewy planes.

Cord, too, felt his reason slipping away. He wasn't supposed to be liking this. He wasn't supposed to be enjoying the pert nubs of her breasts as they rubbed and teased, just begging him to taste them, or the sleek, quivering lengths of her thighs, hot and steamy and eager for a ride.

He tried to remind himself this was a lesson. A payback. He'd wanted her to forget about Zack—and Wes, too, since the boy kept trotting after her like a puppy on a string. He'd wanted to set her blood on fire the way no untried boy could. He'd wanted to *pretend* he wanted her.

The problem was, he hadn't had much practice pretending. Now as he ached to be a part of her, to lose himself in the intimacy that grief and guilt had denied him for so long, he wondered if he had somehow confused his make-believe feelings for his real ones.

An amused "ah-*hem*" brought sanity crashing down around him. He raised his head, blinking dizzily as his surroundings swam back into focus.

"Hate to barge in on you, folks," Wes said, rocking on his heels. He was grinning like a small dog with a big bone, and Cord felt his neck heat. He suspected that the boy hadn't "barged in" at all. The little cuss had probably been standing there, watching him and Fancy smack lips since they started!

Fancy must have thought so too. Suddenly bright red, she rammed her boot into Cord's shin. He yelped, hard-pressed not to hop and curse as she fled from the circle of his arms. He wondered why a professional sinner like Fancy would give a hoot who saw her kissing him.

Unless, of course, he mused a little wistfully, she kind of liked it too.

Chapter Nine

"What is it, Wes?" Cord growled, trying not to wince as he favored his left leg.

The boy's eyes danced. "Well, it's like this. I told Zack he was getting all fired up over nothing, but he flat out insisted that you come and see for yourself. You know how ornery ol' Zack can be," Wes added, winking broadly at Fancy.

Cord frowned at their exchange. "See what for myself?"

"Oh, Zack's gotten it into that wooden head of his that we're being trailed."

Cord's heart lurched. A blue norther whipped through him, icing the blood in his veins. He glanced at Fancy. She'd donned a poker face, but she couldn't quite hide the quickened rhythm of her breathing. He bit back an oath.

"Fetch Zack and the horses. Tell him to keep his rifle handy. From now on, I don't want either of you boys wandering off by yourself. You got that?"

Wes's eyes widened. "You reckon it wasn't just a shadow on that ridge?"

"Maybe." Cord ground his teeth to see how cool and unruffled Fancy looked. "We'll find out soon enough."

As Wes hurried back through the trees, Cord rounded on Fancy. She stiffened. He shot her a look that halted the heady rush of her pulse, and for a moment, she wondered how he could be the same man whose hungry kisses had left her starved for more just a minute earlier. *Fancy, my girl, you're getting soft,* she told herself darkly. *How could you forget, even for a heartbeat, that Cord Rawlins will always think of you as the "lying, cheating thief" he arrested in Fort Worth?*

"I reckon you're feeling mighty smart just now," he said in a low, dangerous voice, "what with your friends on the way. So go ahead. Enjoy your little victory, 'cause I promise you: You won't enjoy much about prison."

Now there's the Cord Rawlins I remember—and hate.

"You have to get me there first, Marshal."

"Oh, I'll get you there all right. Make no mistake about that."

The boys reappeared, leading the horses into the clearing. Cord waved Zack to lead Poco closer.

"Where were the riders?"

"I saw only one—"

"A Comanche?"

Fancy's stomach knotted to consider such a possibility, but Zack shook his head.

"Naw. He was sitting a saddle. The sun flashed off his stirrups. Or his spurs. But he wasn't an Injun, that's for sure. He was wearing a hat."

Cord looked grim as he re-cinched Poco's girth. "Sounds to me like Miss Holleday's friends sent a scout to look us over."

Fancy suspected Cord was right.

"Now hold on just a minute, Cord," Wes said, rising as usual to her defense. "You can't go blaming Miss Fancy. Zack could have seen a soldier heading back to Fort Graham. He could have seen one of those Mexican *peónes* looking for land to squat. Shoot. He could have seen nothing at all. I got a better eye than Zack, and I didn't see anything flashing up yonder. Don't you think I'd tell you if I did?"

His two older brothers exchanged dubious looks.

"Of course you would, Wes," Cord said. "I'm glad you boys are keeping your eyes peeled. You can't be too careful in this country. That's why I'm going to ride up there and do a little scouting for myself."

Preparing to mount, he dropped his stirrup flap back to Poco's side. Zack caught his arm.

"What if that aren't so smart?"

Cord frowned up at the boy, who stood a full three inches taller than he. "What if *what* aren't so smart, Zack?"

The youth reddened. "Well, I was just thinking there might be a couple of outlaws up there."

"You don't think I'm a match for a couple of outlaws?"

"Of course you are," Wes cut in, shooting Zack a quelling glare.

Zack refused to back down. "I just don't think you should go riding alone, is all. Why don't you let me go with you?"

"Much obliged, son, but I need you to look after Wes . . . and Miss Holleday."

Cord glared at her, and she sniffed. She hoped he'd find a whole army of outlaws up on that hill. Or better yet, that they'd find him.

"That ridge is a good half-hour's ride," Zack argued. "It's only an hour till sundown—"

"You cluck louder than an old mother hen," Cord interrupted, hoisting himself into his saddle. "I reckon I know how to keep out of sight. And I'm plenty sure I can handle a gun. I'll be back way before it gets dark. Think you can hold down the fort until then?"

Zack fidgeted. Fancy thought the boy must really be torn between his duties as brother and deputy.

"Yeah. Reckon I can," Zack finally said.

"Good."

Cord smiled down paternally at the boy. Then his features hardened. He drew his rifle from its saddle boot.

"Now, I want you boys to keep alert. Don't go wandering off by yourself. Not for any reason. And I don't want you shooting at rabbits or building a fire, either. Dinner'll have to wait till I find out what's out there."

Wes grimaced. When Cord had cantered out of hearing, he rounded on Zack. "No dinner! You see what you've gone and done?"

Zack said nothing. He was too busy glaring at Fancy to answer.

By the time the boys had scoured the clearing for enough wood to start a fire later for Cord, the sun was well on its way to setting. The clouds, the trees, even the nearby ribbon of stream, had turned a fiery crimson. A bloody crimson.

Fancy shivered. She wrapped the chain of her lucky coin again and again around her finger, but she couldn't shake her feeling of doom. A part of her hoped that Cord and his deputies really were being trailed by Ned Wilkerson's outlaws. Another part of her worried that the Rawlins boys would be no match for Wilkerson's men. What if Ned suddenly decided he wanted her dead?

Fancy blanched at the thought. In truth, she didn't know much about Ned's disposition, although she was inclined to believe that his nickname, the Terror of the Pecos, spoke for itself. If he was anything like his cousin Bart, he would be violent and cruel. He'd hate Mexicans and Indians. And he wouldn't have much use for women.

Fancy chewed her bottom lip.

Perhaps it hadn't been such a good idea, after all, to tell Ned she had hidden her plates and would tell him their location for a price. Perhaps she should have returned to the Barbary Coast, where she could have auctioned the plates to the highest bidder or ransomed them back to the U.S. government.

Then again, she mused darkly, there wasn't much use in second-guessing herself now. She was stuck with her earlier decision. When the time came to act, she'd simply have to find a way to come out on top. Like Diego always did.

She shivered to think of her dead lover. Ever vigilant, Wes hurried to her side with his blanket.

"Are you cold, ma'am? I know it must be kind of rough on you, no dinner and no fire."

She couldn't help but smile. Compared with being left to die in three feet of Nevada snow, sitting on a carpet of clover under a balmy Texas sky was sheer paradise.

"No, Wes. But thank you."

Zack looked disgusted by his brother's chivalry. Rising abruptly, he grabbed his rifle and headed for the bushes.

"Hey! Where do you think you're going?" Wes called.

"Mind your own business."

"Cord said not to wander off alone."

"Yeah?" Zack spun back around and tried to stare Wes down. "Since when did you start following orders?"

"Shoot. You got a chip on your shoulder bigger than the Rio Grande, son." Wes tossed aside his blanket. "What's eating at you, anyway?"

"Look. I've got to take a dump. You want to tag along?" Wes wrinkled his nose. "Hell, no!"

"I didn't think so."

Fancy had to duck her head to hide her smile.

Zack tossed her a withering look. "Just keep an eye on her till I get back."

"Would you just get *going* already?" Wes waved a hand in front of his face. "Whew!"

Fancy nearly choked to hold back her laughter. Zack turned bright red and fled for the trees.

"Poor Zack." Wes's grin was lazy as he winked at her. "He's so goldurned thin-skinned that sometimes I just can't help myself."

Fancy dropped her eyes. In growing bemusement, she realized that she sometimes felt the same way about Cord.

She shrugged away such perplexing thoughts. Shading her face with her hand, she gazed toward the horizon. The sun glared through the trees like a giant, bloodshot eye. It made her feel as if someone crouched out there watching . . . and waiting.

Hastily, she turned her shoulder and tried to think of other things. Cord slipped back into her mind. Surely he had reached the ridge by now. Had he found the outlaws he was searching for? Or had they found him? She was beginning to hope they hadn't. She was beginning to wish he'd hurry back to camp.

A chubby fox squirrel appeared in the live oak above Wes. Squatting on its haunches, it flicked its plush russet tail and scolded him. A devilish twinkle lighted the boy's eyes. Pulling out his slingshot, he searched the grass, found an acorn, and fired. The squirrel screeched and dodged, racing up and around the trunk to settle on a higher limb. Outraged, the little fellow shook a branch. Wes chuckled and reloaded.

As Fancy watched their play, tentacles of guilt crept through her until they squeezed her heart. Dear Lord, what had she done? Wes was a boy. Just a boy, for God's sake! What if Ned Wilkerson really had followed her to this desolate place? What if he discovered Wes sitting here alone?

What if Wilkerson had already found Zack?

Awareness hit her like a speeding train. The grove was too quiet. Aside from the squirrel, nothing moved, nothing chirped. Something was wrong.

"Wes, don't you think that . . . Zack should be back by now?"

He shrugged, his attention on the squirrel. "I reckon you can't rush these things, ma'am."

Fancy bit her lip. She peered into the shadows, but no matter how she tried, she could find no sign of Zack. She tried to console herself that the boy would never have done his business close enough for her to watch. Still, she couldn't shake the feeling that somewhere out there, beyond her vision, danger lurked.

"Don't you think you should check on him, Wes? I mean, Zack's been gone an awfully long time, and, well . . . I'm worried about him."

She *was* worried. She didn't quite know how it had happened, but she was wholly and unequivocally frightened for Zack.

"Please, Wes." She had trouble keeping the panic out of her voice. "Please go look for him."

He sighed and shook his head. "All right, ma'am. All right. Now don't go getting yourself in a lather." He stood and shoved his slingshot back into his pocket.

"Zack!" he boomed, his eyes betraying his mischief. "You got a burr up your butt, son?"

Silence answered him. The humor slowly drained from his features.

"Zack? You okay?"

More silence. Wes glanced at Fancy. In the fading light, he looked uncannily like Cord. His shoulders tensed, his jaw hardened, and his eyes glittered like sea-green jewels.

"Dammit, Zack, this isn't funny anymore. Answer me!"

Fancy climbed to her feet. Wes muttered another oath. Stooping, he reached for his Winchester. His fingers had barely closed over the barrel when a metallic flash caught Fancy's eye.

"Wes! Look out!"

Gunfire spat. The report was deafening. Wes's shriek was lost in it as he slammed to the ground. Blood rapidly stained the shoulder of his shirt, and Fancy rushed to his side.

"Wes! Oh my God." She tore off her neckerchief and sopped frantically at the wound. "Wes, open your eyes. Don't die. Please don't die!"

"Move away from the boy."

The cold, hard voice sounded like Death itself. Fancy gulped, glancing fearfully over her shoulder. She recognized the slouching stance and grizzled beard of Wilton Slade.

"He's just a boy! Leave him be!"

Slade's smile was even more chilling than his voice. "That 'boy' gave me a crooked arm. Doc Tate said there's no telling whether it'll ever be right again."

Fancy saw the bulge in the middle of Slade's left arm, as if his coat sleeve hid a wad of bandages. He was obviously favoring that arm. Her heart speeding, she shifted to hide Wes's head and shoulders from Slade's view.

"Wes?"

To her relief his eyelids fluttered. He stirred.

"Don't move!" she whispered urgently, pinning his unhurt shoulder with her hand.

One glazed eye opened to return her anxious gaze.

"You have to play possum." She silently begged him to understand.

"I told you to move away from that boy," Slade called with greater menace. He snapped his rifle breechblock.

Fancy swallowed hard. Easing her hand from Wes's shoulder, she cocked her wrist. The derringer slid into her palm. The boy's other eye opened wide, and he blinked at her in a mixture of astonishment, comprehension, and growing admiration. The ghost of a smile played across his lips.

"I think I'm in love," he murmured.

"Goddammit, woman, are you deaf?"

Snapping twigs announced Slade's approach. She gave Wes a warning look, and he quickly closed his eyes.

"No, I'm not deaf." Gathering her courage, she slowly rose. She wondered if Cord would hurry back to investigate the shooting. *Please, God, send him back. Send him back now.*

"I was just seeing if the boy had any money," she lied a little less expertly than usual.

"I aren't going to say it again, bitch."

"Okay. Okay, Slade. Whatever you say." She stepped deliberately into his line of fire. "The boy's dead anyway."

"Yeah? You won't mind me pumping another round or two into his gut then, just to be sure."

Dammit, Cord, what's keeping you?

"Of course not. But his brothers might. They're around here somewhere. I say we get the hell out of here before one of them returns."

She advanced toward him. She had to. Cord might not show up for another half hour. She had to rely on her derringer, and the pistol was useless outside of ten feet.

"That's far enough."

She halted, hard-pressed to pose in any kind of alluring way on legs that felt like jelly. Slade sneered at her best attempt.

"What d'ya got there in your hand?"

"The boy's money."

Slade didn't look convinced. "Toss it here."

Her heart stalled.

"Why don't you come and get it?" she rallied, raising her hand and pretending to drop something into her cleavage.

She was gratified to see Slade's eyes narrow, darting from her artfully cupped gunhand to her half-exposed breasts. She hadn't learned to palm cards for nothing.

"You sleazy little whore. I oughta put a bullet through your twat."

She smiled, doing her damnedest not to look nauseous.

"Lest you've forgotten, Mr. Slade, my bounty's only good if you bring me in alive. I daresay five hundred dollars could buy you a lot of pain medicine. Or maybe you'd rather have a fancy new saddle and a couple of Winchesters. Henry repeaters aren't the rage anymore."

"A Henry kills just as good as a Winchester. And lest you've forgotten," he mimicked ominously, nodding at Wes, "it proved itself today. Now bring me the money, or I'll cut your tits off."

"Mmm." Her stomach somersaulted so fast that she thought she might be ill. "How I do love it when a man talks dirty."

Somehow, she kept up her smile as she marshaled her legs. The derringer was growing heavy under her thumb; her palms were hot and sweating. A pistol wasn't much use against a rifle, but surprise was on her side. If she missed, Slade would kill her. He'd kill Wes, too—like he'd probably killed Zack.

Oh God, Oh God, don't let it be true.

A numbing calm washed over her. She couldn't think about Zack just now. She couldn't think about anything but luring Slade's eyes away from her hands. Swaying her hips, bouncing her breasts, she strutted right up to the muzzle of his rifle. One shot, one chance, was all she had. She would make it work because she had to.

"Come and get it, Slade."

Throwing back her head, she straddled her hips with her hands. At last she had the gun in position.

"What's the matter? Aren't you man enough to take it?"

His lips curved in a thin smile. "Think you're something special, eh?"

He shifted the rifle barrel across his bandaged arm. She

stepped closer. She was only three feet away when he reached for her shirt. His eyes were gloating, eager. When they locked with hers, she fired. She could hear his roar of pain above the popping report. Realization dawned hard and fast as his rifle swung toward her. She'd aimed too wide!

"Bitch!"

The rifle butt descended. She ducked. The move saved her head but not her shoulder. Yelping, she stumbled backward as he charged after her, ignoring the bubbling hole in his arm.

"Miss Fancy!"

She heard Wes's cry above a sudden pounding in her ears. Was it her heart . . . or horse's hooves?

Slade whirled, training his weapon on the boy.

"Slade, no!"

She threw herself against him, clawing at his face, his hands, his rifle. He cursed, and the Henry slammed into her stomach. Fancy doubled over. Too winded to move, she could only watch in horror as Wes struggled upright, tugging at the trigger guard on his holster. Slade's face was a mask of feral rage as he aimed again at Wes.

"Hold, Slade!"

Cord's voice rang through the clearing. Slade ignored the warning. He squeezed his trigger, and Cord fired. His bullet drilled through Slade's heart, and the bounty hunter toppled, his cartridge burrowing into the oak trunk just beyond Wes's head. Slade fell lifeless at Fancy's feet. For a moment, she could do nothing more than gulp down air to fight off her sickness. Then, from the corner of her eye, she saw Wes sink back to the earth. Waves of fear crashed over her. Ignoring her dizziness, she stumbled toward him. Cord sprinted after her and yanked her around by the arm.

"Keep away from my boy! So help me God, I'll—"

"Cord . . ." Wes's weak voice silenced Cord's threat. "Is Zack okay?"

Fancy had never seen a suntanned man turn so white. Cord shoved her aside and dropped to his knees beside Wes.

"Dear God." Raising Fancy's sodden neckerchief, Cord

blanched a shade whiter. "Wes, what happened? Where's Zack?"

"I don't know," the boy said thickly. "He wouldn't answer me. He's not hurt, is he?"

Cord shot her a look that would have made any other woman cringe and run for cover.

"Where the hell is Zack?" he shouted as if she were somehow to blame.

"I don't know! In the trees somewhere! He went to relieve himself, and he never came back."

Cord's chest began to heave. He stood and drew his gun. For an instant, she feared he might actually shoot her.

"Help him," he growled, grabbing her wrist and thrusting her toward Wes. Then Cord started running, calling Zack's name.

He paused long enough by Slade's corpse to pick up her derringer before he tossed her another menacing look and thrashed into the underbrush. Fancy released a ragged breath.

"Miss Fancy?"

She gazed down into Wes's worshipful eyes.

"I aren't ever seen anybody so brave. Except maybe for Cord."

She blinked back tears. The praise had been high indeed, coming from Wes Rawlins.

"You're going to be okay, Wes," she murmured, peeling back his shirt.

"'Course I am." His feeble smile turned to a grimace as she gently probed his wound. "Did he . . . hurt you much?"

She wondered for a moment if Wes meant Cord. She'd practically forgotten her bruised ribs in the face of his anger. Perhaps he was right to blame her, she mused. Only . . . why did it have to hurt so much?

"No. He didn't hurt me," she lied.

"Good. I would have felt real awful if he did."

His eyes closed. She panicked.

"No! Wes, stay with me. You can't sleep yet!"

"Wes!"

The cry was Zack's this time. Glancing up, Fancy saw the older Rawlinses emerge from the trees. Zack wrestled himself free of Cord's supportive arm and rushed to Wes's side.

"You aren't gonna die, are you?" Zack whispered, slumping woefully to his knees.

"Naw. I'm too young." Wes dragged his eyes back open. "'Sides. I got to whup you for running off on me."

"I didn't run off!"

Cord joined them. "Zack was struck from behind, Wes. He's got a knot on his head."

"Yeah sure," Wes taunted weakly. "Next you'll be telling me that's why he's so ugly."

Relief flooded Zack's features. He snorted, but he couldn't keep a smile from spreading over his face. "Aw shoot. I reckon he's gonna live, after all."

Fancy noticed dried blood above Zack's ear. "Do you feel well enough to help me, Zack?" she asked anxiously. "I need more water. And bandages. Anything you can tear up."

The boy nodded. She turned next to brave the accusation in Cord's eyes.

"I can't find any sign of the bullet. I think it went through him, but I'm no doctor. We need to get him to Fort Graham—"

"The ranch is closer," Cord said tersely. "Aunt Lally will know what to do. We'll ride just as soon as we can rig a travois to carry him."

Fancy nodded, shutting down that newly discovered part of herself that ached whenever Cord glared at her. "Zack will need his head looked at—"

"I'm fine," the boy said tersely. His gaze wasn't much friendlier than Cord's.

Sighing, she turned her attention to Wes. His fingers had laced through hers. It took her a moment to realize the boy had slipped into unconsciousness. Her heart twisting, she gently retrieved her hand. The ride to the ranch was going to be a long one.

Chapter Ten

"You most certainly are *not* going to lock Miss Fancy up in a bedroom," declared Eulalie Rawlins Barclay, planting her red, work-roughened hands firmly on her hips.

Fancy listened in some bemusement to Mrs. Barclay—or rather, Aunt Lally, as the woman had insisted on being called. The portly, chin-high matron reminded Fancy of a locomotive steaming at full speed.

"Wes told me about last night," she said to Zack. "He told me how Miss Fancy fought off that murdering Slade person with nothing but a pocket pistol. And him packing a Henry rifle!" Aunt Lally shook her graying auburn head. "Miss Fancy saved your brother's life, and she did it with powerful little help from you menfolk. And now you want to lock her up? You ought to be ashamed of yourself, Zachariah Rawlins!"

Zack grimaced, reddening at the use of his full name. "But Miss Fancy's our prisoner. And Cord told me to—"

"So it's Cord who put you up to this, eh? I might have known." Aunt Lally's eyes flashed seastorm-green, the exact shade as Cord's when he started to rage. "Just wait till I get my hands on that boy, getting you to do his dirty work for him. Where'd he run off to?"

Zack looked sheepish. "Reckon he's upstairs visiting Wes, ma'am."

"Well, you just run right up those stairs and fetch him back here. Tell him Aunt Lally's got a bone to pick with him."

"But—"

"Off with you now. You boys aren't too big for me to be taking a switch to your behinds."

Zack's color had heightened to scarlet. "Yes, ma'am," he muttered, slinking from the parlor to the stairs.

Fancy fidgeted as she watched him flee. Threats of a beating always made her uncomfortable. Zack, of course, could easily have overpowered his aunt, but Fancy suspected that fighting back would never have crossed Zack's mind, as it had so often crossed hers when she cowered beneath the brothel madam's fists.

"Those boys," Aunt Lally said, her tone apologetic. "They go bucking in eight different directions at once. Lawd, child, I don't wonder how you kept your patience all those days, what with nothing but menfolk for company. I wonder how I do it myself, sometimes."

She smiled, reaching in a motherly fashion to pat Fancy's arm. Fancy flinched in reflex.

An awkward silence settled between them. Fancy realized her reaction had taken Aunt Lally by surprise—which, in itself, was probably a phenomenon. Those keen, inquisitive eyes weren't likely to miss much. Fancy suspected that Aunt Lally was the kind of person who saw through lies, no matter how skillfully they were told. She also struck Fancy as that rare breed of woman who couldn't be manipulated.

She remembered Aunt Lally's calm businesslike response when she saw her nephew's ashen face and crimson bandages. Heedless of the blood that smeared her calico dress, she'd propped her shoulder under Wes's arm and helped Cord walk the boy into the house. She'd paused for only a moment to order the ranch hands to water her nephews' horses. The vaqueros had obeyed without question. Never had Fancy met a plain-faced woman who could command a man's respect. She sensed that Aunt Lally would be a formidable adversary, despite her fifty odd years.

"You did right by Wes."

The sincerity in Aunt Lally's voice unsettled Fancy. She wasn't used to straight-talking members of her own sex.

"You might not have liked it," Aunt Lally continued. "You might have been more scared than a rabbit in a coyote's back pocket, but you stood by my nephew. And I'm not going to forget that, Fancy, no matter what you might've done last month or last year, or even what you might go ahead and do tomorrow."

Fancy felt her throat tighten. Try as she might, she could find nothing vindictive or deceitful in Aunt Lally's eyes. There must be something in that green Rawlins stare, she thought uneasily, that could see past a person's defenses to the true self that lurked beneath. Hadn't Cord seen through her best charade in the dining car?

Aunt Lally would do the same. Soon she would see just how worthless Fancy Holleday was. Eulalie Rawlins Barclay wouldn't be as impressed with her then.

For some reason, that realization troubled Fancy.

"I'm . . . fond of Wes," she admitted. She was surprised less by the truth of her words than by the relief an honest confession brought her. "He's a good boy."

Aunt Lally nodded, tilting her head as if to study Fancy further. "My nephews are all good boys. It hasn't been easy on them since their ma and pa got murdered."

"Murdered?"

The word tumbled out before Fancy could stop it. She knew that caring was dangerous, but her curiosity proved stronger than her common sense. "How did it happen? I mean . . . it must have come as a terrible shock to you all."

"Yep." Aunt Lally pressed her lips together in a thin, grim line. "Bill and Meg were fine folks. The finest I ever knew."

Crossing to the mantel, she picked up a picture frame and blew away the dust. Fancy edged nearer. She saw that the photograph was of a fair, broad-shouldered man and his diminutive, dark-skinned wife. The couple resembled the boys.

"That's Bill and Meg?" she asked, suspecting that Cord

got his vibrant eyes from his father and his glossy hair from his mother.

Aunt Lally nodded again. She rubbed her sleeve vigorously across the glass. "They were riding on an east-bound stage. Just outside of Houston, some road agents got the drop on the driver. Bill—that's my brother—he tried to keep the robbers from taking Meg's wedding ring. So they shot him down. Shot down Meg too. I reckon that's when Cord made up his mind to be a lawman."

Fancy swallowed hard as Aunt Lally returned the photograph to its place. She felt unaccountably guilty for the couple's fate.

"Wes and Zack weren't but three and four when the killing happened," Aunt Lally continued softly. "Cord kind of took it on himself to be their pa. Then the war came. Me and Seth didn't have but our daughter, Ginny, then, and we had a devil of a time convincing Cord to let us raise those boys.

"*His* boys," she corrected herself with a fond chuckle. "Cord always has thought of Zack and Wes as his. The only problem was that he married Beth, and she never much cottoned to rearing boys who weren't her own. Oh, Beth was plenty good to them after she moved to the ranch," Aunt Lally added quickly, chagrin flickering across her crinkled features. "But she just couldn't love Zack and Wes, not like Cord does. And not like I do, either."

Fancy frowned. She wondered again what Cord had seen in Beth. Wes and Zack had probably been headstrong children, much as they were now, but they'd just been orphaned, for heaven's sake! Why couldn't Beth love them as her own?

Embarrassment bloomed like a rash across Aunt Lally's cheeks. She loosed a sudden belly laugh and winked. Her expression reminded Fancy of Wes.

"How I do go on. And here, you're probably hungry. I reckon trail grub isn't much to a city girl's liking. Why don't I rustle you up some lemonade and a fresh slab of my sweet-potato pie? They ought to tide you over till supper. The boys'll be having beefsteak with biscuits and gravy, and some turnip greens thrown in on the side. 'Course, unless you're good at pushing and shoving," Aunt Lally added, demonstrating a deft elbow jab, "you aren't likely to get a bite after the menfolk stampede the table. Reckon you're up to a good wrastle?"

A smile tugged at Fancy's lips. She had tried her damnedest to dislike this woman, and she had failed. Thoroughly.

"I've managed a few . . . er, menfolk in my time."

"I don't doubt it, child, what with the yarns Wes has to tell." Aunt Lally nodded sagely. "Looks like Cord's gone and met his match in you. Glad to hear it too. That boy needs someone to jingle his spurs. And if you're the one to do it, God bless you."

Dumbfounded, Fancy watched as Aunt Lally headed for the kitchen. She couldn't remember any woman going so far as to bless her—particularly where male relatives were concerned. Just what kind of yarns had Wes been telling?

Left to her own devices, Fancy gazed curiously around her. So this was the house where the Rawlins boys had been raised. She shook her head at the spur gouges on the floor and the tobacco burns on the chairs. Someone had shot a cougar and spread its pelt in front of the hearth; three pairs of mounted steer horns arched above the mantel. The room had a decidedly masculine atmosphere, yet Aunt Lally had made some progress with a vase of wildflowers and a collection of photographs.

Strolling beside the mantel, Fancy pieced together stories from the images on display. There was a slightly younger, less plump Aunt Lally with a lumberjack of a man—undoubtedly Seth Barclay. Fancy remembered the gleaming white cross and the flower-adorned grave under a cottonwood near the Barclay homestead. Saddening a little, she wished she could have met the man who'd won a woman like Aunt Lally for his own.

Next, she gazed at the cameo-faced young woman sitting between Seth and Lally. The girl was probably Ginny. An older Ginny appeared in the next picture, posing with a bookish-looking beau and a toddler-age boy. Ginny had apparently gotten herself married, Fancy thought a little jealously. And she'd moved away. That would account for Aunt Lally's eagerness for female company.

The third frame held a photograph of Cord, perhaps at the age of nineteen, with his battle standard draped behind him. He looked dashing but solemn in his Confederate uniform, and Fancy marveled that he'd worn captain's bars at such a youthful age. She'd heard that the Eighth Texas Cavalry—Colonel Terry's Texas Rangers—had been lauded by Jefferson Davis for its tenacity and fearlessness.

No wonder she had been unable to shake Cord from her trail!

The frame at the mantel's end displayed a bride and groom. As Fancy approached the photograph, she felt her heart quicken. She guessed the identity of the couple even before she drew close enough to examine their faces. Despite what had probably been the happiest day of their lives, neither Cord nor Beth had smiled. Although solemnity was the photographic custom, Fancy thought it prophetic that the couple should look so rigid and cheerless on their wedding day.

Picking up the frame, she blew off the dust and polished the glass much as Aunt Lally had done. She supposed that most men would have considered Bethany Rawlins pretty—in a porcelain kind of way. She looked ethereal. If Fancy didn't already know Bethany's fate, she would have suspected that the bride would never thrive in this hot, dry climate.

Fancy based her conclusion on more than the girl's obvious frailty. There was an air of self-indulgence about Beth. It could be glimpsed in the haughty tilt of her head and the vaguely discernible pout on her lips. Beth had lived a pampered life. Unfortunately, she'd married a man who wasn't inclined to coddle.

The clinking of spurs pricked Fancy's ears. Turning, she found Cord watching her from the doorway. She felt as if she was the intruder when his narrowed gaze darted from the empty corner of the mantel to the frame in her hands.

"What are you doing with that picture?"

She tensed, hearing a threat in his question. Cord hadn't

spoken two words to her since yesterday, when she'd doctored Wes's shoulder. She had hoped that his private visit with the boy would improve his mood.

"I didn't mean any harm, Cord. I was just—"

"Put it back."

"But—"

"I said put it back."

She hiked her chin. "Very well. I've finished looking at it anyway."

His eyes glittered as she obeyed. If he'd been a mustang stallion defending his herd, he couldn't have looked more dangerous.

"You have a heap of nerve, woman, wandering around, poking your nose into what isn't your business, and after all the trouble you've caused."

"All the trouble I've caused?" She gaped. *Stupid girl. Did you think he would actually thank you for risking your life to save Wes?*

"As I recall, Marshal, it wasn't I who dangled that wanted poster in front of Wilton Slade."

Cord stiffened.

"No doubt you'll find this difficult to believe," she went on acidly, "but the last place I want to be is in this dusty rattrap you call home, making nice with your salt-of-the-earth relatives."

"That's fine by me. I'll lock you in the woodshed then."

"Over my dead body!"

Aunt Lally steamed back into the parlor with the pie and lemonade. If she had overheard Fancy's slur, she made no reference to it as she set down her tray.

Cord looked belligerent. "Fancy Holleday is my prisoner—"

"Fancy Holleday is my guest." Aunt Lally wagged a finger under his nose. "You'd best be civil."

"You're forgetting that this woman is wanted for a federal crime, not to mention the rustling and cardsharping she's done since."

"And you're forgetting Miss Fancy saved Wes's life."

Cord's lip curled. "I've got my doubts about that, since Wes's tale grows taller with each telling."

"Oh, so now your brother's a fibber?"

"Hell, Aunt Lally, she's hoodwinked the boy into thinking he loves her!"

"Fiddle." Aunt Lally folded her arms across her chest. "Wes has a mind of his own. Stop blaming Fancy for what comes natural to a boy his age. I seem to recall you getting all calf-eyed over a Miss Bethany Fontaine."

"That's not the same."

"Oh? And why's that?"

"'Cause I was three years older then. And because Beth wasn't . . . well, she just wasn't like Fancy."

"You mean that Beth wasn't likely to throw herself in front of a Henry rifle to keep your brother from getting killed?"

Cord's chest heaved. His eyes locked with Fancy's, but she looked away, unable to bear his cutting stare.

Of course that wasn't what Cord meant, she told herself ruthlessly. He meant that Bethany Fontaine wasn't a lying, cheating thief . . . or a whore.

"Beth isn't the point," he said, his voice gruff. "And neither is Wes. The point is that Fancy broke the law. I'm obliged to bring her in whether you're against it or not. Growing feelings for her won't make things any easier. Not for you, not for Wes, and not for Fancy."

This argument seemed to move Aunt Lally. Her gaze darted uncertainly between them.

"But if we have Fancy's word that she won't try to escape—"

"You can't ask a coyote to stop eating," Cord said flatly. "It'll do what it has to do to survive. If she has her freedom, she'll run. She can't sit still knowing a prison sentence waits for her. You wouldn't expect her to, would you?"

Aunt Lally sighed. She shook her head.

"Good. Looks like we're agreed, then."

He turned abruptly, his shoulders set, his jaw uncompromising. "Zack!" he bellowed toward the top of the stairs.

The boy appeared on the landing. He looked anything but comfortable when Cord gestured him to descend.

"Lock Miss Holleday in my bedroom. Take supper to her when it's ready."

Zack seemed troubled, but he obediently took her arm. She noticed that he refused to meet her gaze.

Cord didn't suffer a similar problem. His features were stony as Aunt Lally hurriedly passed her the pie and lemonade. Taking the tray, Fancy was hard-pressed not to tell Cord exactly what kind of a cur she thought he was.

Her spine rigid, she followed Zack to her makeshift prison. He blushed when she stepped inside, and he made great haste to close the door. She smiled mirthlessly to hear him turn the key.

At least Cord Rawlins had made hating him easy again, she thought bitterly.

Cord's smile was filled with self-loathing as he raised the whiskey bottle to his lips. He'd given up any pretense of civility an hour earlier, when he hurled his shotglass against the mantel. It had shattered with a satisfying crash, and he'd briefly amused himself with the notion that he wouldn't spill any more liquor out of that glass. Or any other, for that matter. Glasses wasted too much time when a man was in a hurry to get drunk. Yep, the gulp and shudder method was the quickest path to forgetfulness.

The only problem was, it didn't seem to be working well that night.

Wiping the back of his hand across his mouth, Cord turned his head to blink up past the gallery-style stairs to the bedroom at the end of the landing. The light beneath his door spun like watery pinwheels, but the knob eventually came into focus. Disappointed, he figured he must not be drunk yet.

He closed his eyes and let his head fall back against the wall. He was going to run out of rotgut before he ran out of thoughts of Fancy Holleday. He didn't much like the idea of her locked in his bedroom, snooping through his personal things. Midnight had chimed a half hour ago, and she still hadn't blown out his lamp. Just what had she found so interesting up there?

Or maybe she was curled up under his quilt after all. Maybe she'd just forgotten to douse the light. Cord imagined all those sable curls fanned across his pillows, and he hastily gulped another swallow. That was one image he'd best forget right away.

He smiled ruefully. Yep, she was dangerous, that girl. She'd gotten under his skin somehow. What was worse, she'd made him feel responsible for his boys getting ambushed.

A grudging part of Cord admitted that he couldn't keep blaming Fancy for his own mistakes. After all, he'd been the careless one, letting a bounty hunter see her posted reward. And he certainly hadn't redeemed himself any when he got decoyed to that ridge.

Even so, there was no telling what had really happened before he galloped into camp. He remembered being too concerned about Wes to see much beyond Slade's rifle, although he did recall a glimpse of Fancy clutching her belly. She'd been pale and shaking, a far cry from the steely nerved gunslinger Wes had described. Knowing the boy's fondness for tall tales, Cord preferred not to believe that Fancy had thrown herself into Slade's line of fire, or that she'd heroically faced him down with a gun.

Oh, he believed she'd hidden a derringer all right, and that she'd misfired in her haste to save her own skin. That would account for the second report he'd heard and the bullet hole he'd seen in Slade's arm.

Still, Cord couldn't explain away Fancy's neckerchief blotting Wes's wound.

His lip curled, and he took another swig.

All right. So once in her life, Fancy Holleday had been selfless. There was yet the matter of her derringer. Just to imagine what she could have done with that pistol while he lay sleeping made his blood curdle. He doubted whether a glimmer of conscience had kept her from shooting his boys. She'd feared his retaliation, pure and simple. And she'd been right to do so. If he wasn't so worried he might forget his purpose in a fit of drunken lust, he would storm his bedroom that very moment to wring her neck.

Cord smiled grimly.

Drunken lust. That was really the issue, wasn't it? He'd guzzled half a bottle of rotgut to convince himself that Fancy was still the conniving, heartless floozie he remembered from the train. Half a bottle should have been plenty to assure himself that she would have ridden off with Slade, left the boys for dead, and plotted to trick the bounty hunter later.

Some small part of him must not have bought the story, though, because here he sat on this hard parlor floor, hating his duty, wishing he could set Fancy free . . . and wanting nothing more than to love her.

Disgraceful, that's what he was. He didn't feel guilty about wanting Fancy, even though he owed it to Beth to feel remorse. In the two years since he'd killed her, he'd swilled gallons of whiskey to forget how he needed a woman. Now he couldn't remember the last time he'd bedded one. Oh, there'd been some harlot back in El Paso four months or so ago, but he'd been so full of spirits then, he fell asleep before finishing the act.

Even when he was drunk, Beth's memory was a powerful deterrent. It rarely let him seek comfort with a whore, much less a decent woman.

Cord's laugh was short and hollow.

Fancy Holleday? A decent woman? Now when had he started thinking that?

"Cord?"

Zack's tentative whisper nearly made Cord jump out of his skin.

"Blazes, boy." Cord flung a guilty—if protective—leg over his bottle. "What are you sneaking around here for?"

"I'm not sneaking."

"When you prowl around softer than an Injun, I call that sneaking."

"Well, if you'd gone and lit a lamp, you'd have seen me

coming," Zack retorted. "Why are you sitting on the floor in the dark?"

Cord glared up at the boy. Between the dim lighting and his bleary eyes, he could barely make out the pale oval of Zack's face high above him.

"That's none of your business."

"Geez, Cord. You're drinking again, aren't you?"

Cord felt his cheeks heat at the blatant disapproval in his brother's voice. "Like I said, it's none of your business."

He imagined the boy's thin-lipped expression.

"It's a good thing Aunt Lally didn't find you. She'd be madder than a wet hornet."

Cord had to agree. That's why he'd waited until his favorite, meddling relative had tucked herself in.

"C'mon." Zack squatted and offered him a hand. "I'll put you to bed."

"Like hell you will."

Zack held his ground. "You know how ornery you get. And it looks like you just about finished that bottle."

"Naw. I got half of it left."

Zack looked skeptical, then his gaze shifted to Cord's hips. "You wearing your gun?"

"'Course."

"Give it here."

Cord thought about arguing, until he remembered how he'd amused himself the last time by shooting moving shadows. He'd nearly put a bullet through the ranch foreman's head.

Drawing his Colt rather sheepishly, he handed it over. Zack stuck it in his belt.

"Now give me the bottle."

Cord's chin jutted. Surrendering his rotgut was an entirely different matter. Aunt Lally had hidden the remainder of Uncle Seth's liquor cabinet, and the saloon outside of Fort Graham was a night's ride away.

"Nope."

"Geez, Cord. What are you drinking for, anyway?"

"'Cause I'm thirsty."

"It's Beth again, isn't it?"

Cord scowled.

"You know she wouldn't have liked you getting drunk. None of us do."

"You're pushing your luck here, boy."

"Well, someone's got to tell you what an ass you're making of yourself."

Good ol' Zack. Cord smiled mirthlessly. Zack could always be counted on to see the bare-bones truth. Wes, on the other hand, saw only the good in the people whom he worshiped . . . like Fancy.

"You've had your say, son. Now leave me in peace before I try and wallop you."

"I'm not scared."

"Well, you should be. I nearly got you killed." He swallowed hard and looked away. "Like I got Beth killed," he added hoarsely. "I reckon I should have listened to you, Zack. I should have taken you with me up to that ridge—"

"Naw, you were right," Zack cut in firmly. "If I'd ridden off with you, Slade would've had time to hurt Wes worse."

"But we could have stopped Slade."

"Maybe—if we'd found him. But we didn't." Zack sat back on his heels. "So what's the point? Wes isn't blaming you, and neither am I. Why are you blaming yourself?"

Cord stared gloomily at the embers in the grate. He didn't rightly know. Maybe because he was afraid he'd forget what a murdering bastard he really was.

A troubled silence passed between them.

"Cord, do you reckon Wes is . . . well, telling the truth about Miss Fancy?"

"No."

Cord figured if he said it enough times, he just might start believing it.

"Do you reckon Wes thinks he is?"

"Yeah." Cord fidgeted. "I reckon."

Zack's brow furrowed. Moonlight spilled across him from the window, and he looked ghostly pale, a painful reminder to Cord that he could easily have found his brother dead, his skull bashed in by the butt of Slade's rifle.

"So what are you going to do, Cord? About Miss Fancy, I mean?"

He drew a ragged breath. "Take her to Nevada. Let the courts deal with her."

"They'll lock her up, won't they?"

"If they find her guilty. Which they likely will."

"Wes isn't going to stand for it, you know."

"He'll have to."

"He won't forgive you for a long spell, either."

Cord hardened himself against a twinge of guilt. "I can't help that."

"But don't you think you could—"

"No! I was sworn to bring her in, dammit. She robbed a train. Men were killed during that robbery. What kind of lawman would I be if I let her walk away?"

Zack swallowed. "But Miss Fancy didn't do the killing, did she?"

Cord sighed. "No," he muttered after a moment. He raised the bottle. Before the whiskey could touch his lips, Zack's hand closed over his arm.

"I understand you're sworn to uphold the law, but . . ."

"But what?"

"You don't have to drink to do it."

Their eyes locked.

"Seems like we've chewed the fat clean off of that one," Cord said.

"Maybe. Maybe not. The truth is, you're holding on to Beth like a dog holds on to its bone. What's got you so scared of letting her go, anyway?"

Cord blinked, incredulous. "You're calling me yellow?"

"Reckon I am."

"That's a helluva thing to say to a man, boy."

"So prove me wrong."

Cord choked back an oath. Shaking Zack off, he climbed to his feet and stood unsteadily. "If you weren't my kid brother, I'd—"

"You'd what? Whup me or get whupped trying?"

"Think right highly of yourself, do you?"

Zack faced him squarely, his hands splayed on his hips. "A man isn't much of a threat when he isn't standing straight."

"You ungrateful little cuss. I taught you that."

"You taught me how to fight too. And I'm not afraid of knocking some sense into you, even if it does take all night. So what's it going to be? Are you going to hand over that bottle, or aren't you?"

Cord bared his teeth in a snarl. Rounding suddenly, he flung his whiskey. The bottle crashed against the firebricks. Flames whooshed toward the flue.

"There's your goddamned bottle. Satisfied?"

Zack nodded, looking a little stunned by his victory. Shoving past him, Cord staggered for the stairs.

"Where're you going?" Zack called in a low, urgent voice.

"To bed."

"But you can't—"

"You're pushing me, boy. You're really pushing me."

Stumbling, Cord loosed a barrage of oaths when he nearly sprawled across the stairs. Zack hurried after him.

"Shh!" the youth warned, steadying Cord as he clung to the railing. "You want to wake Aunt Lally?"

"Hell. What would I need Aunt Lally for? I've got you clucking over me." Cord shook Zack off. "Go pester your other brother for a change."

"But Cord, you can't—"

"You gone deaf or something?"

Cord's hand closed over the boy's collar, and Zack's eyes widened to see a fist shaking in his face.

"All right. All right. I'll leave you be," Zack whispered, raising his hands in defeat.

Cord grunted and released him.

Feeling a little more sober after his climb, Cord cleared the last step and stalked the rest of the way to his room. He was too busy fuming over the wasted whiskey and Zack's highfalooting attitude to divert more than passing attention to the key inside his lock.

It wasn't until he flung the door wide and saw Fancy, standing in one of Aunt Lally's cotton nightdresses, that he remembered why he'd taken such pains to avoid his bed-room.

Chapter Eleven

The door banged against the wall, and Fancy retreated a step, her legs striking the hearth. She didn't know which had unnerved her more, the sound of the door opening or the sight of Cord, steadying himself against the jamb.

"What the hell do you want, Rawlins?"

While he continued to gape at her, a full measure of heartbeats passed. She might have believed the surprise on his face if he hadn't ordered Zack to lock her inside his bedroom, or vaqueros to arm themselves and guard her window. She'd had no hope of escape. Now, as he loomed on the threshold, she felt her spine begin to prickle.

"I asked you what you wanted."

He shut the door behind him. "Keep your voice down. My kinfolk are sleeping."

He swayed slightly as he walked toward her. Fancy's heart crawled to her throat. She couldn't help but notice how he ogled the voluminous white nightdress Aunt Lally had lent her. What a fool she had been to think Cord Rawlins was too honorable to sully his wife's cherished memory by whoring! No, the lout had probably been planning this rendezvous ever since her arrest. The only reason he'd postponed it this long was to hide his rutting from his brothers.

"That's far enough," she said, her voice rough from the sudden dryness in her mouth.

He obliged her, but she doubted whether he would do so for long. She'd seen that hungry, predatory look in the eyes of too many men to mistake it in Cord's.

"Seems to me you could be a bit more civil, seeing as how you're a guest in my room."

"Guest, my rear end," she rallied. "You've locked the door and posted guards beneath the window."

"Saw Juan and Carlos, did you?" Cord laughed as if his sally were the greatest of jokes. "Reckon that means you've been poking your head outside, wondering whether or not to jump and break both legs."

"I've done nothing of the kind."

"Uh-huh."

He flashed his dimples, and his gaze roamed once more over her nightdress. She tried not to wince. He'd clearly been drinking. Just how much was a matter for debate. He retained some semblance of wit, and he wasn't yet crawling on the floor. Even so, Fancy had learned from Diego that a lucid, walking drunk was the most dangerous kind.

"Whatcha got there?"

She started at the playful tone of his voice. He was staring at her bodice now, and she clutched her penny dreadful closer to her breasts.

"A gift from Wes—not that it's any of your business. He thought I might grow bored staring at your walls."

"So you've stayed up late reading about your heroes, eh? Jesse James, Cole Younger, and Belle Starr?" Cord looked inordinately amused. "Learn any new tricks?"

"Do you really think I'd tell you that?"

"Nope. Just making conversation."

"Well, I'm not in any mood to talk to you."

"No?" He raised his eyebrows suggestively. "Just what are you in the mood for, darlin'?"

Her palms moistened at his husky tone. "Get out."

"Now, now. You're forgetting this here's my room."

He reached for her magazine, and she recoiled, tripping over her gown in her haste to sidestep his hand.

He frowned. "Here now. You didn't go and get scared of me all of a sudden, did you?"

God, yes. But she couldn't let him know that. She couldn't let him know how desperate and vulnerable he made her feel. Marshaling her features, she donned her haughtiest glare. "Just because I don't want you groping me, doesn't mean I'm scared."

"Now there's a switch. For days you've done nothing but throw yourself at me every chance you got."

"You flatter yourself."

"I don't think so, but I'll play along. Tell you what. Why don't you put that magazine down and sashay over here?"

"Why on earth would I want to do that?"

"'Cause you're not in the mood for talking, and I'm not in the mood for sleeping."

Dread burned its way to her gut. "You're drunk."

"So?"

"So I'd be wasting my time."

Resentment clouded his features. "I'm not that drunk."

She saw the challenge in his eyes, and she feared she might have pushed him too far. "Come on, Rawlins," she said, struggling to achieve a conciliatory tone. "Don't kid a kidder. Just look at you. You couldn't bed me if you tried."

"I could, all right. And you'd like it."

"I think not."

"Sure you would. You've been wanting me ever since you first laid eyes on me. Remember the train? You got all riled up when I wouldn't pay you any mind. You still do, don't you, Fancy girl? I'm like a burr under your saddle. An itch you can't scratch."

"If you're calling yourself a nuisance, I have to agree."

"You never did much cotton to the truth."

"And you overestimate your appeal."

"Naw." He tilted his head. His eyes were so glazed that they twinkled in the firelight. "Remember our kiss? You liked that sure enough."

"That was pretend," she said loftily.

"Even you don't pretend that good, sweetheart."

She felt her face flame. "You're insufferable!"

"Nope. Just honest."

"Indeed?" She fumed, wishing she dared throw the penny dreadful at his head. "If you're so blessedly honest, you'll have to admit that you've been hot for me ever since Fort Worth."

"Sure. Why not? I'm not ashamed."

The fire in her cheeks quickly cooled. "God, Rawlins." She met his gaze uneasily. "You really are drunk."

"Is that what's got you so spooked?"

"I told you, I'm not—"

"I know what you told me. You'd tell me damned near anything, 'cause you're ornery that way." The humor ebbed from his face. "But the fact is, you're standing over there looking whiter than sun-bleached bones. Geez, girl. Did you really think I'd force you down?"

She fidgeted. In her experience, a man—especially an intoxicated man—didn't much care whether a woman was willing or not. Still, she felt a little guilty for thinking the worst of Cord.

"When I asked you to leave, you refused," she reminded him.

"Aw, Fancy. That's only 'cause I was hoping to change your mind." A tiny, wistful smile played across his lips. "It's been a long time since I wanted a woman, that's all. I kind of missed it."

His confession stunned her. Knowing Cord as she did, she couldn't believe he was lying. Yet what man would admit to such a thing? Was he trying to win her sympathy?

"I'm . . . not sure that's much of an apology."

He had the decency to blush. "I reckon you're right. Sorry 'bout that. Sorry I bothered you too. Maybe I ought to be leaving."

"Wait!"

He paused in midstride. She nearly lost her nerve when he faced her, this time without teetering. Dear God, what if he'd only been acting drunk? What if he hadn't guzzled enough liquor to pass out on the floor?

"I do want something from you."

"Oh?" He hiked an eyebrow. "And what might that be?"

She drew a steadying breath. "My freedom."

Disbelief blanked his face. "Your *freedom?*" He dissolved into laughter. "Now that's the beatenest thing I ever heard."

She stiffened. "Listen to me, Rawlins. I'll cut you a deal."

"You don't say."

"You get what you want, if I get what I want."

Her words sank in, and Cord abruptly sobered. For a moment, all he could do was stare. Then he decided that the rotgut he'd guzzled had moldered his hearing.

"Come again?"

"You heard me right."

"Couldn't have."

Her expression turned grimly earnest. "Then let me speak plainly. You want a woman? I want a horse and the freedom to ride away. Let's make a deal."

He caught his breath. Several moments passed before he released it in a low, soft whistle.

"You're saying you'll rub navels with me if I let you run?"

She nodded.

"And you'll be friendly? You won't scratch my eyes out, or bite my nose off, or do whatever else your mama taught you to do in a Pecos two-step?"

"Your pecker will be in very good hands, I assure you."

He laughed again, not at her joke, but at his own randy foolishness. God help him, he was actually tempted.

"You sure you don't have a scorpion hidden under that nightgown?" he asked half-seriously. "Or maybe a gun stashed up your sleeve?"

"This is business. A girl can't stay in business long if she goes back on her deals."

He wasn't sure he liked the sound of that. Was she acting out a part or speaking from personal experience?

"Supposing I'm not satisfied. You got some kind of

guarantee? As I recall, I walked away with a bootprint on my shin after you got your fill of kissing me."

Her eyes narrowed, betraying her. He was relieved to see the sign. She had no intention of honoring her deal. Most likely she was gambling on the whiskey, hoping it had made him an unfit lover. She'd probably used this ruse on hundreds of lawmen.

"Tell you what, Marshal. Tonight I'll take extra-special care of your legs . . . and everything in between."

Now there was a bluff worth the call.

"But what if things change?" he taunted, unsure whether he was amused or affronted that she thought him so easy to hoodwink. "What if you like me so much you don't want to ride off? What if you get the hankering to do it all over again?"

"Don't worry yourself. The chances of that are rather slim."

"Think so, eh?"

She looked awfully damned sure of herself standing there, with her long, sleek legs silhouetted by the fire. She couldn't have worn a stitch of clothing under that gown, and Cord didn't need much imagination to detect her private parts. He figured a wise man would cut his losses and hightail it down the hall. So what did that say about him?

"Well? Are you ready to deal now?" she demanded.

He smiled wryly. The temptation was killing him. He figured he'd be damned either way.

"Sure I'm ready. Willing and able too, sweet thing."

He strolled closer.

"Not so fast, tin-star. First, your word. You have to swear you'll set me free."

"Okay."

"'Okay' isn't good enough. I want to hear you swear it."

Cord halted before her. His word was his bond. Under ordinary circumstances, he would never have given it. But Fancy Holleday had proven time and again she was only a tease. Things could get downright steamy before she reneged, but that suited him fine. He intended to enjoy himself clear up to the moment she said "stop." No matter what she might believe, he hadn't come there to brutalize her. Violence against women was the one area in which he, as a lawman, sided with the vigilante.

"If you make love to me right here, right now"—he lowered his face on a level with hers—"and if you join in the spirit of things, rather than lying there like a sack of old potatoes . . . Well then." He indulged in a devilish smile. "Come sunup, I'll let you ride out of here. Agreed?"

Her lashes fanned downward. "Agreed."

"Why don't I take this old magazine for you, hmm?"

She caught her breath when his hand lowered to her bodice. For a moment, he was disappointed to think the game might be up already. She recovered her nerve, though, and moistened her lips for an enticing smile.

Yep, she was playing a high-stakes game, he thought. But then, cheaters could afford to.

"Maybe you should start taking off your clothes," she said huskily.

"I'd much rather be taking off yours."

"But I'm only wearing this shift, Marshal. Truly, you're overdressed with all your buttons, buckles, and spurs."

She reached for his belt, but he caught her hand, raising it to his lips. Her fingers felt like velvet against the stubble of his chin.

"The clothes can wait," he murmured, rubbing her palm against his whiskers. "You aren't in a hurry, are you?"

"No . . ."

"Glad to hear it. 'Cause sunup's still a long way off."

Her eyes hooded as he brushed back her hair. God, it felt so silky. He'd been longing to run his hands through it ever since he saw her standing there in front of the hearth. All those fire-burnished curls, spilling over her arms and breasts, reminded him of the feather warbonnets that the Plains Indians wore. He just wished that the war part of his analogy wasn't quite so fitting.

She smelled of soap and summer rain. He lowered his head and breathed deeply, imagining the sheen of water on her skin. Too bad she'd bathed alone. Too bad he hadn't found out in time to, well, invent some really pressing reason to stop by his room. At watering holes along the trail, he'd gotten quite handy at watching her from the corner of his eye. He would staunchly tell himself that he was just doing his job, of course. In secret, though, he was always disappointed that she didn't strip off her chemise and wade into the current. Sometimes he'd thought she knew exactly what he hoped for, and that she spited him just to watch him chafe.

He touched his lips to hers. She tasted like peaches. Weaving his fingers through her hair, he tilted her head back to savor every delectable morsel. He'd never much cared for the fruit until now—until every ripe, luscious inch of her was filling his arms. God, it had been so long. He'd forgotten what a healthy appetite should feel like. She tasted and felt and smelled so good that it was easy, damned easy, not to remember the game she was playing. Or rather, the game *he* was playing.

He cupped her buttocks. She was slimmer and firmer than the women he was used to, but that didn't bother him much. She was fuller on top. He pressed her closer, relishing the feel of her breasts as they flattened against his chest. Longing to fondle one, he slid his hands upward. When his fingers splayed over her ribs, she flinched and gasped, recoiling.

"I thought you weren't in a hurry," she said accusingly, bracing a hand against his chest.

The look on her face was more pained than aggrieved. It confused him. Had he hurt her?

"Fancy, if you want me to stop—"

"No," she said quickly. "We have a deal. I'm not going back on my word. Are you?"

"No, but—"

"Good."

She drew a deep breath and smiled. He was learning how to tell her real smile from her fake one, and he was pretty sure this one was forced.

"Why don't you take off your boots, cowboy, while I turn down the bed?"

She started to flee.

"Not so fast, footloose."

Grasping her around the waist, he dragged her back, but he wasn't prepared when her spine struck his chest. He staggered as his rowels snagged her hem. The floor pitched beneath him, and he muttered an oath as he heard a rending tear. In the next instant, she landed on his lap with an unceremonious "umph."

"Rawlins, you clutz!"

She flailed, which helped his spurs shred the gown further. He realized the fabric had swathed his leg to hers, but it wasn't until his head had fully cleared that he became aware of the creamy white of her thigh against the black bear pelt beneath them.

"I told you to take your boots and spurs off!"

He chuckled. He couldn't help it. She looked angry enough for her ears to start smoking.

"Does all this caterwauling mean you're not hurt?"

She stiffened. Pushing the hair from her face, she glared over her shoulder at him. "Yes, no thanks to you. Look what you've done!"

"I'm trying to, darlin'."

She slapped the hand that reached for her thigh. "The very least you could do is help me, Rawlins."

"I was trying to do that too." He did his best to look grave, but the corners of his mouth kept tilting up instead of down. "Looks like your gown's about ruined. Reckon it'll have to come off now."

"You did this on purpose."

"I did not."

"You most certainly did!"

"Now why would you think a thing like that?"

"Because you're drunk. I'm surprised you didn't just grab me by the hair and shove me down on all fours."

His mirth died. "Is that what you're used to?"

Pain turned her eyes stormy violet once more. "Let's just get this over with."

She tried to rise, but he pulled her back into his arms.

"Fancy, wait."

Her muscles quivered like fiddle strings beneath his forearm. Suddenly, he wondered if he'd misjudged her. Maybe she wasn't a tease who used men to gratify her vanity. Maybe she was a lonely, unloved girl whom men had always used.

"Don't go," he murmured, smoothing back her hair. He pressed a kiss to her temple. "Sit here with me a spell."

"Why?"

"Because I like holding you."

She peered once more over her shoulder. The look on her face was a cross between resignation and disgust. "You want to hump me on the floor?"

"No."

She pursed her lips. "You're backing out of our deal, aren't you? I knew you would. I knew you didn't have it in you."

Cord smiled without humor. Here he was, trying to be tender, and she was doing everything in her power to rub his patience raw. What was wrong with her, anyway? He couldn't believe she preferred harsh treatment.

"Shh. We have all night, remember? Just be still and watch the fire."

She hesitated, eyeing him narrowly before she turned to face the hearth. He waited for her tension to ease and her head to sink back against his shoulder, but many minutes passed, and she still refused to relax. If not for her hammering heart and an occasional, shuddering breath, he might have thought she'd turned to stone.

Sighing, he closed his eyes and rested his cheek against her hair. Its clean, sweet scent helped lull him into a less guarded state of mind. She really was beautiful. He preferred women with wheat-colored curls and doelike eyes, but there was something wild and free about Fancy. It stirred his spirit. As loathe as he was to admit it, he worried that the reformatory would break her.

Gradually Cord realized he was rocking her. He didn't know when she'd leaned back against him or when he'd begun strumming her ribs with his fingers, but her slower pulse and measured breathing led him to believe she'd started to trust him. He touched gentle lips to her cheek.

Casually his hand roamed higher. Slipping beneath the ties of her bodice, he cupped one firm, ample breast. His thumb stroked and rubbed until the nub at last jutted into his palm. He heard the tiny catch in her throat and kissing her again, he wished he could feast on the trophy that overflowed his palm. Since he doubted whether he could stop himself there, he settled on a consolation: the hollow behind her ear. She sighed, letting her head drop back against his shoulder, and he pioneered new territory, his lips eager as they explored the arch of her neck.

Slowly, leisurely, he pushed her gown higher. He trailed his hand along her thigh, pausing every inch or so to massage the goosepimples from her flesh. Only when he was poised to explore the inner side of her leg did he feel her first real stirrings of disquiet. She reached as if to repair her gown, but he caught her hand and raised it to his lips.

"Shh," he murmured again, drawing her middle finger deep inside his mouth. He sucked and licked, and slid and sucked. He felt a tremor ripple through her, and his hand dipped once more between her thighs, his lips and tongue promising above what she might hope for below. She wore nothing to protect her from his finger's wooing, and he felt her legs quiver, as if torn between resistance and surrender.

"What . . . are you doing?" Her voice sounded hoarse as he courted his goal.

"Loving you, sweetheart."

"But that wasn't part of our deal. We agreed that I would make love to—"

She gasped as his forefinger snaked past the velvet entry he'd been seeking.

"Let me touch you," he murmured, ignoring the hand that tried to push him away. She was wet. She was ready. And her efforts to end his petting were feeble at best. He slipped his tongue inside her ear, and her spine arched hard against him. Her hips strained upward; her legs trembled wider. He rewarded her submission with gentle, plunging strokes.

"Damn you, Rawlins."

"Slide off the top of your dress," he urged huskily, searching for that tender spot that he knew she'd like best.

"No."

"Why not?"

"Because it's—" she made a strangled sound as he found her swollen pleasure bud, "it's my turn."

"Not yet, sugar. The night's still young."

She turned her head away from his lips, but she still hadn't told him to stop. In fact, she was putting up even less of a fight now, if that were possible. He propped himself against a nearby armchair, reclining her farther against him. He plumbed her depths with a slower, more serpentine rhythm, and she squirmed. Finally, reluctantly, her hips began thrusting to meet him.

A sense of exhilaration flowed through him. Beth had never let him woo her like this. In fact, Beth had considered sex a repugnant chore. She'd encouraged it only after she realized it could lead to babies. Of course, by that time, he'd been so scared of the consequences that he refused to touch her.

"Cord," Fancy panted, "you said you . . . wouldn't . . . take me on the floor."

His breaths were coming more raggedly too. Whether she'd intended it or not, her rocking was nudging his pecker. He tried to ignore the sensation, but a familiar, pulsing heat surged through his loins. He bit his tongue on a moan.

God, he wanted her. He wanted to press her down into that feather mattress and plunge into her creamy core until they both collapsed into a panting heap. But he didn't dare.

He cursed himself for agreeing to her terms. At the time, he'd figured Beth had made him a master of self-restraint. Now he feared he'd be hopelessly out of control if Fancy got her hands on him.

"Let me turn down the bed," she groaned.

"Can't do that, darlin'," he whispered, surprised to hear how throaty his voice had become. "I'd have to stop, then." He dipped a second finger inside her moist heat. "You wouldn't want me to stop, would you?"

She made an animal sound. He figured she must be very close. Her fingers wrapped around his wrist.

"That's it," he murmured. "Show me. Show me what you want."

"I hate you for this, Rawlins."

"I know," he said soothingly, and obliged her, sliding deeper. Faster.

She gasped. He felt her tiny, trembling shiver. It built to a shuddering quake, and he cradled her closer, stifling another moan. His loins throbbed in time to her careening heart; his rasping breaths echoed her own. He wanted so much more of her, he ached.

He pushed down the neck of her gown. Her breasts were flushed and swollen when they spilled into his hands. He longed to suckle them, but he couldn't risk the change of positions. Not when his need was so great. With a growling, frustrated sound, his mouth fastened to the tender hollow where her neck and shoulder joined.

"Cord, stop."

He hardly heard her plea above the pounding in his temples. Hungrily, he feasted lower. Her shoulder was a poor substitution for the places he longed to taste, but it was all the satisfaction he could take.

"Ow!"

She flinched, and he opened his eyes, blinking back the mists. He couldn't imagine what he'd done to hurt her. A heartbeat later, he was too stunned to find out.

"Fancy, my God. Your back."

Her hands froze in their efforts to pull up her gown. His heart twisted. Pushing aside her hair, he warned himself not to believe his drunken eyes, yet as she knelt there, trembling before him, those long, crisscrossing scars didn't fade away. He touched an incredulous finger to one.

Good God. She'd been whipped!

"Fancy, who did this to you? Santana?"

A shudder rocked her. For a moment, he thought she had given in to a sob until she rounded on him like a boxer in a prizefight.

"What the hell difference does it make?"

Hatred stabbed at him through the unshed tears in her eyes. He winced. Only then did he notice the ugly purple bruise where her neck and shoulder joined. A second blue-green stain marred her abdomen. No wonder she'd been flinching from his hands and lips! He sickened as he remembered Wes's story:

"But Miss Fancy wasn't afraid of going to hell alone. She jumped right in front of Slade's rifle. When she tried to wrastle it away, he hit her with the butt. He hit her plenty hard, too, in the belly and the shoulder. Miss Fancy never cried, though. She never said nothing, but I reckon she was hurting pretty bad."

"Fancy, I . . ." Cord choked, swallowing hard. "I've made a mistake. A terrible, terrible mistake. And I'm sorry."

Fancy gazed into Cord's haunted eyes. She saw his remorse, but more clearly than that, she saw his aversion. She realized then that she, too, had made a mistake. How could she have been so eager to let him love her? And how could she have been so careless? She'd revealed her secret ugliness after staking her freedom on their deal! Hadn't Diego warned her?

"No other man will want you now," he'd jeered as he towered over her, his riding quirt still wet with her blood. "I am all you have. All you will ever have. And I will not be so understanding the next time, *muchacha,* if you disobey me."

Fancy fought back tears. Drunk or sober, Cord would

never want her now. In fact, he looked as if his stomach were turning. She flushed to realize just how grotesque she must appear.

"Quit staring!"

"I didn't mean to," he whispered. "It's just that—"

"You feel sorry?" Her chin trembled as she raised it. "Don't pity me, Cord Rawlins. Don't you dare pity me!"

He paled. Averting his eyes, he staggered to his feet. She guessed that only a miracle saved him from keeling over again.

"Cover yourself," he said hoarsely.

Her tears threatened once more at this newest evidence of his disgust. She jumped up, shredded the remaining fabric from her body, and threw it in the fire.

"There! I'm upholding my end of the bargain, see? You want me? I'm ready."

He shook his head as if clearing away a thick fog. "I won't—"

"Then you forfeit!"

He grimaced, clenching his teeth. "Keep your voice down."

"I'll shout this house down around your ears if you don't give me that key."

"Fancy, for God's sake, I can't—"

"Yes, you can! You gave me your word. Are you going back on your word?"

His eyes were glazed and confused as he backed for the door. "No! I mean . . . I don't have to. Nothing happened. Not like we agreed."

"That's because you wouldn't let it happen. You *refused* to let it happen!"

"No." His shoulder blades struck the door. "Your stakes were too high. I just . . . withdrew."

"You probably do that to all your women!"

Even that insult couldn't shame him into renewing their wager. He turned the knob. She panicked and charged for the door. She didn't consider her nakedness; she thought only that she must dash past him so he couldn't lock her inside. Cord lunged into her path, though. Their collision drove him backward. He grunted, his spine ramming the door shut again, and she sobbed a curse. Desperately she tried to push him aside, to grasp the knob and break for the hall, but his arms had closed around her, and she found herself pinned to his chest.

"Let me go!"

"Fancy, stop." He dragged her hips hard against his own. The strategy saved his groin from her knee.

"Damn you." She writhed futilely, feeling his arms grow tighter and tighter until she could barely struggle at all. "You owe me, Rawlins!"

"Fancy, you don't want to be taken this way. I promise you."

He was right, but he'd seen her scars, so what choice did she have?

"I don't want your promises. I want my freedom!"

"Honey, listen to me. You can't keep running. Somewhere, someday, another Slade will come along. You have to take the price off your head. You have to turn yourself in."

"No!"

"It's the only way."

"They'll lock me up until I'm old and gray and no man will ever want me again!"

"That's not true," he whispered thickly.

"It is true! Diego stopped wanting me. He said I was getting too old. Now you don't want me either. You just want to lock me away for years and years. How can you do this to me when I saved your brother's life?" She broke off on a sob, her fists clenching great handfuls of his shirt.

"Fancy?"

Squeezing her eyes closed against the threatening tears, she sagged, trembling as he stroked her hair.

"You're wrong," he said softly, so softly that she could hardly hear him above her ragged breaths. "I do want you, but not like this. Not when you're in pain. Blazes, girl, why didn't you say something? Why didn't you tell me Slade beat you?"

She winced as his hand skimmed lower, massaging the knotted muscles in her back. She was so ashamed that she could hardly bear for him to touch her there, where she was so hideous.

"Would it have mattered?" she said brokenly. "You didn't believe Wes's story. You would never have believed mine."

His arms tightened around her again. In that instant—and perhaps for the first time in her life—she felt safe. Protected. It was strange to feel that way about one's enemy.

Yet as his breathing matched the rhythm of hers, as their heartbeats mingled, pounding as one, she could summon none of her old malice. He held her for what seemed like the sweetest, most fleeting minutes she'd ever known. And when he sighed, she felt the sensation move through her, shaking the very foundations of her world.

"I reckon I do owe you," he murmured at last, resting his chin upon her hair. "I owe you a sight more than an apology."

She swallowed, afraid she'd heard him wrong. "What . . . are you saying?"

"Come sunup, you're free to ride out of here."

She stirred, venturing a glance at him, but tears could make things look so deceiving. She told herself she was mistaken to think his eyes were glistening with anything more than the glaze of hard liquor.

"Another one of your promises, Marshal?" she asked tremulously. "You'll have to forgive me if I don't take you at your word this time."

He shifted, and she watched warily as he dug a fist inside his pocket. He rummaged for a moment; she heard the faint clinking of coins, or maybe his tobacco tin, then he took her hand and closed it over something small and hard.

The key! She caught her breath.

"A pledge of good faith," he said.

"Truly?" She searched his rugged, sunbaked features for

some covert sign of deceit. "You'll call off your guards? You'll let me ride away?"

He nodded.

"But why?"

A small, heart-stopping smile curved his lips. Raising a hand, he brushed his fingers across her cheek. She flushed to see the glimmer of wetness on his thumb.

"I can't have Wes hating me for the rest of his life, now can I?"

Despite their calluses, his hands were gentle when he grasped her shoulders and eased her body from his. She felt chilled without his warmth, and she shivered, noticing with a twinge of hurt how careful he was to keep his eyes focused above her neck.

"Try and get some sleep now," he said, cracking the door open. "Sunup will come soon enough."

She nodded, uncertain how to respond. He'd taken nothing for himself, yet their deal was clearly done. He'd let her win. She could ride away and leave Cord Rawlins behind her. Forever.

She tightened her fingers around the key. Suddenly, she felt so lost. What would she do with Diego gone? Where would she go? She didn't have a family like Cord's to run home to.

"Cord?"

He paused on the threshold.

"Are you sure you want to—" She bit her tongue. *Sleep alone tonight?* Her face heated as she realized just how close she'd come to humiliating herself again. "I mean . . . thank you. For the key."

He stood quietly without moving. The hall was so dark, she could see none of his features clearly except the chiseled outline of his jaw. Her heart quickening, she tried to imagine his expression.

"Like I said. I'm doing this for Wes."

Just for Wes?

Deflated, she listened as he walked down the hall. She

found herself hoping that he'd change his mind, that he'd come back for her and finish the loving he'd started.

The stairs eventually stopped creaking, though, and she guessed he'd settled in the sitting room, where he could sleep off his whiskey on Aunt Lally's couch.

You're being absurdly maudlin, Fancy Holleday, she scolded herself as she closed the door. *For heaven's sake, you won! What difference does it make why he gave you the key? You have it now; that's all that matters. For the first time in days, you'll get a good night's rest, and tomorrow you'll be free.*

Free and alone.

Chapter Twelve

The smoking cigarette forgotten in his hand, Cord rested his forearms on the back of the chair. Fancy hadn't answered his knock on the bedroom door, and she hadn't stirred when he entered. An aching head and churning stomach had made sleep elusive for him, so he'd straddled the chair at the foot of his bed to wait for her. And watch her.

The first pink rays of dawn crept across her pillow. Brushing her cheek, they stroked some color into a face that looked porcelain white. Sooty lashes and the frame of blue-black curls only emphasized her pallor.

Christ, she looked too fragile for the ordeal that lay ahead. How old was she, anyway? Twenty-five? That was hardly a lifetime, yet last night he'd realized she must know more about hell than any woman, guilty of *any* wrongdoing, deserved to know. Worse, the only future she had to look forward to was prison.

Cord rubbed a throbbing temple. God forgive him. The whiskey was no excuse; he'd been plain stupid. He should never have given her that key. He should never have given her false hope. In a month, maybe two, the price on her head would go up again. The higher the reward, the greater her danger. Soon there'd be nowhere she could hide, no one she could trust. What kind of man would that make him, if he let her ride away?

He pictured Diego Santana, whipping her. He imagined Wilton Slade, beating her. Not for the first time was Cord glad that he'd killed the bounty hunter. He wished now that he'd ignored his conscience back in December and killed Santana too. God only knew when that gutless Spanish whoremonger would finally be healed enough to stand trial. Even then, his hanging wasn't guaranteed. Hangings never were when a defendant could afford to hire a slick lawyer—or fill the election coffers of a judge.

In the meantime, Fancy probably didn't have a penny to her name. Brains and raw grit weren't going to be enough to see her through the weeks ahead. How could he convince her to trust him? How could he get her to turn herself and the plates in, so he could go to the governor for her?

The room slowly brightened. His cigarette burned to a stub. The faint creaking of stairs announced that Zack—or maybe Aunt Lally—had roused for chores. Only then did Fancy stir. Stretching, she yawned. Then she stiffened. She must have smelled tobacco smoke, for her nose wrinkled and she bolted upright, pulling the quilt to her chest.

"How—how long have you been sitting there?"

Wide anxious eyes challenged his, as if she was afraid he might pounce on her at any moment.

"Most of the morning, it seems like."

She reddened. Raising a hand, she hastily smoothed back her hair, but something more important than her appearance must have occurred to her. She turned white again, whiter than starched lace.

"What do you want?"

"We need to talk."

He watched the panic flicker through her eyes.

"We have nothing to talk about," she said harshly. "The deal's done."

"I wish it were that simple, darlin', but this isn't a card game."

Her knuckles tightened on the quilt. "You're going back on your word."

"No. You're still free to go, but . . ."

"But what?"

He averted his eyes. He really hated doing this. "I don't think your running is such a good idea."

"Forgive my frankness, Marshal, but what you think doesn't concern me. Not in the least."

He sighed, rubbing out the cigarette butt with his toe. He'd known this wouldn't be easy.

"Look, Fancy. You and I both know your luck is going to run out. You're worth ten times more than you were in December. Sooner or later, some bounty hunter will track you down, and you're going to wind up—"

"Not in prison. Not ever."

He locked his eyes with hers. "What I was going to say," he finished quietly, "was dead."

A moment passed. She forced a smile. Her expression held none of the saucy bravado he'd come to admire. "Better dead than locked up."

"You don't mean that."

"Oh, yes I do."

He pressed his lips into a thin line. Had Santana locked her up sometimes? Was that why she was so scared?

"You're talking loco," he said sternly, not quite able to rid his voice of the anger he felt toward Santana. "You can't walk away from dead. But you can walk away from prison. In a year—maybe less if I can work it right—you'll be free. No more running. No more looking over your shoulder."

"Assuming, of course, I survive whatever pestilence lurks inside those walls. No thank you, tin-star. Like I told you before, I'll take my chances on the road."

Damn her. And damn himself for caring. When had he started to worry more about trying to keep her safe than about recovering those plates?

He racked his brain for a way to make her see the sense of his plan. Maybe she hadn't fully considered the hardships of the road.

"You realize this means you'll be on the run from now on. Ever give much thought to what your life will be like?"

"Pretty much the same, I'll wager, since you killed Diego."

He frowned. "Diego?" He eyed her in a mixture of bewilderment and surprise. "Santana's not dead. Hell, he hasn't even been tried yet."

Fancy caught her breath. For a heartbeat, she couldn't have been more stunned than if Cord had thrown a bucket of cold water in her face. Confusion, elation, dread, they raced through her veins like quicksilver. *Diego . . . alive?*

Disbelief quickly followed. She remembered the sight of Diego crumpled beside the express car door. He hadn't moved or answered her. True, it had been dark and she'd been frantic, but the sight of his blood had been unmistakable, seeping from his chest and tainting the snow.

"That's low, Rawlins," she whispered, forcing the words past the lump in her throat. "That's about as low as a man can go."

He raised his brows. He looked genuinely surprised. "You think I'm telling a windy?"

"I think you're telling a full-blown hurricane!"

He smiled, but there was no humor in it, only disappointment. "Now why would I go and lie to you about a thing like that?"

"You want to get me to Nevada, don't you?"

He shook his head ruefully. "Darlin', you've been keeping company with too many horse thieves."

"But I saw you shoot him! In the chest. His blood was everywhere, and—"

Cord held up his hand. "I shot him in the shoulder. And the leg. Last I heard, he's been keeping himself out of court by pleading pneumonia or some such thing. He's not likely to die, though. Not until he hangs. Or I get him in my sights," he added under his breath.

Fancy started. She had never heard Cord threaten to kill a man before. A tremor seized her hands, and she had to clasp them together. She supposed he must have been fond of Captain Hamilton, despite appearances to the contrary. Why else would Cord threaten Diego?

"Why didn't you tell me he was alive?" she demanded fiercely.

"I reckon it never came up before."

"For God's sake, Rawlins, I had a right to know. He was . . . I mean, we were . . ." She blushed. She couldn't very well claim they were affianced after she had confessed Diego's preference for younger women.

But those young harlots never stuck by Diego the way she did. She would always be there for him, no matter what. Diego knew it, too, and that's why he would marry her. He had to. Cord Rawlins certainly wouldn't—not with her tarnished reputation and soiled past.

"I love Diego," she declared, raising her chin a notch. The gesture always helped her tamp down the uncertainty that accompanied such affirmations.

"*Love* him?" Cord's jaw dropped. "How the hell can you say that after he beat you?"

She winced inwardly. Even so, she reminded herself that a woman on the verge of her twenty-sixth birthday, a woman who had spent her youth whoring to survive, had to overlook certain shortcomings in her only suitor. Diego was her last chance to have a husband, a home, and children—the kind of life she'd been secretly dreaming of for years.

"My mother beat me too, sometimes," she said defensively. "I didn't stop loving her."

"My God." For a moment, he sat staring at her, his eyes dark and troubled. "Is that what you think love is?"

A prickle of doubt inched up her spine. She staunchly shook it off. "Who are you to question my beliefs about love? You still grieve over a woman so spoiled and selfish that she refused to be a mother to your own kid brothers!"

He drew a sharp breath, his face turning white. Pain pinched his cheeks and hollowed his eyes; Fancy grimaced, instantly regretting her attack. As angry as he had made her by keeping Diego's imprisonment a secret, hurting him brought her none of the satisfaction that it might have brought two nights earlier.

"I'm sorry, Cord. I should never have said that." She

watched uneasily as his chest heaved with barely restrained emotion. "I only meant to say that feelings can be complicated. You should know that better than anyone."

His jaw had tightened so hard, she wasn't sure if he was fighting back rage or grief. She hoped the dam held long enough so she didn't have to find out.

"What do you think you know about Beth?"

Girl, you have really set yourself up this time. "Nothing." She fidgeted. "It's none of my business."

"You've made it your business. So answer me."

She felt her heart skitter. His voice had been quiet, ominously quiet, and laced with a flat, bald grimness. She sensed that saying nothing now would be worse than saying too much. "Well, I've seen her pictures and . . ."

"And?" His challenge burned like embers in his eyes. "What did my family tell you?"

She sank a little lower. The reaction was instinctive. She hardly realized she had done it until she noticed how feverishly her hands were plucking at the quilt. "Only that you loved her. And—" she tried to find words that would stave off an explosion, "and that you blame yourself for how she died. I don't know much about her—or about you, of course," she added hastily, "but it seems to me Beth was lucky. She had a husband who loved her, a big close-knit family, and . . ."

She blinked, her eyelids stinging with sudden tears. "She was having the baby of the man she loved," she finished pensively. "I think Beth must have been happy—deliriously happy—in those final hours. And if she wasn't, then she should have been. You have no cause to keep blaming yourself, Cord. Besides, for what it's worth, I think you would make a wonderful father."

She held her breath. She hadn't planned on saying that. In fact, she'd been surprised when she blurted it out. But to her amazement, she realized she meant it. Every word. Cord *would* make a good father. Now Diego, on the other hand . . .

She chided herself for her disloyalty. People could change,

and Diego could too. After all, he'd been changing almost daily over the last few years. The debonair caballero had become less and less a part of his character after he started dabbling in Barbary Coast politics. And cocaine.

She grimaced as unpleasant memories, mostly having to do with Diego's doped-up rages and his whip, crowded her mind. Maybe if she could convince him to swear off the cocaine, she thought uncertainly, he'd go back to being the man she had fallen in love with. They could be married, then, and she could live a respectable life. Surely that wasn't too much to ask.

A lingering silence settled between her and Cord. She watched him furtively from beneath lowered lashes. He seemed to be calmer now—but not calm enough for her to surrender her guard. What was he thinking? The multiple feelings that flickered over his features moved too quickly for her to identify them. She wondered if she had helped to ease his grief. Surely Aunt Lally, Wes, and Zack had said the same things to him a million times. She was probably flattering herself to think that counsel from a modern-day Jezebel could move him in any way.

But if it did, she thought wistfully, then she'd be square with him for setting her free.

He shifted in his chair. Bowing his head, he rubbed his temples, and she remembered how drunk he had been the night before. His head was probably splitting. At least, that's what she assumed. When he finally raised his eyes to hers again, she attributed the uncommon shininess in his gaze to sickness.

"Thank you," he said gruffly. "I would like to become a father someday."

He was silent for another long moment. Then he sighed. "Fancy, you have to know you can have the same things Beth did. You deserve a loving husband, a family, and children. But I'm not going to lie to you. You have little chance of getting them from a man like Santana."

She swallowed, raising her chin again. She didn't want to hear that. She didn't want to hear anything at all like that.

"You don't know Diego the way I do."

"I don't?" His voice was very soft, as if he were trying to soothe a bristling cat. "Tell me about him."

"Well . . ." She frowned. She really didn't care to be discussing Diego with Cord Rawlins. "He comes from a wealthy Spanish family." Although he'd been disowned after he seduced a novice in the local churchyard. "And he's educated, and clever." That was why he outsmarted all the lawmen. "And he protects me." Because she earned him money as his moll. "We've been together for years and years, and . . ." She swallowed. What else? Could she think of nothing else kind to say?

Cord waited. She felt her face heat.

"And he loves me. That's enough. That's all you need to know. The rest isn't any of your business."

"Maybe not," he admitted in that same gentle voice. "Just answer one more question for me. You say you've been together for years. Has he always beaten you?"

She choked. "That's none of your business, either." She fought back another surge of tears. "We had a deal. I'm free to go. You said so yourself. Diego needs me, and I will not let him down."

"*What?*" He looked as if someone had just punched him in the gut. "For God's sake, Fancy, he needs a lawyer. Maybe even a preacher. But he doesn't need you."

"You're wrong!"

"He's in prison. There's nothing you can do for him."

An old and persistent fear squeezed her heart. "There is. I'll find a way." She'd *make* him need her. To be needed would never be the same as being loved, but at least it was better than being abandoned and growing old alone.

"How?" Cord demanded.

"I don't know yet," she said thickly. "But one thing's for certain: I won't let him hang."

A thundercloud seemed to settle on Cord's brow. His face grew dark. Ominous. Not even her slur against Beth had made him glare at her so fiercely. She wasn't exactly sure how she had aroused such anger in him. God knew, when she had tried, she had failed. Shrinking down again, she braced herself for the explosion.

It never came. Rising with a grim finality, he pushed his chair against the wall. "That settles it then."

"Settles it?" she repeated uneasily, watching the tense squaring of his shoulders.

"You'd best get dressed. You're burning daylight."

"What do you mean?"

"Just that," he said curtly. "You've got twenty-four hours. Come this time tomorrow, I'll be on your trail."

She gaped. "Twenty-four hours?" Her speeding heart threatened to choke her. "But you gave me your word—"

"I said I'd set you free. I didn't say anything about coming after you."

His eyes were hooded. It was the same kind of look professional sharpers wore at the poker table. She thought she might be sick.

"You're cheating! You said you never cheat, Rawlins."

"Reckon you must have rubbed off on me since then."

She gasped, reeling. She wasn't certain whether she was more stunned by his insult or his betrayal. "Why, you lying, no-good, son of a—"

A sharp knock cut short her invective. Her chest heaving, she bit her tongue and watched him cross to the door. When he pulled it open, his sun-bronzed cheeks turned lighter by a shade.

"Wes! For the love of Jesus. What are you doing out of bed?"

"I came to see Miss Fancy."

There was the usual ring of defiance in the boy's tone, but when Fancy glimpsed him standing there, looking more ghostly than human, she grabbed Aunt Lally's robe and hurried to join Cord on the threshold.

"It's all right, Cord. Let him in."

Was it her imagination, or did the glaze in Wes's eyes make them look keener, smarter? He glanced from her to Cord, then back again. Understanding furrowed his brow.

"You're taking her in, aren't you?"

Cord stiffened. A dark red stain crept up the back of his neck. "Wes, you lost too much blood. You shouldn't be walking around yet—"

"Answer my question."

Something about the boy's manner reminded Fancy of Cord, when she'd watched him turn his rifle on Diego. The thought unnerved her. She couldn't think of any other reason why she should feel compelled to defend her enemy.

"I've got twenty-four hours, Wes. Then he rides after me."

"Twenty-four hours? Shoot. She can hardly get to Fort Graham and catch a stage by then. You aren't giving her a fair chance, Cord."

"Fair or not, it's the only chance she's got. And you're using up her time by jawing. Now let me get you back to—"

"She got beat up and nearly killed trying to save me," Wes said harshly. "But it just doesn't matter to you, does it?"

Pain flickered across Cord's face. For some reason, the sight of it moved Fancy. She knew she shouldn't care about his dilemma; if anything, she should use it against him. Unfortunately, she couldn't reconcile herself to the idea of coming between these two brothers.

"Wes." She spoke quietly. "It's all right, I'll manage. You know me." She pasted on a smile. "I've still got an ace or two hidden up my sleeve."

She felt Cord's speculative gaze upon her, and her stomach knotted. She didn't have a damned thing hidden up her sleeve—not yet, anyway. But she would beat him. She had to. If Cord Rawlins wanted to see who was better at cheating, he was in for one helluva showdown.

Suddenly, Wes swayed. Fancy watched anxiously as Cord wrapped an arm around the boy's chest and braced him against the doorjamb.

"You're scaring the hell out of me, son."

"It's nothing. Just my knees. They're feeling a little wobbly is all."

"Wes, you need to sit down," Fancy said, extending a hand.

He nodded, catching her fingers and breathing hard for a moment. Cord muttered an oath. When he tried to help the boy inside, Wes tightened his hand over Fancy's.

"Cord, could you . . . get Aunt Lally for me?"

Cord's gaze darted to her. A warning glimmered there.

"I think . . . I started bleeding again," Wes added hoarsely.

Cord swore. "Fancy—"

"I'll take care of him."

His eyes softened. "Thanks."

As Cord's boot falls faded out of hearing, Wes raised his head and winked at her.

"Well, that was easier than shooting ducks on a pond."

She caught her breath. "Wes, are you faking?"

He grinned, but when he tried to straighten, his knees buckled under his weight. He nearly knocked her over, and she feared he would crumple at her feet until he braced a hand against the wall.

"Well, ma'am." He chuckled weakly. "Maybe not."

She slipped her shoulder under his arm. "Come on, Wes. It's all right to lean on me. You need to lie down."

He let her support him, his cheeks growing pink again when her hip and thigh molded intimately to his. His gaze flew hastily from hers, and she had the sneaking suspicion that Wes Rawlins knew a little bit more about women than his oldest brother probably wanted to believe.

Sweeping aside the quilt, she helped lower him to the bed.

"I'm real sorry, ma'am," he said sadly. "I would have come with you to help cover your tracks and all, but it just looks like I'd be slowing you down."

He lay back on the pillows, and she smiled, brushing a stray lock of hair from his forehead. "The best thing you can do for me is get better. Promise you'll try?"

He nodded. He looked so pained, though, she thought his shoulder must be hurting him. She reached for his bandage, but he caught her hand, holding it close to his heart.

"Will I ever see you again?"

His question startled her. "I don't know," she said truthfully.

His fingers tightened around hers. "You aren't going to prison. I won't let you. I'll do whatever it takes. I'll—I'll marry you."

The intensity of his gaze was unnerving. There was something else behind the fervor, something warm and vulnerable. Something that stole her breath away. No man had ever looked at her like that, not even Diego.

"Wes, you can't marry me." She tried to keep her tone light. "I'm old enough to be your mother."

"You are not. Heck, you aren't but ten years older than me. Cord's even older than you, so that would make you like my sister."

Fancy couldn't help but smile at the irony of his logic.

"Maybe so," she said. "But marriage is a serious business. It takes a lot of work. There's sickness and raising children and sometimes there's money troubles too. You've still got a lot of living to do, Wes. Why would you want to get into such a serious business so soon?"

"'Cause I love you. And I want to take care of you."

She felt her throat constrict. He sounded so sincere. He looked so earnest. But he was only sixteen years old! How could this happen? All of her life, she had wanted nothing more than this: a man to really love her. A man to make her his own for always. Yet now that she had finally been offered her dream, she had to turn it down. It was just so unfair! Why couldn't Wes have been older? Why couldn't he have been . . . Cord?

Her face flamed. Mortified, she hastily pushed the thought aside. Cord Rawlins was her enemy. How could she even *consider* the possibility of spending the rest of her life with him?

"Wes." Ashamed to hear how thick her voice had become, she gulped a bolstering breath. "Thank you. No one has ever asked me to marry him before. But I can't be your wife."

"Why not?" he demanded in wounded tones.

"Well . . ." Dammit, this was hard enough. Why did he have to look at her like she was breaking his heart? "What would Cord say?"

"I knew there had to be more to it," he said, pressing his lips together grimly. "It's not the difference in our ages, it's Cord. You love him."

She felt the heat start in her belly and rocket north and south through her body. She wondered if her cheeks looked as red as they felt.

"Why on earth would you think such a thing? He's trying to put me in prison."

"I've seen how you look at him."

She nearly groaned aloud. Was it true? Did she look at him like a calf-eyed schoolgirl?

"I assure you, Wes. I do not love your brother."

"I saw how you kissed him. And how he kissed you," he added with a tinge of envy. "He didn't ever kiss Beth like that."

"He probably didn't let you see him kiss Beth like that."

"Naw." The wisdom of a man was staring back at her from his young eyes. "He didn't like Beth the same way he likes you."

Fancy swallowed. For a moment, she dared to wonder. Was it true? Then reason returned to set her straight. Of course not. Unlike herself, Beth could inspire finer, nobler feelings in a man, something other than lust.

"Look, Wes. Even if what you think is true—and it isn't— Cord and I have too much bad blood between us to ever build a future. Besides—" she looked him straight in the eye, and she didn't mince words, "I love Diego."

His brow furrowed. "The train robber fella?"

"Yes."

"Shoot." The old challenge crept back into his voice. "If he didn't ever ask you to marry him, why bother?"

She stiffened. Jealousy was probably warring with Wes's adoration for Cord. Even so, he had no right to judge her life —or her tangled feelings for Diego. She tried to remove her hand, but his fingers tightened again.

"Fancy."

His voice had become low and gentle. It reminded her so much of Cord's the night before, when he'd held her close and soothed away her tears, that she felt her whole body quake.

"You have to know I'd rather die than hurt you," he murmured. "If you're set on marrying someone else, well—" he sighed, putting on a brave face, "I won't make a fuss. But don't you go settling for Diego when a man as good as Cord is loose."

Her eyes began to sting. She looked away, trying to laugh, to say something clever. It was useless.

"You can't go around promising your brother to spinsters," she said hoarsely, ducking her head to hide the tears. "How would you like it if he did that to you?"

"I wouldn't mind it a'tall if they were just like you."

Hurried footsteps echoed in the hall, and she blinked rapidly, venturing a glance at Wes. He stretched his freckles into a grin.

"That'll be Cord, coming to my rescue. He couldn't find Aunt Lally, I reckon, since she went down to the pasture to help birth a foal."

True to Wes's prediction, Cord stormed across the threshold. With his narrowed eyes and stone-hard jaw, he looked like a man who realized he'd just been hoodwinked.

"It looks like I'm not the only one you've been rubbing off on." He flung the words at Fancy, but his glare drilled through Wes. "You'd best jingle your spurs, girl. You're down to twenty-three hours and forty-five minutes."

Wes chuckled. The sparkle of mischief returned to his eyes, but it couldn't quite dim the youthful yearning there. "Yep," he whispered. "He likes you all right. Aren't no doubt about it. Looks like I'm gonna have to see the two of you get hitched."

It took another quarter hour for Fancy to get dressed, fill a canteen, and throw food into a satchel. Zack was waiting for her by the strawberry pony. As she approached, he drew himself up taller, and his features, so much like Cord's, formed an unreadable mask.

"You ready?" he asked.

Buckling the saddlebag over her satchel, she nodded.

"I'll give you a boost."

When she was settled, he handed her the reins. He wouldn't look her in the eye.

"There's something you ought to know," he said gruffly. "Cord could track a raindrop through the ocean."

She smiled grimly. She'd suspected as much, considering the man used to ride with the Texas Rangers.

"He'll expect you to ride east to Fort Graham. Your only chance once you leave here is heading south and setting your sights on Meridian."

Fancy remembered the map Wes had put inside her satchel. "Thanks."

"There's something else."

Zack stalled, re-cinching her horse's girth strap, double-checking the length of her stirrups. Fancy waited. She could see the boy was really torn between what he wanted to say and what he thought he should.

Finally, he pulled a Peacemaker from his waistband. She recognized the polished wooden inlay on the butt, and she knew it was one of Wes's.

"You're going to need this." He held tightly to the weapon. "Wes wanted you to have it in case of pumas, coyotes, and such." His brown eyes rose at last, boring through her like agate spikes. "But you have to swear you won't use it on Cord."

She swallowed, her tongue thickening. The .45 was more than she had hoped for. Did Cord have any idea how his romantic, foolish brothers were trying to help her?

She glanced toward the house and saw him, watching them through his open bedroom window. The glow of his cigarette was clearly visible in the shadows. When their eyes locked, her palms moistened. Suddenly she realized that no matter what she promised Zack, no matter where she rode or what she did, Cord would be ready for her. Her hands trembled at the thought.

"I swear," she whispered huskily.

"All right, then." Zack stepped back. "The ammo's in the saddlebag."

She shoved the muzzle under her belt, and an awkward moment passed.

"Zack, I really appreciate—"

"You best get along. Time's awasting."

She drew a slow, steadying breath at his rebuff. "I guess you're right." She stuck out her hand. She genuinely liked the boy, and she wanted to leave as friends. "Say good-bye to Aunt Lally for me. Wes, too."

He eyed her peace offering suspiciously, and she felt the lump return to her throat. Disappointed, she was just about to withdraw her hand when his thick, work-roughened fingers finally wrapped around hers. He gave her a firm shake.

"Keep an eye peeled for diamondbacks. Scorpions too."

"I will." She smiled a little shyly. "Take care of yourself, Zack."

He nodded, then his hand fell with a loud thwack on her horse's rump. "Giddyap!" he shouted at the startled mare. The horse broke into a trot, and Fancy spurred her faster.

As the mare's hoofbeats quickened and the wind whistled past her ears, Fancy thought she heard a faint "Godspeed, ma'am" behind her.

Chapter Thirteen

The next three days were a nightmare for Fancy. She couldn't sleep, she hardly ate, and she didn't dare build a fire to warm her through the unseasonably cool nights. She wished Texas weather was more predictable, and she cursed Cord Rawlins for knowing better than she how to survive temperatures that were too hot by noon and too cold by moonrise. He, of course, could afford the luxury of a campfire. He could even shoot a jackrabbit or ground squirrel for his dinner, if he were inclined. No one was looking for signs of his trail.

Every time a buzzard's shadow swooped, every time a coyote howled or a lizard scurried past, she would jump out of her skin and grab her gun. Her nerves were frayed to the breaking point. She imagined him somewhere out there, watching and laughing. Sometimes, she thought she smelled his tobacco on the wind; at other times, she imagined she heard his horse's hooves or saw the thin gray wisp of his camp smoke curling above the horizon.

She hoped a puma got him. Or better yet, a whole tribe of Indians. The bastard. She'd tried to be nice to him. She'd offered a few words of kindness, shown a little compassion— and what had it gotten her? A kick in the teeth! She had known better. Diego had taught her how to treat her enemies.

She wished she could turn the tables on Rawlins. She wished she could circle back and stalk him, but there was little chance of surprising a man in this flat terrain.

Besides, she'd given her word to Zack. Only God knew why she felt so honor-bound. Diego would be disgusted if he learned she was risking her freedom—perhaps even her life—to earn the respect of some freckle-faced youth. He would tell her she was stupid, like he usually did.

This time, though, she would prove Diego wrong. She would find a way to get him out of jail. He would have to admire her resourcefulness, then. He would be sorry for all the times he had wronged her, and he would finally change. She prayed to God he would. Deep down in his heart, he surely must still love her. They could be happy together—not like Beth and Cord had been happy, or even like Lally and Seth must have been, but happy in the sense that Diego and she had shared past experiences. They knew what to expect from each other.

To Fancy's mind, having someone to care for made all the difference in the world between being a respectable woman and being a whore.

She sighed. Forcing her mind back to her present predicament, she slumped miserably in the shade of a scrub oak and watched her horse guzzle from the stream. With any luck, the animal would save some for her. She wondered if this shallow current was what was left of Honey Creek. She'd given up a day ago trying to make sense of Wes's scrawl. The boy had meant well, but his map was grossly underscale. Either that, or "the split tree" and the "tilting rock" had disappeared from the face of the planet.

She feared she was hopelessly lost. She should have found Meridian by now, which would have put her within two days of Waco and a train. Instead, she sat with numb buttocks and precious few miles to show for them, thanks to the fact that she'd followed a streambed more serpentine than a snake. What was worse, her only company was a horse that got spooked more easily than she did. Yesterday at about this time, the silly beast had stumbled across a nesting roadrunner, and all hell had broken loose. She had nearly been thrown on her head. God only knew what would have happened if the horse had really been in danger, say from a puma.

Or a rattlesnake.

Fancy blanched at the thought. She hated snakes almost as much as she hated Cord Rawlins.

An unbidden image of twinkling green eyes and heart-stopping dimples materialized in the water beside her own reflection. The vision was so vivid, so lifelike and real, she had to glance over her shoulder to make sure he hadn't tiptoed up behind her. Fortunately, nothing but grass, rocks, and a smattering of scrubby trees dotted the horizon. She didn't breathe any easier, though.

Why couldn't she picture Diego? Only four months had passed since she'd last held him in her arms.

Squeezing her eyes closed, she tried for at least the hundredth time to conjure his visage: brown eyes, brown hair, brown mustache and beard.

Dazzling white teeth, sun-burnished muscles, sorrel curls that trailed from his chest to his—

Damn him! She plunged a fist into the watery image. Cord Rawlins already haunted her sleep. Why did he have to prowl through her daydreams too?

Removing her hat—or rather, Wes's—she splashed handfuls of tepid water on her face. She could only rest here for a minute; she mustn't let herself doze off. There would be a full moon tonight, and she had to keep moving. Rawlins wouldn't let exhaustion stop him. He wouldn't let an aching back or an empty belly slow him down. He'd keep tracking. Stalking.

Her stomach knotted. No, she couldn't doze off at all.

Cord's heart quickened as he heard the hunting howl. Ordinarily, he wouldn't have cared about coyotes. Pumas, either. But Fancy was out there somewhere, alone.

Tugging a strip of jerky from his pocket, he ate mechanically as he searched the ground. Thanks to the blowing grasses, her tracks had often been hard to find. Still, he gave her the main credit for hiding her trail. She'd ridden over rocks; she'd detoured through streams; she'd left no ashes, food tins, or other waste behind her. Her pattern was clear to him now, and he was gaining on her—which was a damned good thing. He didn't know where she thought she was headed, but if she kept riding south, she was going to get herself captured by one of the outlaw gangs that hid out in the hill country.

Shuddering, he swung hastily into his saddle.

Old Fort Gates was only a day's ride farther south. There they could catch a stage to Waco, board a train on the Texas Central, and arrive in Carson City by next week's end.

His heart lurched at the thought.

God help him, there were times when he really hated his job. Letting Fancy walk out his door and ride away, when he had no real proof that she could survive on the range, had been one of the hardest things he'd ever done. But setting her free hadn't compared with the moment when he told her he would hunt her down.

How could he reconcile himself to bringing her to trial now? He knew better than to get his feelings tangled up in a prisoner's future. And yet, how could he not care about a woman who had thrown herself in front of a rifle to save his brother's life? How could he not feel anything for a girl who'd been so cruelly beaten with a whip?

In all those months, when he'd been so hell-bent on tracking her down for revenge, he'd never stopped to think about the reasons for her behavior. He'd never considered how brutal, degrading, or frightening it must have been to live as the kept woman of a Barbary Coast kingpin. God forgive him, he'd assumed she *liked* cheating and thieving and poking her gun in a man's loins.

When she'd talked about love and family, though, when she'd talked about the treasure that Beth had once possessed, she'd clearly been talking from the heart. And something inside of him had stirred. It was as if a mountain of granite had been lifted from his chest. Although Beth had begged him to take her away from an overbearing father, she had never been happy without her fandangos and balls. She had always wanted more than he, a hired gun, could provide. He'd been ashamed that he couldn't give his wife the kinds of luxuries to which she'd been accustomed.

To hear Fancy talk, though, maybe he hadn't been such an awful husband after all. Maybe giving Beth his heart and his family had been a greater gift than the occasional froufrous he could afford.

And maybe, just maybe, he'd been punishing himself a little too hard, and a little too long, about the child.

In any event, he'd clearly been unfair to Fancy. She wasn't the crass and heartless floozie he'd thought she was. He didn't know everything there was to know about her, and he certainly didn't understand why she professed love for a man who beat her. Still, he was absolutely certain about one thing: She deserved a hell of a lot better than Diego Santana.

Sighing, Cord urged Poco to a faster pace. He knew Hog Creek lay just beyond the horizon. Fancy seemed to be headed that way. With the sun in the four-o'clock position, he still had several hours of daylight left. With any luck, he would find Fancy and water by nightfall.

Fancy woke with a start. Something was wrong.

At first, she tried to convince herself otherwise. She was merely on edge again because she had wasted precious hours of daylight. The sun was nearly touching the horizon.

The sun wasn't the only thing out of place, though. Knuckling the sleep from her eyes, she blinked uneasily at the wind-tossed grasses. Was it her imagination, or was that her belt lying a few yards away?

The belt moved. Every hair on her arms stood on end. A triangular head took shape, rising from the earth to sway above a rippling neck. Fancy felt her throat constrict. For a moment, nothing in her body worked—not her heart, not her lungs, not her brain. All she could do was stare, transfixed by two glittering eyes that were colder and blacker than Satan's.

Coil by coil, the serpent drew itself higher. Then came the

rattle: portentous. Menacing. Fancy tried to scream, but nothing came. Not even a squeak. Icy trickles of sweat dribbled down her spine. From somewhere deep inside her, terror rose, a shrieking, manic assurance that she must flee or she would die.

She jumped up, and the viper lunged. This time when she screamed, the sound ripped from her throat until it turned raw.

Cord's blood curdled. Never had he heard such horror in a woman's cries.

"Fancy!"

Gunshots followed. Again and again came the reports; he saw the fire spitting in the thicket up ahead. He drew his .45, and Poco broke into a dead run.

Merciful God, what was it? What was attacking her? A puma? Rustlers?

His heart climbed to his throat. Was she being raped?

Four, five, six—he counted the reports. Then came the silence, an ominous, gut-wrenching silence.

"Fancy!"

Time crawled. He hit the ground running, but he couldn't drive his legs fast enough. If she was hurt, if she was dead, Christ, he would never forgive himself. He charged past a prickly pear, heedless of the spines that slashed his sleeves, heedless of his danger from whatever lay ahead. His lungs hammered in time to the pounding of his blood.

The first thing he saw was her face, white and wild, a mask etched of terror. He looked frantically around her. There were no cats. No outlaws. No signs of struggle. Her horse stomped nervously, but it looked safe.

He heard a clicking and trained his eye on her hand. She was pulling the trigger again and again on empty chambers. The gun shook so violently he couldn't immediately tell where it was aimed. He half expected to spy Old Scratch himself—horns, pitchfork, and all—crouching in the bushes.

Then, beneath the shadows of a creosote, he saw the diamondback. Or rather, what was left of it. The snake's three-foot body was so riddled with lead, it looked like a sieve.

"Fancy." Cord forced the word past the lump in his throat. "It's dead, darlin'. You can stop shooting now."

"No." She shook her head frantically. Her eyes looked more black than purple in her fear. "It can't be."

"It's in pieces."

"It makes no difference," she insisted, her teeth beginning to chatter. "Snakes don't die. Not until sundown."

He blinked, uncomprehending. Then one corner of his mouth twitched. Why, she actually believed that old wives' tale!

"I'm telling you, sweetheart, it's deader than Davy Crockett. Look."

He bent to reach for the viper, and she stumbled backward, clapping a hand over her mouth.

"Don't!"

"Aw, they're good eating, hon. That is, if you don't have to spit out bullets." He grinned, picking up the prized tail in his glove. "Too bad you only shot yourself a baby. Rattlers grow up to seven feet, you know."

She turned green, and the gun slid from her fingers. His mirth ebbed.

"You weren't bit or anything, were you?"

She staggered away from him.

"Fancy? Were you bit?"

She turned and began to run. He muttered an oath. If there was venom in her veins, the last thing she should be doing was pumping her heart harder.

"Fancy!"

She didn't answer, and he sprinted after her. She was faster than he had figured, but he managed to cut her off from her horse.

"Give it up, girl! There's nowhere you can go."

She veered toward Poco, and he gulped down air. His sharp whistle sent the gelding trotting out of her reach.

"Cut it out now, you hear?" he called, his worry verging on anger. "You're just making this harder on yourself!"

Fancy sobbed, closing her ears to his cries. She wouldn't be caught. She wouldn't go to jail! Visions of iron bars filled her mind, and terror crackled down every nerve.

She raced back toward the trees. His boots pounded hard behind her. She could feel his heat spreading over her; she glimpsed the shadow of his outstretched arm. She feinted, but he was faster, and she shrieked when his hand grasped her collar.

She rounded with swinging fists. The first whizzed harmlessly past his ear; the second collided with a gut as taut as saddle leather. He tripped up her legs, and they crashed in a tangle of limbs. When he deftly rolled her, she was crushed by a mountain of muscle. She fought back desperately, kicking, scratching, jabbing. Her nails raked his neck, and she heard the hiss of his oath.

"So help me God, girl, if there's no poison in your blood—"

"What do you care? You're going to leave me to die in prison anyway!"

"Dammit, Fancy, that's not true."

He pinned one wrist, then the other. His weight began to take its toll. Her breasts heaved, rubbing her nipples against his chest; her thighs trembled, fused in steamy intimacy to his own.

"Were you bit?"

She sobbed, unable to bear his touch. His heat. His maleness. Three nights ago, she had let his tender petting and sweet words of concern woo her trust. Now she knew that he had set out to use her. The only difference between him and all the other bastards was that he had wanted her minting plates, not her favors.

"Answer me!"

"No! I wasn't bitten."

She bucked, straining and writhing. No trick could set her free. Finally, she collapsed, her breaths coming in great, shuddering gasps. She was mortified to feel tears spilling down her cheeks.

"I hate you, Cord Rawlins," she whispered brokenly.

For a moment, he looked shaken. She felt how his heart hammered, slamming against her ribs. Then the sea storm in his eyes ebbed, and an inner light rolled back the clouds. She had never seen anything quite like it before. It wasn't the gleam of lust or the glare of anger. She blinked, trying to see more clearly past her tears, but his eyelids drooped, and she was thwarted.

"Sorry, darlin'," he murmured, his voice soft and husky in its breathlessness. "I've learned better than to believe a damned word you say."

A quarter hour later, Cord had coffee bubbling and snake simmering on the campfire. Fancy, who'd shown no interest in the preparation of the meal, now huddled as far from him as he would permit. He hadn't bothered to cuff her; she was acting nothing like the spitting wildcat who'd tried to scratch his eyes out.

In truth, her sagging shoulders and downcast eyes troubled him. He suspected she had revealed something that she never wanted anyone to see. That's why she'd told him she hated him. The words had cut deeply—more deeply than he cared to admit. Still, there was a part of him that wanted to hold her, to soothe her fears and assure her that things would get better.

"Reckon you're tired of cold beans and jerky," he said, trying to coax her out of her fortress of silence.

She ignored him.

"A hot meal ought to make you feel better."

He would have had more response from the ghosts at the Alamo.

"'Course, if snake's not to your liking—" he peeled back the waxy green skin of a prickly pear cactus and set it on a plate, "you can try nopales."

She refused to acknowledge the delicacy he handed her. He shrugged, trying to ignore the hurt in his chest.

"Suit yourself."

Sitting, he spooned out a hearty portion of snake meat, but he couldn't keep his mind on his hunger. His gaze kept drifting to Fancy. The Texas sun, so deadly to Beth's complexion, had dusted the bridge of Fancy's nose with freckles. Her cheeks had turned a coppery brown, a shade that made the violet of her eyes more startling, the ivory of her teeth more vivid. Her curls, wild and unruly, had slipped from her braid when she struggled with him earlier; now the sheen of blue black wreathed her face like a mane. She looked like some exotic jungle cat sitting there, with her amethyst stare fixed on the fire and golden flames dancing in the center of her eyes. He wondered what she was thinking.

"So." He scooted backward, propping his spine against his saddle and balancing the plate on his knee. She was out of his reach now—which was good. He wasn't sure he could trust himself not to touch her. Or worse, to let her go. "Is it the snake or the company that's got you well muzzled?"

She tossed him a scathing look. "They're pretty much related, aren't they?"

"Naw." A smile tugged at the corner of his mouth. "My daddy was a hurricane."

She pursed her lips and looked away.

"Now that we're on speaking terms again," he continued, swallowing his first bite of what turned out to be a damned tasty meal, "why don't you tell me where you hid those plates?"

"After the scam you pulled at the ranch? Forget it."

He winced inwardly. He might have known she'd refuse to forgive him. To her way of thinking, he was probably the most despicable kind of cad.

"C'mon, Fancy. Even you have to admit my finding you was for the best. Otherwise, you'd be lost, hungry, and short on ammo, smack in the middle of desperado country."

Her jaw hardened. Turning her shoulder on him, she began to spread her bedroll in short, jerky movements. She was wearing the look she'd worn at the ranch, when she'd called him "lying" and "no good."

"You're going to need a friend once we reach Carson."

She turned her back this time. He sighed. He was

beginning to think spitting and clawing was preferable to this mulish show of silence.

"Look, Fancy. I'm trying to help you. Don't you think it's time we called a truce?"

She tossed him a withering look. "You mean you want to make another *deal?*"

Jesus, was that why she was spreading her blankets? He pressed his lips into a grim line. She really didn't think much of him, did she?

"Be reasonable, Fancy. If the only thing I wanted from you was sex, I could have had it a dozen times by now."

She winced, biting her lip. He felt the creep of guilt. Now what? Had he hurt her feelings? He hadn't meant to. Hell, he thought she'd be relieved to know he wasn't going to jump her bones the first chance he got. Besides, she'd made it more than clear she preferred Santana—although God himself probably wondered why.

Pushing his plate away, Cord dragged a hand through his hair. Why couldn't she be reasonable?

He might come to regret his decision, but he wanted to help her. He knew he could never forgive himself if she died of some disease behind prison walls. Or if she emerged with her spirit shattered beyond repair. Telling himself that he'd only done his job would be poor consolation then.

Somehow, he had to find a way—a legal way—to keep her out of jail. The problem was, he didn't have the power to acquit her, much less pardon her. He was as helpless as she was when it came to her future, unless she agreed to help herself.

"Fancy, you don't have to be alone in this."

Her hands hesitated, hovering above the fold she'd been smoothing. It was the smallest of signs, the briefest indication that she was wavering, but it gave him hope.

"I can't help you if you don't give me the chance."

A small tremor moved through her. She bowed her head. For a long moment, she knelt there so still, so silently, that he thought she'd stopped breathing.

"Darlin', you're going to have to trust somebody

sometime," he said gently. "It might as well be me. Whether you want to admit it or not, I've been trying to keep you alive these last couple of weeks. And when we're in Nevada, I'll do everything I can, within the limits of the law, to keep you out of jail too. I promise. I swear it. I just don't know what else I can say to convince you."

Fancy swallowed hard, brushing a shameful tear from her cheek. He would keep her out of jail? Truly?

She drew a ragged breath. Trusting had never come easily to her. In truth, she couldn't remember the last time it had come at all. She'd learned to find an element of safety in cynicism, especially where men—even Diego—were concerned.

"Wit and heart, that's all a woman can call her own, Fancy." She could almost hear her mother's bitter voice. *"A man will try to rob you of them. Once he does, he'll leave you behind. You have to hold something back. You have to keep something for yourself."*

The advice had worked with Diego. She had always stayed safe, no matter how bad things got, because she had kept a piece of herself away from the hurt.

Now here was Cord, asking her to put her life in his hands. He promised her freedom, but he had made that pledge to her once before. She had trusted him, and she had been hurt. Deeply. Dare she play the fool again?

God help her. Did she have any other conceivable choice?

She pulled her blanket more tightly around her. Turning, she sat again and willed herself to face him. The effort to hold his gaze took every scrap of nerve she possessed. Did this plain-speaking lawman with the bottomless eyes and the heart-tripping smile realize just how much he was asking of her?

"All right." She forced her reluctant tongue to move again. "I'll take you to the plates. They're in a hollow tree, just outside of Carson. But you need to know that—" she hesitated, at war with her doubts, "I only have two of the plates. Wilkerson rode off with the other pair, and the silver too."

Crouching lower beneath her blanket, she watched him warily, searching for traces of subterfuge. The moments passed, and she couldn't detect a single sign of deceit.

"So you and Wilkerson—"

"Wilkerson's dead," she cut in flatly. "The sonuvabitch left me to freeze to death in Nevada. He was a small-time operator, hoping to capitalize on Diego's contacts. He headed south, trying to reach Mexico. But he never made it past Fort Worth."

"So those plates are in Tarrant County?"

She hesitated. In truth, she didn't know.

"They could be in Tarrant County," she admitted, thinking their location depended entirely on where Ned Wilkerson was hiding out.

"Does Applegate know?"

"No. At least, he didn't two weeks ago. Marshal Brand and Sheriff Applegate are square—unless you count weakness for loose women as a crime."

Cord pressed his lips together. She had the distinct sense he'd disapproved of the loose woman dig, which was more in keeping with the ethical Cord she'd come to know.

"Looks like I'll be heading back to Fort Worth, then," he said.

A ray of hope broke through the chinks in her doubt. "Tomorrow?"

"No." His voice held a note of apology. "Tomorrow I wire Clem Applegate. Hopefully he's had enough time to cool off since the jail break. Then I'll be taking you to Carson."

"But—"

"Fancy." He spoke with that firm, caring tone he usually reserved for the boys. "I'd have to jail you at Fort Gates if I didn't take you north. This way, I can talk to Governor Underwood in Nevada. I can tell him how you've turned the plates over and try to work out some kind of deal. A *legal* deal."

Disappointment dragged her back down to earth. She should have known better than to aspire so high. A deputy

U.S. marshal didn't have the power to pardon her, even if he really did want to see her go free. So whether in Fort Gates or Carson City, she didn't see how she was going to avoid jail time. Unless . . .

"I think I know who has the plates," she blurted.

Cord arched an eyebrow. She tried to appear calm, even though her heart was hammering so hard against her ribs that she could scarcely catch her breath.

"If I tell you who it is, you can't come back to Texas without me. That's the deal," she added hurriedly. "They're my contacts. They can smell the law a mile away. I have to go in for you. And I have to have Diego's help. In exchange, I want our pardons."

"What? Pardon Santana?"

She winced at his vehemence. Still, she thought Diego might cooperate if the charges against him were dropped.

"Diego knows all the tricks. And he has a reputation in the underground. My contacts will accept him. Besides, it could take months for some agent like a Pinkerton to earn their trust. By that time, the plates will disappear again."

Cord reined in his temper, but just barely. Pardon Santana? God in heaven. Had she forgotten how the bastard tried to put a bullet through her head?

Filling his lungs, he held his breath for a judiciously long count of ten. Then he spoke again.

"Robbing a government train is the least of Santana's offenses. You're talking about loosing a murderer. And I won't stand for that."

"I can't let him hang, Cord."

"Why? After what he did to you, hanging is too good for him."

She stiffened. He imagined he saw a flicker of pain cross her face before she turned away.

"It's true that Diego and I have had our differences—"

"Differences? Lady, Diego Santana's not good enough to lick your boots."

She started. For a moment, she looked genuinely surprised. Then doubt crisscrossed her features. She tucked her chin and pulled her blanket closer. "You just don't understand. Diego was the only person who ever saw something in me. Something worthwhile. There's no escaping what I am, Cord."

He frowned. "What are you talking about?"

"You said it yourself. Back in Fort Worth."

He must have looked as puzzled as he felt, because she smiled mirthlessly.

"A lying, cheating thief. Don't you remember? And a whore, Cord. I'm also a whore."

He flinched. God in heaven. Had he really called her such things? To his mortification, he remembered he had.

"Fancy, I'm sorry," he said, his heart climbing to his throat. "I was angry. That's no excuse, of course. I should never have—"

"Called a spade a spade?" she whispered hoarsely. "But that's what you're good at, Cord: the truth. My talents lie elsewhere."

His face burned with his shame. If he could have taken back every careless word, every unkind thought, he would have. He couldn't bear to know how she'd taken them all to heart.

"It takes more than talent to be honest," he said, his tone gruff with remorse. "It takes courage. And you've got that, Fancy. You proved it with Blood Wolf, and you proved it with Slade."

She bowed her head. "Maybe I need a different kind of courage, then."

Her voice sounded so tiny and ashamed, it nearly ripped his heart out. "Fancy . . ." He crossed to her side and knelt, reaching out to hold her.

She cringed. "Please. Don't touch me. I . . . couldn't bear it."

He dropped his hands instantly. Frustration welled up inside him. He remembered the scars on her back, and his frustration surged to anger. Had Santana made the simple touch of kindness something for her to dread?

Damn him. Damn the bastard to hell.

"Fancy." He struggled to keep the helpless outrage from his voice. "Maybe once, a long time ago, you didn't have a choice. Maybe you couldn't change the kind of life you led. But you have different choices now. As long as Santana stays in jail—"

"No. You don't understand," she broke in tremulously. "Diego didn't make me a whore. I was born to it. My mother was one, and when she started getting too old to attract regular customers, she threw herself over the balcony. I didn't want to end up like her, so I tried to run away . . . many times. But they always found me and forced me to come back."

Cord's gut knotted to hear this newest evidence of the horrors she had lived through. "Who? Who forced you?"

"The madam. Old Barrows, the owner. All their thugs." She shrugged bravely, but her face had paled with private torment. "Even if I could have found a lawman who wasn't in Barrows's back pocket, Barrows had a contract for my services. My mother signed it, and I was bound by it until my twenty-first birthday.

"One day," she continued wistfully, tears glimmering on her lashes, "Diego started visiting me at the house. He said if I went away with him, if I helped him work the suckers and the fools, I would never have to whore again. Ever. At the time, it seemed like a dream come true. He staked his casino for my freedom, and he won. While Barrows stood there red faced and fuming, Diego lit a cigar and burned my contract. I thought he was the most wonderful man in the world. And I fell in love with him that day."

Cord swallowed. *Love.* She'd said it again. And this time, he had reason to believe her.

"But Fancy, surely your feelings have changed. I mean—" he fidgeted, trying to find a delicate way to discuss an indelicate situation, "Santana didn't treat you with kindness. Or respect."

Her chin trembled. She hugged her arms across her chest and refused to meet his gaze. "Diego may have done hurtful things, but he never went back on his word. He never forced me to whore. That in itself was like saving my life. I can't turn my back on him now. He needs my help."

Cord felt his patience slipping away. He grappled with the intense desire to grab her shoulders and shake her until some sense rattled loose in her brain.

"Fancy, Diego Santana beat you within an inch of your life. And he would have shot you down if I hadn't fired on him first during the robbery."

Her head jerked up. Too late, he realized his mistake. Santana's treachery was something she had carefully blanked from her memory. He could see the resentment smoldering like branding irons deep inside her eyes.

"I don't know why I expected you to understand," she said harshly. "All you're really interested in is hanging outlaws. And recovering the plates so you can cash in on the reward."

"Fancy, that is not true."

"So prove it."

He ground his teeth. He thought he *had* proved it. Several times.

"All right," he said. "I might be able to get Santana's charges reduced. But that's as far as I'm willing to go."

"You said you would help me!"

"I am helping you, dammit. Setting Santana free is the absolute worst thing that could happen to you. He'll talk you into running away with him again. He'll have you cheating and robbing, maybe even killing a few men. Where's it all going to end, Fancy? And what are you going to do next time if I'm not around to stop him from putting a bullet through your head?"

A big silvery tear rolled down her cheek.

"Go to hell," she whispered fiercely, snatching up her bedroll.

She stalked to the other side of the fire, spread her blankets, and flopped down, tugging the wool to her chin.

Then, as if sensing the heat of his glare, she turned her back on him.

Chapter Fourteen

Cord had been too frustrated to sleep well that night. To lie in such proximity to Fancy, her lush curves silhouetted by amber flames and violet shadow, had been only part of the distraction. True, he'd been sorely tempted to bridge the space between them. With no brothers, no aunt, no dishonorable promises to come between them, the only way to keep his mind off the simmering heat in his loins was to repeat silently over and over that she hated him. With a passion. And that wasn't the kind of passion he wanted from a woman.

He didn't understand why his best intentions always went wrong where Fancy was concerned. She seemed determined to misinterpret or flat out disbelieve everything he said. What was worse, she seemed equally determined to put all of her faith in Santana. He couldn't fathom such a blind loyalty.

Thinking there must be something more he could say to hammer the truth home, Cord tried once more on their way to Fort Gates. In vivid detail, he pointed out all the dangers of living life on the run—especially with an inveterate sinner like Santana. He pleaded with her to supply her contacts' names so he would be bargaining from a position of power when he went to the governor.

Reasoning with the woman proved just as futile as before. Half the time, he suspected she'd turned deaf as well as blind.

She wore a stony, indifferent expression during their entire ride. When he fired off telegraphs to New Mexican lawmen, seeking information about Bart Wilkerson's old cohorts, she didn't even bat an eye in challenge.

During their stage ride to Waco the next day, she proved even more unreachable, if that was possible. His hopes of coaxing a confession out of her were dashed the instant the wife and daughters of Fort Gates's commander all clambered aboard the coach. They spent most of the ride giggling about charivaris and honeymoons and debating the merits of taffeta over satin for wedding gowns. As their chatter droned on and on above the jolts and bumps of the road, Cord thought he had never seen Fancy looking quite so grim . . . or so resigned. He imagined she was thinking of Santana again. The thought gnawed at his gut all the way to Waco.

The stage pulled into town late in the afternoon, just as the commercial district was closing down and the saloons were picking up. Cord watched the proliferation of swaggering young gunslingers with a wary eye, but he didn't anticipate trouble. He guessed they had stopped in Waco on their way to Austin to sign up for the Rangers. Now that Yankee Reconstruction had finally released its stranglehold on Texas, the legislature had proudly reactivated the state's legendary law force. Cord suspected half the rowdies in town were eager recruits.

Main Street was bustling with people, most of whom were headed for the hotels or the saloons. The rare exception seemed to be their own traveling companions. The belles of Fort Gates set off briskly for the dry goods store, which, they had confided earlier, carried a far better selection of nuptial fabrics than the trading post.

Fancy said nothing as the ladies hurried away, but Cord glimpsed the longing in the look she cast after them. The store's window was dressed with colorful bolts of calico, muslin, and silk. Even the plainest cloth made her own flannel and denim look shabby. His heart went out to her.

"Maybe the store has some traveling clothes," he said

impulsively. "Let's take a look. I know the owner. He'll float me the money."

Her head snapped back around. Considering the glare she gave him, one would have thought he'd offered to fit her with a hair shirt.

"If my clothing embarrasses you, Marshal, you have no one to blame but yourself. You sailed my gown down the river. Remember?"

He felt his face heat. Of course he remembered. He remembered her burlesque only too well. Most nights, he had a dream about it.

"No offense, Fancy. It's just that Zack's shirt and jeans aren't . . . well, you know. And I thought you might have a hankering to get gussied up."

Her eyes narrowed.

"Or maybe get more comfortable," he corrected himself hastily.

This attempt at conciliation only kindled a brighter, more dangerous gleam in her eyes.

"I mean . . ." He fidgeted. Confound it, why did she always have to get so ornery? He knew he was digging a deeper hole for himself, but he didn't see any way of backing out now. "Look. I just thought you'd like to wear the kind of clothes that come natural to a lady, okay?"

She laughed. The sound came suddenly, and it startled him. Harsh and explosive, it was as bitter as day-old coffee.

"Save your money, tin-star. I'm no lady. Besides, where I'm going, I hear they wear uniforms."

"Fancy—"

"Let's just get this over with, shall we?"

She spun on her heel and marched toward the town marshal's office. The shadow of a nearby picket fence fell across her path—like bars, he thought uncomfortably. He felt his stomach roil.

"Wait!" Hurrying after her, he grabbed her arm and pulled her back against his chest. "I said I'd keep you out of jail, dammit, and I meant it."

He felt her shiver. Her breathing quickened, and a pale flush crept up her neck.

"Then where—?"

"The hotel."

She stiffened in his arms. A twinge of hurt stabbed his chest. He wished she would let him hold her. He didn't care that a hundred eyes might be watching. To hell with them all. He wanted to stroke her hair and taste her lips and swear that he would never let anyone hurt her again.

She wrenched herself free and rounded on him. Her eyes pierced through him like violet steel.

"You forfeited your chance at the ranch, Rawlins. Don't presume I'll deal you that hand again."

"What?" He gaped. His neck heated so fast under his collar, he thought his ears might steam. "That's a helluva thing to say to me, woman. A *helluva* thing to say."

"Oh? But I thought you liked honesty."

He ground his teeth. Honesty, yes. Contrariness, no. "I was going to put you under house arrest. Your own room. No bars. *No deals."*

Her head tilted skeptically, and she folded her arms across her chest. "Do you really expect me to believe it never crossed your mind to—"

"Yes! Yes, I do, dammit. And frankly, I'm tired of paying for every bastard whose mind it *did* cross. When are you going to cut me some slack, Fancy? Even you've got to see I'm not out to do you wrong."

She looked chagrined then, but he was too furious to listen to an apology. He led her to the hotel across the street, locked her in a second-story room, then asked the town marshal to post a deputy beneath her window.

Thanks to Fancy's obstinacy, Cord spent most of the night sending out wires and piecing together information about Bart Wilkerson and his estranged family. Messages arrived for him almost hourly from lawmen in New Mexico Territory and counties across Texas. He finally deduced that Bart's cousin, Ned, was the man Fancy was protecting.

While watching her the next morning in Waco's train depot, Cord felt certain he had guessed correctly. A far cry from her usual poker-faced self, she turned whiter than bleached bones when he casually dropped Ned's name.

"You're shooting in the dark, Marshal," she retorted coolly, but her eyes held a wary, cornered look as he stood over her on the loading platform.

"I am, eh?"

She shrugged, clasping her hands over her knee, but she couldn't quite hide the tremor in them. Although he had relieved her of Wes's six-shooter, he hadn't bothered to cuff her, even here, among the crowds. He'd figured she would stick by his side to avoid getting dragged off by a vigilante. Her wanted poster was staring down at them from every corner of the depot. So, too, were some locals who had dollar signs dancing in their brains.

"Well now." Propping his boot on the bench beside her, Cord leaned an arm across his thigh and pushed his hat back with his thumb. He couldn't help but notice the gray hollows under her eyes. He suspected she hadn't slept much. She hadn't eaten much, either—for dinner or for breakfast. She was scared out of her mind, knowing she was on her way to Carson, but she'd rather be damned than trust him. Her smoldering hostility was beginning to stick in his craw.

"Your friend, Sheriff Applegate, doesn't think I'm following a cold trail," he said. "Fact is, Clem's been having a regular Wilkerson stampede. First Bart. Then Ned and the boys. Kind of makes you wonder what all those New Mexican outlaws find so consarned fascinating about Tarrant County."

Her pulse leaped, pumping hard in the hollow of her throat. She rallied quickly, though. "Perhaps they're paying their respects to Bart's grave."

He felt the corners of his mouth twitch. She really was at her wit's end. He didn't know whether to be disappointed or amused that she would try to divert him with such a weak excuse.

"Now that would be a switch, wouldn't it? Ned finding

some Christian charity? 'Course, I'm not saying it isn't possible. Maybe he did ride to Fort Worth to forgive ol' Bart for gouging out his eye."

She reddened. She apparently hadn't known the reason behind the Wilkersons' bad blood. Maybe she'd never met Ned. That latter suspicion helped confirm in his mind that he'd made the right decision when he decided to hide Fancy at Aunt Lally's ranch. He didn't like the prospect of lying— and to Nevada's governor, of all men—but he just didn't see how he could keep her out of jail unless he insisted she was necessary to help him infiltrate the Wilkerson gang.

Of course, detective work was much too dangerous for a woman. He had no intention of taking her into that pit of vipers.

Watching her stare north along the tracks, he could almost feel the worry she tried to conceal. An outlaw usually wanted to talk when his back was against the wall. Fancy had been more stubborn than most, but her time was running out.

He took pity on her.

"Maybe you know something more about Ned you'd like to tell me," he prompted gently, trying to make confessing easier on her pride.

She refused to look at him. "What would I know about some New Mexican outlaw?"

Dammit, Fancy, come on.

He leaned closer, so close that he inhaled the just-washed scent of lilac in her hair and the sweetness of sun-dried flannel. After she refused his offer of clothing, she had holed herself up naked in her hotel room to wait for Zack's old shirt and jeans to dry. He'd deduced that when he saw her bloomers fluttering from the window. The rest of the night, he'd wiled away the hours imagining all the creamy, sun-shy flesh that lounged on the bed next door.

If he hadn't learned to be such a consarned celibate, he might have beat down Fancy's door. God knew, he'd stood on her threshold and thought about it long enough. In the end, though, he'd kept his promise and gone back to his room. He'd decided he wanted all of Fancy, not just some little piece she'd learned to give away.

"I'll tell you a secret," he murmured, letting his breath tease a curl above the pinkening lobe of her ear. "I got a wire from the territorial marshal yesterday."

Her own breath released in a ragged rush. "So?"

"So . . ." Damn, but she had the moistest strawberry-red lips. "I know all about Ned's career as a wartime counterfeiter. And how Reconstruction came to Missouri, spoiling his dreams of grandeur. I know that he and the boys hightailed it to New Mexico Territory to mine for silver, except that they found thieving and murdering more profitable. Easier, too, since the law's still scrabbling for a foothold there. And I know that a gang of Wilkersons has been terrorizing Tarrant and Johnson counties ever since ol' Bart kicked the bucket last month."

"Now then." He forced himself to retreat an inch or two. The temptation to kiss her was just too strong. "Don't you think it's time you came square with me?"

He sought her eyes once more. He spied a softness there, a misty uncertainty that bordered on yearning. It stole his breath away.

"Fancy." He laid his hand on top of hers. It felt so tiny. So soft. It quaked at his touch, and he tightened his fingers around it. For one precious moment, her thumb gripped his fingers in return.

"Help me, Fancy. Help me so I can help you."

She blinked back tears. He sensed she was close, so very close to trusting him. That was all he cared about now.

"I'm afraid," she said hoarsely.

"I know, darlin'. But you don't have to be. This is one gamble you can't lose."

The telltale clatter began on the tracks. She tensed, and he gripped her hand harder.

"Fancy."

A high, hooting whistle stirred the crowd. A frenzy of parasol-snapping and bag-grabbing ensued. Among all the hugging, kissing, and good-byes, the black hats of the porters could be glimpsed bobbing toward their stations.

Fancy's eyes locked with his. "This is it? The train to Carson?"

He nodded.

The floorboards began to vibrate, rattling beneath their feet.

"Can you really do what you said you would?" She leaned closer, raising her voice to be heard above the clamor. "Can you really keep Diego from the gallows?"

"I'll do everything humanly possible."

Her eyes were pleading. "And you'll get me permission to see him?"

He frowned. He had reservations about visits, not the least of which was his fear that seeing Santana again would reaffirm her love for him. Nevertheless, he didn't see how he could deny her request without being cruel. Besides, one brief visit couldn't do too much harm, could it? She wouldn't see the snake again for twenty years.

"I'll talk to the warden," he said grudgingly.

Her chest rose and fell on a long, tremulous breath. At last she nodded.

"All right, Cord." Her voice was almost lost in the squeal of iron brakes. "I'll tell you whatever you wish to know."

Fancy couldn't sit still. Up and down, back and forth, she paced. She could feel Cord's speculative gaze on her as she prowled the suffocating box he'd called the Nevada State Prison's interrogation room. He said nothing of his thoughts, though. He simply sat with his boots outstretched, his ankles crossed, and his arms folded over his chest. She imagined he was counting the number of times she passed by.

She stole a glance at his face. Etched in sunbronzed relief, the chiseled features betrayed nothing of his feelings. She wondered if he was worried. He didn't look it—not since he assured her he had a plan. She couldn't help but wonder what it was. She just hoped his scheme was better than his last idea to establish headquarters at Aunt Lally's ranch.

His negotiation with the governor hadn't gone as well as she had hoped. Even though Cord had been armed with her pair of minting plates and all the information she had on Bart and Ned Wilkerson, he achieved nothing better than a draw at the governor's office. She'd known his news was bad the minute she threw open her hotel door and saw the thunder on his brow.

"The governor agreed to your pardon," he'd announced in a gruff, frustrated voice, "as long as you cooperate fully in my search for Ned Wilkerson and the other pair of plates."

She nodded, holding her breath, bracing herself for the worst. "And Diego?"

He frowned. "If I were you, I'd worry a little more about Fancy. Governor Underwood only gave me a month to bring the plates back in."

She choked, clutching the back of a chair for support. "But that's ridiculous! We'll need a week just to reach Wilkerson's place, and another week to get back to Carson!"

"I know. I'm working on that. But for now, we've got to move fast. Our train leaves for Texas in an hour. You don't have much time, but if you absolutely must see Santana, I'll take you to the prison. He'll be standing trial for aggravated robbery with intent to commit murder. The judge won't hang him on those charges, but Santana will be seeing the inside of a jail cell for a good, long spell."

Fancy shuddered. *A good, long spell.* That translated to ten, maybe twenty years, according to the prison warden. He had also told her Diego spent most of the last four months in the infirmary. She'd been surprised that the chief administrator of a state prison could be so easily hoodwinked by Diego's scams. She supposed she shouldn't have been, though. Once again, her lover had proven himself the king of all frauds.

But what if Diego really wasn't milking his injuries for all they were worth?

She bit her lip as the voice of guilt needled her. The image of a crippled, broken Diego filled her mind, and she wrestled with the feelings that image evoked. Perhaps she shouldn't be so cynical. She herself had thought his wounds were bad enough on the night of the robbery to conclude that he was dead. Would he believe her when she explained that was why she'd deserted him?

She swallowed, clutching her cipher closer. Though she tried to tell herself her worries were absurd, that Cord had deliberately put these thoughts of danger into her head, there was no denying she was scared. Even with the best intentions, Cord couldn't possibly save her if Diego decided she had betrayed him. Diego had an inordinate fondness for revenge, and she knew he would find her, no matter how long or how far he had to look.

Fancy smiled grimly to herself. Not for the first time did she wish she had attracted the attention of an upstanding, trustworthy man like Cord on that fateful day seven years ago, when Diego first came to the whorehouse. Being a practical woman, however, she had learned to make the best of the hand fate dealt her.

She had also learned to guard her back.

Certain that any conversation she might have with Diego would be monitored, and assuming that any letter she might try to pass to him would be censored, she had planned for their meeting by preparing a cipher. She had paid a visit to the hotel's desk clerk and had sweet-talked him out of his copy of *Tales of the Grotesque and Arabesque* by Edgar Allan Poe, a work eerily suited to Diego's tastes. By underlining words on random pages, she had composed a message.

Cord, of course, had been suspicious. He'd riffled through the volume, searching for straight razors and knives. She'd held her breath as he handled the book. But whether he didn't have the patience for reading, or whether he was too preoccupied with plans for their mission, he'd never challenged the book after that.

Thus, using one of Diego's oldest tricks, she'd been able to smuggle her message inside the prison. She'd explained in the book how she must accompany Cord back to Eulalie Barclay's ranch; how she must work with him to find Ned Wilkerson; and how she must return the plates and all the silver, even if it meant the end to Diego's dream of a counterfeiting empire.

"I agreed to cooperate with Rawlins only because he promised me you wouldn't hang," she assured Diego. "I tried every trick I knew to get you pardoned; I swear it. But the governor wouldn't deal. The best I could do was get your charges reduced."

And to get her own pardon.

She didn't tell him that, though. She didn't dare. There was still the chance, albeit a long one, that he would be acquitted.

Even though a lonely, wistful side of her prayed for such a miracle, she had another side, a confused and guilty side, that dreaded the possibility. What if Diego blamed her for his capture? What if he came after her?

The sound of approaching footsteps jarred Fancy back to her harsh surroundings. Spinning toward the door, she hugged her book and listened. An odd tapping and clanking accompanied the ringing bootfalls. She had a moment to wonder at those sounds before the door was thrown wide. A burly guard pushed his prisoner into the room and slammed the door behind him.

"Diego," she whispered in horror.

Gone was the cocky caballero she had adored in her youth. In his place was a gaunt and bitter man who looked at least ten years older than his thirty-five years. Dressed in the inevitable black-and-white prison garb, he leaned heavily on a cane as he shuffled forward, dragging his ankle chains. His uniform hung from his shoulders like a great striped sheet; his knuckles were skeletal knobs beneath skin that looked more saffron than olive.

She felt the sting of tears as he halted before her. The lustrous blue highlights were gone from his dark hair, dulled now by threads of iron gray. His once pencil-thin mustache, which he had always taken such care to groom, drooped over his lip like a piece of frayed rope. Only his eyes seemed the same, holding the spark of deviltry that had first endeared him to her. When he gazed past her to Cord, they burned like hellfire.

"Diego," she whispered again, trying to keep the anguish from her voice.

An eternity passed. She swallowed, feeling Diego smolder. She felt the fury and hatred he'd bottled up, all directed at the lawman who had robbed him of his freedom. She imagined she could see the rapier-keen mind working on the other side of those pitch-black eyes, and for a moment, her concern for Diego's health dissolved into fear. Fear for Cord.

"*Querida.*" Diego's gaze turned her way at last. It settled on the book at her breast, and a cunning smile curved his lips. He straightened, holding out an arm to her. "*Por fin, estamos reunidos.*"

We are reunited at last. Her vision blurred with tears. She had waited so long to hear his voice, to feel his arms around her again, so why were her feet suddenly rooted to the spot? She forced herself to step forward, and he reached for her, plucking the book from her hands before he clasped her to his chest. She felt his ribs, like iron rails, jutting beneath his shirt.

Oh God, she thought, look what prison had done to him. She wished she could honestly say his suffering wasn't deserved.

Dutifully, she raised her head for his kiss. When his mouth covered hers, it felt as dry as paper, as cool as moss. Her lips responded, but her mind reeled. What had happened? Where was the spark?

Diego's hands gripped her buttocks, dragging her hips hard against his own. The nudge of his swelling manhood embarrassed rather than tantalized her. She knew she shouldn't mind that Cord watched as she was fondled; she knew she shouldn't wonder what he thought, or if he cared. Diego was the man who wanted her, the man whose need for her was clear. Even so, it was difficult to forget how her pulse had skyrocketed and her insides had throbbed when Cord's hungry lips feasted on her own.

What was wrong with her? She shouldn't compare. Trying

to atone, she let Diego rub his manhood against her mound. She let him arch her spine and crush her breasts and thrust his tongue inside her mouth. She waited for the fiery throb that used to make her knees go weak with wanting, but the best her female parts could do was give a nervous twitch.

"*Querida*," Diego murmured again, raising his head. He held her face captive and fixed her with his shrewd, questing gaze. "*Te eché de menos. ¿Dónde*—"

"He understands Spanish," she whispered quickly, trying to distract him. She needed time to collect her thoughts. If Diego sensed the ambivalence of her ardor, he would definitely think she had betrayed him. She needed time alone with him, time to feel the old way, before she'd met Cord.

"*¿Sí?*" A tiny smile tugged at Diego's lips. She had a moment to worry about what he was thinking before his hypnotic stare released her.

"*Buenas noches, señor federale*," he mocked in his lilting Castilian. "The señorita and I wish a moment of privacy. Is there not someone else you can shoot and arrest?"

"You're to be watched at all times," Cord said brusquely.

"Ah. You wish to learn from my lovemaking, no?"

Cord felt his jaw twitch, despite his struggle to suppress his anger. Ignoring Santana's taunts was going to be a true test of forbearance. His patience had already been tried while he watched the outlaw maul Fancy. But watching her subject herself to all the slobbering and pawing—that had been far worse. He'd had to grip the arms of his chair to keep from tearing the lovers apart.

"You've got ten minutes, Santana," he said coldly. "Don't waste it by trying to goad me."

"Ten minutes? That is all?" The outlaw looked stricken. Wrapping his free arm around Fancy's waist, he molded her possessively to his side. "But we are affianced, señor. We planned to be married before your bullets shot me down and shattered my knee."

Fancy started; Cord tensed. Was it true? he wondered. Had she really promised herself to the snake? And if so, why hadn't she said as much?

Hastily, he sought her eyes. She was too busy gazing at Santana's cane and blinking back tears to notice his concern.

"Won't you reconsider, señor?"

Cord thought he might be sick when he saw the outlaw smirk above Fancy's head. For her sake, he had actually been ready to consider Santana's request. But now he had confirmation that Santana was using her. He was trying to turn her into a weapon—and she was too caught up in her own heartache to recognize the truth.

"You're wasting time," Cord bit out acidly. "Nine minutes, Santana."

The outlaw shifted sad eyes to Fancy. "Señor Rawlins is a cold man, *chiquita*. He brings you here only to torment me, I think."

She fidgeted, and a frown marred her brow. "Diego—"

"Let us sit awhile," he murmured, raising her hand to his lips. "For these brief minutes, I would not have you think of me as crippled."

Cord felt his gut roil. Glimpsing the distress on Fancy's face, he imagined Santana had just racked up another point against him. The outlaw looked downright pathetic, hobbling with his walking stick, stumbling over his chains. Cord suspected that proclaiming Santana a fraud now would do little to even their score.

Each of the next eight minutes dragged by like an eon. Sitting with his teeth clenched and his eyes narrowed, Cord watched as they whispered. An occasional tear would spill down Fancy's cheek, and Santana would brush it away. Or stroke her hair. Or kiss her hand. They sat knee to knee, their fingers laced upon the table, their foreheads all but touching. It made Cord's blood boil.

Finally, after every single one of his nerves had been stretched to their utmost limits, the eighth minute drew to a close. Fancy must have sensed her time was up. Choking back a sob, she threw her arms around Santana's neck.

"Don't give up hope, Diego," she pleaded thickly. "You won't have to live out the rest of your life in prison. There are always appeals. We—we can still be wed."

Cord stood so quickly, his chair banged against the wall. "Time's up, Santana."

"Surely it cannot be, señor. Check your timepiece again, *por favor*."

The outlaw hugged Fancy close to his murderous heart. He had the audacity to smirk again, when she couldn't see it, and Cord felt his fingers flex over an empty holster. Too bad he'd surrendered his gun to the guard.

"I said your time's up, Santana. Fancy, wait for me outside."

She blinked uncertainly at him, but he had used the tone even Wes dared not disobey.

"You . . . aren't coming with me?"

"I have questions for Santana."

Reluctance etched her features, but she withdrew from Santana's arms. The criminal rose with her, leaning heavily on his cane. He let Fancy cling to him for a moment longer, gave her one last hungry kiss, then smiled, raising a hand in sad farewell.

Cord didn't think the leather-brained guard would ever close the door.

"So." Santana turned slowly, putting on a great show as he limped back to his chair. "You have questions, señor. Do you wish to learn more about kissing, or—" he sat, his lips twisting in oily mirth, "do you need instruction in the use of your prick?"

Cord managed a cold, tight smile. He reminded himself that Santana's only weapon was his tongue.

"What do you know about Wilkerson?"

"Wilkerson?" Santana rolled the name around his mouth, giving the *r* an exaggerated trill. "It is Anglo, no?"

"Ned Wilkerson," Cord persisted, ignoring the man's sass. "Do you know him?"

Genuine surprise flickered through Santana's eyes. They were as black as the devil's back pocket—and concealed twice as much sin.

"What would I know of a cattle rustler?"

"So you've never met?" Cord asked skeptically.

Santana shrugged, his expression mocking. "I am a businessman, señor, not a thief."

Cord let that wisecrack slide by too. With the train leaving in twenty minutes, he had precious little time to verify the names of Santana's contacts in the Mexican underground. Fancy had told him what she could, but her information had been sketchy—no doubt due to Santana's plan to double-cross her. Although there were few men in Mexico with the kind of money necessary to purchase all four minting plates, Cord knew he wouldn't have time to track them all down if his plan to infiltrate the Wilkerson gang backfired.

"Wilkerson's in Texas," he said to Santana. "I thought you might have an idea where."

Santana cocked his head, as if trying to fathom Cord's reasoning. *"Tejas?* The bowels of *el diablo?* My condolences to Señor Wilkerson."

Cord frowned. Slurs against his homeland never failed to fry his patience. He thought of Fancy, though, and how her freedom could depend on the information he gleaned. Somehow, he reined in his temper once more.

"Who will Wilkerson try to sell those plates to?"

Santana laid his cane across the table. "Ah yes. The plates."

Leaning back in his chair, he steepled long, aristocratic fingers—fingers that looked too soft to dig a fence-post hole or plow a field. Cord had seen fingers like that before: They often belonged to men who destroyed what others built.

"These plates are a popular topic among you *federales.*" Santana wore the trace of a sneer. "It is the reward money, no? Three thousand dollars would seem like a fortune to a man who earns two hundred dollars a month."

Cord felt his own lip curl. "I reckon you *would* think it's the money, seeing as how you'd sell your best friend." He couldn't quite stop there. "Or kill her," he added in a low, gravelly voice.

Santana chuckled as if Cord's accusation were the most amusing of sallies.

"Now we get to the heart of the matter. I must confess, *mi amigo,* I thought you a man of more discerning tastes, a man of loftier standards. But you have developed a weakness for my fancy little whore."

"You sonuva—"

Something inside Cord snapped. He sprang forward, and Santana leaped upright, his chair crashing to the floor. As agile as a viper, he grabbed his cane, but Cord ducked, blocking the blow that would have smashed his skull.

"It's not the same when your victim fights back, eh, *amigo?"* Cord wrenched Santana's arm back. The cane went flying.

"Guard!" the outlaw shrieked, his eyes dilating as Cord's fists closed over his collar.

Santana was tall and rangy, but fury was pumping through Cord's veins. He heaved, dragging the writhing felon across the table.

The door crashed open. "Cord!"

He hardly heard Fancy's cry. He was too busy readying a fist to smash Santana's face in. He'd borne insults to his manhood, his profession, and Texas. But he would not stand by and let Fancy be used.

"Marshal!" Two guards hurried into the room.

"Madre de Dios, get Rawlins off me!"

Burly arms wrapped around Cord's chest. "Back off, Marshal. Back off I say!"

It took both guards to drag Cord from Santana, who rolled to his feet, crimson and wheezing. Determined to rearrange the outlaw's face, Cord strained for a moment longer, until he felt the stab of violet eyes from across the room. They cut through the fog in his brain like a hot knife through butter.

"Diego! Diego, are you hurt?" Fancy rushed to Santana's side, her hands anxious and shaking as they searched for bruises.

"No, my little dove," he panted, steadying himself against the table. "Shh, now. I am not in danger," he murmured in Spanish. He caught her fingers and pressed them to his heart.

"It is you I worry for while you are in the custody of this mad-dog policeman."

"Hell, Rawlins," one of the guards boomed behind him, "you trying to cheat the hangman of Santana's neck?"

Cord shook the man off. His pulse was crashing in his temples, and his breaths were harsh and ragged. What the devil was wrong with him? he wondered. He didn't beat prisoners. He didn't even call them names, most times. Yet he suspected that if he'd been given a second chance, he would have bypassed the collar and gone straight for Santana's throat.

"Take him to his cell," he bit out.

Santana staggered away from the table. He made up for his earlier show of fitness by letting his left knee buckle. The guards braced him. Sucking in her breath, Fancy hurried to retrieve the walking stick.

As she swept past him, Cord felt her gaze knife through him once more. Her concern for Santana hurt—really hurt— and he was hard-pressed not to grab the cane from her hands and break it over his knee. *Santana's using you,* he wanted to shout. *He doesn't love you, can't you see?*

He restrained himself, knowing he wasn't likely to change her opinion of him, much less of Santana, after what she'd just witnessed. So he stood there fuming, feeling cheated and monstrous and confused.

That's when it hit him. It hit him harder than a cannon ball in the gut.

I'm the one who's in love with Fancy!

"Gracias, mi amada." Santana gave her an unctuous smile, but he didn't waste additional time by wooing what he clearly thought he'd won. He turned his back on Fancy.

"I shall remember this night, Mr. Rawlins," he said in Spanish, his words made even more ominous by his deceptively pleasant tone. "And you will remember it also on the day I send you to hell."

Cord snorted. He didn't put much stock in threats made by a man in stripes and chains.

As Santana clanked down the hall, Cord picked up his hat and dusted it off. He used the moment to gather the nerve to face Fancy and her certain tirade.

When he did, he was surprised by what he saw. She didn't look angry. She looked whiter than death.

Chapter Fifteen

During the long ride back to Texas, Cord didn't say much about the fist fight. Fancy tried a couple of times to pry the full story out of him, but the best she ever got was a fierce glare and a snappish "Nothing happened that he didn't deserve."

So what *had* happened? she wondered. She had no illusions about Diego's part in the scuffle. Doubtless he had thrown cruel words one after the other like dueling knives until he hit Cord dead center in the heart. Part of her was angry with Cord for letting himself get bled. Another part was afraid for him. Diego was like a bulldog when he got vengeance between his teeth.

Dear God, she thought. Didn't Cord know better than to betray his secret weakness to his enemies?

Cord would be in dire danger if Diego ever got out of prison. A twenty-year sentence might be the most likely outcome of the trial, but a shorter punishment was also possible. Acquittal was too. What if she couldn't stop Diego from going after Cord?

The idea frightened her. The fact that it frightened her scared her even more. Why was she so worried about Cord? Why was she being so disloyal to Diego? For heaven's sake, *Diego* was the man who had asked her to marry him.

In truth, after seven years of waiting and hoping, she had

secretly begun to despair. But after their four-month separation, Diego had realized how much he loved her. Prison had made him a new man—that's what he claimed.

Well, she wasn't so sure, especially after the way he had threatened Cord. She supposed a man couldn't completely reform in four months—particularly a man who had as much reforming to do as Diego. But at least he had asked her to marry him. That was a good sign. Becoming Mrs. Diego Santana had always been her most cherished dream. She should be deliriously happy now that it might finally come true.

So why did the prospect of spending her whole life with Diego suddenly seem so . . . ominous?

She pondered that question a great deal on the journey back to Texas. She had little else to do, since Cord was so untalkative. He seemed to be concentrating on his strategy to locate Wilkerson and the plates. He'd made a hasty stop at the telegraph office just minutes before boarding the train in Carson, and he'd disembarked to visit the wiring stations in Abilene, Kansas, and in Dallas. Fancy had assumed he was hoping one of the prison guards would have better luck interrogating Diego than he, and had followed his last-minute orders to wire the names of Diego's buyers.

But Fancy didn't finally glean the full purpose behind Cord's errands until they arrived by stage at Fort Graham. Wes and Aunt Lally were waiting for them at the livery stable with horses.

"Got your wanted poster just like you asked, Cord, hot off the press yesterday," Wes said cheerfully, although he still looked a shade too pale to be out of his sickbed. He tossed Fancy an uncharacteristically shy smile. "Reckon that poster was your idea, ma'am. And a darn fine one it was too."

Fancy frowned. A poster would set Cord up as a target for every bounty hunter in Texas. Why would he risk his life like that when she could easily have vouched for him to Wilkerson? Uneasily, she sought Cord's eyes, but he was quick to avoid her gaze.

"What in tarnation are you doing out of bed, boy?" he

demanded, glaring up at Wes. "I can see clear to Kansas through that hole in your shoulder. Aunt Lally?" He turned to his bonnetted relative, gave her a quick peck on the cheek, and scowled down into her sun-crinkled face. "Why isn't the boy back home healing, where he belongs?"

"I'm no boy," Wes snapped before Aunt Lally could open her mouth. "And I am healed. I'm plenty healed. I'm not some no-account deputy who lollygags in bed while there's outlaws on the prowl. 'Sides. Someone had to keep Zack from turning vigilante. He's been madder than a rained-on rooster since we got twenty of our best steers rustled. He's laying odds the Wilkersons are to blame."

Lally turned to Fancy and winked, raising her brows in mock despair. "I must apologize for my nephews, my dear. I really did try to raise them better." Planting her hands on her hips, she glared up at Wes and Cord both. "Where are your manners? Did it ever occur to you fine gentlemen that Miss Fancy could use a bit of help with her bags? Or that she might like a moment's peace after listening to clattering rails and galloping hooves for days on end?"

"I just have my saddlebag," Fancy said, warming to Aunt Lally's thoughtfulness.

"A saddlebag? Good gracious, child, you can hardly fit a change of shoes in that."

"I'll get it," Wes volunteered, springing up onto the driver's box of the stagecoach.

Lally glared at Cord again. "You mean to tell me you let this poor child travel across three states and a territory wearing nothing but an old beat-up shirt and a pair of patched jeans?"

Cord pressed his lips together, and Fancy couldn't help but think he looked like a mutinous Wes.

"It's not like I didn't offer to buy her some lady's clothes," he said.

"*Offered?* Young man, you should have insisted."

Retracting the finger she'd been wagging under Cord's nose, Aunt Lally caught Fancy's elbow and marched her toward the trading post. "Come along, Fancy. Looks like we womenfolk have some spending to do."

Fancy wasn't given the chance to retreat. She wasn't even given the chance to protest. Aunt Lally haggled like a peddler, pointing at the store's only two skirts and shirtwaist blouses and barking orders to the blushing, bespectacled young man who scurried to find suitable drawers and stockings somewhere in the back room. Wes lounged against the counter. Grinning from ear to ear, he added his manly two-bits worth concerning the store's limited supply of unmentionables until Aunt Lally shooed him out the door. Cord had already made himself scarce.

Fifteen minutes later, Fancy owned new clothes, thanks to Aunt Lally's generosity. The skirts, which turned out to be full-legged riding pants, had been tailor-made in Saint Louis for a Mrs. Montgomery, who had neglected to claim them when her husband was transferred to Fort Phantom Hill. Judging by the ample waists of the blouses, Fancy suspected she was about ten pounds lighter than the intended owner, but Aunt Lally assured her a quick needle could put the ensembles to rights.

Cord was waiting for them by the family buckboard, which was loaded with bags of flour and other supplies for the ranch. Fancy hoped for a moment alone with him. She didn't want to alarm Aunt Lally, but she didn't like the sound of the plan he was hatching. Outlaw life was fraught with danger—not the least of which was a bullet in the back from another outlaw. Cord didn't need to bring the law down on his head as well. He was going to have enough trouble cheating and lying with the kind of conscienceless ingenuity that was necessary to keep himself alive.

Fancy never got an opportunity to challenge him, though. Wes was too determined to play suitor. He found numerous reasons to hover at her side—carrying her armload of packages, assisting her across the quagmire that stretched before the livery, handing her up into the wagon. Aunt Lally winked as she settled beside her.

"There isn't an unmarried girl within a hundred miles that

Wes hasn't sweet-talked at one time or another," she said. "Best watch your heart, Fancy, or else that young skirtchaser will try and steal yours too."

Fancy shifted uncomfortably. She wasn't exactly sure what Wes saw in her to make her worth his devotion—or to make him glare so fiercely at the brother he adored.

If Cord sensed the challenge in Wes's manner, he didn't show any sign. Fancy sighed, chastising herself for her twinge of disappointment. What had she been expecting? Unlike Wes, Cord would never see anything in her worth fighting over. Not after she'd been so foolishly honest and told him she was a whore.

Cord pressed the horses hard in his eagerness to make good time. Even so, the Barclay homestead was a good twelve hours away. Wes's gossip helped to pass the time, but his reminiscences of his brothers and their childhood scrapes made Fancy feel lonely. She began to realize just how much she had missed by being raised without a family.

Oh, she had had her mother to look out for her every now and then, when Mama hadn't been angry with her for getting under foot or jealous of her for growing up too pretty; and she had had the whores to act as her older sisters when they weren't nursing their own bruises. But every one of them had been too afraid of Barrows to stop him from beating her or locking her up—or forcing his way into her bed on the night of her twelfth birthday.

"You're a woman now," the whoremonger had jeered, "and it's high time you started earning your keep."

She shuddered, remembering his rum-soured breath and sweaty hands, and the pain that seemed to go on and on, not just between her legs but inside her soul, as if it had been fouled and blackened forever.

"Ma'am?"

She started, blinking rapidly, and noticed Wes leaning down from his saddle. He was peering at her under her hat brim.

"You all right, ma'am?" Worry etched his freckled face.

"Did I say something wrong? You aren't, er . . . crying, are you?"

"Of course she's not crying," Aunt Lally said briskly, but the glance she slid Fancy's way was motherly and full of concern. "You boys are forgetting this here's a city girl who's not used to the prairie sun. Seems like we ought to find ourselves a watering hole and give Miss Fancy a rest."

"I'm fine," Fancy said quickly. "Really," she added, her face heating beneath Cord's appraising stare.

"Reckon Aunt Lally's right," he said, shifting in his saddle. "A rest would do us all a bit of good."

"Honey Creek's not but a mile or so to the west," Wes said.

"Good idea, son. We'll stop there."

Wes made a face, despite Cord's compliment. Fancy guessed Wes was taking offense to being called "son," even though Cord had used the term as an endearment, as he always did.

Honey Creek proved to be a gushing torrent after the recent bout of spring thunderstorms. Wes, never far from her elbow, was quick to advise her another storm was on its way.

"Hear them bullfrogs croaking? They're singing to call down the rain."

Cord chuckled as he filled his canteen. "Son, that's nothing but an old wives' tale. You know that."

"Gnats are swarming low to the ground too," Wes retorted. "Gnats aren't ever wrong about rain. Right, Aunt Lally?"

Lally nodded solemnly, but she couldn't hide the twinkle in her eyes. Wes's mouth tightened. Fancy thought she'd better change the subject.

"So tell me, Wes, where's Zack today?"

He flopped down by her side among the blue and scarlet wildflowers. "Hard to say. He took some of the hands up north two days ago just in case them Wilkersons are hiding out near Comanche Peak."

Cord's head shot up, his face dripping with a handful of

creek water. "I thought I wired you boys to stay put and let me worry about the Wilkersons."

"Well, you know ol' Zack. He's about as tame as a tabby until somebody messes with his beeves. Then he kinda turns into a tiger. 'Sides, someone had to nail up your wanted posters in case them Wilkersons come back this way. I shipped the rest to Sheriff Applegate, like you said."

Fancy cast a sharp look at Cord, who was quick to evade it again. So that was what the wanted posters were for. With Cord's face hanging from every tree in Tarrant County, Wilkerson was likely to see the "proof" of Cord's crimes before the two men ever met. Cord probably thought those wanted posters were enough to gain him entry into Wilkerson's hideout, wherever that might be. But Wilkerson was really looking for her and her plates. Cord wasn't likely to get past Wilkerson's sentries without her.

"So who is this Frank Harris feller, Cord?" Aunt Lally asked. "Some name you made up for the wanted poster?"

"Naw, he's a counterfeiter," Wes said, "and a gambler too. He ran a saloon as a front out in Houston. Now he's serving time in Huntsville. That's why I put 'escaped' so big on the wanted poster."

Lally quirked a graying eyebrow. "And how do you know so much about Frank Harris, young man?"

"'Cause it's my job as Cord's deputy," Wes replied loftily.

He scooted closer to Fancy and leaned toward her. "Reckon we got our work cut out for us, huh, ma'am? I mean, passing Cord off as a sharper isn't gonna be easy. He's not any good at dice or poker since he won't cheat."

"Thanks, Wes," Cord said dryly. "I reckon I'll take that as a compliment."

"Wes does have a point," Fancy said, wondering how best to voice her reservations without alarming Aunt Lally—or exciting Wes. "Can you palm cards? Or shave dice?"

"Don't know. Never tried."

"Shoot." Wes fished in his shirt pocket and drew out a box of playing cards. "Then it's a good thing I bought these pasteboards for you in Fort Graham."

Lally's brow furrowed as she watched her youngest nephew fan the deck. "Wes, those cards are marked."

"'Course they are. Cord would lose the ranch if he had plain old pasteboards."

Cord gazed in amazement at his aunt. "You can read marked cards?"

"Well . . ."

"Sure she can," Wes said cheerfully. "She taught me."

Cord's jaw dropped. "You taught my kid brother how to cheat?"

Lally's face turned crimson. "Well, boys just aren't interested in quilting," she said, hiking her chin. "'Sides, Wes only does card tricks for the ladies. He's no more a cheat than you are, Cordero Rawlins."

Wes snickered, winking at Fancy. "Cordero. That's what Mama always used to call him. It means 'little lamb' in Spanish."

Cord grimaced. Fancy bit her lip and tried not to laugh.

"Now the way I see it," Wes breezed on, shuffling the deck like a Barbary Coast blackleg, "we only got about forty-eight hours to turn Cord into a sharper. Zack too."

"Now hold on a minute, son." Cord was frowning again. "Zack's got cattle to drive. If you're strong enough for long riding, then you're strong enough to prod beef."

"But I'm your deputy!"

"And a mighty fine one too. But Aunt Lally's depending on you boys to sell those beeves. I'd do it myself, if I didn't have to round up outlaws."

Wes looked mutinous. "Zack's got Juan and Carlos and the rest of the hands to drive cattle into railroad cars. Zack doesn't need me. 'Sides, I've never been as good at cutting and roping as he is. I'm better with a gun. Seems like I proved it, too, back in the alley against Slade."

Cord and Lally exchanged uneasy looks. Fancy shared their concern. Even if Wes could hold his own in a gunfight, she knew the boy would be no match for an ambush.

"Wes," she began gently, "no one is doubting your

ability. Or your courage. But you have to know you'll be putting Cord and me in danger by going undercover."

"Fancy's right," Cord said. "Besides, Aunt Lally will need your help keeping Fancy safe from the bounty hunters once you and Zack get back to the ranch."

"What?" Fancy's head snapped around. She stared incredulously at him. "You're going to leave me behind?"

"I'm going in alone," he said firmly, and rose.

Wes's face brightened considerably, but Fancy felt as if a fist had just smashed into her gut. Dear God, he wasn't joking.

"Cord, you can't go in alone. It would be—" She glanced at Aunt Lally and bit back the word *suicide* just in time. "It would be too risky. You need me to cover your back."

"The day I need a woman to cover my back is the day I turn in my six-shooter."

Lally snorted. "We ought to box his ears for that, Fancy."

He chuckled, shaking his head. He was wearing the same patient I-know-best smile that he always wore when his brothers protested his authority. Fancy understood now why Wes took such offense to it.

"We're wasting time, folks. I want to be back at the ranch by nightfall so I can ride out first thing tomorrow morning. Wes, why don't you go help Aunt Lally into the wagon."

"Cord!" Fancy jumped up, catching his sleeve. "Dammit," she said in a low, fierce voice, "I thought we had a deal. I said I would give you the plates only if you took me with you."

He looked surprised by her vehemence. "I would never hold you to a deal like that."

"Why?" Her heart slammed against her ribs as she imagined all the terrible things that could happen to a lone lawman inside a den of thieves. "Don't you trust me?"

His features softened, and he placed his hand over hers. "I trust you just fine, Fancy. I want you to be safe, is all."

He released her, and she swallowed. She couldn't ever remember Diego putting her safety before his own.

"Cord, you have to listen to me. You don't realize your danger—"

"Fancy." He looked vaguely amused—and irritated—that she doubted his ability to fend for himself. "It's settled. Now let's get a move on."

She bit her tongue on another protest. No matter how right she was, he would never back down. Not in front of an audience. She would have to continue this argument when she got him alone. Besides, she didn't want Wes and Lally worrying about him any more than they already were.

"All right, Cord," she said quietly. "For the sake of your family, I'll let this be settled." She looked him square in the eye. "For now."

Chapter Sixteen

Fancy prowled restlessly up and down the length of Cord's bedroom. She couldn't have slept even if she wanted to, knowing that he planned to get himself killed. If he rode alone, the only way he'd come back was in a pine box. Fancy knew that as surely as she knew she would never forgive herself if Wilkerson shot him. She had to stop Cord. The problem was, she didn't know how. Nothing she or the boys said had been enough to change his mind.

"Cord, I'm going to be frank," Zack had told him. "Riding alone is a dumb idea. Sure, you've been a Ranger, but you've never been a gambler. And you sure aren't any liar. Now, I can see why you wouldn't want to trust *her* any further than the nose on your face—"

"Hold on a minute, son," Cord interrupted, folding his arms across his chest. "Am I to understand this 'her' you're talking about is Miss Fancy?"

Zack frowned. The look he shot her left no doubt in her mind that things still had not been thoroughly patched between them.

"All I'm saying, Cord, is if you need someone to ride to hell for you, you can count on Wes and me. We're your brothers. She's a stranger. And an outlaw, at that."

"I see," Cord said coolly. He nodded toward the door. "Well, you've said your piece, Zack. Go wash up for dinner."

The boy's spine went rigid at this cursory dismissal. "Dinner can wait. This is important, Cord, and you aren't listening."

"No, Zack. You aren't listening." Cord's eyes glittered like shards of green ice. "Go cool off."

Zack's face darkened. Grabbing his hat, he stomped past her, nearly bowling over Wes, and slammed the back door. Wes started after him, looking for all the world as if he meant to start a brawl in her honor, but Cord caught his arm and spun him in the other direction.

"Go and fetch my bedroll, will you, Wes? I'll be sleeping in the stable tonight so Miss Fancy can have a bed."

Later that evening, after the dishes were cleared, Aunt Lally had apologized for Zack's surliness throughout dinner.

"You can't take anything Zack says or does in a personal way right now, Fancy. The boy can be a moody cuss whenever a dogie is missing. You see, Seth entrusted those beeves to him, and Zack blames himself whenever something bad happens."

Fancy suspected the rustled steers had little to do with Zack's attitude—toward her, anyway. He hadn't forgotten how she betrayed his confidence, using what he'd said about Beth to hurt Cord. Now with Cord's life at stake, Zack had made it clear he would fight her tooth and nail, if that's what he had to do, to keep his brother safe.

The whoosh of wind and the snap of curtains startled Fancy from her disturbing thoughts. The air felt wet and cool. A low, grumbling sound rolled around the horizon, and she realized Wes's prediction would soon come true. The storm was moving in fast. She needed to find Cord. She needed to talk some sense into him—and soon, if she didn't want to get drenched.

Another dewy gust scuttled apple blossoms across the windowsill. The tree's great gnarled branch bobbed just outside, knocking against the house. She thought she had better shut the window, unless she wanted to return from her mission to sleep on sopping quilts.

When she tried to slide down the glass, though, she found

the frame had jammed. She muttered an oath, pushing and tugging, then pounding with a fist. Every pane rattled, but the window wouldn't budge. Her mood wasn't improved any when the first drops of rain splattered against her cheek.

"Need help?"

The call came from below. She would have recognized that lazy, amused drawl anywhere, but she couldn't see him with her hair whipping around her face. She tried to shove the shorter, more rebellious curls behind her ears, but she only had two hands to fend off the silken horde. She heard him chuckle, and she wondered what entertained him more: her struggle with his window or her battle with her hair.

"Just what do you think you're doing down there, lurking under my window?"

"My job, footloose."

"Well, you're not going to see much of anything from down there," she said.

"Is that an invitation to come up?"

"Didn't you offer to help?"

He chuckled again. Suddenly, she saw him in a flash of lightning. Shirtless and barefoot, he lounged against the apple tree. He'd positioned himself just beyond the splash of lamplight that pooled beneath her window. She had a split second to wonder how long he'd been standing there, spying on her, before the darkness returned to blind her. She heard a rustle and a thump, and she caught her breath.

"Cord, you aren't climbing that tree, are you?"

"Sure am."

"Are you mad? There's lightning!"

"Well, ol' Mr. Crabbie here seemed the quickest route to reach a lady in distress."

"Mr. Crabbie?" She could see him again now, walking up one bowing branch after another with the swift, surefooted grace of a marten.

"My cousin Ginny used to sleep in this room, before she got married and moved away. She always used to call this crabapple tree Mr. Crabbie 'cause it groaned."

He sprang to a bough above her. Wrapping his hands

around the branch, he let his body drop. She bit back a shriek.

"Be careful!"

"Aw." He flashed a winsome, boyish grin as he swung unabashedly before her, every muscle in his arms and chest rippling in display. "You still worried about me? Why, that's two times in one day. I must be doing something right."

She pressed her lips into a thin line. Wes wasn't the only Rawlins who possessed a mischievous charm.

"Quit clowning around," she whispered fiercely.

He relented, hauling himself back up by sheer arm strength to crouch in the crooked elbow of the tree. With his hips wreathed in snow-white petals and greenery, he looked like some virile sylvan god who'd come to partake in the rites of spring. Her heart quickened at the thought.

"Cord, it's starting to rain."

"Uh-huh."

"The wind—"

"It's picking up, isn't it?"

He plucked a blossom from the tree. Inhaling, he let his gaze linger on her mouth as he drew the petals downward, touching them to his lips. He smiled. The expression was soft and tender, with just a trace of longing. It made her pulse flutter.

In spellbound fascination, she watched as he reached toward her, unfolding his long, sun-coppered torso, lowering himself abreast of the sill. His lips were only inches from hers when he stilled. Her curls snapped and blew, wrapping like tiny fingers around his wrist, but he defied their best attempts to draw him closer. A deft stroke of his hand swept her hair back, and he anchored it behind her ear with the flower.

"Better?" he whispered.

She nodded, unable to speak. For a moment, one fleet and precious moment, his palm lingered, resting against the throbbing vein in her throat. She thought he was going to kiss her. She waited, half-closing her eyes, not daring to let herself breathe. He touched her cheek. His smile turned wistful. Then he reluctantly withdrew.

"Good. Reckon you're not a lady in distress anymore."

Her breath released in a ragged rush. She tried to stem her disappointment. She tried to remember all her arguments and rationales, and why she had called him to the window. But it was hard to focus on such unimpassioned thinking when he sat there before her, warm, vital, and potently alive. She wanted to keep him that way.

She wanted something else too. Right now, this very moment, she wanted him to want her the way he had that other night, when he came to her in this room . . . before he knew she was a whore. God help her. Was that wrong? Diego had finally said he would wed her. How could she stand there, still wanting Cord?

Guilt wrapped around her. Guilt and desire. She drew a deep breath and tried to steady the rush of her pulse. "I'm getting wet."

"Me too."

She blushed at the husky timbre of his voice. It brought to mind another, steamier wetness—one, she was sure, that a man like Cord Rawlins would never discuss with a woman.

"I . . . need to close the window. You came here to help, remember?"

"Can't do it from out here."

"Then you'll have to come inside."

His dimples showed. "Think we can call a truce that long?"

Her gaze slid lower, to the dusky fur upon his chest. Her fingers itched to walk through it, and she couldn't quite suppress her sigh. "I can let bygones be bygones—if you can."

"Sure." He grinned. "It's my job to keep the peace."

He swung down beside her. Apple blossoms tumbled from his jeans as he turned to face the panes. She tried not to ogle the damp fabric that fit so snugly to his buttocks. Her appreciative gaze traveled over him, roaming up the V that extended from his waist, broadening at his shoulders, and finishing with the sinewy arms he'd raised overhead.

He made a fist, unconsciously treating her to a show of biceps. Two sharp raps later, the window frame fell with a rattle and a clank. He turned then, and she knew another twinge of disappointment. She had hoped to admire him in secret for a little while longer.

"You didn't tell me you had a trick for it," she said.

"Well now, you see? Even I have one or two hidden up my sleeve."

The glow from the lamp had turned him golden. The last beads of rain slid across his chest like the finest threads of silver. She could only imagine where those droplets finally pooled. The images that filled her mind heated her belly. She chided herself that she was promised now, but the reminder did little to stop that kindling warmth. *This is business, Fancy girl. Keep your wits about you.*

"Cord, we have to talk about your plan." She clasped her hands together to keep from touching him. "Going alone after those plates is too dangerous."

"I thought we called a truce."

"We did. It's just that—" her chest heaved with her frustration, "I can't keep quiet about this. You're talking about entering my world now, a world that's very different from your own. Men like Wilkerson don't think like you. And you won't be able to second-guess them."

"I won't, eh?"

"No! You're too honorable."

He raised his brows. "Why, thank you, darlin'."

He was smiling at her. He had the most sensual, spell-binding smile of any man she'd ever known. She thought the dimples must be to blame, since they gave him that rare combination of boyish mischief and hypnotic masculinity.

"Cord, listen to me," she said, trying not to sound as if she'd just run a city block. "Every blackleg has a knuck. Someone to help him swindle a mark. That's why cons are so successful. Without one, you can't win."

"A knuck, huh?"

"Well, in my case, a moll."

Amusement shone in his eyes. They danced and twinkled like jade-colored stars, making her feel giddy and not quite as sure of her argument. There was something unsavory about turning Cord into a crooked creature like her and Diego. But if she didn't, he wouldn't survive. And then a part of her might die with him.

"So what you're saying is," he drawled in his slow, rumbling baritone, "you want to come with me to be my guardian angel."

Angel? Well, not exactly.

"That's one way of looking at it, I suppose."

His gaze had shifted to her mouth. She felt every nerve in her body tingle. How was it that she, a jaded temptress, could still let a simple look from him stir her?

"Cord, you need me."

He leaned closer.

"We can be good together."

"Good together," he repeated in a mesmerizing whisper.

His breath touched her lips. It was warm and moist and faintly scented with an aromatic tobacco. She felt herself sway. Calling upon every fiber of her self-control, she restrained herself from bridging the final inch between them. Too much was at stake to play the wrong card. She'd already learned the hard way that seducing Cord would get her nowhere.

"So," she said, "do we have a deal . . . partner?"

Something dark flickered in his eyes. Something like regret, or frustration. She wasn't sure. His lids lowered, veiling the shadow underneath. She had a heartbeat to wonder if she'd made the wrong play, then he raised a hand to pluck the flower from her hair. Her curls spilled in wild disarray, but his fingers were gentle, combing the mass, tilting her head back so he could gaze into her face. She recognized a new determination in his eyes, as if he'd come to some kind of decision.

"Tell me, darlin'. Have you ever made love to a man?"

She blinked in surprise. What kind of question was that? She thought they'd been talking about a partnership to get the plates.

"Well, of course I have. You know I have."

"No." His tone was firm, but his smile was tender.

"There's a difference between making love and making business."

She returned his gaze uncertainly. What was he talking about? Some new kind of method? Surely she knew them all.

"I'm not sure I understand."

"Then let me show you."

He lowered his head and kissed her. It wasn't the impatient, domineering plunder she'd come to expect from Diego. Rather, Cord's lips stroked hers, persuading, wooing an invitation to let him taste more.

Pleasantly distracted, she welcomed the tip of his tongue. He didn't taste of whiskey or cocaine, which was a welcome change after Diego.

Diego. She cringed inside. She was supposed to be talking sense into Cord, not kissing him! Dare she continue this love play? Cord hadn't given her his word. He hadn't agreed to take her with him. And yet, what harm could one little kiss do?

His probing deepened, and she closed her eyes, feeling breathless. Possessed. He smelled of rain, blossoms, and newly cut hay, but another, more elusive scent clung to him too. It was heady. Earthy. A fragrance that was his alone. She liked it. She wanted to fill her senses with it.

She pulled his head lower. God, but she'd wanted to run her hands through his hair for so long. Its copper highlights had tantalized her even in the dining car, when he swaggered, spouting wisecracks at her. The memory made her smile. Still, she found it hard to be satisfied with hair when so much exquisite, unexplored flesh beckoned below.

She lowered her hand to stroke his chest. The hair there was damp with rain, but the skin was soft and warm. It quivered beneath her fingertips, and she hesitated, thinking she was being too bold. Cord was a family man. Perhaps he liked his women sweet, shy, and complacent—as Beth must have been.

He pressed himself against her palm, though, urging her caress. Temptation got the better of her. She splayed her hands downward, over his ribs and belted muscles, along the sinews of his thighs. She liked the way they tensed, anticipating a more intimate fondling. She would have gladly obliged them, but he'd gripped her buttocks, lifting her hips against his. She gasped, falling against his chest. The raindrops steamed between them, and her nipples tingled, growing hard with the sensation.

Oh, yes. He felt so good.

Unable to resist, she shimmied closer, reveling in that primal pleasure of flattened breasts against hard male musculature. A feral growl rumbled in his throat, and his mouth slanted across hers, hungrier, more predatory. She swayed, the flurry in her stomach creeping south to shake her knees.

His hands seemed to be everywhere then, gentling, tantalizing. She wasn't exactly sure when they unpried the hooks of her blouse. She couldn't remember how the lamp got doused, or how his jeans and her skirt fell in a heap at their feet. He clasped her close in a sweet, intimate kiss, and she marveled at his tenderness. His caring to woo her was a new experience, for she was in the habit of giving pleasure, not receiving. Yet the moment she tried to drag her wits back and curb her renegade body, the hot, velvety wetness of his mouth fastened on her breast.

She groaned. She arched her spine. Her every inch was burning now, and she yearned to smoke against his rain-cooled length. When she rode her thigh across his hip, he balanced her weight, running his hand along her limb's quivering underside. Her mound was already smoldering when his fingers dipped inside. Probing and teasing, they fueled her tender places with such volatile energy that she began to combust, consumed by the fever to become one with him.

"I want you, Fancy," he whispered, his voice low and raspy. "I want to love you the way a man *should* love a woman. I want to teach you what 'making love' means. From now on, there won't be any deals between us. I—"

Thunder crashed—or was that earth-quaking sound the pounding of her heart? She couldn't say. She strained to hear the rest of his words, but they were swept away by the rumbling echo. He carried her to the bearskin, that same erotically plush bearskin where he had pleasured her before. Only this night would be different, her reeling senses told her. This night, he wanted her. After all those maddening bouts of frustrated desire, she would finally make him her own.

But tomorrow he would ride away, a voice knelled inside her brain. *And he won't come back to you unless he's in a pine box.*

"No!" she gasped, jolting as if a bullet had ripped through her heart. *My God, no.* How could she have lost control? She had known what was at stake.

The room shook with the next crash. A blaze of light turned night to day, but just as quickly, night resumed. She was blinded. She wriggled, her foot striking the floor, but his hand gripped her buttocks, and she couldn't pull away.

"Cord, no—"

"I'm sorry, darlin'," he whispered. "I know you prefer the bed, but it creaks, and Wes is next door."

I don't care about the bed, she wanted to say. *I don't care about Wes; I care about you.* The heavens boomed again, though. Her ears were buzzing, her eyes were dazed. She groped for his arms, and he eased her beneath him, his mouth unerring in its descent to meet hers. Her shoulders sank into the pelage of the bear; her nipples were buried in the fur of his chest. *Don't let this be our last night together,* she wanted to cry out. *Don't leave me behind.*

But she needed every gasp of air just to breathe. His mouth was delving lower, moistness on the prowl. His hands chased scintillating shocks down her spine. When his tongue flicked between her thighs and his finger joined the thrust, she thought she'd go mad from the electric jolting inside her.

"Cord, please." She was panting now. "You have to stop. You have to—" She cried out, her hips leaving the floor, as he found that tiny, pulsating trigger once more.

"Don't hold back," he growled. "I want all of you, Fancy. All of you."

The storm was upon them now. She couldn't escape. It

was inside and outside, crashing and blazing. He locked an arm around her hips and pulled her beneath him. He was hot; she could feel the thunder in his veins. Feverishly, she groped for his rod.

He groaned. "That's it, darlin. Ride it out with me. Ride it out."

He thrust into her, driving deep. Lightning flashed inside her. The current crackled between them, showering sparks across her flesh. She cried out his name, but his mouth swooped down to silence her. Moaning, she could do little more than rise and fall, tossed by the tempest building inside her. She hardened the grip of her thighs, and he pitched faster, pushing her higher, higher, until she teetered somewhere in the stratosphere, ready to fall.

A tendril of panic anchored her there. She'd never fallen before. The drop looked too far.

"No," he whispered. "Don't be afraid. Come with me, sweetheart. C'mon."

She heard herself sob. How did he know? How could he tell? She strained against him, thinking she could pretend, but the storm clouds only rolled faster, carrying her closer and closer to the precipice. She found herself battling to hold on again.

"Fancy . . ." His breaths were ragged in her ear. "You're cheating yourself, darlin'. You're cheating yourself, and I won't let you."

He was slowing his rhythm, rolling inside her now like leashed thunder. "Look at me."

She turned her face away, trying to hide her tears, but he kissed her lips and gripped her chin, gently pressuring her to obey. She blinked. Through the mists, through the darkness, she saw a light. It was shining from his eyes, a radiance so warm and tender, it stole her breath away.

He smiled, brushing back her hair. "Let me love all of you, Fancy."

She nodded, mesmerized by that golden glow. She'd had a reason to hide her true self away, but she couldn't remember it now. He touched his lips to hers. His tongue only wooed her at first, but as its probing deepened, so too did the thrusting below. Bolts of energy crackled over her nerves. She squirmed, twitching helplessly as the electricity built. Soon she was fully charged again, a shaft of lightning ready to hurl into the abyss. He braced himself against the deluge that would drive him over the edge without her.

"Trust me," he gasped. "Trust me and let go."

He plunged faster, snaking his thickest finger into her wetness. That double penetration was more than she could bear. She cried out; the clouds burst; and she plummeted, tumbling through a shower of sensation.

An eternity of heartbeats later, she finally struck solid earth. Her breath tore from her lungs in great, shuddering gasps. Thunder receded from her limbs; sparks cooled upon her flesh. She didn't know whether to think or to feel. The maelstrom had ended, but she couldn't move. *My daddy was a hurricane,* he had teased her once. God in heaven. Now she had proof.

Many more minutes passed, yet still he lay buried inside her. His arms and legs wrapped around her as if she were a treasure he might never let go. If not for his still-pounding heart, which echoed the tumult of the rain on the roof, she might have thought he'd fallen asleep.

At first uncertain, then increasingly anxious, she waited for the cue to collect herself and leave him in peace. She wasn't used to being so wholly possessed, much less cherished after the taking.

"Cord?"

He sighed, a long and gusty contented sound.

"Cord?" she whispered more urgently.

It was over, all over, and the fear was settling in. Just like her mother warned, he had taken a piece of her. She feared she might never get it back if she let him ride away. Raising a shaking hand, she touched his hair. He finally lifted his head. She had no sooner opened her mouth to speak than his eyes slitted and his lips swooped down, fastening over hers.

She was gasping again when he finished his wicked, toe-curling kiss. Grinning, he shifted to her side and propped his head up on his hand.

"You were saying?"

"Stop doing that!"

He smirked. "Need a rest, huh?"

She felt her cheeks burn. The scalawag. Who would have thought that upstanding, duty-driven, salt-of-the-earth Cord could make her pant and thrash, screaming out his name in a paroxysm of maddening desire? Thank God for the thunder peals. Otherwise, the whole household might have heard.

She gazed into his eyes. They were so open and honest, filled with a genuine warmth. A lump built inside her throat. Embarrassed, she dropped her gaze, letting it run over his lean length. He was so beautiful. So breathtaking. She swallowed, her fingers touching his breast in a feather-light caress. She could feel the steady, vibrant thrumming of his life force, and a tear threatened to spill. She couldn't bear to know she might never feel his heart again.

"Cord," she said quietly, and as firmly as she could, "I'm not going to let you ride off this ranch without me."

Cord sighed, catching her fingers in his hand.

Did she have to bring up that again? he thought with a twinge of frustration.

He touched her hand to his lips. He had hoped they could spend their last hours together making up for the thirty days they must spend apart. In truth, he hadn't climbed through her window with the intent to bed her. But after wanting her for so long, and after realizing how cold and hard the next few weeks would be without her, he hadn't been able to help himself.

A part of him said he was selfish—not to mention morally bankrupt—to seduce a woman who thought she was promised. Another part of him refused to accept the idea that Fancy and Santana were engaged. Back in the prison, when she agreed to wait for Santana's release, she couldn't possibly have known that the bastard still thought of her as his "fancy little whore."

As much as Cord longed to warn her that her engagement

was a lie, he couldn't bear to hurt her that way. He feared she was just stubborn enough to run to the prison and get Santana to marry her. No, he had to find some other way to make her realize the outlaw was no good for her. But how could he possibly hope to turn her heart and head around in the space of a few hours?

She finally raised her eyes back to his. He smiled. The light of the hall lamp was slipping beneath the door, bathing her in its soft, golden glow. Just to see her lying beside him with her tumbled curls and flushed breasts and moist, kiss-swollen lips was enough to kindle a heat inside his belly. He knew it wouldn't take much for that warmth to spread south to his loins.

"Did you hear me?" she asked, her chin jutting in a show of resolve.

The storm flashed inside her eyes, and he had the almost overwhelming desire to kiss her nose.

"Yeah," he said softly. "I heard you."

"So it's settled."

"Not quite," he murmured, skimming a hand down her belly. The velvety flesh shrank and quivered at his touch. He found himself longing to taste it again.

Her lashes fluttered downward. He had the sense she was hardening herself, steeling herself against something. Then she slowly met his gaze again. Her lips curved in a luscious smile—one that made his breath catch.

"You know, Marshal," she drawled, trailing silken fingers along his breast, "you're being terribly shortsighted about all this. I could be most valuable to you as your deputy. Your *undercover* deputy."

His lips quirked in a lopsided grin. "Well now. There's an interesting idea."

"Yes," she said, her voice throbbing with an earthy resonance. "I thought that might interest you." She shimmied closer, so close that her heat warmed his flesh. "I'm most adept at handling guns."

"Is that so?" He arched a brow.

"Oh, yes. Would you care to see?"

She didn't even have to shift her hand. Just the sound of her voice and the light in her eyes was enough to make him harden.

"But I thought you were all tuckered out," he teased.

"Me? Never."

Suddenly, she pounced. He was so stunned when her weight slammed into his chest that he could only fall back, the air whooshing from his lungs. She grabbed his wrists, stretching his arms above his head, and locked her slinky thighs around his hips.

"Now then, let's see," she said, her voice rumbling deep inside her throat. "Where were we, lover?"

He drew a shaky breath. To be pinned by all that silken flesh was the most heady, pulse-firing sensation he'd ever known. She'd become the jungle cat again, her eyes ablaze with amethyst fire, her mane gleaming with indigo shimmers. When she smiled, revealing wicked, feline teeth, he felt every nerve in his body jolt, reveling in the danger.

He evened out his breathing enough to grin up at her. "Well, the last thing I remember was you calling out my name."

Her eyes slitted in that sultry, catlike way that never failed to start his blood smoking. "Indeed?" She eased lower, brushing her nipples across his chest. "Funny. I don't remember you calling out mine."

Her head dipped, trailing fragrant curls across his nose and throat. He closed his eyes, expecting a kiss. When her teeth fastened on his bottom lip, he gasped at the sharp prickle of sensation. She pushed her tongue into his mouth. There was nothing ladylike about her kiss. Brazen, demanding, she sucked and nibbled, parried and thrust, as if she were waging some kind of battle. *A battle of wills.*

The warning had barely knelled in his brain when he felt her hips rise. She was already moist and hot like melted butter. When the fur of her mound stroked his shaft, a current of sparks jerked through his loins.

"There. You see?" Her fingers twined through his. "Making business isn't all that bad, is it, Marshal?"

Her tongue thrust into his ear, and he made a strangled sound, half laugh, half groan. "I ought to turn you over my knee."

"Oh no, then I couldn't do this." She positioned herself, sliding slowly, artfully, until she'd buried him deep inside her wet heat. "Or this," she added softly, tantalizing him with tiny false starts as she crept back up the trail. "And you like it when I do this, don't you, Cord?"

He nodded. He couldn't help himself. She grinned triumphantly. Sheathing and stroking, she took him again. Down and up, in and out, and he groaned, feeling his control slipping away. He knew she was toying with him. She had some nefarious scheme in mind, and he'd be eating crow the second he let himself give in. But she was sucking him deeper, gripping and gliding with her muscular walls. Her rhythm was driving him mad. He began to strain, rising to meet her. She rewarded his cooperation with a hungry kiss.

"Now then," she whispered huskily, her breath hot and moist against his lips. "Let's make a deal."

"No," he panted. "No more deals."

She slid out of reach. He bit his tongue in frustration.

"Then a promise," she said. "Between very close friends."

She rubbed and teased. He felt his blood surge, engorging him further. A moan escaped him, despite his best efforts.

"Fancy, sweetheart, please. Don't make me lie to you."

"But that's just it, don't you see?" She brought her face back down to his. "You can't lie well enough to save your life. That's why you need me. And if you won't take me with you, then I'll help the boys track you down."

She meant business. He could read the determination in her eyes. Nothing short of tying her to the bed would keep her safe at the ranch. He would have to choose between risking her or risking his brothers. And that was an impossible choice.

"Fancy, don't do this," he pleaded. "I'm scared you'll be hurt."

"I'll be skinned alive if I stay at this ranch. Your family will never forgive me if something happens to you. I'd rather face a judge and jury. Now quit being so stubborn. Besides, it's my damned future riding on those plates."

So it was the plates she was worried about? The plates and his family?

A sliver of pain sliced through him. Why couldn't she just admit that she cared about him? She didn't love Santana. If she did, she wouldn't have screamed "Cord" in her passion. He'd touched a part of her no other man had ever touched. He knew he had. He'd learned long ago in his marriage bed the signs of when a woman was holding back. He had never dreamed that Fancy, of all people, would be a fledgling to her own erotic pleasure, but he was delighted that he—*he, by God*—had taught her how to fly. She had given all of herself to him, and that meant she cared. And she wanted him too. He would prove it to her.

With a shove and a deft roll, he switched their positions. She was light; it didn't take much effort to pin her hips to the bear pelt. She tried to tear her hands from his, but he held on, smiling smugly at her oaths as he stretched her arms above her head.

"Not so loud, darlin'," he drawled. "Aunt Lally might hear and come wash your mouth out."

Fancy squirmed, twisting to no avail. She didn't know whether to be outraged or amused. How dare the wretch use her tricks against her? The expression on his face was positively gloating. If she hadn't had so much invested in the outcome of this duel, she might have laughed and called him a peacock. But as it was, she wanted to wring his neck. Her own too. *Fancy, my girl, you are a fool. You know better than to gamble with sex when Cord Rawlins is the player.*

Finally, she subsided, glaring up at him. As much as she hated to admit it, his weight and strength, the sheer beauty of his virility, were arousing. She had to bite back a moan as he positioned himself, his shaft probing the slick, trembling flesh that sought to guard her opening.

"You know, I'm beginning to think you're more of a scoundrel than you pretend," she said, but her show of anger did no good. It was belied by the tiny shocks of anticipation that jerked along her inner thighs.

"You do?" he taunted softly. "Why's that?"

He pushed. The thrust was clean and deep, and she arched helplessly. His second thrust nearly had her crawling out of her skin. She tried desperately to brace herself, to hold herself back from the dizzying vortex of sensation. But when she would have twisted away, he added the weight of his chest, burying her beneath flint-hard planes and fleecy fur.

The room began to reel. Everything was spinning out of focus except his face. His eyes were like a beacon, drawing her to him. They shone with that same golden radiance that had wooed her to surrender before. There was something else lurking in their beguiling depths, though. It was primitive, a hunger, and it devoured her every move. Dimly she realized he watched her for signs, altering his rhythm to escalate her desire, taking primal satisfaction in learning the greatest source of her pleasure.

She might still hold the ace after all, she thought.

"Oh, yes," she moaned, her head rolling in a feverish frenzy. "Take me, Cord. Take me with you."

"I'll take you as far as you can go, sweetheart."

He plumbed to her furthermost depths. She gasped, digging her heels into the bearskin, pitching her hips higher. Molten fire exploded inside her. She cried out, and his mouth silenced her, possessing her yet again with the quick, plunging thrust of his tongue.

He was still shuddering when she collapsed beneath him. She gulped down air, reveling in the raw, pulsating power of his masculinity. He was magnificent. A seasoned lover whose caresses offered paradise. She couldn't help but smile.

Yet despite his undeniable skill, he was still a rank beginner when it came to love games.

She kissed his hair. "Darling?" When he didn't immediately stir, she tapped his shoulder. "I think we should leave before dawn, to avoid a showdown with the boys."

He raised his head. "What—"

"You said you would take me, remember?"

Realization gathered slowly, rolling like a thundercloud across his brow. "I didn't mean—"

"You said 'as far as I can go,'" she interrupted silkily.

A slow blush crept up his cheeks. "The hell I did."

"Now, now. Don't be a sore loser. With practice, you'll get better at these games. Someday, with a lot of hard work, you might even be as good as I am."

She smirked, and his lips twitched. A reluctant smile spread across his face. Suddenly, he threw back his head and laughed.

"I have to hand it to you, sweetheart." His eyes turned wistful as they met her gaze once more. "You really are good."

Chapter Seventeen

Seventy-two hours later, Cord was still smarting over the way Fancy had tricked him into giving his word, but even he had to admit he preferred a female long rider by his side than one of his wide-eyed, overeager brothers. At least Fancy had no illusions about the dangers of their mission. And he'd learned from experience that she kept a cool head in heated circumstances.

God knew, he needed a cool head beside him now.

Using intelligence supplied by the Texas Rangers, Cord had tracked the Wilkersons to Comanche Peak, in Johnson County, where Ned was holed up after Sheriff Applegate's posse cost him three men. The Johnson County sheriff appeared in blissful ignorance of the renegades hiding in his jurisdiction—either that, or the lawman preferred to chase drunken, mischief-making cowboys rather than risk his hide by tracking cold-blooded killers. In any event, Ned and his men had taken refuge in Johnson County, nursing their wounds and, no doubt, plotting their revenge against Clem Applegate.

Since Cord figured Ned would need recruits to bolster his ranks, he was counting on the outlaw being less suspicious of outsiders than he might normally have been. Even so, Cord couldn't help but wonder at how readily Ned had agreed to negotiate after Cord sent him a message, ostensibly from

Frank Harris. He guessed Frank Harris's reputation as a counterfeiter had preceded him, thanks in part to the mock wanted posters; and that the reminder of Fancy's earlier correspondence with Ned, promising Mexican silver for U.S. minting plates, had wooed the outlaw further.

After only twenty-four hours of silence, Ned sent his younger brother, Jake, with the message that he was willing to hear Cord's proposal.

The game had officially begun.

Jake was a scowling, uncommunicative bear of a man, to whom Cord took an immediate dislike. The fact that Jake was a known sheriff killer had less to do with Cord's resentment than with the way the man stared at Fancy's buttocks, swaying so enticingly in her saddle. Cord tried to remind himself that in the past, Fancy had handled far worse than leers from randy men, yet at least twice he came dangerously close to punching the renegade's lights out while Jake directed them with grunts and nods along the rocky ribbon of trail.

Scaling the bald face of the butte, Jake at last rode ahead of Fancy, leading her horse beneath towering boulders and slabs of avalanche-ready stones, many of which—Cord was certain—had been gathered and strategically placed by the gang's sentries to protect their hideout. Cord could occasionally glimpse a rifle barrel glinting from the craggy shadows above.

Fancy, too, must have noticed the guns trained on them, but rather than show any uneasiness, she sent him a dry smile and a shrug over her shoulder. Apparently Santana had made similar death threats routine for her. Considering how she rode into a den of thieves with a lawman rather than a crime boss, Cord couldn't help but admire her nerve. He also prayed he could keep her safe. He prayed, too, that he could end this nightmarish quest soon. Two weeks of the governor's four-week reprieve had already ticked off the clock.

As they reached the scrub-brush summit of Comanche Peak, Jake gestured for them to dismount. Cord reached automatically to help Fancy, but she gave a small, fierce shake of her head. He was surprised by her reaction, but the clinking of spurs distracted him, and he spied a lanky denim-encased leg dangling from a nearby boulder.

"So you're Harris the Hustler, eh? Houston's big-time sharper." This challenge came from the boulder's sentry, a thin-haired, long-necked man with a bulbous Adam's apple. He grinned, lazily swinging his boot about an inch from Cord's hat brim. "Reckon prison's been good to you, Harris. You got yourself a nice tan."

Cord felt the back of his neck heat. The sentry's wisecrack could mean trouble, considering how Frank Harris had been locked up in the state penitentiary for more than two years.

"Reckon I do," he retorted, drilling the outlaw with an unflinching stare. "What of it?"

Fancy laughed. Dismounting, she made a point to hike her buttocks in the process. Cord couldn't help but notice how easily her ploy stole the attention of both outlaws.

"You should see what else hard labor did for Frank," she drawled in her whiskey-smooth alto. "You ought to try it, boys."

The sentry's face split into a lewd smile. "I'd much rather try you, sweetheart."

"The hell you will, Goose," Jake said in his guttural bass. "I saw her first."

Cord steeled himself against a growing desire to crack both outlaws' skulls against the rock. "Where's Wilkerson?" he demanded brusquely.

"You mean Mad Dog?" Goose chuckled as he ogled Fancy's breasts. "Well, lessee. Blisse ain't skinning the rabbits Cass shot for her, so—"

"Christ." Jake's scowl deepened. "Grub's gonna be late again." He drew his six-shooter and fired into the air. "Ned! Quit your goddamned screwing and come out here. I brought Harris back to deal. You want a cut of that silver or don't ya?"

Two other men dropped eagerly from the rocks. Cord realized they'd been lying in ambush, and he suspected the promise of silver was the only thing that had kept them from shooting him in the back. Judging by the way they ogled Fancy, he worried she would face another kind of danger.

"Mighty nice piece you got there, Harris," called the first bushwhacker, a dark, slanty-eyed scorpion with a drooping mustache. "And I ain't talking 'bout your six-shooter."

Goose snickered. "Just wait till you see her tits up close, Lash."

"Hey, Harris." This came from the second bushwhacker, whose long snout and sly grin reminded Cord of a coyote. "Where's the rest of your women? Don't tell us you only brought one."

"Hell, Cass," Goose said. "If she ain't to your liking, you don't have to poke her. I'll take your turn." He winked at Fancy.

Cord sensed rather than saw her tense. She was too good at playacting to show revulsion, but he suspected she was remembering other campsites, other outlaws. He leveled his coldest, hardest stare at Goose. "The woman's mine."

The wiseacre's grin ebbed. He glanced at Jake, whose face had darkened with resentment.

Before either outlaw could challenge Cord's claim, though, a heavyset man lumbered out of the bushes. Hurrying in his wake was a skinny, disheveled redhead of about sixteen. The girl's steps faltered when she spied Cord—or perhaps Fancy—but Cord's gaze was quickly drawn from the surprise on her gaunt face to the bruises on her shoulder, which was too bony to hold up her chemise strap. His gunhand twitched at the proof of her abuse, and he glared narrowly at the heavyset man. Even without the patch covering the outlaw's left eye, Cord would have recognized the Terror of the Pecos instantly. Ned Wilkerson's bulldog jowls and the list of his atrocities had taken up prominent wall space in the U.S. marshal's office the last time Cord had reported there.

"You're Harris?" Ned halted before Cord and crossed his arms over a barrellike chest.

Cord nodded curtly.

"And this here's your *puta?*"

Cord ground his teeth as Ned appraised Fancy as if she

were a piece of raw beefsteak. But if Ned's Spanish taunt of "whore" had insulted her, she didn't show it. She merely donned the sultry, closed-lip smile Cord had watched her use to such advantage at the Diamondback Saloon. He felt his temperature rise.

Apparently he wasn't the only one who didn't like Fancy's game. The redhead's fists clenched, and she stepped possessively to Ned's side, her storm-colored eyes flashing in warning.

"Me and Harris were just discussing the lady," Goose said in an oily voice. "Seems like he don't want to share her with nobody."

A breathless silence fell as Ned sized up Cord again. Cord imagined he heard Fancy's heart picking up its pace. As for the redhead, her gaze flickered uneasily from him to Ned, as if she feared they might start a shootout. Suddenly, she flounced between them, sticking out her boyish chest in a futile attempt to attract Ned's notice.

"Why would you want to go and hump her for, Mad Dog?" the girl said, her tone falling somewhere between sullen and wheedling. "That whore's got a twat as old as Methuselah."

"And yours is ten times as worn," Cass said, wrinkling his snout.

"Shut up!"

"Aw, Dusty." Goose chuckled, and the girl turned as red as her hair. "Why don't you go skin them rabbits? We got business to discuss."

"The name's Blisse," she fired back. "And you can go skin 'em yourself."

"You cook?" Ned shot this question at Fancy.

She met his basilisk stare with flawless aplomb. "Among other things."

"Then go make yourself useful."

Blisse sneered. "Yeah."

"You too." Ned grabbed the girl's shaggy hair, and she yelped as he yanked her around, shoving her toward the campfire.

Cord felt his blood boil. He stepped forward to protest Ned's treatment of the girl, but Fancy tossed him a quelling look and moved quickly to bar his way.

"Serving you gentlemen would be a pleasure," she purred, lavishing her come-hither smile on the outlaws. "But don't keep me waiting for long."

Goose hooted. Cass snickered. Cord bit back an oath as he watched Fancy saunter after Blisse. He didn't know whether to be relieved or worried that Fancy played her part so well. Jake and Lash were practically drooling.

Although Cord told himself Fancy was just playing her old high-stakes game, he couldn't quite discount the hurtful twinge inside his chest.

He recognized it as jealousy.

That night, Fancy spent what seemed like hours cooling her heels, waiting for Cord. He had forbidden her to leave his sight, which irked her to no end. She supposed she should be flattered that he cared enough to worry about her. On the other hand, she wasn't sure she liked the implication that she was weak and helpless, and that he was the only thing that stood between her and bodily harm. God knew, she'd been handling men like Goose and Lash since she was thirteen years old.

Her gaze drifted back to the campfire. A lively game of poker was underway. Cord was losing badly. Since he didn't have much of a purse to wager, she guessed he was staking his share of the loot from the minting-plate sale he had supposedly arranged with Mexican nationals. Over dinner, in an attempt to get Ned to reveal where he'd hidden Bart's plates, Cord had claimed that his contacts would deal only if all four plates were available for sale. Ned had grunted something noncommittal and wandered off to urinate. He hadn't said another word about the matter, but whenever he was out of earshot, his men started muttering.

Boredom always took its toll on a group of holed-up outlaws, but Fancy sensed the tension in the Wilkerson gang stemmed from resentment. Lash had grumbled that hiding out was worse than prodding steak-on-the-hoof; at least when the gang rustled beeves, they made money. Jake had also had enough of lying low. Showing a tendency to dispute his brother's leadership, he'd complained that Ned was going soft and ruining the gang's reputation for retaliation. They should be riding back to Tarrant County to make an example of Sheriff Applegate, instead of hiding out.

Applegate's posse must have turned up the heat pretty high for Wilkerson's men to go underground for five weeks, Fancy mused. She remembered thinking that Wilkerson would try to track her down after her escape from the Fort Worth jail, but apparently Applegate's pride had been too great to admit publicly that a federal marshal had stolen his prisoner. At least, that's what Applegate had confessed to Cord during one of their recent correspondences. No doubt that was why Ned had readily bought Cord's lie that he, as Frank Harris, had ambushed and killed the bounty hunter who'd been sent to track her.

Privately, however, Fancy couldn't understand why Ned hadn't cut his losses after learning she'd slipped through his fingers and had fled with Bart's plates to Mexico. For a band of men who had access to thousands of dollars worth of silver bullion—not to mention the cool million each of Bart's minting plates should bring in—the outlaws were leading un-necessarily spartan lives. They could have been drinking sipping whiskey and entertaining high-class whores in some gilded casino. Instead, they were sitting on this godforsaken rock.

She couldn't blame Ned's men for harboring ill will toward him. He'd let them pull off a few small highway rob-beries, and they'd stolen a horse here and there, but for the most part, Ned had ordered them to stay put until local lawmen considered them old news. It probably was boredom that made Lash and the others speak so nostalgically of rus-tling. Even so, why would thieves who could conceivably mint their own fortunes want to go back to the drudgery of herding stolen cattle?

Fancy was distracted from her speculations when Ned suddenly threw down his cards in disgust. Rising, he grabbed Blisse's arm and pulled her to her feet. The girl glanced longingly at Cord—much to Fancy's irritation. Blisse's hungry gaze had been feasting on his chest, crotch, and buttocks all day. When Cord failed to notice Blisse's latest appeal for sex, she hid her obvious disappointment and let Ned drag her into the shadows.

It was then that Fancy remembered Blisse's bruises. She was just thinking she should try to rescue the girl when the sound of Blisse's soft, seductive laughter drifted toward her. Moments later, Fancy heard tell-tale thumps and the sounds of satisfied grunting. She thought she might be ill.

Jesus. Ned urinated in plain view. Did he have to screw in public too?

Fancy couldn't bear to listen anymore. As casually as she could, she climbed to her feet, trying not to let her hand quake as she unlatched the safety on her Colt.

A path led to a stream, and she followed it. Thankfully, the chirping of crickets and the whispering of wind at last drowned out the noise of rutting. Squeezing her eyes closed, she battled the bile that had risen to her throat. She'd forgotten what it was like, what it *really* was like, to be in Blisse's shoes.

Swallowing hard, Fancy gulped down ragged breaths and gazed around her. She had to stay alert. Vigilant. Otherwise, one of the bastards would sneak up on her and try to mount her too.

Shuddering, she hugged her arms around herself. The day had been typical of other days she'd spent with lecherous, pecker-proud outlaws, but difficult, nevertheless. Each time Cord had lapsed into a display of his well-ingrained gallantry, every hair on the back of her neck had stood on end. Somehow, she had to make him understand that kindness to women made him suspect. Even Blisse had begun to eye him suspiciously.

"Have you ever been to Miss Lottie's?" she'd asked, spooning dinner onto his plate.

He'd glanced up sharply, his features frozen. "Miss Lottie's?"

"Yeah. She runs a cathouse in El Paso."

He'd held Blisse's gaze for a long, breathless moment. Then his lids had drooped, hooding wary eyes. "Why would I be wasting my money in some El Paso crib? I've got Houston's finest bawds working for me."

Blisse had frowned, looking thoughtful. She had probably considered his answer a challenge—or maybe an employment opportunity. For the rest of the evening, she had dogged Cord's heels, rubbing his shoulders, stroking his thighs, and generally trying to map his private parts in spite of his gentlemanly resistance.

Five weeks earlier, before Fancy had come to care about him, Cord's predicament might have amused her as much as it had Goose and his coyote pal, Cass.

"Someone shoulda told you 'bout befriending whores, Harris," Cass had said.

"Yep." Goose had winked at his friend. "You just can't seem to get rid of 'em."

Is that what Cord will think about me when this whole scam is finally over?

Fancy struggled to ignore the sinking feeling that followed that thought. Cord had proved himself a tender, caring lover, but she knew better than to expect more than a few bittersweet nights in his arms. She had no illusions about their arrangement. They were business partners, pure and simple. When the plates were found and she was free, he would go back to his family and his upstanding way of life. He would begin the search for another lily-white woman to marry. And she . . .

Well. She smiled mirthlessly. She would do what she had to do to survive. Just like she'd always done.

Just like Blisse did now.

A furtive footstep made her jerk around, her hand on her Colt.

"Fancy?"

She smelled Cord's tobacco before she saw him, hesitating

in the shadow of a scrubby live oak. She released her breath and dropped her hand. To her consternation, she realized it was shaking.

"Are you all right?" he asked.

She swallowed as he stepped into the starlight, his eyes seeming to fill with that soft, shimmering glow. She wondered why she always got a lump in her throat whenever he drew near.

"Of course."

He didn't look convinced, and she averted her gaze. She couldn't let him see how scared she really was. In three days, she would turn twenty-six years old. Diego might not be freed until she was forty-six. What would she do in the meantime, when her looks started to fade and none of the casinos would hire her to deal faro?

Her vision blurred. The answer was painfully obvious: She would have to live like Blisse.

Blinking rapidly, she pushed past Cord and walked beside the stream. She tried not to think of the future stretching out before her, all those bleak, empty days. Instead, she focused on the night, with its gentle, south-born breezes, its heavenly vista of blue-black and silver, and the companionship of the quiet man who had fallen into step beside her.

The farther they walked from the camp, the purer the air seemed to be—and the slower her heart seemed to beat. She breathed more easily, but Cord remained guarded. She could see the tension in his shoulders and the cast of his jaw. His gaze darted constantly over the bushes, and he kept his hand near his gun. She wished his vigilance wasn't quite so necessary. She wished they were far from this place, perhaps strolling along the docks by San Francisco Bay . . . or holding each other again on the bearskin by his hearth. She knew she would never forget that night, no matter how much time or distance came between them. In truth, a part of her refused to let go of the memory.

"I'm sorry I left without you," she said finally. "I just couldn't bear to—to sit there anymore and—" she swallowed, "and listen."

"I know." His features softened, and his gaze held hers for a precious moment. "I would have come sooner, if I could have."

He understands. Gratitude mixed with her growing sense of wonder. She had a hard time dragging her wits back about her. The task became more difficult each time she melted into the sea-green depths of his eyes.

"It will be hard for us to speak in private like this," she said, "except perhaps at night, when we can always say we wandered off to—"

He glanced at her sharply, and she felt her face heat.

"—make love," she finished more diplomatically than she had intended. "You'll be tested in the days to come. Someone will set you up, and you'll have to behave like the rest of them, without honor or integrity. And certainly without chivalry."

"I thought I was," he said dryly. "Except maybe for the chivalry part." Grimacing, he tossed his cigarette into the current. "Dammit, Fancy, one of them hit Blisse. How am I supposed to stand by and do nothing if someone does it again?"

Her throat constricted. *When* someone hit Blisse again was more likely. "I'm not saying you should let them beat her," she said, thinking how special he was to worry about a whore —a nobody—that way. "But you have to understand. These men consider kindness a weakness. In a way, it is. If they realize you care about Blisse, they'll try to force your hand by using her against you."

Cord felt his gut churn at Fancy's unspoken implication. "Or by hurting you," he whispered hoarsely.

She shook her head, but his fears were confirmed when she wouldn't look him in the eye.

"Don't worry about me," she said. "As long as they think I'm the one with the plates—and you're the one with the contacts—we're both safe."

Oh God. He pulled her against him. A tremor rocked her, and he tightened his hold, uncertain whether the pounding against his ribs was his heart or hers.

"I should never have let you come with me," he said.

"You didn't have a choice, as I recall."

Her attempt at humor failed. He still felt like the rear end of a donkey. "No, I had a choice," he berated himself harshly. "I chose to believe I could protect you—"

"Stop it." She raised her head from his shoulder. The glare she gave him was watery. "That's not your job. Your job is to be a scoundrel. With any luck, I'll rub off on you."

"What if I rub off on you instead?" he whispered, transfixed by her glimmering stare.

"Don't be ridiculous. There's too much at stake."

He managed a fleeting smile. She was changing already, although she refused to admit it. The woman who had trained a gun on his private parts was not the same woman who now stood close to tears in his arms.

"So how can I be more like a scoundrel?" he asked.

"Well, for one thing, don't offer to help me down from my horse. And don't help Blisse stack her wood. And for God's sake, don't ever give up your seat by the fire, even if I have to sit in six inches of mud."

"Hmm." He strove to put some levity into their conversation. "That sure is a lot to remember on top of the shuffling, the double dealing, the card palming—"

"Which you *still* aren't doing right," she interrupted, pressing her lips together.

He was secretly pleased by her disapproval. During their three-day journey to Comanche Peak, she had spent hours teaching him how to impersonate a sharper. She'd only been obliging his request for advice. Still, he'd grown resentful—in truth, jealous—wondering if she was being a bit too dedicated in her efforts to turn him into a replica of Santana. The final straw had come when she suggested he carry a riding quirt.

"The day I carry a whip to beat horses and women with, is the day I go to hell," he'd growled, only to regret his outburst a heartbeat later. He'd seen how the remark had hurt her.

Diego Santana was a bastard. Clearly, she knew it too. But

getting her to admit Santana was a louse was going to require plenty of patience. And a lot of love.

"Well . . ." He tried to think of a response that might coax a smile from her. "I figured if I got too good at cheating, none of those penny-pinching outlaws would let me play their game."

She sighed, looking troubled. "You're a good man, Cord. That's why all this pretense is hard for you. But in a few weeks, your mission will be over, and you can look back fondly because . . . well, because you were only playing a role. Not acting out your life."

A lump swelled in his throat. She was the only reason he would look back fondly on the spring of '74. Until Fancy blazed into his days and nights, he had forgotten how cold his marriage had been. He had forgotten the real reason for letting his badge take him so far from home. Irksome and bawdy, clever and brave, Fancy lived and loved with the intensity of a wildfire. He wanted her heat in his life. Always.

He chose his next words carefully. "Fancy, you don't have to keep living like an outlaw if you don't want to."

Her chin quivered, and she dropped her eyes, staring at the top two buttons of his shirt. "I don't think prison has changed Diego much."

Santana again. Damn. How could a man confess what was in his heart if the woman he loved kept mooning over some flashy sharper who didn't even remotely resemble the fantasy she had dreamed up?

Cord struggled with his frustration. As much as he wanted to tell Fancy he loved her, he still needed some sign that she was ready to let Santana go. Winning for keeps had become too important to him to risk a high-stakes gamble in this game.

He tried another tactic to woo her.

"I expect you're right," he whispered huskily, brushing a curl from her cheek. "You don't have to worry about Santana for a good, long spell, though. We have the whole night ahead of us now. And you know what? You were right about another thing, Fancy. I need you. I need you something fierce."

His words were plain and simple and blessedly welcome to Fancy's ears. She wanted so much to believe Cord spoke the truth. She raised her lips to meet his, returning his hungry kisses with a fervor that left them both breathless.

Her senses were spinning when he tugged her blouse from her waistband. Eagerly she reached for the buckle on his gunbelt. A breath of wind gusted across her tingling nipples and shivering thighs. It took a precious moment longer to free herself from her boots. When she at last straightened, naked except for the shimmer of starlight, she was disconcerted to see how he had stepped back to gaze at her.

"My God, Fancy," he breathed. "You are so beautiful."

She was beautiful? She felt her throat tighten. Truly?

She saw the truth shining in his eyes, but it was hard to believe after everything Diego had said and done. *You don't have to flatter me,* she wanted to assure Cord. *We both know what I am.*

Her throat ached too much to free the words, so she took the hand he offered and waded with him into the stream, where tumbled slabs of limestone formed shields against prying eyes. The water glided over her skin like liquid satin. It was warmer than she had expected, or maybe the warmth was Cord's, flowing over her, seeping inside her, wrapping around her heart. When he drew her closer for his kiss, she felt as if a ray of sunshine had crept inside her soul to thaw the year-round winter that had frozen her secret self.

He smelled of pine smoke and tasted of salt, the essences of earth and man, yet his pulse throbbed around her with the primordial rhythms of the sea. He pulled her deeper into the current, and she felt herself sinking, sable waters sliding over her flesh, waves of wanting lapping at her core. As the moon rose, so did her tide of desire. Every touch, every sensation was new, now that the fortress inside her was melting. His arms buoyed her hips higher; he braced his weight against the stone. When he let her sink again, she felt the hot, sweet swell of life that flowed from the font of his being.

"Cord . . ." She squeezed her eyes closed, wanting to be every part of him, wanting to feel, for the first time in her life, the heart and soul of a man. "I love . . . how you love me," she finished hastily, biting back the truth just in time.

She heard his breath catch, but when she would have raised her head to search for the reason, he tangled his hand in her hair, holding her cheek close to his, plunging her hips faster and deeper.

"I love to love you, Fancy."

The waves were cresting inside her. He pushed them higher and higher, until at last the dam broke and she was rushing with the tide, flowing outside of herself to that special place near the star-spangled horizon, where heaven touched and became the sea.

The sweetness of that moment never faded. He loved her again and again through the night, kissing her as if she were a delicacy to be savored, holding her as if she were more precious than gold.

The third loving came before dawn. Lying beside him on the bank of the stream, she had been longing to hold him as the stars faded, leaving Venus to wink like a diamond in the indigo blue. She had been too shy to reach for him, though, thinking she should be satisfied with two heavenly journeys and that to ask for a third would remind him of her past.

He woke to catch her watching him. His slow, wicked grin made every nerve in her body jolt and spread a languorous heat from her head to her toes.

"Why did you let me waste time sleeping?"

She laughed when he pulled her across their nest of denim and lace. "You have to be the healthiest man I've ever known," she retorted, squirming with delight when his hard body pressed her down, and she felt the sweet, hot throb of his stirring masculinity.

"I have to admit, darlin'," he drawled, "you do powerful things to me."

Later when she lay spent and wistful, cradled in the safety of his arms, she wondered if any man had ever loved her the way Cord did. She couldn't remember anything like the dizzying pleasure he gave her, or his tender possession afterward, when the loving was done. She cherished every moment, every heartbeat that he shared with her.

But the most treasured time of all came during the long and spiraling aftermaths, when he clasped her close and held her tight, refusing to let her go. She could imagine then that he truly cared about her, that she meant more than a few torrid nights of relief from his work. In those quiet, blissful moments, when their every fiber was joined as one, she began to nourish the seedling of hope that Cord would not grow tired of her as Diego had.

Squeezing her eyes closed, she reached beyond herself, daring to breathe the first prayer she'd offered to heaven in years.

Father, please forgive me for my wrongs. Please help me to be worthy of this man. I humbly place myself in your hands. Amen.

Chapter Eighteen

The next two days passed in an agony of dread for Fancy. Every minute of every hour was a test of her nerve. Arguments erupted often between members of the gang, who sought a reprieve from their boredom. Men who weren't waving guns or throwing fists at each other often amused themselves by trying to decoy Cord from her side.

When she wasn't worrying about being stalked or ambushed, she was worrying about Cord. The outlaws didn't trust him, as evidenced by Ned's demand that Cord leave her behind in good faith and go arrange a rendezvous with his Mexican *compadres*. Cord had countered that he first wanted proof of Ned's plates and silver. And so the dance continued.

The strain was enormous. Ned was planning a stage robbery, ostensibly to keep his men from killing one another, but Fancy suspected his real motive was to test Cord. She'd never feared for Diego this way, probably because Diego had been so slick. But Diego's strength—his lack of principle—was Cord's weakness. He had a tendency to tense his jaw when he lied. The habit made him appear harder, more dangerous, but she knew him well enough to realize that dishonesty was like a needle in his gut. The strain showed in the harsh angles and deepening hollows that seemed to be marking his face of late. At any moment, she feared he might expose his true identity.

Sometimes, she was the one who nearly gave him away. She'd choked back his name on more than one occasion before the ever-present, ever-vigilant Blisse. Calling him Frank had not become any easier with the passage of time; in truth, Fancy was loath to keep up the pretense. Cord could never truly be cruel or depraved, and yet, the more she watched him behave the way he imagined a desperado might, the more she wanted the old, mischievous Cord back.

As if the fear of Cord's discovery weren't wreaking enough havoc on her nerves, she still had the governor's deadline to worry about. It was only twelve days away. Terse and suspicious by nature, Ned had apparently confided Bart's minting plates' location to nobody, not even his brother. At least, that was Jake's complaint. She hadn't seriously hoped to find the plates in camp—Ned would have been a fool to tempt thieves with such a booty—but she thought she might glean a clue to their hiding place by allying herself with Blisse.

Blisse, however, wanted no part of female companionship. The day before, when Fancy was collecting firewood for breakfast, she had found Blisse sniffling in the bushes with a split lip and a blackened eye. Fancy had tasted bile to realize how brutal the girl's night must have been. Kneeling at her side, she had offered to salve Blisse's wounds, but the girl had slapped her hand away.

"We ain't friends, *puta*," she had hissed like a cornered animal. "I know what you're trying to do. This here's my camp and my men. Stay outta my way, or you can kiss that fancy man of yours good-bye."

Fancy still wondered what Blisse had meant. Did the girl hope to seduce Cord and make him her protector? Or was her intent far more sinister?

Remembering how Blisse had challenged Cord about being in an El Paso crib, Fancy had waited impatiently all day to question him in private. In truth, she had trouble picturing him in some low-class brothel, but she understood how great a man's need could be, and she wondered if he might have given in to loneliness one night after his wife's death. She couldn't exactly fault him for longing to be held. After all, wanting Diego's affection had frequently driven her to do things she regretted. But the thought of Cord fornicating with Blisse made her heart sick.

Cord, however, assured her he remembered nothing of Miss Lottie's. "Fancy," he said, frowning as if being reminded of past lovers was the greatest possible offense to him, "don't you think I would have gotten you the hell out of here if I thought Blisse might be a threat to you? Or me? Or us?"

"But what if you just don't remember?" she whispered uneasily. "What if you've had so many women over the years that you just can't recall their faces—"

Suddenly, he laughed. He threw back his head and roared with mirth. Her face flamed. She glanced uneasily around them for eavesdroppers until he finally caught his breath.

"Why, Miss Fancy Holleday," he drawled, raising an eyebrow and flashing sinfully provocative dimples, "you're jealous."

If she hadn't been so worried about him, she would have punched him in the gut.

In fact, Fancy couldn't stop worrying, despite Cord's reassurances. Blisse was sharp-eyed, keen-eared, and quickwitted. What if the girl really had recognized him from some fleeting encounter in El Paso?

And what if he'd been wearing his badge?

May twentieth ticked off the third frustrating day of negotiating for the plates.

It also marked Fancy's birthday.

Conditioned by her former profession to think of twenty-six as ancient, she had deliberately kept the occasion a secret from Cord. Still, she felt disappointed when she woke to find he was missing from the bedroll beside her. She had thought that they might . . . well, sneak off for a private celebration.

She glanced hopefully around the campsite. Dawn hadn't quite crept over the cliff face, so most of the men were still snoring. By the glow of the campfire's embers, she could discern a few empty bedrolls among the darker shadows, the most notable one being Blisse's. But then, Blisse rarely slept. She shared that trait with Cord.

Fancy fidgeted, disliking where her thoughts were straying. Cord had stopped reaching for her at night, but that was perfectly understandable, wasn't it? After all, they had no privacy, and he wasn't one to do his lovemaking in front of drooling spectators.

As for his gruff tone, his rare glances, and his aloofness, all were part of his desperado guise—a guise she had instructed him to create. It was foolish, not to mention dangerous, to crave reassurance from the old, tender Cord. The problem was, she'd had so few genuine demonstrations of affection in her life that Cord's sudden coolness felt like a hard freeze. His behavior left her wondering. Did he still think she was special? As special as she had been to him that night by the stream, when she was a year younger?

She sighed. Stretching stiffly, she rose and grimaced. When had it become so hard to sleep on the ground?

"Sleep well, Caliente?" Cass was leering at her across the campfire with his incessant, coyote grin.

She nodded, trying not to scowl. Cass and his confidant, Goose, had been quick to christen her "hot whore" in Spanish, then had shortened Caliente to Callie. All the outlaws had a nickname, it seemed. Cord's was Randy, since he refused to share her bedroll with the others.

"Too bad," Cass drawled. "I thought Randy had more juice in him than that." He smacked his lips like a hungry mongrel. "Now, if you was my woman, you wouldn't be sleeping much a'tall—if you catch my meaning."

Oh, she caught his meaning, all right. It was as obvious as his lack of personal hygiene. One couldn't walk within five feet of Cass, Goose, or the others without smelling some part of their bodies. She suspected Cord would never have crawled into his bedroll, much less a woman's, caked in dust and sweat. Watching him bathe had become the highlight of her days.

She smiled wryly. "Next time I want a sleepless night, Cass, I'll keep you in mind."

"Quit your gabbing, woman," barked a squarish lump in another bedroll. "We don't got wood for the fire. And I sure as hell don't see my breakfast."

Mad Dog. Her smile turned wan. Yes, womankind would certainly be better off if Ned Wilkerson died heirless.

She crossed to the soup kettle.

"And you'd best tell that other one to get her lazy ass up," Ned said, "if she knows what's good for her."

Fancy frowned in mock confusion. "Oh, dear. So much to do. Which would you prefer first, Mr. Mad Dog? The wood, your breakfast, or Blisse?"

Ned's lip drew back in a snarl.

Cass chuckled. "He's had Blisse. You'd best go fetch his breakfast, Callie."

Fancy hid her revulsion.

The red-orange disk of the sun was finally edging above the cliff face when she started toward the stream with the unwashed kettle in her hand. Furtively glancing at each shadow, she hoped for a glimpse of Cord. He seemed to have disappeared. Blisse too. But then, Blisse usually went where Cord went.

Fancy swallowed, carefully turning her mind away from the obvious conclusion. She wouldn't believe that of Cord. She couldn't. It was her birthday, and she was feeling old. Snubbed. That was all.

Suddenly, she was distracted by the sound of a high-pitched male voice. It seemed to come from the sheltering boulders that had tumbled down beside the path.

"I didn't haul your scrawny ass out of Miss Lottie's to do you any favors," the man snapped. "Now go do like I told you."

Fancy stumbled to a halt. She couldn't immediately place the speaker, although she thought it might be Goose. The menace in his tone was unusual and distorted his oily tenor.

"I don't got to listen to you." The second voice was

unmistakably Blisse's, angry, defiant, and just a bit scared. "I'm not your whore no more."

"You'll do like I said, bitch, or your whoring days are through."

"Ha! I ain't scared of you. Not when I got Randy—"

The ominous crack of flesh on flesh bounced off the limestone wall.

"Blisse!" Fancy's pulse skyrocketed. "Is that you? Ned's been looking for you."

A tense silence filled the seconds that dragged by. Fancy felt her skin grow clammy.

"Blisse!"

More silence. Dear God, had Goose killed her?

And what had Blisse meant by "I got Randy?"

Hastily, Fancy set down the kettle and slipped off her holster's trigger guard. She tried to keep the panic from her voice. "Dammit, Blisse, I'm not cooking breakfast by myself again!"

She waited uneasily. A faint whimper sounded, then the scrabbling of rock. Goose strolled out from behind the tumbled monolith. He wiped his hand on his pants leg, and Fancy's stomach flipped when she spied the tell-tale stain of red that his knuckles left behind.

"Well, well, well. Looks like Callie's lost her man." Goose's face split into an obscene grin, but his eyes stayed narrowed and dangerous. "You been standing there long, Callie?"

Blisse stumbled out from the other side of the rock. A trickle of blood spilled from the corner of her mouth. She braced herself on the limestone, pressing the back of her hand to her split lip, and shot Fancy a warning glare.

"She ain't looking for you, Goose. Or didn't you hear?"

"I hear just fine, Blisse. How 'bout you, Callie? You didn't answer my question."

Fancy willed herself to return his stare. Although his lean boyish body made him less physically threatening than Ned, Goose had proven himself the canniest member of the gang.

By watching Diego, Fancy had learned that clever men with slight builds were the most dangerous of all.

"Sure I heard you, Goose. We all hear you when your pants are down." She wanted to retch at the very idea, but she had to protect herself. Blisse too. Fortunately, she had more to flaunt than Blisse, so she used it—hips, breasts, smile, and all. "You make the others sound like schoolboys. Not one of them can ride as long as you."

"Yeah?" He smirked, but his conceit wasn't quite as great as his suspicion. It smoldered like twin embers in his eyes. "Even longer than Randy, eh?"

"Oh, yes, much longer," she purred. "I've counted."

Blisse stalked forward, her hands balled into fists. "I told you these men are mine, damn you. *Mine!*"

Fancy shuttered her features, trying not to telegraph her frustration. When she was sixteen, had she acted this way? She repressed a shudder. Up until that moment, she had considered Blisse wise beyond her years. Now she saw the glimmer of childishness in the girl's ravaged face. *For God's sake, Blisse, I'm trying to help you.*

"Yes, well . . ." Fancy lifted a provocative shoulder and beamed her most enticing smile at Goose. "I suppose you did. A pity they don't have a choice."

"They got a choice, bitch. And it's *me!*"

Shrieking like a banshee, Blisse charged. Startled, Fancy could do little more than throw up an arm against the claw-like fingers that reached for her eyes. Blisse's bony frame slammed into her chest, and the next thing Fancy knew, she was toppling to the ground with Blisse trying to rip her hair out.

"Catfight!" Goose whooped.

Sitting on the lookout rock with Lash, Cord didn't immediately hear the commotion. He'd approached the taciturn sentry on the pretext of sharing a cigarette. Goose was Cass's *compadre,* and Ned kept company with Jake, but Lash was the odd man out. Like the scorpion he resembled, he watched and waited, keeping largely to himself. Cord had hoped to maneuver Lash into a conversation that would eventually lead to the plates.

Goose's gleeful cries brought that plan to a screeching halt.

"C'mon, boys!" Goose trumpeted like his namesake. "Blisse and Callie are going at it good! They're tearing out hair and ripping up shirts. There's gonna be tits everywhere, boys. Come see!"

Merciful God, Cord thought. Was it true?

He rose hastily, but Lash stepped to block his way.

"What's your hurry, Harris?" the outlaw drawled, darting Cord a sly look through the haze of cigarette smoke. "Don't you think your woman can lick little ol' Dusty?"

"I got twenty dollars riding on Blisse," Cass called up to them as he ran down the path beneath the lookout rock. "Your whore won't last five minutes, Harris, once Blisse pulls out her knife."

Cord's heart stalled. He shoved Lash out of the way. The outlaw's mocking laughter floated after him as he jumped down to the trail, but he didn't care. The time for pretense had ended. Fancy's life was at stake.

He pushed his way through the circle of hooting, cheering outlaws, slamming a fist into Cass, who tried to hold him back, and another into Goose, who tried to trip him up. By the time he finally won access to the arena, Fancy and Blisse were rolling in a cloud of dust, their legs flailing. Fancy was muttering oaths, Blisse was shrieking curses, and they both were gouging and scratching. Never had he seen such a spectacle.

"Fancy!" he shouted, wading in. "That's enough now, dammit!"

By virtue of her weight, she had rolled on top. He grabbed her by the collar and yanked her to her feet.

Blisse scrambled up in a heartbeat. With tears trickling down her cheeks, she charged again. This time, steel glinted in her hand. Lunging to intercept her, he grabbed her wrist and spun her hard against him. The outlaws hooted as she kicked and clawed.

"Blisse!" he yelled.

She hesitated when she realized whose private parts she was trying to gouge with her knee.

"Drop the knife."

She sobbed, struggling in earnest again.

Her boot struck his shin, and he bit back an oath. Half-carrying, half-dragging her, he wrestled her a few yards away and pinned her against the face of the cliff. The pressure of his fingers finally forced the knife from her hand.

"It's over, Blisse," he said in her ear. "Settle down now, or you'll get yourself hurt."

"You don't care about me," she sobbed. "No one cares about me. You only care about *her.*"

"That's not true," he murmured, trying to soothe her with his hands.

She blinked up into his face, looking pathetically hopeful, and he felt his heart twist. The girl was a wild card, and he didn't trust her. But she'd been so brutalized by the other men that he didn't have the heart to shove her away while she still gulped down tears.

He let her cling to the front of his shirt as he glanced at Fancy. For now, it was more important to assess her injuries than to demand what the hell she'd been thinking to let herself get goaded into a knife fight. Other than a torn sleeve and a scratch on the bridge of her nose, she didn't seem any the worse for the brawl. He breathed a sigh of relief—until he saw the resentment smoldering in her eyes.

"What'd ya go and stop the fight for, Harris?" Cass growled, his face wiped clean for once of its habitual smile. "You didn't have no right. And now you owe me twenty dollars."

"That's right," Goose said, his cheeks mottled with anger as he clutched his gut where Cord had punched him. "You owe every one of us twenty dollars. In gold. And a turn on the woman too."

"I told you she's mine," Cord snapped.

"You can't have both of them, Harris," Lash taunted from his perch on the rock.

"That's right," Cass said. "And it seems like he made his choice, don't it, boys?"

There was a general rumble of agreement. Only Fancy said nothing. Her chest heaving, she continued to regard him with that scathing stare. Goose stepped forward and reached for her arm.

"Back off," Cord warned.

The outlaw sneered.

"Back off, I said."

The gun was in Cord's hand so quickly, Goose didn't have time to blink. Cass, Lash, and Jake all drew belatedly. Blisse caught her breath. She edged nervously from the circle of Cord's arm.

Fancy's brittle laughter broke the tension.

"You aren't fool enough to shoot the only man who can bring you four million dollars in Mexican silver, are you, boys?" she said. "Because if you are, you'll be sitting on other godforsaken rocks just like this one, swatting flies and baiting scorpions for the rest of your lives."

"Put your guns away," Ned growled, glaring at each of his men in turn. "Christ, your brains are the size of your peckers. And that ain't saying much."

He leveled his baleful eye at Cord. "As for you, Harris, keep that whore of yours on a leash, or I'll put a bullet through her snatch. Then no one's gonna have her. Got that?"

It was the longest speech Cord had ever heard Wilkerson make. He nodded curtly.

"Now get your horses ready." Ned was quick to divert his followers from their itchy trigger fingers. "That stage route is a good three-hour ride from here. And I want biscuits and coffee for every man in ten minutes." He snapped that last order at the women.

Blisse nodded hurriedly, slinking away to do his bidding. Without so much as a glance at Cord, Fancy turned on her heel and stalked after the grumbling outlaws toward the campfire.

"Fancy!" he called sharply. He saw her halt, her spine as

rigid as an oak board. God, he hated this pretense, but he knew the others would watch and listen. He didn't dare soften his tone just now, yet he couldn't let her walk away without trying to communicate his concern. He could see how badly the brawl had shaken her.

"We aren't finished, woman," he said in his brusque Frank Harris voice.

Fancy swallowed hard, digging her nails into her palms to fight back tears. She wouldn't humiliate herself. Not this time. She'd been a fool much too often where Cord Rawlins was concerned.

How could she have been so naive? She should have known better than to think he cared about her, *really* cared. "I got Randy," Blisse had said. For once, the girl seemed to have spoken the truth. If Fancy hadn't seen it with her own eyes, she would never have believed Cord could turn against her that way.

Clearly he blamed her for the fist fight. He'd seen Blisse's tears, and he'd taken her side. Never mind that the little savage had tried to stick a knife inside her chest! He'd gone to comfort Blisse. He'd let her hug and fondle him in front of Goose, her whoremonger, and the entire Wilkerson gang.

And to think I almost told him I love him that night by the stream!

Unable to bear the pain of her newfound feelings, Fancy rounded on him. "Christ, you were stupid," she hissed, leaping to the attack. "If you want to get yourself killed, that's fine by me. But leave me out of it."

She saw him stiffen. His eyes flickered to Lash, who was pretending not to eavesdrop on the rock overhead.

"You want to explain yourself?"

"Well, let's see. Pulling a six-shooter against five armed men—"

"I seem to recall you needed help."

"I don't need anything from you . . . *Frank,*" she added acidly.

He stepped closer. His eyes were practically slits under the brim of his hat. She couldn't read them.

"This isn't a poker game, sweetheart," he said, his voice low and throbbing with some restrained emotion. "You heard what Wilkerson said. Keep your nose clean."

"What about you?" she wanted to shout. "What about keeping your *hands* clean?"

"You forget, *Frank.*" She used the name like a flogging. "I know my way around men. And if I were you, I'd watch my back."

She started to turn, but he caught her arm, pulling her hard against him. She could feel his heart hammering against her back, his quickened breaths gusting against her cheek.

"Dammit, Fancy, what does that mean?"

Her throat thickened. She almost regretted her words, for she'd meant them as a warning, not a threat.

Then she recalled the image of Blisse, her tear-streaked face pressed against his shoulder. She remembered how he'd clasped the girl's waist and crooned words of comfort to her. Blisse had been pitiful, like the hurt and frightened child she really was. And Fancy had never felt as old as she did at that moment.

"It means," she said harshly, fighting her traitorous tears, "that you're vulnerable, Frank. Very vulnerable. Hold on to that knife to protect yourself, because your little redheaded friend probably has another one waiting for you under her skirts."

"Where the hell is Caliente?" This bellow came from Ned, whom she could see towering before the campfire with his fists on his hips.

Cord muttered what sounded like an expletive. "Fancy," he whispered quickly, his fingers tightening over her arm, "this thing between me and Blisse, it's not what you—"

"You deaf or something, woman? Get your ass up here!" Ned was toying with the trigger guard of his holster. "I ain't saying it again!"

Fancy tugged free of Cord's grasp. Twenty-six years of deceit—of hiding who she really was and what she really felt —saved her now from a gross display of feminine weakness.

She masked her features, falling back on the old habits as easily as she used to fall onto Diego's feather mattress.

"Save your breath, Frank," she said. Smiling seductively at Wilkerson, she headed for the campfire. "Ned needs me now."

That day was perhaps the longest one of Cord's life.

The stage robbery had troubled him deeply, so deeply that he almost wasn't able to go through with it. Seeing the passengers' terror when the gang had swooped down, when Ned had ordered the baggage burned and the stage rolled, when Goose had talked about killing the men and raping the pregnant woman—all had brought home to Cord the realization of how his parents must have suffered before they were gunned down in another stage robbery thirteen years earlier.

If Fancy hadn't been by Ned's side, pointing out that no one would get much pleasure from humping a pregnant female, or that the Mexicans might refuse to deal with a man whom every Texas Ranger was hunting for murder, Cord might have lapsed back into his old lawman role. As it was, he'd been sorely tested not to put a bullet through Ned every time the bastard tried to grope Fancy.

Or every time she had whispered in Ned's ear, smiling her loins-stirring smile and playing the game she'd played with Cord himself when he'd tried to arrest her in Fort Worth.

With Ned, Cord wasn't so sure Fancy was just playing.

She'd flirted outrageously with the man all afternoon and had ignored Cord completely. At sunset, when the outlaws stopped to make camp, she had enticed Ned into a game of poker. The others had all gathered around, laughing, betting, making lewd comments. Cord was sure Fancy had cheated during her deals, working him out of the game.

He wanted to believe she had some plan in mind, that she was trying to ingratiate herself with Ned to learn the location of the plates. But it was hard, damned hard, especially when she refused to join him when he made movements to retire. Waiting what he thought was a discreet period of time, he'd tried to attract her attention once more. Finally, he'd had to rise, looming over her in the midst of her play, and demand that she accompany him to bed.

He'd never forget the look in her eyes when he later reached to hold her.

"Go to sleep, Frank," she had said in a low, biting whisper. "You wanted to retire, remember?"

Now she was gone. Her hat, saddlebag, and change of clothing were all cleverly arranged to form a mound beneath her blankets.

Damn her. How could she have sneaked off without his noticing?

"Poor Randy," a lilting soprano voice taunted behind him. "You weren't really expecting to find Caliente in her own bed, were you?"

He swung around, choking back another oath. *Blisse.* He'd thought she was off in the bushes somewhere with Goose. Or Cass. Cord cringed inwardly. The only time those two seemed to separate was to urinate or fornicate.

"Where is she?" he demanded.

Blisse cocked her head and smiled. It was the slow, inviting smile that Fancy had often used to drive him mad. But from Blisse, with her swollen lip and missing tooth, the come-on looked pitiful. He tried to step past her, but she caught his arm.

"You know, I ain't never thanked you proper," she murmured. "For being so nice to me, I mean."

He managed not to make a face at the husky timbre of her voice. Where did a girl her age learn to flirt like a bawd? Miss Lottie's? He made a silent vow to shut that clap trap down the next time he passed through El Paso.

"You cook my meals, Blisse. That's thanks enough."

Nodding, he tried to move on. She wouldn't let go.

"I thought maybe we could be more friendly. You know, get acquainted."

He scowled. Where the hell was her father? he wondered fleetingly. With her mop of red hair and her dusting of freckles, she reminded him poignantly of Wes. She was just a kid. If he didn't have Fancy to worry about, he would have marched the girl to her blankets and sat shotgun on her himself.

"Now isn't the time," he said brusquely, prying her fingers free.

"Why? Ain't I lady enough for you?" She stuck out her chin. "Ain't I *fancy* enough?"

He steeled himself against his growing alarm. He didn't at all relish the way she competed for his affection. Even so, he knew now was not the time to tell her she could never take Fancy's place in his heart. No woman could.

"I have business to attend to."

"Yeah? Well, you ain't much good at lying, Marshal. Didn't your woman never tell you that?"

Cord's heart stalled. When it started up again, he felt dizzy from the rush of his pulse.

Blisse smiled smugly. "Still don't remember me, eh? Well, I remember you, Marshal. We met about five months ago at the cathouse. 'Course, you were red-eyed drunk then, and mooning over some picture card of a prissy blonde. You wouldn't take no one to bed, not even Miss Lottie. All you wanted was whiskey, you said. And Miss Lottie had the finest."

Her smile turned wistful. "Don't you remember? There was this man, a big-fisted bastard, who claimed I stole his purse. 'Course, Miss Lottie was the one who rolled him, but I couldn't let on or she would have killed me. So he started hitting me. And everyone laughed.

"Everyone except you," she said softly. "I'll never forget it. Not as long as I live. You stood up. You were weaving all over the place, but you pulled your gun and you shoved it in his face. He got a good look at your badge then. He turned all pasty-faced and hightailed it for the door, just like a jackrabbit."

She clasped her hands and giggled, turning big, adoring eyes on him. *"Now* do you remember?" she whispered hopefully.

Cord swallowed hard. In spite of the bottle of whiskey he'd consumed, he could vaguely remember that night because it had been the anniversary of Beth's death. He'd been so busy trying to drown his guilt and sorrow that he didn't think twice about drawing his gun. Or his reason for doing it. He'd reacted instinctively, because it was his habit to protect people who couldn't fend for themselves.

Jesus. Had Blisse really been the whore he saved that night?

He drew a ragged breath. Whether or not she was, she clearly knew he wasn't Frank Harris.

"What do you want?" he asked curtly.

She blinked, looking wounded by his tone. "I—I want you to take me with you," she said in a hesitant, childlike voice. She raised her chin a notch. "And I want you to get rid of that whore."

He bit his tongue. His immediate impulse was to tell her she asked the impossible, then fear snaked through him. Fear for Fancy. He fought it back down.

"If you want my help, Blisse, then you'll have to prove you can be trusted. Like I trust Fancy."

Her eyes narrowed to hear him compare her to her rival. "Yeah? How?"

"Tell me where the plates are."

She laughed uneasily and shook her head. "Why don't you ask *her* if you trust her so much?"

"Because I'm asking you."

Their eyes locked. Blisse fidgeted.

"Well, I don't know," she finally admitted in a sullen voice. "Ned won't tell me nuthin' and Goose is awful mad about it." She grimaced, wrapping her arms across her chest. "Now Goose isn't even sure Ned has the plates. He said Ned's been lying in wait all this time, not lying low. He says Ned was sneaking out nights to talk to the local folk, trying to get wind of where your woman was, before you and she got here. That's why Goose sent me to hump Ned all those nights, to find out what he learned."

Cord felt his gut knot. So Ned had set up Fancy?

"Where is she?" he demanded more urgently.

Blisse looked mutinous. "You said you'd get rid of her anyway, so what does it matter?"

Her implication iced Cord's blood. With the speed of a gunfighter, he caught her chin. Surprise registered on Blisse's face, then fear. She grabbed his wrist, trying to wrench herself free until she realized he wasn't hurting her.

"Now you listen to me, Blisse. If anything happens to Fancy, anything at all, I'll hold you personally responsible." He leaned closer, drilling her with his gunfighter glare. "Do you understand?"

Her eyes filled with tears. "I don't see why you're so worried about *her* all the time—"

"If you take care of Fancy, then I'll take care of you. That's the deal. Are you in?"

Her bottom lip trembled. He felt like the world's mangiest mongrel. In her eyes, he could see her love for him warring with her fear for her life. He had no right to ask Blisse to make such a sacrifice, and if Fancy's life hadn't been at stake . . .

Dammit. Plates or no plates, he had to get them out of camp. Tonight.

"Okay," she whispered thickly. "I'm in."

"Good. Now I want you to wait for me by the horses."

"But—"

"Do as I say. Where's Fancy?"

She sniffled. "You ain't gonna like it."

He ground his teeth, wanting to shake her. "Tell me anyway," he said in a voice that cracked with impatience.

Blisse winced. "She went to see Ned."

His mouth went dry. He must have conveyed his dread somehow, for he saw the tiniest flicker of triumph in Blisse's face.

"Yeah. That's right. And if I were you, I wouldn't be trusting her so much, neither. I heard them talking. That fancy woman of yours is trying to cut you outta the plate loot."

Chapter Nineteen

Fancy glanced up in surprise when Cord, looking madder than hell, crashed through the bushes to find her and Ned sitting cozily on the lookout ledge.

Cord, however, couldn't possibly be as angry to see her as she was to see him. Damn the man. What did it take to shake him? She had no time—or patience—for his lectures on personal safety. As of midnight, the governor's deadline would be only ten days away. While Cord might feel free to let a teary-eyed sixteen-year-old distract him, Fancy couldn't afford to forget the urgency of their mission. She had a prison sentence hanging over her head. Time was running out to get Ned to spill his guts about those plates.

"Am I intruding?" Cord asked curtly, his gaze raking over her unbound hair and immodestly buttoned shirt.

"Are you here to take the watch?" Ned growled.

Fancy shot Cord her best "go away" glare, but it didn't seem to affect him.

"Hell, no," he answered. "I'm here for my woman."

"Then you're intruding."

Fancy let her laughter tinkle in Ned's ear. "Frank's a jealous man," she purred, rubbing herself against the outlaw to distract him from the gun he was fingering.

"Let's go, Fancy," Cord said, extending his hand. The other hung loosely at his side, ready to draw.

Dammit, Cord, you have the worst timing. If he had waited five minutes, just five minutes more, she knew she could have had Ned where she wanted him. He'd already admitted to keeping the plates' location a secret from everyone, even Jake, "that scheming bastard." And he'd thought he might like to "shack up with a skirt like her," just the two of them, with four million dollars to spend. Apparently Ned wasn't above humbugging his own brother.

"We still need Frank for his contacts," she whispered in Ned's ear. "He's suspicious now. I'll have to go. Let's talk later of how we'll spend all those millions, just you and me, together."

She started to rise, but Ned caught her wrist. Something cold and cunning flickered in the depths of his coal-black eye. She felt her heart crawl to her throat.

"I'll deal with you later," he said.

Deal? She swallowed. Was Wilkerson referring to the mock bargain she had proposed . . . or something else?

She nodded weakly at him and stumbled to Cord. He pulled her behind him.

"The only deal you'll be making is with me, Wilkerson." Cord's voice was low and laced with warning.

Wilkerson's lip curled in response. "Yeah. That's right, Harris. With you."

Fancy didn't wait to hear more. She hurried down the path, her pulse racing. Something had gone wrong, terribly wrong, judging by the way Wilkerson had eyed her. Had she somehow botched the scam?

Cord's anger seethed like a black storm cloud giving chase. She could hear his footsteps falling fast and hard behind her, and she quickened her pace. She needed time to think, to plan. She didn't want to admit to him she might have lost his precious minting plates. After all, that was all he really cared about.

She cursed herself for the hundredth time. In truth, she had no one else to blame. She'd gotten her hopes up. She'd allowed herself to believe Cord might actually come to care about her in spite of her age, her past, and all the odds. Now she understood he had merely been compassionate when she had been in need. Chivalry was so ingrained in the man that he treated her the way he would treat any woman—or sixteen-year-old—whom he felt obligated to protect.

Her eyes stung, and she stumbled, blinded for a moment by the memory of his tenderness. She would never forget that night of lovemaking by the stream. Never. But her month with Cord was nearly over. She had to start thinking of her future—without him. Without Diego too. After watching Blisse and Goose together, Fancy knew she could never go back to Diego. She could never live that kind of life again. Cord had taught her there was a better way, and she wanted to find it.

One day, perhaps, she would meet a man who'd love her. Someone who'd care about her as she had secretly hoped Cord would. For the rest of her life, she would nurture that ember of hope. But no matter how many days turned to months, and months into years, she knew she would never stop loving Cord. He was the man she would always want, the one against whom she would measure all others.

Fortunately, after twenty-six years of hardship and disappointment, she had learned to accept she could never have what she wanted.

"Fancy."

His voice was low and strained. She interpreted the tone as accusatory and walked faster, fleeing as much from Cord as from the ache in her heart.

"Dammit, girl, slow down."

"I'm perfectly capable of walking down a hill in the moonlight, I think."

He caught her arm, but she yanked free.

"Let go of me! I'm not helpless without you." If she concentrated on the anger, she wouldn't have to feel the pain. . . .

"Is that what this race is all about?"

His arm locked around her waist this time. She tried to push free, which did little good, and she muttered an oath as he pulled her off the path, where the bushes closed around them and the trees rose as silent sentinels of judgment.

"Fancy, we have to talk," he said in a low, warning voice. "Settle down now."

She remembered how he'd used the same words to quiet Blisse. The memory was so hurtful, she began struggling again. All she wanted was her freedom, her dignity, but he denied them both to her when he pressed his body into hers. She found herself pinned between the rigidity of oak bark and the hardness of his chest, and she fought back tears. Three days ago, she would have been exhilarated by their closeness. Now all she could do was hate herself for letting him into her heart.

"Damn you," she said, "you ruined everything!"

He stiffened, his heart hammering hard against her breasts. *"Ruined* everything?"

"That's right! I had Wilkerson eating out of the palm of my hand until you blundered in with your misguided sense of chivalry!"

His fingers tightened over her arms. "Fancy, for God's sake, you have no idea how close you came to—"

"To what?" she interrupted in a ragged voice. "To meeting our deadline? Or have you forgotten my freedom's at stake now that you're busy protecting Blisse?"

He made an exasperated sound and gave her a small shake. "Fancy, *listen* to me."

"No, you listen, *Frank*. How dare you heave me around like your saddle? You don't own me."

His patience finally snapped, and he caught her chin in his hand. "Maybe you want me to own you, is that it? Is that why you're so spitting mad?"

She almost died to hear him come so close to her secret desire.

"You know very well what I want," she snapped, thinking of her freedom.

"Do I?" His jaw hardened in that stubborn look he got when he would have his way, and only his way. He pressed nearer, flattening her beneath his raw masculinity. "Seems like we've been dancing around this issue for so long, I got confused. Why don't you tell me plainly, so I'm sure."

"What do you *want* from me?" she flung back, nearly choking on a sob.

"The truth, Fancy. Just the truth. When are you going to admit you love me?"

She gasped. How could he be so cruel? He had never— and never would—say those words to her in return. If he had driven a knife through her, he couldn't have struck a deeper wound.

"I would never lie about something like that. Not *ever.*" She shoved him from her with a force that surprised them both.

For a moment they stood staring at each other. Then she spun away, dodging the hand he flung out to keep her from bolting down the hill.

Cord caught up with her minutes later, mortified by what he had done. He had promised himself he wouldn't push her into a confession she wasn't ready to make. And yet, when he saw her sitting beside Wilkerson with her hair down and her shirt undone, he'd nearly gone loco. He supposed the strain was responsible—the constant battle to suppress his need to look at her, to speak to her, to hold her in his arms. That, and the overwhelming fear that he would find her dead on the lookout rock.

Cord tried not to let his jealousy blind him to the truth. He liked to think that, in her own way, Fancy had been trying to protect him from Wilkerson when she'd rubbed so enticingly against the bastard. After all, if she had told Wilkerson who he really was, Cord would be shoveling coal for the devil's furnace by now. No, Fancy must have thought she had a good reason to face that killer alone. So why had she acted so defensive when he found her, as if she had something to hide?

He fell into step beside her. She had slowed her pace. Her shirt was buttoned and her hair was pulled back; he sensed he was dealing with a calmer, more controlled Fancy now. At least she wasn't running from him.

"Can we talk now?" He was careful to keep his voice quiet and even. They were too close to the camp to risk another argument.

"I think that would be wise," she said coolly.

He winced. He supposed he should be glad for her concession, but he had hoped for a little more warmth. He still had to tell her about his bargain with Blisse. Too much was at stake to hold back that information until Fancy was in a more receptive mood. Even so, he worried that at this particular moment, he would be doing irreparable harm to their apparently fragile trust.

"I'm sorry I upset you," he said. "I was pretty upset myself. After what Blisse told me, I thought I'd find you dead."

Fancy stiffened, glancing up at his face. She might have felt better if his apology had been devoid of yet another Blisse reminder.

Funny, she mused. Five months ago, when she had been fighting so desperately for Diego's favor, she would have done every underhanded thing in her power to rid herself of a younger rival. Today, she had realized Blisse wasn't a rival. She was the tragic reflection of every hurt, fear, and mistake that Fancy had ever experienced. In the eyes of a man like Cord, Blisse was someone to be pitied.

And so it went without saying that Cord must pity her too.

"You underestimate me," she said dryly. "And so does Blisse."

"Fancy."

He caught her arm once more, halting her. She felt his warmth, his worry, flowing through her, and she wanted to run again. Why couldn't he just let her be? She didn't want his pity. Anything—even his contempt—would be more bearable than that.

"I know you're angry," he said, "but you have to listen to me."

She hardened her jaw, training her gaze over his shoulder. She couldn't face his knowing eyes. "Very well."

"You were set up, Fancy. Ned set you up," he added more gently.

She felt her gut knot. Goosebumps scuttled down her spine. "What are you talking about?"

"He doesn't have the plates. He never did. He's been playing you, me, his brother—hell, his entire gang—for fools."

"That's preposterous." But was it? Hadn't she herself wondered why Ned hadn't fled to Mexico by now? "Why would he do such a thing?" she amended uneasily.

"For four million dollars in Mexican silver."

Fancy's heart began to slam against her ribs. She had wondered why Ned accepted her and Cord so readily into the gang. And she had thought Ned was taking an uncommonly long time to agree to ride with them to Mexico. If he had no plates to retrieve from some secret cache, then his procrastination would be explained.

Her mind whirred with speculation. Ned must have thought his men would refuse to believe Bart had died without handing over the plates. So he had pretended to bury them somewhere, trusting no one with his secret, not even Jake, for fear his brother's tongue might slip. If the outlaws had ever lost faith in Ned's leadership, they would have turned on him like wolves.

"But if Ned doesn't have the plates, where are they?"

"My guess is, you're the only person who can answer that, Fancy."

"No!" She shook her head, not wanting to believe she'd come so close to earning her freedom, only to have it snatched away. "I told you everything. I swear! I don't know where they are."

"You must," he said urgently. "Think. Think hard, Fancy. There has to be some clue you've overlooked, some conversation you had with someone."

She frowned, fear and frustration whirling in her brain. Surely she had followed every lead to its logical conclusion—

She caught her breath. A sudden spark of insight flashed as she recalled the conversation she'd had with Bart Wilkerson's physician.

"Dropped like a rock, Bart did, when he hit his head on the stone wall outside of Cattleman's Bank," Doc Tate had confided as she'd plied him with whiskey. "Yep, that's what finally did him in."

At the time, the site where Bart had lapsed into a coma didn't seem significant.

"Maybe you're right," she whispered. "Maybe there is something. I was talking to Bart's doctor back in Fort Worth, and he said Bart visited the Cattleman's Bank right before he died. Maybe Bart left the minting plates there."

Cord frowned. "But that doesn't make sense."

"Of course it does," she said eagerly. "It makes perfect sense. Bart was too weak to bury the plates. He needed somewhere to stash them, and the vault is like a fortress—the safest place in town. Of course, being an outlaw, he never would have deposited valuables under his real name. That's why no one ever wired his relatives to come get the sack or the strongbox, or whatever else he might have used to conceal the plates."

Cord shook his head in amazement. "The man was an idiot."

"Or a genius," she murmured. "Take your pick."

Cord gazed deeply into her eyes. For a heart-stirring moment, he seemed poised on the brink of some confession. Some sweet affirmation of feeling. She held her breath.

Suddenly, a night creature darted through the brush. Cord tensed, his gunhand flexing. Pebbles scrabbled, and she swallowed, standing like stone. For a long moment, they both strained their eyes, searching the vegetation for some sign of human intrusion. Nothing else moved, though. Nothing else breathed.

Cord frowned. She was disappointed to see his tender mood had been destroyed. He caught her elbow and guided her several steps farther down the trail.

"There's something else you need to know," he said, halting her once more.

She felt her pulse quicken. His voice sounded so grim. "What? What is it?"

"It's Blisse." He looked monumentally uncomfortable. "She . . . er, remembers me fairly accurately from El Paso."

Fancy felt her stomach churn. She knew this would happen. She knew Blisse would be trouble.

"So you did whore with her."

"No," he said quickly, meeting her gaze again. "No. Not that. Apparently I saved her from a beating. I'd finished off at least half a bottle of whiskey at the time, so I don't even remember. But she does."

Fancy swallowed hard. So Blisse knew he was a federal marshal. God help them both.

"Fancy, I'm sorry," he said hoarsely, apparently guessing at her thoughts. "I don't normally make it a habit to, er, visit places like Miss Lottie's. But it was the anniversary of Beth's death, and I was drunk out of my mind. So drunk, in fact, that I couldn't do anything. With anybody. Much less a child."

His eyes pleaded with her to understand. She wanted to shake him.

"Blisse is no child," she said in a tightly controlled voice. "She is a very real threat. And it's high time you started thinking of her that way."

Someone chuckled, and a match flared behind Cord. He whirled, drawing his gun and shielding her, but it was too late. Rifles gleamed in the moonlight.

"Imagine that, Cass," Goose drawled. "Little Blisse being a threat."

He shoved the girl forward. She was shaking visibly, despite her best efforts to look fierce and unconcerned. Cass grinned, snapping the lever on his Winchester.

But it was Ned, unarmed and unemotional, who frightened Fancy most of all. He puffed for a long blood-chilling moment on his smoke. Then slowly, deliberately, he raised his head. Her knees turned to rubber when his Satanic eye drilled through her.

"Looks like we're gonna rob us a bank, boys."

The ride to Fort Worth took two days. Two days of nerve-rending stress. Cord didn't understand why Wilkerson didn't just kill him. Clearly, his position in the gang had deteriorated to prisoner. They'd taken his gun. They'd bound his wrists. They'd even roughed him up. But they'd allowed him enough food and water to stay alive. And so far, they hadn't raped Fancy.

Blisse helped to shed some light on the situation shortly before dawn on the third day. Sneaking to his side, she slipped him a derringer.

"They still think you might have rich friends down in Mexico," she whispered. "And they don't want trouble from those bastard Rangers. I told them Fancy's daddy owns the Texas Central Railroad. I told them they could get a lot of ransom out of him if they played their cards just right. But if Fancy went home bruised or bloody, I told them her daddy would go and hire the whole damned Ranger force. And then there wouldn't be nowhere on this earth that Ned could hide."

Cord's heart warmed to the girl. "Thank you."

She nodded, darting a nervous glance toward his snoring guard before slipping back into the shadows.

So Blisse hadn't told them he was a federal marshal, he mused—or rather, no one had beaten it out of her yet. He worried what would happen to her when they learned how she had lied for him.

But if he worried about Blisse, he agonized over Fancy. During the last three days, when the outlaws stopped to make camp, they had always tied her opposite him at the site. Wilkerson, perhaps out of boredom, perhaps out of spite, played cruel games to trigger her darkest female fears. No one else was allowed to touch her. Wilkerson always stopped short of the final depravity—thank God for Blisse's quick thinking—but Cord suspected Wilkerson enjoyed terrorizing Fancy far more than he would have enjoyed the actual rape. Cord's only consolation during his helplessness was small: Fancy had resisted every one of Wilkerson's attempts to reduce her to hysterics.

If it's the last thing I do, he vowed in deadly earnest, *I'm going to kill that sonuvabitch.*

As for Fancy, she was far more worried about Cord being shot or lynched than she was about the few bruises Wilkerson gave her. She'd been pinched and prodded, slapped and bitten, and even ejaculated upon before, and certainly she'd suffered far worse at Diego's hands. Of course, she wondered why Wilkerson didn't rape her outright—or let any of the others take a turn, for that matter—but she didn't force the issue by indulging in morbid curiosity. The humiliation of having Cord witness the outlaw's perversities was far worse than their physical discomfort.

After two days and nights of this abuse, the morning of the robbery dawned. Fancy anxiously watched Cord's wrists being bound to his saddlehorn while Wilkerson finally revealed his plan.

"Goose, Cass, and Lash are gonna go into the bank posing as customers. Fancy here, being such a fine-looking distraction, is gonna change a twenty-dollar bill. When the cashier's back is turned, you boys'll jump him and any tellers, and get them to open that safe. The rest of us'll keep the townsfolk busy."

"What about me?" Blisse asked quickly. "I could guard Harris while you're hurrahing the town."

"Good thinking." Goose sneered at her. "Now that he's all trussed up and can't fight you off, you can finally get your hands in his pants."

Blisse reddened. Wilkerson drilled her with his baleful eye.

"You hold the horses," he told her.

"A hitching post can do that," she retorted sullenly.

"She's got a point, Ned," Jake said. "We can't be watching Harris and shooting up windows at the same time."

A cold, cruel smile curved Ned's lips. "We don't need to be watching Harris. He's gonna watch himself. When we do the swoop and hurrah, he's gonna ride between us with an empty gun."

Fancy's stomach curdled at the harrowing image his words conjured. But Cord didn't flinch a muscle even though he had to know he would be caught in the crossfire when the shootout began.

At four o'clock that afternoon, the gang separated at the city limits sign. Lash and Cass rode for the north side of town; Wilkerson's group headed south. By the time they crossed the Trinity River, Fancy's heart was pounding so hard she could scarcely breathe. Goose stopped her mare to slash her bonds. For a moment, one fleet and agonizing moment, her horse stood beside Cord's, and she was able to clasp his hand.

"Come back to me, Fancy," he whispered, his heart shining in his eyes.

She choked and nodded, unable to force her answer past the sob that welled in her throat. *I love you, Cord. I love you!*

Riding away, she battled tears as she watched him over her shoulder. She stubbornly fixed her eyes on his form until he was no more than a speck in the cloud of dust kicked up by the horses. *Dear God, please. Please don't let this be the last time I ever see him alive.*

To avert suspicion, Goose turned his and Fancy's horses down First Street; minutes later, Blisse spurred hers down Weatherford. By the time Goose and Fancy reached the center thoroughfare, they found Lash had already arrived. Puffing a smoke, he leaned indolently against the wall of the hardware store and watched as they rode by. Cass was tethering his horse farther down the street.

The wind had picked up. Ominous purple clouds were rolling in from the north. In anticipation of the storm, the townsfolk were shooing children off the street, shuttering windows, and slamming doors. Goose checked his watch as the sun was swallowed whole.

"We got ten minutes till the hurrah." He fixed Fancy with a keen, hard stare. "Get down."

She obeyed, trying not to let her knees quake visibly. He

swung down beside her. Catching her elbow in a viselike hold, he propelled her past the alley where Blisse crouched, waiting to round up the horses. Fancy felt the girl's resentful gaze stab through her. Or perhaps it was stabbing through Goose. It was hard to say.

"You do what I tell you," the outlaw said in a low growl, driving her up the bank steps and reaching for the doorknob. "Understand?"

She nodded weakly, feeling Ned's twenty-dollar bill smolder like a brand inside her pocket. She had the briefest of moments to wonder why this robbery should seem so different from the train's. Just as before, she was playing decoy. She knew what to do, how to behave. If she had to, she could outfox any hayseed cashier alive. But maybe that was the key. She didn't want to. Cord had really fixed her this time. He'd made her too upstanding for her own good.

Searching for escape routes, she took stock of the bank. The lobby was big and rustically appointed, with steer-horn chairs, cowhide hangings, and a mounted wolf head above the teller windows. Behind the counter, she glimpsed the vault, easily as tall as she, and wide enough for three men to step inside. Beyond the safe, there appeared to be some kind of clerk's office. Or maybe it was a door to the back alley. She remembered vaguely from her last visit to Fort Worth that stairs led from the building's rear story to the dusty street below.

Two other customers were in line. They were staring at her, and Fancy tried not to balk when Goose put his arm around her waist, drawing her close like a sweetheart. Lash wandered in a couple of minutes later. Then Cass. The three men were the most attractive in the gang and, Fancy supposed, the least likely to be regarded with suspicion. Cass even tipped his hat when the first customer, a matron, turned to head for the street.

A lean, boyish figure pushed past the woman as she tried to exit. The matron hurrumphed, excusing herself in disapproving tones, even though the youth had clearly been the one at fault. Fancy supposed it was the boy's rudeness that made him remarkable to her.

Goose muttered an oath. "Dammit, Dusty . . ."

Blisse had stuffed her hair under her hat and turned up her collar. Even so, her bruises could be glimpsed despite the shadows of her Stetson. They easily made her the most suspicious character there. Blisse glared back at Goose, then at Cass, both of whom were gesturing in a furtive, angry way for her to return to her post.

For God's sake, Blisse, Fancy thought. Would the girl get herself killed trying to prove she was more valuable to the outlaws than Fancy was?

The last customer was walking out the door. Fancy quailed as Goose tightened his arm around her waist and pushed her forward.

"Good afternoon, folks," the cashier greeted them jovially. "And how can I help you today?"

Fancy swallowed. She couldn't remember ever feeling so nervous, even in the early days, when Diego used to make her rehearse before him to make sure she wouldn't botch the con.

"I'd like to change this twenty, please," she said hoarsely, her tongue only slightly more pliant than sun-dried leather.

"Of course, ma'am." The cashier gave her a reassuring smile, no doubt thinking she was shy. "Won't be but a moment."

He stooped, reaching for the money box under the counter. Fancy caught her breath. Only then did she spy the wanted poster that had been hidden behind his shoulder. The face belonged to Diego. "Escaped Killer" was clearly discernible beneath "$1,000 Reward."

Cord! she thought with heart-stopping force. What would Diego do to Cord?

The cashier abruptly straightened. Adjusting his spectacles, he frowned down at the greenback she'd handed him. "Ma'am, I'm sorry to have to tell you this, but your bill is counterfeit."

"Yeah? Well, what d'ya know?" Goose stuck his revolver under the man's plump chin. "This .45 ain't, mister."

Gun hammers clicked as Cass and Lash both drew. One teller, growing whiter than chalk, sank to his knees; the other must have lost his senses. Turning tail, he bolted for the rear of the bank. Lash cursed, vaulting over the counter. The teller threw open the back door, and the footrace ended in gunshots. Fancy heard the ominous thudding when the teller's body bounced down the stairs.

Lash sneered as he turned back around. "Hell. He coulda put up a better fight than that."

Fancy fought down nausea. The insidious creep of panic threatened to bring her to her knees. *Caring is weakness, and weakness is death,* the old chant pounded in her ears. She couldn't let them know she mourned the teller's death. She had to think about Cord.

Her gaze strayed back to Diego's wanted poster. Somehow, she had to get through this robbery alive. She had to warn Cord he was in terrible, terrible danger.

Sitting on his horse nearly two blocks away, Cord heard the gunshots. With the gut-level instincts of a lawman, he knew the reports had come from the bank. *Fancy!* He tasted bile. *Dear God, keep her safe.*

Sputtering the foulest curses known to man, Ned slashed at Cord's bonds with a knife.

"Idiots! They're shooting too soon!" Ned pulled his neckerchief over his nose and spurred his horse down Main Street.

Jake cocked his Peacemaker and tossed Cord his gun. "Ride or die, Harris."

Cord ground his teeth. Donning his own mask, he kicked Poco after Ned's fleeing horse. His .45 felt uncommonly light without its bullets. He switched it to his left hand.

Frightened townsfolk shrieked and fled before the galloping horses. On either side of him, the Wilkersons loosed blood-curdling whoops. Cord had a fleeting moment to notice that Jake, who rode at his left, protected Ned's blind side. Then someone fired from a hotel window. Ned took aim, and the sniper jerked, tumbling streetward through a shower of glass. He hit the street like a rag doll, and Cord bit back an oath of outrage.

That's another one I owe you, Wilkerson, you bastard.

"Applegate! Brand!"

People were shouting for their lawmen as the Wilkersons swooped out of the Acre, arriving at the center of town in a tumult of dust, smoke, and noise. The sheriff's own window splintered into a thousand pieces. But Applegate, canny old codger that he was, had already hotfooted it to safety. Cord glimpsed the sheriff beneath a stairwell, tossing a rifle to a red-haired youth, before the two men ran their separate ways, firing and shouting for deputies.

More snipers appeared in windows, on rooftops, around the corners of buildings. Fort Worth was fighting back, but Cord could take no civic pride in the rally. He was terrified that somebody would defy chivalry and gun down Fancy. What the hell was taking so long inside that bank? He'd foiled a dozen or more robberies in half this time. Why weren't the outlaws running for their horses?

Suddenly, Ned's mare screamed, spouting blood. The beast reared, and Ned cursed. Instinctively, Cord swerved Poco, and the gelding rammed the mare's shoulder. Ned snarled, and Cord lunged, knocking the outlaw from the saddle. They crashed earthward in a hail of gunfire, rolling under flailing hooves.

Ned was heavier; he ended up on top. Bullets zinged off the ground near Cord's head. A red fog pounded in his brain as he grappled for Ned's loaded gun. When the yawning blackness of that muzzle turned toward him, Cord snapped back his wrist, freeing Blisse's derringer, and fired. Ned jolted, making a gurgling sound. He slumped across Cord's chest.

"Ned!" Jake howled with fury, charging back to his brother's aid.

Cord heaved frantically, pushing free of the dead man's weight. He reached for Ned's gun, but his fingers fell short. Jake took aim.

"Cord!"

A deafening report sounded. Blood spurted from a bullet wound in Jake's leg.

As startled to be alive as to hear his name, Cord glanced up at the grocer's roof. Only then did he realize his neckerchief had torn free. The red-haired youth was firing fast and furiously, driving a now bloody Jake back toward the shelter of the hardware store.

My God, that's Wes! Cord thought. *What the hell is Wes doing here?*

In the bank, time had slowed to a crawl. Fancy knew enough about robberies to realize this one was being bungled. They shouldn't be worrying about the cash box. They shouldn't be stuffing grain bags full of silver. They couldn't possibly carry it all.

Dimly she was aware that the clattering of gunfire had increased outside, as if the outlaws were no longer the only ones shooting. The moment was upon them. The time had come to flee. But Goose, relishing his command—or perhaps sotted with greed—was still shouting orders.

"Hold that bag wider," he snapped, shoving her so hard that she collided with Blisse, who was dashing past her with a chin-high stack of bills. The money went flying, and Goose reached for his Colt.

"I found them!" Cass cried eagerly from inside the vault. "I found the plates, Goose!"

Goose seemed to forget his quarrel with Blisse. "You sure?"

"Sure I'm sure! This here's Bart's old strongbox. What else could be inside?"

Reports shook the building as Cass shot open the lock.

"Lash!" Goose was barking orders again. "Go help Cass. I'll guard the tellers."

Lash muttered an oath as he hurried inside. "For Christ's sake, Cass, let's go! You're taking too damned long."

Another gunshot echoed inside the safe. Fancy started, her stomach crawling to her throat. Someone laughed. It proved to be Cass. He emerged seconds later with two bags and a smoking gun.

Goose grinned. "One down, eh, Cass? That leaves just Jake, Ned, and Harris."

Goose rounded on the cowering bank employees. "Time to say your prayers, boys." He fired once, twice. The cashier and the teller dropped dead where they had knelt. Cass snickered. Goose's grin faded as he noticed Fancy edging toward the door.

"Where the hell d'ya think you're going?" He caught her by the hair, jerking her back against his chest, jabbing the red-hot muzzle of his gun beneath her ribs. "Hold that silver real close now, precious, and it just might keep those pretty tits of yours safe."

Cass was peeking out the door. "All's clear!"

"Let's go."

Cass was the first one to reach his saddle. Goose moved more slowly, wheeling Fancy as a shield, firing back at the sniper on the bank's roof. Above the din of the shoot-out, Fancy heard Cass shout something. It sounded like a warning about Blisse.

Suddenly Goose jolted. He wheezed in her ear, and his arm slid free of her waist. Spinning, she felt the rise of sickness as he crumpled, falling facedown at her feet.

Blisse's lip curled above her smoking gun. "Reckon you won't be beating me ever again, you bastard."

For a heartbeat, Blisse's eyes—and her revolver—trained on Fancy. Then she made a savage gesture. "Run, stupid!"

Fancy stumbled backward, dropping the coins. She feared the girl would shoot her, but Blisse had already turned with her bag of loot, racing through the bluish powder haze.

"Bitch!" Cass shouted, his bullets peppering the ground at Blisse's feet. She fired back, and he spurred his horse after her. A shell zinged dangerously close to Fancy's boots, and she fled, unable to watch more.

"Fancy!"

She heard her name as she vaulted the hitching post. The cry seemed to come from above her—behind her—she wasn't certain. Gunsmoke burned her eyes so much that they teared. Blinded, she tried to fling herself across her horse's back, but the skittish mare bucked, throwing her to the ground. More bullets whizzed past, splintering the wooden post above her ear. She rolled, scrambling to her feet.

From out of the haze, a human locomotive charged. Steely arms drove her backward as a rifle blast shattered the bank window. She realized dimly she would have been in the bullet's way if her savior—or her attacker?—hadn't slammed her into the wall. Terror flooded her veins. Sobbing, she twisted frantically, trying to break his hold.

"Fancy!"

"Cord?"

He shoved her into the grocer's alley, dragging her down behind a stack of drygoods boxes. She reeled, falling into his lap, half-afraid to believe the sight, the sound, the *feel* of him. "Cord?"

"Stay down!"

A bullet whistled near her ear and burrowed into the rain barrel beside them. She flung her arms around Cord's neck as water showered them both.

"Cord, don't leave me!"

"I won't, sweet. I won't. Stay close, now."

She hugged him desperately, fearing he might change his mind, terrified that he would lose his life in the fight raging just beyond the alley.

"Cord, I was so scared," she sobbed, clinging to his neck. "I thought I would lose you. I thought I'd never see you again!"

He rocked her, stroking her hair. "Me too," he whispered huskily.

You were? she thought, swallowing hard. Then, feeling the sticky dampness of his shirt, a new fear strangled her like an iron noose. Rearing back, she clutched his collar and ran her frantic gaze over his chest. "My God! You were hit! You're covered with blood—"

"It's not mine," he said soothingly. "I'm fine, darlin'. Just fine. I'm safe. And you are too—but you have to stay down."

He pulled her back against him, and tears streamed un-heeded down her cheeks. Even if she had wanted to, she couldn't hide the truth from him anymore.

"Cord, I . . ."

She gulped a shaky breath. Raising her head, she gazed into his eyes. Their glow—that warm and tender glow that always touched her core—melted the last of her self-conscious fears.

"I love you, Cord."

He caught his breath. With a hoarse sound, he pulled her face to his. "My God, girl, if you only knew how long I've been waiting to hear you say that!"

His mouth fastened hungrily over hers. Hot and fierce, his kiss possessed her with all the pent-up longing of the last five endless days. She began to quake, as much from the feelings that tore through her breast as from the aftershock of their ordeal. When she sagged against him, he cradled her, wrapping his arms and legs around her.

Still, she was unable to quell her tremors. She buried her face in his throat. "Goose, he—he was going to kill you," she whispered brokenly. "And Blisse. And all of them—"

"Shh," he murmured, pressing her close to his heart. "It's over now. We can go home soon."

Home? Had she heard him right? She had hardly dared to hope . . .

"But the plates! Cass has them."

He sighed, pushing her head down to his shoulder. "Let me worry about Cass, love."

She bit her lip, struggling to stave off a fresh flood of tears. He'd called her love. *Love!* But now he wanted to ride away and be a lawman again. How could she bear it if he got killed?

God, please, don't let it start again. Please don't take him from me now.

She shivered, listening to the gunfire. It was fading away. So were the shouts and the galloping hooves. The entire shoot-out had lasted less than ten minutes, but she felt as if another year of her life had just passed.

Cord stirred beneath her. "Wes. I have to see if . . ."

Something in his voice made her gut knot. She glanced up sharply. "Wes is here?"

He nodded, looking haunted.

Oh no, she thought. Not Wes too. But why? What was he doing there?

She bit her tongue as Cord helped her to her feet. They would know the answers all too soon.

She clung to his hand, waiting behind him as he peered cautiously around the corner.

"No one's moving yet. I can't see him." He frowned, glancing anxiously over his shoulder at her. "Wait for me here. You'll be safe."

But she didn't want to be safe. She wanted to be with him —especially if Wes was out there hurt. Or worse.

Cord eased out into the cloud-choked light. She crept after him. She had intended to shadow him all the way to the city's limits, if necessary, but the carnage spread before her stopped her cold. She nearly retched on the spot. The smoke was clearing now, leaving behind thrashing horses, broken glass, and twisted bodies. Ned, Jake, Lash, Goose—all dead. Only Cass seemed to have cheated the undertaker. She shuddered. When she spied the blood that followed his horse's hoofprints out of town, she wondered darkly if his wounds would kill him . . . or if the coyotes would.

"Wes!" Cord bellowed.

Thunder rolled. In the accompanying flash of lightning, she spied a boyish form with red hair lying motionless before the hardware steps. She pressed her hand to her mouth.

"Wes!"

"Over here, Cord."

The air rushed from Fancy's lungs as she saw the youngest Rawlins, his rifle slung over his back, sliding down a pillar on the grocer's battered porch. He was unhurt. He was alive.

She blanched at her next thought. *Blisse.*

Battling the wave of sickness that washed over her, she stumbled to the girl's side. Blood was oozing from Blisse's chest and hip; her breaths tore from her lips in great, wheezing gasps.

"Blisse?" Fancy whispered, dropping to her knees.

The girl's lashes flickered, and she slowly turned her head. "Fancy." A tear rolled down her ashen face. "Is he . . . alive?"

The gray eyes were glazing over. Fancy nodded quickly, taking the girl's hand.

"Hold on, Blisse. They're bringing a doctor—"

"No." Her fingers tightened over Fancy's ever so faintly. "It's better this way. You know."

Fancy choked on a sob. No. It *wasn't* better. No matter how bad things got, she had never given up hope. Never.

"Cord!"

He'd been walking toward Applegate. Turning to see her holding Blisse, he ran to join her. When he fell to his knees at the girl's other side, Fancy saw the anguish on his face.

"Blisse." He took her free hand, and a tiny spot of color bloomed on the girl's cheeks.

"I didn't tell nobody who you were," she whispered. "And I kept her safe for you. I did just like you said. Did you see?"

"Yes. Yes, I did," he said thickly. "Thank you."

Fancy felt her throat constrict.

"Just once . . . before I go . . . do you think you could . . . kiss me like you do her?"

Cord glanced at Fancy. She nodded.

Her vision blurred as she watched him lean forward, gently touching his lips to Blisse's. It was a sweet, tender kiss of good-bye, the kind one might give a child before she drifted to sleep. When he straightened, Blisse smiled, closing her eyes.

"Now I can say I had a gentleman," she murmured weakly.

The girl's hand grew limp. Fancy wept, stricken by the terrible, unfair waste. Cord bowed his head.

Finally, someone cleared his throat. Dashing away tears,

Fancy saw Applegate patting Cord awkwardly on the shoulder.

"I'm real sorry about the girl, son. But you've got other problems. Bigger problems."

Cord's brow furrowed, and he climbed to his feet. Struggling to regain her composure, Fancy hurried to join him. She nearly jumped out of her skin when Marshal Brand galloped by, followed by a dozen heavily armed, vengeful-looking men. Cord turned, whistling for Poco, but Applegate caught his arm.

"Now hold on, son. That desperado ain't going far. Not with his wounds. And not with that storm blowing in. Brand's my best deputy when he ain't busy being the town marshal. He'll bring the renegade in."

Cord pressed his lips together. "I never thought I'd see the day when you let a town marshal do your job, Clem."

"Now don't you start with me, Cord. I got my reasons."

Cord crossed his arms, waiting expectantly. Applegate glanced at Wes. Fidgeting, the boy dropped his eyes. When the sheriff cleared his throat again, Fancy realized she had never seen Applegate at a loss for words.

"You know, Cord," the sheriff boomed suddenly, "Wes here is going to be a real fine lawman someday." He slapped the boy on the shoulder. "Why, he wasn't here but ten minutes after tracking those bastards all the way to Blue Mountain, and yet he put up a helluva fight on that roof without a wink of sleep—"

"What bastards?"

Applegate grimaced, clearing his throat and averting his gaze. Cord's eyes narrowed.

"Clem?"

Wes finally raised his head. Fancy was stunned to see how close the boy looked to tears. He squared his shoulders and clenched a fist.

"It's my fault," he said. "I should never have let Zack ride home alone after the droving. Me and the boys stopped off at Fort Graham for a couple days of drinking and . . . well, you know. I only spent the night, but when I got back to the ranch—" His voice broke.

"Some sonuvabitch nabbed Zack," Applegate said quietly. "Lally too."

Fancy's heart lurched. The blood drained completely from Cord's face.

"Who?" he asked.

Wes fished in his shirt pocket. "We don't know yet. There weren't any names. Just this pasteboard with a dirk stuck through it."

Fancy edged nearer. Peering over Cord's shoulder, she recognized the flowery pen strokes that defaced the ace of spades.

"Diego," she breathed.

Her blood turned to ice.

Chapter Twenty

Thunder rocked the house as Fancy quietly closed the door on the Applegates' spare bedroom. From below, she heard the rumbling bass of the sheriff himself, telling his wife he was going to town to wait for Brand. She heard the porch door bang, and she thought she heard the squishing of horse's hooves. It was hard to tell, given the din of the rain on the roof.

She bit her lip as she glanced once more toward the bedroom. Poor Wes. He'd spent three sleepless days tracking Diego north from the Barclay ranch. He'd needed rest so badly that he dozed off twice during the short ride to Applegate's homestead, yet nothing short of Cord's threat to exclude him from the posse could convince him to retire to a bedroom. The boy had been the unfortunate one to find the smoking ruins of the ranch and the slaughtered hands who'd stayed behind to help Lally run it. He'd also found Diego's note stabbed to the charred remains of Ginny's crabapple tree.

I have the old woman and the boy. Bring me the plates. Signale Mountains, near Wild Horse Creek. Come alone or they die. I'll be watching.

Diego was headed for Indian Territory, where lawlessness reigned. Rustlers, smugglers, murderers, and counterfeiters were known to seek refuge there. No wonder Wes had been

so desperate to catch the kidnappers before they crossed the
Red River. But he hadn't dared risk Zack and Lally by trying
their rescue alone. Hurrying back from Blue Mountain station, where Diego had holed up, apparently to ambush the
next day's stage, Wes had made the two-hour ride south to
Fort Worth in record time. He had hoped to enlist Applegate's help with the rescue, and somehow send word to
Cord.

When Cord learned the full story, he'd had nothing but
praise for the boy's quick thinking and grit. But Wes had
refused to take solace in either Cord's or Applegate's assurances that he could have done nothing more. Fancy's heart
had broken to see the way the boy punished himself. Unable
to bear the sounds of his anguished pacing, she had finally
gone to the bedroom to try to ease his mind.

"Please stop blaming yourself, Wes," she'd murmured,
taking his freckled fingers tightly in her own. "Zack has ridden home alone hundreds of times. You couldn't possibly
have known this was the one time he would be ambushed.
No one blames you, Wes. No one. It's not your fault."

It's mine.

She hadn't had the courage to speak the truth, though.
Clearly, it was her message to Diego, not Wes's harmless
night of revelry, that had placed Zack and Lally in danger.
When she composed that message, she had never dreamed
Diego could break out of a state penitentiary. She had never
imagined he might set a fire two days after their meeting and
escape with six inmates. But she should have known better.
She should have known.

Today, tomorrow, the truth would come out. It was inevitable. Cord would learn how she'd betrayed him, and he
would hate her. She had risked the lives of his family, even
though she hadn't meant to. How could she plead innocence? She had lied to him. She had smuggled Diego a message outlining her destination and her mission.

Oh, God, how could she have been so stupid?

Squeezing her eyes closed, she dragged a shuddering
breath into her lungs. Telling herself she was an idiot was a

waste of time. The book, the message, the deceit—she could do nothing to change them. But she could save Zack and Lally. The damage between her and Cord was irreparable, but maybe, just maybe, if she rescued his family, she could live with herself.

She finalized her plan. She had already pilfered a knife, revolver, and ammunition from Applegate's desk. Wes's compass was in his slicker, which he'd left out to dry. Blue Mountain wasn't that long a ride, really. She knew the lay of the land, because she had spent several days in the hospitality of the lonely station master there, cheating the honest stagecoach passengers who'd stopped for a meal. That station was the only real shelter within ten miles of Blue Mountain. In a storm like this, Diego and his men were bound to seek the building out a little earlier than they had planned.

She knew she had to move fast. Diego would continue riding north after tomorrow morning's robbery. Fortunately, Applegate had convinced Cord not to give chase without a posse to back him up.

"You, me, and a sixteen-year-old against seven inveterate killers? That ain't good odds, son. Not when you got kinfolk under the gun."

Fancy had wholeheartedly agreed. Zack and Lally were nothing more than lures; Cord was the one Diego wanted. But Fancy also knew Diego would kill the hostages once he had Cord as his audience. That was why she couldn't let him ride. She had to go in alone. She had to face Diego herself.

Shivering, she carefully turned her mind away from her own danger. What happened to her didn't matter. Only Zack and Lally did.

Slipping past the parlor, where Mrs. Applegate was trying to lose her own worries in a book, Fancy hurried to the kitchen for biscuits, coffee, and molasses. During their last dinner at the ranch, Cord must have spooned two or three dollops of molasses into each cup of java that he drank. Fancy did so now. Then, squelching her flare of guilt, she hastily retrieved the vial of laudanum she always strapped beneath her garter. She poured the entire dosage—two spoonfuls—

into the cup. It should be enough to knock Cord out. He would taste only the molasses, and by the time the drug took effect, it would be too late for him to stop her.

With a last glance at the parlor, she padded back up the stairs with her tray.

Applegate's considerable carpentry skill had turned the second-story veranda into a solarium. She found Cord pacing there, streaks of lightning flashing behind him like jagged spears. For a moment, she stood absolutely still, awed as she watched the sky through the shutterless windows. The storm raged around him in all its elemental ferocity, as raw and electric as his mood. It was such a change from that other storm, that other Cord, who had loved her with tender hands and hungry lips. He had trusted her then. She swallowed painfully. He would never trust her again.

"I . . . brought you some coffee and biscuits."

He glanced up. When he saw her standing on the threshold, the thunder on his brow lifted somewhat. "Thanks, but I'm not hungry. How's Wes?"

Closing the door to keep her imminent crime from the household, she crossed to a table. She could hardly bring herself to look him in the eye. "Better, I think. He finally fell asleep."

"Good."

He began pacing again. Up and down, back and forth, he prowled the creaking floorboards. She wished there was something she could say to ease his mind. He had never once lashed out in word or deed to punish her for Diego's infamy. In truth, neither he nor Wes had said a single thing against Diego while she was present, even though she knew their fear and outrage must be killing them inside. It was as if they had secretly agreed to spare her. To spare *her,* when she was the one to blame.

Diego, you bastard, you went too far this time. You'll pay for Zack and Lally. I swear you will.

She pasted on a smile, hoping it would hide how sick she felt inside. "Mrs. Applegate's biscuits are the best in town. Clem's always bragging about them."

He shook his head.

"Cord, please. You turned down dinner and you had no lunch. You have to put something in your stomach to keep your strength up. You've got a long ride ahead. Could you at least try the coffee? Please?"

He sighed, turning on his heel and crossing to her. She handed him a plate, but he reached for her instead, pulling her close, hugging her to his heart. She felt its strong and steady rhythm against the perfidious skittering of her own, and she nearly cried.

"Clem wired Nevada," he murmured, resting his cheek on her hair. "He asked for an extension. It doesn't look like I'm going to get the plates back to the mint by week's end."

"It doesn't matter."

"Of course it matters. *You* matter. But I have to bring back Zack and Lally. I have to make sure they're safe. Do you understand?"

She nodded, too choked to speak. How could he possibly think of her when his loved ones were at stake?

"Thanks," he whispered, kissing her brow.

He released her, and she thought she'd died. Right then, right there. Hell was the torment in her chest.

He managed a smile as he picked up the cup. Turning to walk the floor again, he slowed dutifully every now and then to sip. Fancy perched on a chair and dug her nails into her palms. She felt like a black widow spider, lurking, watching, waiting. *Oh God, please let it end soon. I can't bear this. I can't bear to hurt him this way . . .*

The pounding assault lessened on the roof. The rain was falling almost leisurely when he took his first staggering step. He rubbed his eyes and set the cup down. The coffee was gone.

She fought back tears. Another few minutes passed. The clock in the hall chimed eight when he staggered again. This time his knees buckled, and he gripped the side of the table. She hurried to his side and touched his sleeve.

"Cord . . ."

He was shaking his head, as if to clear it of fog.

"Maybe you should sit down."

He frowned, swaying as he held a hand to his forehead. "I feel kinda like . . . a poisoned pup."

Guilt hit her like a knife in the gut. Her hand quaked on his sleeve. "You've had a long day," she said, hating herself so much that she could barely force the words out. "You need to rest."

Slowly his eyes rose to hers. Understanding flickered behind the dull green glaze. "What did you put in the coffee?"

She couldn't lie. She owed him that much. "Laudanum," she whispered hoarsely.

He did little more than grimace, but to her, the reaction was worse than any physical blow she had ever suffered. It marked the end of every hope, every dream. It marked the end of them.

"Dammit, Fancy . . ." He started to pull away, but the drug was relentless. He stumbled. She threw her arms around his waist to brace him against the fall.

"Why, Fancy? Why?"

"Because he'd kill you. Zack and Lally too." *And I might as well have pulled the trigger myself.*

His breathing was ragged now, shallow. Try as she might, she couldn't support his weight. She oozed with him to her knees, and he slumped against her chest.

"Are you saying—" he blinked, trying to focus on her face, "are you saying you set me up? All this time, you—"

"No!" She felt the tears surge, finally breaking their dam. "Not all this time. You were right about him, Cord. Everything you said. But I'll make him pay. I won't let him hurt Zack or Lally. I promise."

The hurt in his eyes was snuffed out by horror. "No!" He gripped her arms so hard that she winced. "Fancy, no! I won't let you go."

"I have to," she whispered, "don't you see? I love Zack and Lally too."

He was shaking his head and reeling. "Santana will kill you!"

"No," she said soothingly, even though she knew he

spoke the truth. If he still cared enough to worry, she wouldn't torture him with the reality. Besides, Diego had to catch her first. "He trusts me. He thinks we're engaged. I'm the only one who can bring them back alive."

"No! Oh, God." He made a strangled sound. Trying once more to rise, he nearly toppled them both. *"Clem! Wes!"*

"Shh." She wove a restraining hand through his hair. "They can't hear you," she murmured, forcing the words past her aching throat. "Don't make this harder. On any of us."

His breath was hot and labored against her neck. She felt him sink another inch, and she squeezed her eyes closed, spilling more tears. *Forgive me, Lord. Forgive me, because I'll never forgive myself.*

He wrapped his arms around her in a ferocious hold, as if sheer strength alone would keep her there while he slept. "Fancy . . ."

Her name was a groan, a plea. He slipped lower, and she cradled him, stroking his hair with tremulous fingers.

"I know this is hard for you to believe right now," she said brokenly. "But I love you. I do."

His hands clutched at her shirt, sliding down the fabric, wadding excess folds.

"I'm so sorry, Cord. So terribly sorry . . ."

Slowly, gradually, his deathlike grip eased. His breathing became more regular. She hugged him closer, burying her face in his hair.

And she wept.

An eternity passed in the space of a heartbeat. Fancy didn't know how long she held him there, but the thunder was receding, and the rain was trickling to a sporadic drizzle. She had to go. She had no choice. Diego might stay at the station through the night, but certainly no longer.

Blinking back tears, she eased out from under Cord's weight. He muttered, grasping, but her gentle touches quieted him once more. She found his linen duster slung across a chair and pillowed it beneath his head. Then she dragged one of Mrs. Applegate's half-finished quilts from her work shelf and tucked it around his body.

For a moment longer, she lingered, feeling his steady pulse beneath her fingertips, wishing she could see his dimpled smile. Just once. Just one last time.

Then she dug down to the rock-hard bottom of her soul. She dredged up the old Fancy, the one who felt nothing. The one who lived by animal instinct. That was the Fancy Diego had taught her to be. It was the Fancy she needed now to survive.

Rising, she donned Wes's slicker, pulled up the hood, and walked out into the rain. When she descended the veranda steps to the muddy yard below, she didn't look back.

She knew she would not be seeing Cord Rawlins again.

Clouds were racing like furies across the sky. Rumbling, crackling, they threatened a second deluge with every passing heartbeat. The drizzle had long since stopped, as if the storm were gathering strength for another assault.

Fancy coughed, swallowing painfully. The ache in her throat was second only to the pounding in her head. Although she had ridden north as quickly as possible in the sodden, pitch-black terrain, the storm had moved faster. Now, as she squinted through the trees at the station's lighted windows, she battled the illness that muddled her thoughts.

Horses. She had to rid the grounds of horses.

Tethering her mare, Fancy tore off Wes's slicker. She was sweating bullets, but whether from nerves or fever, she couldn't say. The air felt cool, heavy. Gulping a deep breath, she pulled her knife to cut a quirt from a tree.

The animals were hobbled under a wooden overhang at the rear of the building. Diego had posted no guard. But then, why should he? He was hiding out in the middle of nowhere, in a storm that would soon rival Noah's. "No one will be so foolish as to hunt us down this night, *amigos*." She could almost hear his arrogant assertion. She smiled mirthlessly. If Diego had ever had a weakness, it was arrogance. His overconfidence this night would finally give her the weapon she needed against him.

As she crept up beside them, the horses nickered. She tried to whisper soothing words, but an oath slipped her lips every now and then as her shaking fingers fumbled. She expected to be discovered any moment and shot from behind. The flashing lightning exposed her again and again, and she counted her heartbeats to keep her mind from her fear.

Eventually she'd freed five of the animals. Shooing them away, she looped the reins of the last two horses over the post. Zack and Lally would need them to escape.

So far so good.

She dropped her switch. Drawing her gun, she ran in a crouch across the open yard. By the time she reached the building, her heart was hammering so hard she could scarcely breathe. She gulped several bolstering breaths before she peered inside the window.

The renegades had discovered the proprietor's store of lightning whiskey. Three men sat swaying in their chairs, hooting bets and throwing cards. Two more were sprawled facedown under the table. Diego was not among them. Uneasily, she wondered where he was. She preferred to play the cat to his mouse. Was he watching her from the privy just a few yards away? Or was he amusing himself by tormenting the prisoners?

Her stomach clenched at the thought.

Hurrying to the next window, she could clearly hear the sounds of snoring. She glanced inside. The proprietor's bedroom. She made out the figure of a man on the bed, but the snorer wasn't Diego. The body was much too bulky. As for the station master . . . She shuddered. He had most likely been murdered and thrown down the well.

Damn you, Diego. Where are you hiding?

She crept around the building's corner. There was a third window, the kitchen's. The lighting was dim, yet she could still make out two huddled forms. They were propped shoulder to shoulder on the floor beneath a table, as if they had been tied to one of its legs.

Lally and Zack.

Her breath released in a rush. They were alive, but from this angle, it was impossible to tell if they were hurt.

She waited impatiently for the next crack of thunder, then eased the window open. Zack tensed, his head snapping around. His dark eyes glowed dangerously in the lantern's gleam, but they widened when he recognized her. She pressed a finger to her lips, and he nodded.

The sounds of carousing, so alarmingly close now, made Fancy's palms moist. She had no step or toehold, so she had to throw her chest over the sill. Pushing and kicking, she finally worked her hips high enough to swing a leg inside the room. For a moment, she wondered why such a simple exertion had made her pant so hard. Then the sill heaved to life. It spun beneath her like a wheel of fortune.

"Fancy!" Zack hissed anxiously.

She dug desperate fingers into her perch. The dizziness passed quickly, and she stopped swaying, but the bout left her trembling. She nodded weakly at the boy. Fever or no fever, she couldn't let him down. She wouldn't.

Somehow, her brain took command of her limbs again. She climbed over the washbasin, miraculously disturbing none of its food-encrusted pans, and lowered herself to solid ground. She took a moment to steady herself, praying she could climb through that window again. The only other escape was through the poker game.

She knelt. Avoiding Zack's searching gaze, she cut him free. Her hands trembled when she saw the bloody slashes in his shirt, the swollen bruises on his jaw.

Lally looked none the worse for her ordeal, except for a torn skirt and a few tear-streaks on her dirt-smeared face. The woman's arms wrapped hard around her, and Fancy cringed, unable to bear for Lally to think of her as some kind of savior.

"Good Lord, child, you're hotter than Hades," Lally whispered, drawing back.

Fancy shook her head. She instantly regretted the motion as Lally's face blurred.

"Where's Cord?" Zack whispered urgently.

"Fort Worth."

"You came alone?" Lally asked.

The older woman finally swam back into focus. Fancy smiled grimly to see Lally gaping at her.

"I'm not much of a posse," she admitted. "Now listen. Two horses are left at the hitching post. You have to run for them."

Lally nodded. "And you?"

"My horse is in the trees, a few yards away."

Zack's brows knitted. "Any lookouts?"

"Not that I could see. Three men are passed out; three are playing poker. I don't know where Diego is."

His young features hardened. Her heart tripped to see how much like Cord he looked.

"All right," he said. "Let's go."

He reached to help his aunt, but she bounded to her feet, far spryer than Fancy would have imagined after being tied on a dirt floor all night long. Determination glittered in her green eyes, and not for the first time did Fancy find herself admiring Eulalie Rawlins Barclay.

Zack was the first one through the window. With a sizzling crack, the heavens opened up, loosing water in sheets. He floundered, sucked down by the mud, and Fancy held her breath until he caught his balance. Dashing the sodden hair from his eyes, he raised his arms to his aunt. Fancy watched nervously, her attention alternating between Lally's trailing petticoats, which threatened to sweep crockery to the floor, and the door leading to the poker game.

Somehow, Lally made it through the opening without so much as a creak from the sill. Zack whispered, and she nodded. Hiking her skirts, she ran toward the horses.

Next Zack held out his arms to her. She shoved her pistol into her waistband. *If Lally can do it with skirts, by God, I can do it with fever.*

Gritting her teeth, she stretched across the basin and grabbed the sides of the window. But where Lally's boots had been dry, Fancy's were slick with mud. She stifled a cry as her foot slipped. Her chest slammed into the basin, and the air rushed from her lungs. Only Zack's quick reflexes saved her from crashing into the pots. She sagged, wheezing, and the window whirled out of focus.

"Fancy!" He leaned over the sill, his hands grasping her under her arms. He tried, but he couldn't haul her up, and she slid another inch down the basin.

"Go help Lally," she gasped, the rain pelting her in the face.

"Dammit, I'm not leaving you here!" His fingers dug into her flesh, as if to infuse her with his strength. "C'mon, Fancy. C'mon, girl, stay with me now."

She smiled weakly. He sounded so much like Cord.

"I . . . have to . . . catch my . . . breath first."

Thunder shook the room. Zack muttered something about rain and fevers. "Fancy." The water streamed down his face, into his collar, plastering his clothes to his long, lean frame. "You gotta try again now. Harder. C'mon. I got a hold of—"

Suddenly, a door banged. They both gasped, their eyes locking.

"*Madre de Dios*. Curse this rain."

The voice was Diego's. He *had* been in the privy!

Another Spanish oath rang out about the missing horses. "You there! Old woman! You want to meet your maker?"

Fancy's heart stalled. "Help her, Zack, *help her!*" she whispered, shoving him away.

Hesitating less than a heartbeat, he churned at breakneck speed through the mud to Lally's rescue. She was struggling with Diego. Through the rain, Fancy couldn't see whether Diego carried a revolver or his bullwhip, but she knew he always had a pocket pistol. Zack and Lally were in deadly danger.

"Diego!" She heaved herself onto the sill, ignoring the pots and pans that crashed around her.

His head jerked up. For a split second, the fist he had drawn back faltered, and Lally rammed a knee into his loins. He doubled over, and Zack grabbed Diego's collar, deliver-

ing a double punch that knocked the outlaw flat on his buttocks. Lally fled for a horse. Fancy drew her gun.

"Run, Zack! For God's sake, mount up!" She fired, and
Diego scrambled for cover, sputtering blood-curdling Spanish.

The kitchen door crashed open. Whirling, Fancy spied the
glint of metal in the renegade's fist. Instinct took over, and
she fired once more. The man teetered, and she leaped to the
ground. She expected to feel the bite of lead at any moment.

"Fancy!"

She heard Zack's warning above a crack of thunder. A pair
of outlaws rounded the station. The mud wreaked havoc on
their drunken legs, and she was able to drive them back with
two more bullets. Their own shots went wild.

"Idiots!" Diego's voice came from the other side of the
building. "The whore is mine, you understand? Mine!"

Oh God.

She began to run, having no choice but to brave the open
yard. Her horse was tethered less than twenty yards away. But
those yards stretched like miles when her feet were sucked
again and again into the mud. She could hear the labored
charge of Zack's horse as he rode after her. Gunshots exploded. She glanced fearfully over her shoulder. Zack jolted,
crying out, and nearly toppled from his saddle. Lally screamed
his name.

Fancy spun. She could hear the ominous squishing of
Diego's boots, but she couldn't waste her last shots on him.
She fired at the first outlaw, who jumped back around the
station. The second dived behind the well.

"Ride, Zack, dammit! Leave me and ride!"

He managed to hold his seat. "Fancy, no!"

More bullets sprayed mud around his horse's hooves. The
animal stumbled, fighting its bit.

"Save Lally!" She fired her last shot and ran, unable to do
anything more for the boy. Despite his valor, bullets were
chasing his frightened horse back.

Just ahead, through the gray veil of rain, she could see her
horse stomping and snorting. The beast was salvation, teth-

ered by a thread. If she could just reach the mare before it broke free and bolted, she knew she'd be safe. Diego's der-ringer was useless over ten feet, and the outlaws had no way of giving chase.

She closed the distance. So did Diego. She could hear him panting behind her. Thirty feet, twenty feet—she was almost there. She stretched out her hand.

A sinister whir whispered behind her.

The bullwhip! That insidious, nerve-rending sound raised every hair on her scalp. She veered, but the rawhide cracked, lashing around her ankle. She yelped as her foot was yanked out from under her. Pitching forward, she tried to kick free, floundering in the mire as she grabbed for her knife.

"Bitch!" Diego's fist swung, and her blade flew. *"Ramera!"*

He pulled her up by the collar and slapped her back down. It was the first time he had ever struck her in the face. The realization filled her with a nerve-numbing fear.

"You will pay, *puta*. You will pay dearly!"

He stomped on her shoulders. Mud filled her nose and mouth, and she nearly drowned in the òoze. Above the roar-ing in her brain, she heard Zack and Lally calling. Their cries seemed to come from the protection of the trees. They were safe then—or at least they would be, if the outlaws would stop shooting.

"After them, you idiots! Her horse. Take her horse!"

With Diego momentarily distracted, she crawled to her knees, swiping the mud from her vision. She got no farther. His fingers dug into her hair, and her head snapped back. Her eyes flew wide as a stiletto glinted, descending for her throat.

"Where's Rawlins?" he hissed.

She gagged on the rain that was rolling into her nose and mouth. "He's dead!" She watched helplessly as one of the outlaws galloped off in pursuit of Zack and Lally. *Please God, please let them escape.* "Wilkerson killed him. For the plates!"

"You're lying."

Lightning flashed, turning Diego into a blazing-eyed

demon. His blade pressed harder, and she bit back a whimper, feeling the tender flesh slice.

"Why . . . would I lie . . . when you have . . . the knife?"

He snarled. Suddenly, he pulled her face to his, so close that his hot, whiskey-tainted breath made her head spin.

"It is unfortunate for you, *querida,* that your lawman is dead. Most unfortunate indeed. *Amigos!*"

He turned, wrenching her around to face the remaining outlaws. Dimly, she recognized the bleeding one as the man she had shot in the kitchen. Then she stumbled, and her fever —her blessed, God-sent fever—turned the world into a kaleidoscope of whirling blacks and grays.

"See the prize I have for you?" The sneer was unmistakable in Diego's voice. "A finer whore you'll never find. Come, *muchachos.* Let us take our pleasure!"

Chapter Twenty-One

Standing on the ledge that overlooked Blue Mountain Station, Cord checked the barrel of his revolver for the last time. Applegate and his men should be in position by now. The sheriff had agreed to give him ten minutes. Ten minutes to ride in first and rescue Fancy. Then the shoot-out would begin.

Flanking him in stoic silence, Wes and Zack waited with him for Applegate's signal. Their young faces wore a mixture of dread and grim resolve. They had each lived a personal hell in the last seventy-two hours, and he sensed a change in them. His boys had turned into men. As much as he feared for them in the showdown to come, he couldn't keep them from this fight. They had lost their home and many ranch-hands whom they considered family. Wes and Zack wanted Santana as much as he did.

Cord snapped closed the cylinder of his gun. He could see the pale orange tendrils of dawn creeping up the eastern sky. A few minutes earlier, two outlaws had headed for the trees, one on foot, the other on Fancy's pony. Presumably, they'd gone to round up their missing horses. Cord trusted Applegate to make short, silent work of them. The more outlaws who were disabled before the shoot-out, the less risk there would be to Zack and Wes.

Of course, if his brothers even suspected he was thinking such a thing, they would try to cuff him to a tree.

Cord shook his head. If the situation weren't so grim, he might have smiled. Despite their stubborn assurances to the contrary, the boys were in poor shape for a shoot-out. Wes needed two days of sleep just to look human; Zack was carrying a bullet hole in his arm. Although being drugged had been humiliating, Cord had to admit that his rest had, ironically, left him the most capable of all the men. Brand and his deputies hadn't returned to Fort Worth until two-thirty in the morning. They'd ridden in with a wounded Cass and both minting plates. No doubt their exhilaration had helped Applegate convince them to head back out again. Hungry, tired, and soaked to the bone, every single man had nevertheless mounted up for the two-hour ride to Blue Mountain. Cord knew he owed these Fort Worthers one hell of a debt.

He owed Fancy one too.

His gut knotted just to think of what might have transpired in the five-and-one-half hours since she'd freed Zack and Lally. During the ride north, the posse had intercepted the former hostages fifteen miles from the station. Zack, uncommonly defiant, had refused to stay with his aunt at a nearby ranch house, where his arm could be properly bandaged.

"It ain't nothing but a powder burn," he had insisted tersely. "Fancy risked her life for us. And while there's still a breath in me, I'm going back to make those bastards pay."

Wes had paled at Zack's uncharacteristic fierceness. "What did they do to her?" he asked hoarsely. "Is she hurt?"

Zack and his aunt exchanged uneasy looks.

"Fancy had a real bad fever, son," Lally said quietly. "She put up a fight you would have been proud of, but I reckon the sickness finally got to her. She fainted."

Cord frowned. Swooning wasn't like Fancy. He suspected there was a lot more to the story than Aunt Lally wanted him or Wes to know. He drilled his eyes into his brother. "Is that all that happened, Zack?"

The boy swallowed and looked away. "That's all as far as I

could see. There wasn't anything we could do for her, Cord.
Santana carried her inside, and a gunman started riding after
us. We were lucky, 'cause he was too drunk to do much
tracking."

The boy had lied about Fancy, of course.

Carefully keeping his features composed, Cord held his
rage in his gut, where it would drive him. If Zack and Lally
both thought they should keep Fancy's condition from him,
then she had been in dire straits indeed. At the very least,
Santana had beaten her. Cord didn't want to think about the
worst that might have happened. This morning there could
be one thing, and one thing only, on his mind: getting Fancy
out alive. To that end, he would do whatever was necessary.
Even if that meant leaving Blue Mountain in a pine box.

A double flash of light from the trees caught his eye. The
signal came again. He shoved his gun into his holster. Both
his brothers tensed.

"Now, boys," he said quietly, "you know the plan. The
clock doesn't start ticking till I'm inside that door. Even if
you hear shooting, I want you to sit tight. I need the full ten
minutes before the posse charges. You got that?"

They nodded.

"All right, then."

He started for the trail.

"Cord!"

His heart wrenched at the panic in Wes's voice. Turning,
he saw that neither of his brothers looked quite so stoic now.
A lump rose in his throat. Crossing back to clasp their shoulders, he drew them into a huddle, much as he had done that
day at the saloon, when he told them how to arrest Fancy.
The irony wasn't lost on him. He swallowed hard.

"I'm a lawman, boys," he said gruffly. "This is all part of
the job."

"We know," Zack said thickly.

He squeezed the boy's shoulder.

"Dammit," Wes said, "ten minutes is an awful long time
to be waiting for you, Cord."

"Well." He forced a smile. "Maybe so. But I've stayed

alive a lot longer and in worse spots than this. So do me proud. Okay?"

Wes nodded, his eyes glistening. Zack drew a shuddering breath and nodded too.

"Okay." He gave them a fierce hug.

Hurrying for the trail, he honed his eyes and ears. He was a predator now, hunting predators. He ran in a crouch, his teeth bared as he headed for the foot of the hill. The outhouse sat a few feet farther on. The stench was riper than usual since the rain, but he took little notice. His gaze was fixed on the unarmed renegade who was reeling across the yard. When the man reached the privy, he threw the door open and retched. Cord never hesitated. He struck the outlaw from behind, slammed the door shut, and shoved a stick through the outer door handle. The renegade would be a prisoner when he roused again.

One down. Four to go.

He ran across the yard. A second outlaw stood on the porch, rolling a cigarette. Cord stole closer until he could press the muzzle of his gun against the man's temple.

"Make a sound," he hissed, "and you're dead." He draped his neckerchief over the man's shoulder. "Gag yourself."

The outlaw obeyed stiffly.

"Hands behind your back."

When the man hesitated, Cord cocked his revolver. The man's hands couldn't come back fast enough, then. Cord cuffed the outlaw's wrists, ordered him into the shadows, and struck him over the head. He shoved the body beneath the porch.

Two down, three to go.

He glanced inside the window of the main room. In the flickering lamplight, he made out a table that was littered with broken glass and cigarette butts. Behind the bar, the door to the kitchen had been splintered as if from a kick. At the rear of the mess room, a second door stood ajar. Lamplight pooled inside, and he spied movement. A few bedrolls were haphazardly spread outside this door, but no outlaws slept in them.

The burn in his gut raged hotter. He pushed open the main door. Above the groaning of its hinges, he heard wagering and raucous laughter. Then came a whimper and the creaking of a bed. Every one of Cord's nerves fired. Seeing nothing but red, he charged across the room and flung back the bedroom door. A man knelt over a writhing form, his pants down around his ankles. Snarling, Cord fired.

A second man, whose face was scratched and bleeding, straightened above Fancy's struggling body. He drew, and Cord gunned him down too.

Cocking his hammer a third time, he saw Santana himself, pale and panting after he'd dived headlong for a shield. Now he pinned Fancy's back to his chest and jammed his derringer under her chin.

"Drop your gun, Rawlins."

For a heartbeat, the only sound in the room was Fancy's wheezing. Cord's insides blazed with a fury that threatened to incinerate him. He couldn't look at her. He couldn't look at her shredded shirt and bruised flesh without exploding like a gun.

"Drop it," Santana repeated more savagely, "or I'll blow her brains out."

Her head made a tiny, protesting gesture, but any words she might have uttered were silenced by the pressure at her throat. Cord bit back a feral sound. He tightened his grip on his gun butt so hard, it sawed into his flesh. He knew Santana was bluffing. The bastard wouldn't waste his only bullet on Fancy. But the outlaw could flinch. The pistol could go off by mistake. Cord didn't dare take that chance.

Easing the hammer on his gun back into place, he fastened the safety and let the Colt slip from his fingers.

Santana's chest heaved, as if he were relieved. "Kick it here."

Slowly, deliberately, Cord placed his instep along the revolver's barrel. Keeping his eyes locked with Santana's, he shoved the gun beneath the bed.

A red stain crept up Santana's cheeks. "You will regret your impudence," he hissed.

"Yeah?" Cord sneered, strolling closer. "So what are you waiting for? I don't see any ball and chain holding you back this time. Or maybe you're just a pretty Nancy-boy who can't lick anything more than a swooning woman."

"You dig your grave, lawman. You dig your grave and hers."

"That's mighty big talk for a mudsill dandy."

Fancy whimpered, her eyes rolling in warning, but he knew a derringer's range. He planned to step well within it. Fifteen feet, twelve feet—he continued his advance. Santana was trapped between him and the wall; the bed barred his escape to the right. Santana was many things, but he wasn't a fool. Eventually, he would have to train that pistol on him. And Cord wasn't about to let some lady's popgun slow him down.

Fancy squeezed her eyes closed. The room kept whirling in and out of focus. She struggled to concentrate, to warn Cord again, but her head ached so much and she was so thirsty. She should never have called to Diego. She should never have begged him for water. When he heard she was awake, he'd brought the other outlaws.

Why did he have to be so cruel? And why did he always want to hurt her? She had loved him once. She had tried to make him happy. Lying to Cord, she had even risked her freedom to keep Diego from the gallows. Did none of that matter to him?

The question confused her. Diego confused her. If he cared so little about her after all she had done, then why did Cord care so much?

She spilled a tear. Cord. He had come to save her. Even though she had nearly cost him his family, he had come. She didn't understand. He must not realize how she'd betrayed him. Someday, somehow, he was sure to find out. But she would rather lose him to her lie than lose him to Diego.

She forced herself to cling to that thought, drumming it again and again through her brain. Fear for Cord was the one thing that could stave off the darkness. She had to stop Diego.

"Your tongue is the first thing I will cut off," Diego said, his voice harsh and ragged in her ear. "Then I will cut off your so-called manhood."

"Why's that, Santana? Are you needing one of your own?"

Diego snarled, cocking his gun beneath her chin. Cord halted an arm's length away. His smile was truly terrible. Fancy had never seen anything quite like it before. Even at Diego's most diabolic, he had never looked so feral. So ferocious. In that moment, Cord was afraid of nothing. Not pain, not death, not Satan himself. It was the first time—and perhaps the last—that Diego had ever faced a fearless victim. She could feel Diego's heart careening against her spine.

"So what are you going to do, Santana?" Cord taunted in a low, guttural voice. "You got one bullet. You kill her, you got me left over. And I'm your express train to hell."

"Then die first, like the pig you are."

Diego's fist swung out. Cord lunged to the side, and Fancy screamed. She tried to throw herself against Diego's arm, but the bullet found a piece of its mark, ripping into Cord's shoulder. She nearly died to see his blood, but his charge hardly faltered. He slammed Diego into the wall, and the whole room shook. She found herself crawling over dead outlaws, trying desperately to get out of the way, trying even more desperately not to retch—or worse, faint. She had to get to Cord's gun, but the floor kept heaving beneath her.

The grunting and cursing seemed to be moving past the window now. She heard the shattering of panes, the tinkling of glass. Crimson smeared the frame, and the combatants moved on. Fists and elbows flying, they crashed from the wall to the door to the mess room beyond. Diego was taller, and he should have had the advantage against a wounded man. But Cord's fists were a blur, pounding with the force of twin hammers. She saw the spray of spittle; she heard the howl as Diego lost one of his perfect teeth.

The outlaw was scrappy, though. He would not go down. Gouging, kicking, he jammed a palm into Cord's nose; he clawed at the torn flesh of Cord's shoulder. Cord yelped, and Fancy flinched, shuddering to her core to hear his cry of pain. Dimly, she realized Diego was cheating—like he always did. But cheating seemed to have little effect against Cord's greater skill. She sagged against the doorjamb, thinking Cord would not be needing her help, thinking she might be able to rest after all.

Suddenly, Diego reared back. He rammed his knee between Cord's legs. Stunned, Fancy could do no more than gape as the color vanished from Cord's face. He doubled over, staggering. In the next instant, Diego's whip wrapped around his throat.

It all happened so quickly. Fancy blinked, and Cord was trapped. Choking, wheezing, he arched his back, clutching at the rawhide that sought to crush his windpipe.

"Diego, stop!"

She heard him laugh. Sadistic, gleeful, the sound made her heart freeze. She stumbled forward, thinking she must do something—anything—to break his stranglehold. Then her mind rallied against the fog.

Cord's gun!

She whirled, nearly collapsing on the spot as the walls wheeled around her. Gritting her teeth, she reeled toward the bed. Her foot tripped over a dead man's leg, and she cried out, falling. The floor rose fast to meet her. She grabbed frantically for blankets, but her buttocks struck wood, and the collision jarred every bone in her spine. Darkness swept past her mind's defenses. She fought back desperately, pushing a shaking hand against the mattress that threatened, at any moment, to topple down and smother her.

"I've waited a long time for this, Rawlins." Diego's ragged taunt came from the light beyond, piercing the pitch-black cyclone in her brain. "A long time to watch you die. A pig should not live half so long, eh?"

"No!" Fancy cried, and the darkness lifted. *Hold on, Cord. Please, hold on.*

She crawled to her belly, sticking her head beneath the bed. She could see the Colt gleaming in a ray of sun that had filtered past the dust and the cobwebs. She stretched a hand. She couldn't reach it. Shimmying closer, she tried again. Her fingers strained, quaking from the exertion, but it was too far. *Too far!*

". . . Such a fool," Diego was jeering. "I expected so much more from a mighty *federale*. To throw your life away for a common *puta* . . ."

The dead man. A new solution whirred past the panic in Fancy's skull. *The dead man's .45.*

She beat a graceless retreat, banging her head, scraping her shoulders. Splinters dug into the fleshy part of her palms, but she hardly noticed. She had to get to the gunbelt. The gunbelt on the other side of the bed . . .

"Ah, but my Fancy, she is so good when she ruts, no? Señors Carson and Jacks, they must have died happy men."

She scrambled to Carson's side. He was large and bulky and heavier than a wagonload of bricks. She struggled to roll him, forcing herself not to inhale too deeply or look too closely at the unwashed mountain of bleeding flesh. Sweat poured down her forehead. Her eyes stung from the salt. *Hold on, Cord. I almost have it. I . . . almost . . . have it!*

The corpse fell back. The holster popped free of its weight, and she grabbed the .45.

"Diego, stop!" She hurried on shaking legs to confront the man she'd once loved. "Let him go!"

Diego sneered at her. Cord was on his knees now, his veins bulging, his fingers white and straining beneath his scarlet face. He tried to rise, as he must have countless times in the eternity that had just passed, but his strength was bleeding away. His strength and his life.

"Diego, I have a gun!"

Diego's lip curled. "And what is that to me, eh? Your hand trembles. Your knees quake. Fire away, *querida*. It is the lawman you are likely to hit."

Her heart lurched. It was true. Cord was in equal danger from her bullet. *Oh, God, what should I do?* She bit her lip. Cord's gaze swiveled her way. To her horror, she saw his eyes were glazing.

She clamped another fist over the gunbutt and braced her

back against the wall. "Don't make me do this, Diego. Don't make me kill you."

"Kill me?" He laughed. "You are a frightened rabbit."

The stiletto flashed in his hand. "And now, *amigo*," he said to Cord, "it is time for *adiós*."

He raised his fist above Cord's throat. The time for doubt had passed. Taking aim, Fancy fired. The bullet ripped into Diego's shoulder. He staggered, snarling in pain, but he wouldn't drop his weapons. When he raised the knife again, Fancy squeezed the trigger. This time, the bullet slammed into his chest, and Diego jolted backward, dropping both blade and whip. He crashed into the wall, slowly sliding down. His eyes were wide and dark with shock.

"But . . . Fancy," he wheezed, his head shaking weakly in disbelief. "You . . . love me."

Hot tears streamed down her face. "No, Diego," she whispered brokenly. "You killed my love a long time ago."

He blinked, his mouth gaping. Then his head lolled, and he toppled to the floor.

Oh, God . . .

She had killed him.

The gun fell from her numbing fingers. She tried to push herself from the wall. She tried to go to Cord, to bind his wounds, but she didn't have the strength. The room was spinning again. Her legs wouldn't support her. Gunfire sounded in the yard, and she reached out fearfully. "Cord . . . ?"

His arms wrapped around her.

"Someone's shooting—"

"It's the posse." His voice cracked. His arms trembled as he hugged her fiercely, burying his face in her hair. "Fancy, I'm so sorry."

"Sorry?"

He sounded close to tears. She tried to raise her head, but his hold only tightened, as if he were ashamed.

"Those men," he said. "What they did. Fancy, I—"

"Shh." She shook her head, choking back a sob to see the

whip burns, raw and bleeding, on his throat. "They did nothing, Cord. Nothing happened. You came in time."

"I did?" He drew back to look at her, and she saw his tears. They were trickling past the stubble on his face.

She nodded, trying to smile, to reassure him, but it was so hard. She was shaking so badly. All of her muscles seemed to be in mutiny against her commands. She felt herself sinking. She wanted to hold on, to cling to the moment, but it was floating away from her on a tide of darkness.

"I'm so c-cold." Her teeth were chattering now. "So terribly, terribly cold. C-could you hold me?"

Panic flickered through his eyes. "I am holding you, sweetheart. Real tight. Can't you feel it?"

She shook her head. "T-tighter then."

He was practically crushing her.

"D-don't let me go. P-please?"

"I won't, Fancy."

"P-promise?"

"I promise, love. Hold on to me, now. Hold on, and I'll get you a blanket."

His voice came from high above her. It seemed to be fading. She couldn't hear it when her ear was pressed against his heart. Soon even that comforting sound was drowned in the roar. The waves of darkness were breaking.

They pulled her under at last.

Chapter Twenty-Two

Fancy could hear the hum of voices, fading in and out, giving tongues to the faceless visitors who came to her bedside.

". . . the poor child. Three days now. Three days, and still her fever's raging. . . ."

". . . Cordero." Aunt Lally's voice floated into her dreams, replacing the husky whispers of Mrs. Applegate. "Now you listen to me. You got wounds that need healing. You can't sit here night after night by her bed without rest."

An age passed away. Or was it only a minute?

Another shadow loomed over her. A gruff masculine voice cleared. "Got the wire from Nevada, son. It doesn't look good. The governor ain't a patient man. And he's not going to be decent about this. . . ."

Decent? Of course not. Whoever heard of a decent politician?

The light slipped away. When it stole back again, an hour, maybe a day later, strong young fingers were gripping hers.

"That damned old gov'nor. He's not going to jail Fancy, is he, Cord? 'Cause Zack and me won't stand for it. We'll go up there and boot that Yankee's butt clear to California if we have to."

Fancy turned her face into the darkness. She didn't want to listen. She just wanted to fall back into that sweet, soothing blackness where governors didn't matter, and jails didn't exist. . . .

And hearts didn't break when they felt too much pain.

A beam of light filtered through the shadows. She tried to will it away, but it refused to vanish. Creeping closer, it spread and brightened, pushing her further and further from her sleep. Suddenly her mind was flooding with memories she'd been trying so desperately to repel. *The plates. The book. Diego* . . .

Cord.

Dimly she remembered him clasping her hand and mopping her brow, urging her to fight back, begging her to get well. But the governor had summoned. Cord had argued with Clem, saying the plates could wait, saying the whole damned state of Nevada could wait, but in the end, Clem had convinced Cord that the best thing he could do for her was get her that pardon.

Later, when her fever abated and she was starting to make better sense of the nightmare she had lived through, Aunt Lally came with motherly advice and chicken soup.

"Don't you fret, Fancy," she murmured, spooning broth down her patient's throat. "Cord's taking those plates back personally so there can't be any mix up. He'll get your pardon, make no mistake. He'll see that everything's put to rights."

Dear Lally. She couldn't possibly know how those words knifed through Fancy's breast. To put everything "to rights" could only mean that Cord would do to her what she deserved. All of Carson City must still be talking about the prison fire and the inmates' escape. Someone would surely mention the book. He would be outraged. And when he returned to Fort Worth, he would ride her out on a rail.

How sad to come so close to love . . . only to watch it slip away.

Two men, two loves. She'd lost them both. In truth, she was glad to be free of Diego, but she couldn't be glad she had killed him. She hadn't wanted vengeance; she had only wanted Cord to be safe. Pulling that trigger the second time had hurt her far more than any beating she had ever suffered at Diego's hands.

If she tried hard enough, she supposed, she could hate him. But she'd learned from years of experience that bitterness never brought peace. Better to forgive him and move on. Better to feel nothing and forget.

So in the days that followed, she nodded dutifully every now and then to please her visitors. She said little, and she listened even less. She preferred to let their chatter drone on and on while she stared into the fire. It was June in Texas, yet she felt nothing of the heat. All she could feel was emptiness. It was like a winter in her soul. Cord was gone. Diego was gone. And soon she must be going too.

Wes's plaintive voice floated back to her from the shadows in the hall.

"She won't talk to me, Aunt Lally. How come she won't talk to me? She don't laugh anymore, either. I tried every story I know to cheer her up, but she just keeps staring into that stupid fireplace—"

"Now don't take it personal, son," Lally said gently. "Fancy's had a hard time of it, and she's not . . . well, she's not quite back to her old self yet."

"You mean she's still sick? She don't look sick," the boy said suspiciously. "What's wrong with her, anyway? You said she doesn't have fever anymore. Do you reckon that fire's gone and fried her brains out? It's gotta be a hunnert degrees inside there."

The door closed. Fancy's breath freed in a rush of relief. *Bless you, Lally.*

She loved Wes dearly. Truly she did. But in his wake he'd left a silence that was heavenly. She sighed, closing her eyes. Only then did she sense the presence of another visitor. The rustle of movement was so faint that she almost missed it in the popping of the logs. Her eyes flew open, and she saw Zack settling cross-legged on the floor beside her chair. His visit surprised her. She couldn't remember him coming before. But then, she couldn't remember a lot of things about the days of her fever.

She turned her face back to the fire. Zack wasn't one to share gossip, and he didn't spin yarns. She couldn't imagine what he might have to say to her. They had never had the camaraderie that she and Wes shared, not even in the early days, before their friendship had been nipped in the bud. Zack was, and always had been, shy at heart. Maybe that was why the boy said nothing now.

Minutes drifted into a quarter of an hour. She stole another glance his way. He was sitting in the same pose, his gaze fixed upon the fire. His quiet was a welcome respite from Wes's endless banter, yet she found she was nervous. Such lengthy reticence was unusual, even for Zack. He must have something important to say. She couldn't believe he had come simply to roast before her hearth on what Wes had assured her was a blistering summer day.

"Zack?"

He tilted his chin to gaze at her. "Yes, ma'am?"

"Do you . . . have something you want to say?"

He smiled faintly, shaking his head. "I reckon you've heard all the jawing a body can stand for one day. I just thought you might like some company, is all."

His consideration touched her. She felt her throat constrict. "Thank you."

"No, ma'am," he murmured, his eyes soft with gratitude. "Thank *you*. I reckon I never got to tell you that after you helped me and Aunt Lally. I said some pretty unkind things about you a few weeks back. And I was wrong. Real wrong. I just wanted you to know I'm sorry."

She nodded, too overwhelmed to speak. She tried to hide the clouds forming in her eyes. Never had she dared to hope that she and Zack might become friends. As fond as she was of Wes, she knew she had to keep a certain distance from him, because his feelings for her were more than brotherly. But with Zack, things could be different. He didn't idolize her. She didn't have to worry about breaking his heart or appearing frail and human in his eyes. He already knew she was fallible. Coming here today must have been his way of showing that he accepted her, all of her, both the good and the bad.

But then, he doesn't know the full extent of your badness, does he, Fancy?

An unbidden tear rolled down her cheek. Then a second. And a third. Despite her best efforts, the dam broke. Her resistance to feeling was swept away, and the pain surged in, breaker after breaker. It racked her with sobs. She might have drowned in her tears if Zack hadn't reached up to hold her. His arms closed around her waist, and she clung to his shoulders as she would to a lifeline.

Eventually the truth spilled out. In great, shuddering breaths, she told him how scared she had been that Diego would be acquitted and that he would come to kill her. She confessed how she'd tried to appease his murderous rage by tricking Cord, by smuggling information about the lost plates into the prison. Finally, she admitted how she had told Diego that Cord was headed for the Barclay ranch.

Helpless to stop the tide of guilt and grief, she wept harder, knowing she must now face Zack's recriminations. But if the boy thought she was heinous, he didn't say so. He didn't push her away or jerk himself free. He simply held on, resting his chin on her hair, letting her tears soak the front of his shirt. She poured herself out in his stoic embrace until every last tear was spent.

Finally, she was reduced to hiccupping sniffles. She slumped, exhausted, against him. His neckerchief dangled before her eyes, and she took it sheepishly, too ashamed to meet his gaze. She was grateful when he didn't speak, allowing her the dignity to gather her composure.

For another measure of heartbeats, she dared to cling to him, taking comfort in his silence. She knew it was wrong to pretend, and yet, with his arms so warm and sweet around her, it was easy to imagine he was Cord. It was easy to make believe that Cord had forgiven her.

Zack wasn't Cord, though. He was a seventeen-year-old boy who had been kind to her in her moment of need. She should never have repaid him with a burden. *Her* burden. She had no right to pit the boy against his brother.

Forcing herself to withdraw, she sank back tremulously into her chair. "I'm sorry, Zack," she whispered hoarsely. "For your shirt, for your neckerchief . . . for everything. I didn't mean to tell you these things. At least, not this way."

His eyes were brown, not green, like the rest of the Rawlins clan's, but tiny jade flecks glistened in their depths as he gazed at her in understanding.

"I'm glad you did," he murmured. "Holding back a truth like that can eat a body from the inside."

He sat back on his heels. After a long moment, his brow furrowed. "I reckon you haven't told Cord about this?"

She quailed at the idea. "No." Wringing his neckerchief through shaking fingers, she added hastily, "Not yet."

Concern vied with the empathy on his face. "You weren't going to, were you?"

She stared at her lap. Actually, she'd been thinking about writing a letter. . . .

"Fancy." His hand covered her own. "Maybe there's other facts you don't know about. I mean, Cord ain't the kind to jump to conclusions. He'll withhold judgment until he's investigated all the evidence. And . . ."

She held her breath, waiting in an agony of dread, hoping he would give her some concrete reason to believe Cord might forgive her. "Yes?"

He fidgeted. "Well, he has the right to know."

His words fell around her like shattered glass. He was right, of course. She knew he was. She nodded glumly, and his hand tightened over hers.

"Now don't go giving up hope. I can't speak for Cord, and I can't speak for Wes or Aunt Lally, but I believe you. I don't think you wrote that message out of spite. And you don't have to worry about me carrying tales—"

"Oh, Zack—"her voice broke, and she pressed trembling fingers to her lips, "I can't ask you to keep what I've told you a secret."

His chest rose and fell on a sigh of relief. "Well . . ." The concern returned, weighing his young features with an ancient solemnity. "I won't say anything anyway. Not until you need me to stand up with you when you're telling my kinfolk."

She managed a weak smile. She hadn't thought beyond her responsibility to tell Cord. How was she supposed to tell Lally? And Wes? How did she admit to the boy that she'd cost him his home and nearly robbed him of his family?

Something inside of her shriveled and died. She thought it must have been her courage.

"Thank you, Zack." She tried to work the croak from her voice. "You're very kind to offer your help. It's . . . more than I deserve."

"Naw." He gave her hand a firm squeeze. "You're like family to me, Fancy. 'Sides. I'm not forgetting that you saved every one of our lives at least once."

He withdrew his hand. "Now I reckon you'll be wanting to rest. Try not to fret yourself sick again. Cord should be riding into town any day now. Maybe even tomorrow. Between the two of us, I betcha we can get him to see things your way."

He unfolded his long legs and rose. "I'll come back after dinner, if you want to talk more."

She nodded dutifully, until a second thought stopped her. "Er, no. I think I'd like to turn in early. Right after dinner."

"Okay." He touched her shoulder. "Reckon this is good night, then."

"Good night, Zack."

And good-bye.

She listened, her throat aching as his footsteps faded down the hall. If she had a single tear left, she would have shed it. Zack had all the tender chivalry of Cord. Wes had all the love of family. Between the three of them, the world was a kinder place to be a woman. Someday, each of the Rawlins brothers would turn a lucky girl into a happy bride. She wished fervently that she could be Cord's.

Oh, Cord. How different my life would have been if I had fallen in love with you, not Diego, when I was eighteen.

Sighing, she pushed aside her futile dreams. She forced herself to rise, dragging her feet to the box of writing papers that Mrs. Applegate kept stocked for guests. Lowering herself heavily to the bed, she balanced the writing board across her lap and gazed blankly out the window. She could see the prairie stretching to the west in a rippling wave of burnt orange. Soon the sun would set. Soon Cord would return to knock on her door. . . .

Her vision blurred. Blinking rapidly, she dipped her pen into the inkwell and began a shaky scrawl:

> *My dearest Cord,*
>   *I'm so sorry. You must think me cowardly to write, but I couldn't bring myself to face you. After reading this letter, I'm sure you'll agree that my leaving was for the best. . . .*

The sun was edging toward its zenith when Cord trotted Poco through the gate of Applegate's spread. He'd had a long two weeks of travel—Carson by way of Abilene. He supposed cities must be fine for some, but he'd never been one for the smell. That's why the fresh, clean scent of a wind-swept prairie was enough to bring a mist to his eyes.

That, and the thought that Fancy was waiting for him in the ranch house just ahead.

Poco, like any good pony, picked up his pace when he smelled oats and sweet hay. Soon they were in the yard, scattering chickens and dogs. As Cord stepped gratefully down to Texas soil, he heard the porch door slam. He glanced up to see Zack and Wes hurrying down the steps to greet him, just as they used to do as boys, when he'd ridden home from the war on an occasional leave. He smiled at the memory.

"Morning, boys."

They exchanged uneasy glances.

"Er . . . morning, Cord. How's that shoulder of yours?"

"Just fine, Zack. Thanks."

Wes hovered nervously at his elbow. "Glad to see you back so soon. Did you get the pardon?"

He nodded wearily, tapping his breast pocket. He'd gotten

it all right. He'd had to raid a cathouse and catch the governor butt-naked, taking his pleasure from two—yes, two —whores, but he'd gotten Fancy's pardon, by God. Fortunately, Governor Underwood had a hankering to keep his office, and the election was only two weeks away.

Tossing Poco's reins over the rail, Cord tried to step around Zack. Wes squared off with him instantly.

"Uh . . . do you think you're fit for another ride, Cord?"

He quirked a brow at his youngest brother. Now there was a suspicious question if he'd ever heard one. "If you've got something to tell me, son, you know I'd rather hear it straight."

Zack pulled a folded paper from his pocket and solemnly handed it to him. Cord frowned at the boy before dropping his gaze to the female handwriting on the page.

"She says she left us 'cause she thinks you blame her for the ranch burning down," Wes blurted out. "Something 'bout a book and a message."

Cord glanced up sharply from Fancy's guilt-ridden prose. So *that* was the matter?

Frustration welled hard and fast in his throat. Why on earth would he blame her, when Santana had threatened to torch the ranch on the night of the train robbery?

Cord crushed her letter in his fist. Yes, he knew about the message in the book. When he'd returned to Carson, the warden had shoved the book in his face, making nasty accusations. Upon studying the so-called cipher, Cord had found nothing to make him believe Fancy had assisted in Santana's escape. Quite the contrary. The message had been laced with fearful platitudes. She'd been clearly worried that Santana would blame her for his capture and come to kill her. Why would she have wanted to help him escape?

Cord muttered an oath. If she had put a little more faith in *him,* none of this foolishness would ever have happened.

"When did she leave?"

" 'Bout dawn, best that we can figure."

"Six hours ago?" He glared at Wes, and the boy blushed. "And y'all didn't ride after her?"

"We tracked her to the station," Zack said hastily. "The master said she took the late morning stage to Dallas. She'd been asking lots of questions 'bout the fastest route to Abilene."

Cord's heart lurched. "Abilene?" He pulled off his hat, running a rough hand through his hair. "Jesus."

"Now don't get yourself in a lather, Cord," Wes said, patting his shoulder. "We'll find her. 'Course, you'll probably have to do some sweet talking to make her come back. Seems to me you could have saved us all a heap of trouble if you'd just gone and done it right the first time."

"Yeah?" He turned withering eyes on his kid brother. "And what's that supposed to mean?"

"The way I figure it, Fancy would never have run off on you if you'd gone and told her you love her."

He stiffened, feeling the heat creep up his neck. "Well, of course I—"

He hesitated, biting his tongue. Maybe the boy had a point. He'd never really said he loved her in so many words. Between Santana, the robbery, the kidnapping, and her sickness, the timing had never seemed right. But surely Fancy knew he loved her. Didn't she?

Wes folded his arms across his chest. He was shaking his head in mock disgust. "Son," he said gravely, "it looks like you need to come to ol' Uncle Wes for advice on the womenfolk. Just like Zack does."

"Oh, yeah?" Zack turned a fiery shade of crimson. "And what makes you think you're such a sagebrush Romeo?"

"Just never you mind," Wes retorted loftily.

Cord might have laughed at their jesting if he wasn't so worried about Fancy. Did she really know what she was getting herself into? Abilene, Kansas, made Hell's Half Acre look like a churchyard social. Damn that girl's wild streak. He should have hog-tied her back when he had the chance.

Squinting up at the sun, he refigured the hour to be closer to eleven. "What time did you say that stage left, Zack?"

"Around ten-thirty."

He shook his head and donned his hat. He supposed it could have been worse, but a half-hour's start would be hard to beat.

"You *are* riding after her, aren't you, Cord?" Zack asked, his gaze growing dark with reproach. "'Cause it wouldn't mean the same to her if Wes and me brought her back. She's hurting real bad, thinking you can never forgive her. But you ought to know the girl you arrested at the Diamondback ain't the same girl who rode off this ranch."

Cord blinked, stunned by Zack's scolding. After a moment of reflection, though, he recognized concern, not anger, in the boy's words. Apparently Fancy had won Zack over. Cord smiled to himself. He had been a little worried about the way the two of them were getting along. He'd even begun to wonder how he was going to tell Zack there would soon be a new Mrs. Cord Rawlins.

"Reckon you're right, son," he said solemnly.

Wes was grinning from ear to ear. "Well, Marshal, it looks like you got another lady renegade to bring in." He saluted smartly, clicking his heels. "Deputy Rawlins reporting for duty, *sir!*"

The tension eased from Zack's shoulders. He smiled. "Make that two deputies, sir."

Cord felt his lips twitch. Well, now. A 'sir' from each of them, and on the same day. He just might get used to this deputy stuff.

He flipped two bits at them both. "'Fraid I don't have any badges. But you can consider yourselves sworn in now."

They caught the substitute tin-stars, their eyes shining with eagerness.

"Mount up, men," he said in his gruffest, long-rider voice. He tipped his hat brim to hide his smile. "We're going to catch ourselves a woman."

Fancy gazed gloomily out the window, gritting her teeth with each bounce of the poorly sprung stage. Every now and then she had to grab her hat to keep it from flying off and getting lost forever in a hail of earth. The dust was almost unbearable. Thank heaven she'd thought to buy a veil with the money she won—squarely, for once—in a poker game at the Diamondback. She had piddled away most of the morning there, waiting more than three hours for her coach's axle to be repaired.

In truth, she had bought the veil because she feared she might encounter her wanted poster at the train depot. Unfortunately, her notoriety caught up with her long before Dallas. The fifth passenger had no sooner wedged her into the last fifteen inches of seat space on the stage, when a gangly, pale-complected man clambered aboard. At the time, she hadn't observed him too keenly—preachers never held much interest for her. But he'd caught her attention an hour or so later when he began a blistering denunciation of rail travel.

"I assure you, brothers," he said as they rolled past the laborers who were laying tracks toward Fort Worth, "a railroad is not the godsend you might think. I for one shall never trust body or limb to a train! Why, shortly after Christmas, I was Carson-bound when my train was derailed by a gang of Barbary Coast cutthroats and their vicious soiled dove! I cannot begin to describe to you, my friends, how truly decadent was that daughter of Jezebel. She shot and looted with the rapacity of a corsair. And when acts of savagery were committed against us passengers, she looked on with fiendish glee!"

Fancy grimaced at the memory.

Naturally, after Parson Brown delivered that sermon, she had kept her face turned religiously to the window. She supposed she deserved every word, but she had trouble comparing herself to the "corsair" of the robbery. The girl who had lived by guts and wits back then had since learned she owned a heart.

It was true: She had become a new person. She never imagined it would be possible, but then, she had never dreamed a man like Cord Rawlins would come into her life. His tender caring had turned her around. He had given her a chance to know real loving. She wished she could thank him and show him how she'd changed. Was it still too late to pray for a miracle?

She was almost tempted to ask Parson Brown that question, but the gentleman was leaning out the opposite window and wringing his hands.

"Oh, dear. Oh, dear me. Riders seem to be following us."

Fancy squinted into the blaze of late afternoon. Hazy ripples of heat rose from the dust, distorting the scrub brush landscape, but she had to admit the old man's spectacles were not conjuring mirages. There were, in fact, three horsemen. Galloping hell-for-leather out of the west, they were slowly gaining on the coach.

"Gentlemen, this is most unusual, is it not?" Brown asked the other passengers in a high, quavering voice. "Why would riders be following the stage? Do you think . . . ? Oh, good gracious me! Do you think they could be road agents?"

Well, that would certainly be ironic, Fancy thought. She shaded her eyes and turned back to the road. She had committed countless thefts before, but she had never been the victim of one.

"They've come within rifle range," another passenger observed with considerably more calm than the preacher. "Since they haven't started shooting yet, they're probably just wild young cowpokes, racing the stage for a lark."

Fancy hoped he was right. Her new life was going to be bleak enough without Cord. She didn't need a robbery to start it off.

Suddenly, something metallic flashed on the middle rider's vest. She decided the object couldn't possibly be a button; he was wearing it too far to the left. In fact, he was wearing it above his heart, as if it were a . . .

As if it were a tin-star!

"Goddammit, reinsman, pull up," bellowed that stocky middle rider. "I'm a federal marshal. I got business with the lady in the coach!"

Cord? Her heart soared and then, just as quickly, sank. He'd said "business." What kind of business? Had something gone wrong in Nevada?

The driver must have heard him. Amid the clamor of cursing, neighing, and the screeching of brakes, the stage slowed down. Soon the riders were abreast each window. Wes grinned, waving gaily at her, before he galloped to the front of the team and grabbed the lead harness.

"Whoa!"

Fancy's pulse was speeding so fast she could scarcely breathe. She sank back against her seat. Six speculative pairs of male eyes drilled into her from every corner of the coach. She cringed, thankful for her veil.

Abruptly the door was jerked open. Cord stood glaring up at her, a fist on each hip.

"And just where do you think you're going, footloose?"

She wanted to laugh but nearly cried. He looked so angry, but she didn't care. Even angry, he was still a welcome sight. *Oh, Cord. Cord. I never thought I would see you again.*

"You'd best get down off of that coach, 'cause you don't want me coming in there after you."

Was he jesting? She bit her lip. He didn't look like he was jesting. She placed shaking fingers in the hand he offered her. His grip was firm and reassuring, despite the sternness of his features. Confused by his mixed message, she stepped down and retrieved her hand. "Am I under arrest?"

"You bet you are."

She swallowed, her heart careening. She had hoped for his denial because she wanted to throw her arms around his neck.

"I see." She forced the lump from her throat. "Forgive me, Marshal, but this all comes as quite a surprise. You see, I thought I was pardoned and—and free to go." She hiked her chin. "What are the charges against me this time?"

"Running out on your man."

She blinked dumbly. She had never heard of such a thing. Then she heard a snicker—undoubtedly Wes's—and she glimpsed Zack, smiling and shaking his head. She caught her breath. Was she being humbugged?

Cord swept back her veil. "Well, I'm your man, right?" he growled.

The light in those green eyes was like a burst of sunshine to her soul. She felt dizzy in the sudden flood of warmth that flowed through every fiber of her being.

"Yes," she whispered, half-afraid that speaking would somehow rob her of her dream come true. "You are my man."

"And you love me, don't you?"

She blinked, her vision turning watery. "Oh, yes."

"Well, you've got a damned fine way of showing it." His dimples peeked at last, belying the gruffness of his tone. "And I'm getting mighty tired of chasing you down, woman. This time, I'm bringing you in for good. Preacher!"

Brown jumped so hard, his spectacles bounced on his nose. "Er . . . yes, Marshal?"

"Get your book and come here. I've got a job for you."

"But—"

"You'd best do as he says, Preacher," Zack said gravely, unlatching the coach's other door and swinging it wide. Brown quailed to see the youth towering over him with a rifle in his hand. He scrambled to the ground, hurrying around the rear of the coach to join Cord.

"Marshal!" He gasped, his eyes bugging out when he got his first good look at Fancy. His cheeks mottled to a wrathful crimson. "Do you know who this woman *is?*"

Cord shot him a look that made the parson's Adam's apple bob a half-dozen times. "Damned straight I do. She's the woman I love. Got that?"

Her knees went weak to hear the words.

Cord turned to her, and his features softened. "I do love you, Fancy." He caught her face between his hands. "And I don't plan on ever letting you forget that."

"Oh, Cord." A tear slid down her cheek. "But I cost you your home. Can you ever forgive me?"

His eyes grew a misty meadow green. "There's nothing to forgive, sweetheart. There never was. The things Santana did can never be laid at your door."

A bubble of joy floated to her brain.

"Fancy Holleday, I love you," he said loud enough for

every passenger to hear. "And I want you to marry me. Right here. Right now. Will you be my wife?"

Happiness fizzed like cherry sarsaparilla through her veins. She nodded, too dazed to speak.

Brown went into conniptions.

"I protest!" he cried. "Marshal, I cannot condone a marriage under such circum—"

"Yeah? Well, I'm the lawman, padre, and I say the circumstances are legal. Binding too. Open your book."

Wes grinned, coming to her left side and giving her hand a squeeze. Zack crossed to Cord's right and winked at her.

Brown raised a mutinous chin. "This is all highly irregular. *Highly* irregular, and I cannot—"

Suddenly, he was staring down the barrels of three guns. He gulped, turning whiter than his collar. With all those dizzy bubbles dancing in her brain, Fancy nearly giggled. The poor man! No doubt he was making history. This was probably the first wedding on record where the preacher—not the groom—was standing under the gun.

"Er . . . since you put it that way, gentlemen." He glared at them all. "Very well." Clearing his throat, Brown opened his book and smoothed a page. "Dearly beloved—"

"Aw, hell, Preacher, speed it along," the driver grumbled. "I got a run to make, you know."

"Yeah!" one of the passengers bellowed. "Hurry up so we can watch the kissing part!"

Hoots and snickers rocked the stage. Cord grinned down at her, lacing his fingers through hers. Brown harrumphed. Thumbing forward through several pages, he frowned, readjusting his spectacles.

"Miss . . . er, Holleday, is it?"

She nodded, too happy to care if he disapproved of her.

"Very well."

Brown raised his eyes to hers. Maybe it was just her delirium, but his displeasure seemed to lessen when his gaze touched hers.

"Miss Holleday. Do you take Marshal Rawlins to be your lawfully wedded husband . . . for better for worse . . . for richer for poorer . . . in sickness and health . . . and forsaking all others . . . for as long as you both shall live?"

Cord's hand tightened over hers. "I do," she whispered giddily.

"And do you, Marshal Rawlins, take Miss Holleday to be your lawfully wedded wife . . . to have and to hold . . ."

She stared up at Cord, and he smiled. It was the warmest, tenderest smile a woman could ever hope to know. In that moment, she knew she had found a love to last a lifetime. Never again would her heart be on the run. Together they would rebuild the ranch and start anew. She wasn't afraid of hard times because she'd worked through so many. Cord was hers, and she was his. That, quite simply, was enough.

Parson Brown had stopped speaking.

"I do," Cord said quietly.

"Then by all the powers invested in me, I now pronounce you man and wife."

Hoots and whistles shrilled from the stage. Amid the clapping and stomping, the whooping and backslapping, Cord pulled her into his arms. He kissed her as if she, and she alone, were the only light in his life. The world began to spin, flashing around her. The prairie became a kaleidoscope of rainbows, a symphony of sound.

And above it all—the music, the laughter, the heartbeats, the clamor—she heard an impish chuckle.

"You see?" Wes whispered near her ear. "I *told* you I'd see the two of you get hitched."

ABOUT THE AUTHOR

After earning more than thirty awards for journalistic ex-
cellence, Adrienne deWolfe finally gave into her love for
fiction and put her pen to writing romance. Adrienne is a
native of Pittsburgh. After receiving her journalism degree
from Ohio University, she migrated to central Texas,
where the rolling hills and lush green belts are reminiscent
of the Pennsylvania woods she still loves. When she isn't
hiking, she volunteers for numerous civic organizations.

For Adrienne, writing historical fiction is one of her greatest joys. She welcomes correspondence and invites readers
to write to her in care of Bantam Books, 1540 Broadway,
New York, NY 10036.

*Look for the next thrilling historical romance from
Adrienne deWolfe as she delivers the passionate and
captivating follow-up to TEXAS OUTLAW.
TEXAS LOVER coming soon from Bantam Books.*

To Texas Ranger Wes Rawlins, settling a property dispute
should be no trickier than peeling potatoes—even if it does
involve a sheriff's cousin and a headstrong schoolmarm on
opposite camps. But Wes quickly learns there's more to the
matter than meets the eye. The only way to get at the truth
is from the inside. So posing as a carpenter, the lawman
uncovers more than he bargains for in a feisty, gun-toting
beauty.

*Here is an excerpt from
this exceptional romance.*

A gunshot exploded to the west.

Wes sat bolt upright, nearly blinded by the rising sun. The report had come from the direction of Boudreau's homestead. For a moment, his vision swam with the image of frightened little faces, of trembling little bodies racing for the storm cellar.

The children.

He was on his feet, grabbing for his gunbelt and his cartridge case even as the second report rolled down from the hills. He choked out an oath.

Grabbing Two-Step's reins, he vaulted onto the gelding's back and spurred him to a gallop. Wes left behind his saddle, bedroll, and even his hat. He would retrieve them later. All he cared about now were the children.

And getting his sights on any bastard who might have ridden out to hurt them.

"Sons of thunder."

Rorie rarely resorted to such unladylike outbursts, but the strain of her predicament was wearing on her. She had privately conceded she could not face Hannibal Dukker with the same laughable lack of shooting skill she had displayed for Wes Rawlins. So, swallowing her great distaste for guns—and the people who solved their problems with them—she had forced herself to ride out to the woods early, before the children arrived for their lessons, to practice her marksmanship.

It was a good thing she had done so.

She had just fired her sixth round, her *sixth round,* for heaven's sake, and that abominable whiskey bottle still sat untouched on the top of her barrel. If she had been a fanciful woman—which she most assuredly was not—she might have imagined that impudent vessel was trying to provoke her. Why, it hadn't rattled once when her bullets whizzed by. And the long rays of morning sun had fired it a bright and frolicsome green. If there was one thing she couldn't abide, it was a frolicsome whiskey bottle.

Her mouth set in a grim line, she fished in the pocket of her pinafore for more bullets.

Thus occupied, Rorie didn't immediately notice the tremor of the earth beneath her boots. She didn't ascribe anything unusual to her nag's snorting or the way Daisy stomped her hoof and tossed her head. The beast was chronically fractious.

Soon, though, Rorie detected the sound of thrashing, as if a powerful animal were breaking through the brush around the clearing. Her heart quickened, but she tried to remain calm. After all, bears were hardly as brutish as their hunters liked to tell. And any other wild animal with sense would turn tail and run once it got wind of her human scent—not to mention a whiff of her gunpowder.

Still, it might be wise to start reloading . . .

A blood-curdling whoop shook her hands. She couldn't line up a single bullet with its chamber. She thought to run, but there was nowhere to hide, and Daisy was snapping too viciously to mount.

Suddenly the sun winked out of sight. A horse, a *mammoth* horse with fiery eyes and steaming nostrils, sailed toward her over the barrel. She tried to scream, but it lodged in her throat as an "eek." All she could do was stand there, jaw hanging, knees knocking, and remember the unfortunate schoolmaster, Ichabod Crane.

Only her horseman had a head.

A red head, to be exact. And he carried it above his shoulders, rather than tucked under his arm.

"God a'mighty! Miss Aurora!"

The rider reined in so hard that his gelding reared, shrilling in indignation. Her revolver slid from her fingers. She saw a peacemaker in the rider's fist, and she thought again about running.

"It's me, ma'am. Wes Rawlins," he called, then cursed as his horse wheeled and pawed.

She blinked uncertainly, still poised to flee. He didn't look like the dusty longrider who'd drunk from her well the previous afternoon. His hair was sleek and short, and his cleft chin was bare of all but morning stubble. Although he did still wear the mustache, it was the gunbelt that gave him away. She recognized the double holsters before she recognized his strong, sculpted features.

He managed to subdue his horse before it could bolt back through the trees. "Are you all right, ma'am?" He hastily dismounted, releasing his reins to ground-hitch the gelding. "Uh-oh." He peered into her face. "You aren't gonna faint or anything, are you?"

She snapped erect, mortified by the very suggestion. "Certainly not. I've never been sick a day in my life. And swooning is for invalids."

"Sissies, too," he agreed solemnly.

He ran an appreciative gaze over her hastily piled hair and down her crisply pressed pinafore to her mud-spattered boots. She felt the blood surge to her cheeks. Masking her discomfort, she planted both fists on her hips.

"*Mister* Rawlins. What on earth is the matter with you, tearing around the countryside like that? You frightened the devil out of my horse!"

"I'm real sorry, ma'am. I never meant to give your, er, *horse* such a fright. But you see, I heard gunshots. And since there's nothing out this way except the Boudreau homestead, I thought you might be having trouble."

"Trouble?" She felt her heart flutter. Had he heard something of Dukker's intentions?

"Well, sure. Yesterday, the way you had those children

running for cover, I thought you might be expecting some." He folded his arms across his chest. "Are you?"

The directness of his question—and his gaze—was unsettling. He no longer reminded her of a lion. Today he was a fox, slick and clever, with a dash of sly charm thrown in to confuse her. She hastily bolstered her defenses.

"Did it ever occur to you, Mr. Rawlins, that Shae might be out here shooting rabbits?"

"Nope. Never thought I'd find you here, either. Not that I mind, ma'am. Not one bit. You see, I'm the type who likes surprises. Especially pleasant ones."

She felt her face grow warmer. She wasn't used to flattery. Her husband had been too preoccupied with self-pity to spare many kind words for her in the last two years of their marriage.

"Well," she said, "I never expected to see you out here either, Mr. Rawlins."

"Call me Wes."

She forced herself to ignore his winsome smile. "In truth, sir, I never thought to see you again."

"Why's that?"

"Let's be honest, Mr. Rawlins. You are no carpenter."

He chuckled. She found herself wondering which had amused him more: her accusation or her refusal to use his Christian name.

"You have to give a feller a chance, Miss Aurora. You haven't even seen my handiwork yet."

"I take it you've worked on barns before?"

"Sure. Fences too. My older brothers have a ranch up near Bandera Pass. Zack raises cattle. Cord raises kids. I try to raise a little thunder now and then, but they won't let me." He winked. "That's why I had to ride south."

She felt a smile tug at her lips. She was inclined to believe a part of his story, the part about him rebelling against authority.

"You aren't gonna make me bed down again in these woods, are you, ma'am? 'Cause Two-Step is awful fond of hay."

He managed to look woeful, in spite of the impish humor lighting his eyes. She realized then just how practiced his roguery was. Wary again, she searched his gaze, trying to find some hint of the truth. Why hadn't he stayed at the hotel in town? Or worse, at the dance hall? She felt better knowing he hadn't spent his free time exploiting an unfortunate young whore, but she still worried that his reasons for sleeping alone had more to do with empty pockets than any nobility of character. What would Rawlins do if Dukker offered to hire his guns?

Maybe feeding and housing Rawlins was more prudent than driving him off. Boarding him could steer him away from Dukker's dangerous influence, and Shae could genuinely use the help on the barn.

"Very well, Mr. Rawlins. I shall withhold judgment on your carpentry skills until you've had a chance to prove yourself."

"Why, that's right kind of you, ma'am."

She felt her cheeks grow warm again. His lilting drawl had the all-too-disturbing tendency to make her feel uncertain and eighteen again.

"I suppose you'll want to ride on to the house now," she said. "It's a half-mile farther west. Shae is undoubtedly awake and can show you what to do." She inclined her head. "Good morning."

Except for a cannily raised eyebrow, he didn't budge.

Rorie fidgeted. She was unused to her dismissals going unheeded. She was especially unused to a young man regarding her as if she had just made the most delightful quip of the season.

Hoping he would go away if she ignored him, she stooped to retrieve her gun. He reached quickly to help. She was so stunned when he crouched before her, his corded thighs straining beneath the fabric of his blue jeans, that she leaped up, nearly butting her head against his. He chuckled.

"Do I make you nervous, ma'am?"

"Certainly not." Her ears burned at the lie. "Whatever makes you think that?"

"Well . . ." Still squatting, he scooped bullets out of

the bluebonnets that rose like sapphire spears around her hem. "I was worried you might be trying to get rid of me again."

"I—I only thought that Shae was expecting you," she stammered, hastily backing away. There was something disconcerting—not to mention titillating—about a man's bronzed fingers snaking through the grass and darting so near to the unmentionables one wore beneath one's skirt.

"Shae's not expecting me yet, ma'am. The sun's too low in the sky." Rawlins straightened leisurely. "I figure I've got a half hour, maybe more, before I report to the barn. Just think, Miss Aurora, that gives us plenty of time to get acquainted."

His grin was positively wicked as he stretched out his hand. She realized if she wanted her bullets back, she would have to pluck every single one from his palm. And that meant *touching* him. She glared up into his laughing eyes. Fortunately, she was no longer a green girl, and she'd learned a good deal over the years about diverting young men from their less-than-wholesome urges.

"I don't have time to get acquainted," she said tartly, fishing for new bullets inside her apron. "I must finish my practice before my students arrive."

"Let's see what you've got, then."

"I beg your pardon?"

"Show me what you can do."

He pocketed her cartridges, and her jaw dropped.

"You can't mean to stay and watch!"

"Well, sure. Why not? I figure with all the gunpowder you've been burning, that's got to be the fifth bottle you're about to blow to Kingdom-come." He rocked back on his heels and hooked his thumbs over his gunbelt. "I reckon I might even learn something."

Oh, he really was a cut-up.

"Watching me would not be a good idea . . ."

"Why's that? You said I don't make you nervous."

Rorie bit her tongue. She'd never been good at the polite little falsehoods that nice people told. Her lie always seemed to backfire when she tried to spare another person's feelings.

"The truth is, Mr. Rawlins, I'm not very accurate—"

"Oh, don't worry about me. I'll stay out of harm's way."

"—And Shae is the teacher I prefer." She couldn't think of a single better excuse.

"Shae, eh?"

"Yes. He's a crack shot."

"Well, even I've been known to hit a bottle once or twice at fifty paces," he said dryly. "Go ahead. Draw your bead."

Rorie scowled. She would have much rather called him a name and marched into the sunrise. However, her father, a German immigrant with political aspirations, had drilled her rigorously in the essentials of decorum.

Feeling out-foxed and out-maneuvered, she stalked to her marker. Rawlins whistled to his horse. She had hoped to use the gelding as another excuse, but when it trotted obediently out of the line of fire, she could only mutter an uncharitable epithet and pump bullets into her revolver's cylinder. She took her time, checking and re-checking the chambers, adjusting and re-adjusting her stance.

If she had hoped her delay would irritate Rawlins enough to drive him away, she was disappointed. He folded his arms across his chest and watched her ritual without comment. She suspected he was highly entertained by the whole procedure—a fact that irritated her to no end.

Resigning herself to the inevitable, she clamped her left fist over her right, raised her gun, and took aim. The .44 exploded, she jolted, and a ripping, cracking sound came from the canopy of leaves above the barrel.

Rorie waited for the smoke to clear, then ground her teeth and tried again. This time, nothing ripped, nothing cracked, and the bottle stood as staunchly as a soldier. She longed to vent her frustration.

Rawlins, no doubt valuing his hide, refrained from his usual smirk.

By the time she was drawing her fifth bead, her palms had grown so sticky and her muscles were quivering so badly, she could scarcely hold her arms straight. She tried locking her elbows, and Rawlins finally spoke.

"Er . . . Miss Aurora?"

She tossed him a withering look.

"Would you mind if I gave you a piece of advice?"

"I most assuredly would!" she wanted to snap, but the side of her that esteemed self-control subdued her tongue.

"Very well," she said. "What do you suggest?"

"First of all, you gotta loosen up. You're sweatin' bullets over there when you ought to be firin' them."

She blew out her breath. Shae had told her the same thing, several times. Only Shae had never put it quite so colorfully.

"And second?"

"Well . . ." Rubbing his chin, he seemed to consider. "I reckon you might try some dry firing next. You know, without any beans in your wheel. That way, you can get used to squeezing the trigger rather than jerking it."

"But how can I ever learn to aim straight if I don't fire bullets?"

The plaintive note in her voice made her wince. She wished she could contain her feelings as well as Papa had. Every morning since Gator's death, she had dragged herself to this clearing for the dreaded practice. She felt obligated to put the children's safety before her own principles. The problem was, her aim wasn't improving.

Shae had tried to help. He had accompanied her every few days to give her suggestions, but his patience would inevitably wear thin, and she wound up feeling clumsy, foolish, and a trifle stung by his exasperation. As fond as she was of the boy, she had to concede that Shae was no teacher.

Rawlins, on the other hand, was smiling at her. Smiling kindly, in fact. The expression was in such contrast to his usual roguery that she wondered what he could possibly be thinking. After all, she was a woman with a gun. In Cincinnati, females with firearms were considered no better than floozies.

"Aiming isn't so hard," he said. "It just takes practice.

You don't want to rush a shot. That's the secret. Right now, you're anticipating the recoil, and that makes you jolt before your bullet clears the muzzle."

She considered this advice. It sounded legitimate.

"If what you say is true, then how do I correct the problem?"

"Here. I'll show you."

Two strides brought him to her side. He seemed even taller with his chest scant inches from her shoulder. She felt her pulse leap, and it was all she could do not to flinch when he drew his gun and dumped out the bullets.

"See?" Turning, he extended his right arm on a line with her target. Now his broad chest was facing her own. "Nice and relaxed, an easy pull." He demonstrated a few times, clicking empty chambers.

It was amazing what one noticed when under duress, Rorie thought. She could scarcely keep her eyes on his trigger. Her gaze kept stealing to the unfastened button at his neck, where red-gold hairs trailed into the well-planed shadows below. She noticed the way his shirt, a faded cornflower-blue, hugged his ribs and accentuated the leanness of his waist. She indulged in a shy glance at his gunbelt, noting the way it wrapped his hips like a lover might.

The indecency of that thought made her insides flame, so she hastily raised her eyes. His arm should have been safe to observe, except that all its rippled musculature bore testimony to a supple strength, one that no doubt stemmed from long hours of cattle roping and log-splitting. Or whatever else young men did on ranches near Bandera Pass.

She found herself wondering more about him. Studying his profile, she decided he was handsome in a rugged, robust way. His attraction went far deeper than physical good looks. A magnetic energy surrounded Wes Rawlins, something that emanated from the core of his being and twinkled like starshine in his eyes. That something reminded her of laughter. And youth. And all the other things she secretly missed in her life.

". . . The slow and steady way. You try it this time, ma'am."

She started, flushing. He'd been speaking, and she hadn't heard a word. What was the matter with her, letting him disturb her concentration so?

"Go on. Give it a whirl."

"Thank you," she said primly.

She moved away from him and took her stance. Her arms were more rested now, and when she fired, she managed to strike the barrel. Splinters flew into the air. The bottle trembled.

"Better," Rawlins said. "But try not to grip the gunbutt so tight."

She nodded. Shae had given her the same advice.

Focusing all her concentration, she fired her last shot. The bottle actually jumped, but she still had come no closer to shattering it.

"Foot." She pressed her lips together and fished for more bullets.

"Never mind that," he said. "Come back over here."

She eyed him uncertainly, but he waved her forward, still clearly bent on his lesson.

"Are you locking your knees? I can't tell."

He'd been staring at her skirts! She hastily shook her head.

"Good girl. Now all we've got to do is get you to hold still. Let's try something. Hold out your arm, like you were taking aim."

She bit her lip and obeyed.

"Good." He stepped behind her. "Your bead's on target. Now go ahead and pull the trigger."

The barrel clicked.

"See how your muzzle's jumping up?"

No, she hadn't. She was too worried about what he was doing—or going to do—behind her.

"But the gun's lighter without the bullets," she protested weakly, glancing over her shoulder at him.

"Doesn't matter. You're still trying to compensate for the kick. Here, I'll show you."

Before she could stop him, before she could even think to stop him, his arms had circled her shoulders. His chest fused to her back. She was so stunned by this intimacy, this *audacity*, that she was rendered motionless as he clamped his hands over hers, holding them prisoner around the butt of her gun.

"See this?" He pushed her arms up, out of alignment with the bottle. "This is what you've been doing."

"*Mister* Rawlins—"

"Now this," he continued, fitting his finger over hers and squeezing the trigger, "is what you want to do. Feel the difference? See how your elbow takes the shock after you fire?"

Her heart, which had nearly catapulted out of her chest, was now slamming painfully against her ribcage. He held her so firmly, so steadily, she couldn't have broken free if she'd tried.

Her perverse side resurfaced then, noticing curious things. There was the off-key rumble of his deep voice in her ear, and the way his breaths teased an errant curl, spreading shivers from her neck to her toes. She couldn't help but note how snugly his arms wrapped her shoulders, and the pleasant, if scandalous, heat that pooled between her buttocks and his thighs.

A woman with a less hardy constitution might have fainted dead away at such a trial. But Rorie had always disdained displays of weakness.

"I see precisely," she replied in her best no-nonsense voice. "You may release me now."

"Why don't you give it a try first."

Was there the faintest hint of amusement in his tone?

"Very well."

Obeying his directions, she fired, reasoning that the sooner she could satisfy him, the sooner she could flee with her last shreds of dignity.

A strange thing happened, though. With his arms as buffers, she realized he was right. Each time she pulled the trigger, her spine butted ever so slightly against his chest. Shae had never mentioned she'd developed this bad habit.

"I'm . . . not recoiling quite as much now, am I?"

"Nope. You're squeezing that trigger like a professional lead-chucker now."

It was high praise indeed, she thought, judging by the warmth in this voice.

"Here." He pulled his left gun, the loaded one, from its holster. "Try it with bullets."

He passed the weapon to her, and their hands brushed. The touch was electric, shooting tiny sparks through her limbs. She felt her stomach flutter, so she told herself that his gun was to blame. Tentatively, she wrapped her fingers around the cool walnut-inlayed butt. It was a work of art, a custom-made piece. The butt itself had been designed for the hand that used it most.

Forcing such distractions from her mind, she aligned the gunsight with the bottle. He was still behind her, around her, his heat flowing through her. The sensation was unnerving—and strangely comforting too. She realized then just how much she wanted to strike that bottle. She wanted to do well, really well, and not only for the sake of the children.

Releasing a ragged breath, she focused. She relaxed. She did everything he had instructed her to do. And when at last she pulled the trigger, she forced herself to stand like stone.

The bottle exploded into a hundred pieces.

"I did it!"

She laughed, spinning toward him, so excited she nearly danced. *"I did it, Wes!"*

He smiled, and she caught her breath. For a moment she stood spellbound, absolutely dazzled by the coppery shimmers that sparked like fire in his hair. In that instant, with the rays of morning ablaze around him, he looked like Apollo stepping out of the sun.

"Want to try again?"

His voice had turned husky. She felt rather than heard it, a wave of tingles gusting over her skin.

"Uh . . ." She realized, to her embarrassment, that she was staring. "I don't have another bottle."

"Too bad." He cocked his head, and his gemstone eyes,

peridot-green with a trace of wistfulness, seemed to delve past all her pretenses. "Tomorrow, then?"

She nodded, still too dazed to command herself.

He chuckled, retrieving his Colt. With a speed and a flare that appeared second nature, he spun the .44 over his forefinger and into its holster.

She felt her heart trip, then it sank to her toes. Clearly, she'd been nursing false hopes.

Her Apollo was a gunfighter.

DON'T MISS THESE FABULOUS
BANTAM WOMEN'S FICTION TITLES

On Sale in November

AMANDA *by bestselling author* Kay Hooper

*"Don't miss a story that will keep your reading light on until
well into the night."*—Catherine Coulter

With her spellbinding imagination and seductive voice, Kay Hooper is the
only author worthy of being called today's successor to Victoria Holt. Now
this powerful storyteller has created a stunning tale of contemporary sus-
pense that begins with a mysterious homecoming and ends in a shattering
explosion of passion, greed, and murder.___ 09957-4 $19.95/$24.95 in Canada

MASTER OF PARADISE *by* Katherine O'Neal

Winner of *Romantic Times'* Best Sensual Historical Romance
Award for THE LAST HIGHWAYMAN

*"Katherine O'Neal is the queen of romantic adventure,
reigning over a court of intrigue, sensuality, and good
old-fashioned storytelling."*—Affaire de Coeur

Katherine O'Neal unveils a spectacular new novel of romantic adventure—
a tantalizing tale of a notorious pirate, a rebellious beauty, and a dangerously erotic duel of hearts.   ___ 56956-2 $5.50/$7.99

TEXAS OUTLAW *by sparkling new talent* Adrienne deWolfe

Combining the delightful wit of Arnette Lamb and the tender emotion of
Pamela Morsi, this spectacular historical romance is a dazzling debut from
an author destined to be a star.   ___ 57395-0 $4.99/$6.99

New York Times bestselling author Sandra Brown's

HEAVEN'S PRICE

Now available in paperback   ___ 57157-5 $5.50/$6.99

- -

Ask for these books at your local bookstore or use this page to order.

Please send me the books I have checked above. I am enclosing $___ (add $2.50 to
cover postage and handling). Send check or money order, no cash or C.O.D.'s, please.

Name _____

Address _____

City/State/Zip _____

Send order to: Bantam Books, Dept. FN159, 2451 S. Wolf Rd., Des Plaines, IL 60018
Allow four to six weeks for delivery.
Prices and availability subject to change without notice.   FN 159 11/95

THE VERY BEST IN CONTEMPORARY
WOMEN'S FICTION

SANDRA BROWN

____28951-9 Texas! Lucky $6.50/$8.99 in Canada

____28990-X Texas! Chase $6.50/$8.99

____29500-4 Texas! Sage $6.50/$8.99

____29085-1 22 Indigo Place $5.99/$6.99

____29783-X A Whole New Light $5.99/$6.99

____56768-3 Adam's Fall $4.99/$5.9

____56045-X Temperatures Rising $5.99/$6.9

____56274-6 Fanta C $5.50/$6.9

____56278-9 Long Time Coming $4.99/$5.9

____57157-5 Heaven's Price $5.50/$6.9

TAMI HOAG

____29534-9 Lucky's Lady $5.99/$7.50

____29053-3 Magic $5.99/$7.50

____56050-6 Sarah's Sin $4.99/$5.99

____29272-2 Still Waters $5.99/$7.5

____56160-X Cry Wolf $5.50/$6.5

____56161-8 Dark Paradise $5.99/$7.5

____09961-2 Night Sins $19.95/$23.95

NORA ROBERTS

____29078-9 Genuine Lies $5.99/$6.99

____28578-5 Public Secrets $5.99/$6.99

____26461-3 Hot Ice $5.99/$6.99

____26574-1 Sacred Sins $5.99/$6.99

____27859-2 Sweet Revenge $5.99/$6.9

____27283-7 Brazen Virtue $5.99/$6.9

____29597-7 Carnal Innocence $5.99/$6.9

____29490-3 Divine Evil $5.99/$6.9

DEBORAH SMITH

____29107-6 Miracle $5.50/$6.50

____29092-4 Follow the Sun $4.99/$5.99

____29690-6 Blue Willow $5.99/$7.9

____29689-2 Silk and Stone $5.99/$6.9

____28759-1 The Beloved Woman $4.50/$5.50

Ask for these books at your local bookstore or use this page to order.

Please send me the books I have checked above. I am enclosing $_____(add $2.50 to cover postage and handling). Send check or money order, no cash or C.O.D.'s, please.

Name _____

Address _____

City/State/Zip _____

Send order to: Bantam Books, Dept. FN 24, 2451 S. Wolf Rd., Des Plaines, IL 60018

Allow four to six weeks for delivery.

Prices and availability subject to change without notice.

FN 24 1/96